Cracking the Ice

To my wife, Brenda,
who believed in me when it made no sense at all.

This one's for The Kid.

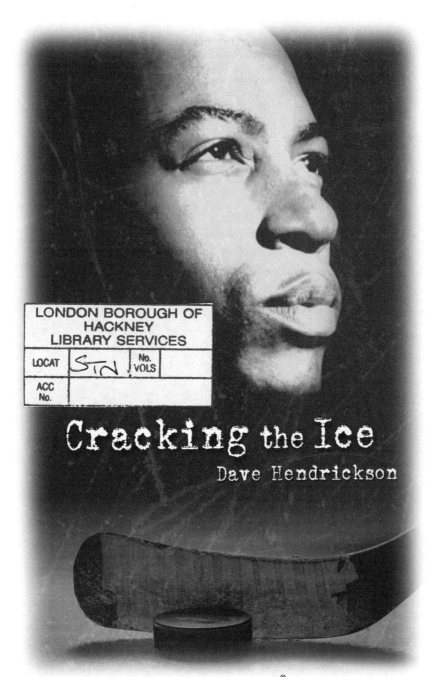

Cracking the Ice

Dave Hendrickson

WestSide Books
Lodi, New Jersey

Published by WestSide Books
60 Industrial Road
Lodi, NJ 07644
USA

This is a work of fiction. All characters, places and events
described are imaginary. Any resemblance to real people,
places and events is entirely coincidental.

Library of Congress Cataloging-in-Publication Data

Hendrickson, David H.
  Cracking the ice / by David H. Hendrickson. -- 1st ed.
    p. cm.
  Summary: In 1968, when fourteen-year-old Jessie Stackhouse wins a hockey scholarship to an elite New Hampshire boarding school, it seems the only thing standing be-
tween him and his dream of one day being the second African American to play in the
National Hockey League is the bigotry of the coach, some students, and townspeople.
  ISBN 978-1-934813-55-3
  [1. Hockey--Fiction. 2. Racism--Fiction. 3. African Americans--New Hampshire--Fic-
tion. 4. Boarding schools--Fiction. 5. Schools--Fiction. 6. New Hampshire--History--
20th century--Fiction.] I. Title.
  PZ7.H38568Cr 2011
  [Fic]--dc22

                                                                            2010053729

International Standard Book Number: 978-1-934813-55-3
School ISBN: 978-1-934813-56-0
Cover design by Chinedum Chukwu
Interior design by Chinedum Chukwu

Printed in the USA
10 9 8 7 6 5 4 3 2 1

First Edition

1 2 3 4 5 6 7 8 9 10

Cracking the Ice

Tuesday, April 2, 1968

What the two white men on the front porch were saying made Jessie Stackhouse's head spin. He'd heard of other fifteen-year-old boys leaving home to play hockey in places like Canada, but he'd never even considered boarding schools for himself. That was for rich white kids, who'd go on to colleges like Harvard or Yale, and then become millionaires like their parents.

Pop ushered the headmaster and the coach into the house and hung their expensive-looking, full-length coats in the hall closet. Next to the Stackhouses' well-worn garments, the two new coats looked as out of place as if a Rockefeller had moved next door.

"Our school offers an extraordinary opportunity for young men like Jessie," Mr. Whitney, the headmaster of Springvale Academy, said. The younger of the two men by at least twenty years, he wore a dark suit and tie and held a thin leather briefcase. "It's a life-changing opportunity, as I think you'll see."

For a second, Jessie's mom looked as though a poisonous snake had just slithered inside her house; but then she smiled and said, "Come, have a seat in the dining room. I'll fix you something."

"Oh, that isn't necessary," Mr. Whitney said. "We don't want you to go to any trouble."

"It's no trouble at all," Momma said. "Coffee?"

"That would be great, Mrs. Stackhouse. Thank you," the headmaster said. "It'll keep me awake for the drive back to school." He turned to the coach. "Frank?"

Coach Stone just shook his head and said nothing.

As Mrs. Stackhouse rushed off to the kitchen, Mr. Whitney lingered in the hallway, stopping to examine the array of framed photographs that lined the hallway. The center one showed Dr. Martin Luther King Jr. speaking before the masses at the Washington Monument. Flanking that photograph were action shots of Jackie Robinson, Bill Russell, Muhammad Ali, and Willie O'Ree, with a bronze nameplate beneath each photo.

"An impressive grouping," Mr. Whitney said. "Although I have to say, I don't know much about this O'Ree fellow."

"He's the first black man to play in the National Hockey League, and so far, he's the only one," said Jessie's father, Dr. Stackhouse, who Jessie called Pop.

"I want to be the second," Jessie blurted.

They all laughed except for Coach Stone, whose face remained hard and impassive. Broad-shouldered and muscular, but with a paunch that hung over his belt, the coach looked to be about fifty years old. He smelled of stale cigarette smoke and broken blood vessels crisscrossed the lower half of his bulbous nose; a surefire sign of a heavy drinker, Pop had once said.

"I'm surprised you have a picture of Cassius Clay up here," Coach Stone said.

"Muhammad Ali," Jessie's dad corrected, reminding the coach of the boxer's Black Muslim name.

"Yeah, him," Coach Stone said, a sour look on his face. "He'll fight for himself, to get rich, but he won't fight for his country in Vietnam."

"*Frank*," Mr. Whitney said, the look of warning on his face matching his tone.

"And Willie O'Ree?" Coach Stone said. "Instead of Gordie Howe, or even Bobby Orr? Why? Just because he's colored?"

"*Frank!*" The headmaster's tone came across as an order.

Stone's bushy eyebrows furrowed as his eyes narrowed and his nostrils flared. Gritting his teeth, he said nothing more on the subject.

Jessie held his breath. He didn't like Coach Stone, but figured that these two men arguing couldn't be good news for him.

"We are *black*, Mr. Stone, not *colored*," Pop said. "Black and very proud of it. Not Negro, nor any of those other words that begin with the letter N. We are *black*. We need no euphemism for that which is beautiful."

The headmaster jumped back into the conversation, saying, "Yes, of course." He shot the coach an icy look, then turned to Jessie's dad with a conciliatory smile. "No photographs of Jessie up here?"

"Not yet," Pop said. "Everywhere else in the house, but not up on that wall. Not yet." He smiled. "But he's next."

Everyone slid into their chairs; Jessie's dad sat at the head of the dining room table, the two men on his right, and Jessie on his left. They could hear the clatter of plates in the kitchen as Mrs. Stackhouse bustled about.

Mr. Whitney popped open his leather briefcase and pulled out three glossy color brochures. He slid them across to Dr. Stackhouse, Jessie, and put one before the empty place beside Jessie. The headline on the brochures read, "*Springvale Academy, a tradition of excellence since 1876.*"

"Go ahead," he told them. "Take a look while we wait for your mother. The information about our sports teams starts on page twenty-three."

Jessie skipped right to that page, then flipped through from one page to the next, each showing eye-catching photographs with glowing descriptions of all kinds of teams, from football to golf to swimming.

"We were New England champions in seven sports last year," Mr. Whitney said. "Seven! We don't settle for second place." He smiled.

"Impressive," Dr. Stackhouse said, flipping the pages in his copy of the brochure.

"Jessie, are you familiar with a hockey player at Princeton named Carl Tibbetts?" the headmaster asked.

Jessie shook his head.

"He's one of our graduates, Class of '66; we've been told he might have a career in the NHL after he graduates."

Jessie felt his heart being to pound. The NHL. Professional hockey. His dream.

Mrs. Stackhouse rushed in and set heaping plates of strawberry shortcake in front of the two visitors. After a trip back into the kitchen, she returned first with the coffee, and then with two more plates for Pop and Jessie, and a third one with a tiny portion for herself.

She sat down next to Jessie and said, "Dig in, gentlemen," surprising Jessie, who'd expected her to ask someone to say grace first.

But Jessie couldn't even think about Momma's strawberry shortcake, baked from scratch, with fresh strawberries, sharp and sweet, and topped with a curling mountain of whipped cream. Normally, his mouth would be watering, his fork ready to dig in, but all he could think about was what the headmaster had just said. The NHL for a Springvale Academy graduate out of Princeton.

Jessie had dreamed of playing in the NHL ever since he was a child and saw Willie O'Ree skate for the Boston Bruins. Jessie had watched a lot of Bruins games on the local station, TV38, even when he'd fiddle with the rabbit ears to get a picture that wasn't all snow. But he thought he couldn't make that dream become reality without moving to Canada, something his parents would never allow.

But now . . . maybe it could happen for him.

"My goodness!" The headmaster said after taking a bite of the dessert; he closed his eyes and shook his head. "Oh, my, Mrs. Stackhouse. Your baking is every bit as outstanding as your son's athletic prowess." He winked at Jessie. "And that's saying something."

Momma bowed her head ever so slightly, smiled, and said, "Why, thank you."

11

His voice cracking, Jessie said, "The NHL? Really?" He didn't know what else to say.

Mr. Whitney waved his fork. "Dr. and Mrs. Stackhouse, you have a remarkably talented son. But he needs to be challenged to get to the next level. He's already close to six feet tall and built like a linebacker, playing against boys half his size. He's not just bigger and stronger than they are. He's also faster and has better skills. He needs tougher competition than he's getting here. The game Coach Stone and I saw him play this weekend was a perfect example. He scored five goals, and it was like watching a man play against boys. Isn't that right, Frank?"

Coach Stone nodded; he hadn't touched his strawberry shortcake. "That's right," was all he said.

The headmaster waited, expecting the coach to go on. But when he didn't, Mr. Whitney said, "Frank might have had the opportunity to play professionally himself, if not for a knee injury. Like Jessie, he was bigger, faster, and stronger than the competition. He had to leave home at the very same age as Jessie so he could face other kids who were at his level. Otherwise, he wouldn't have grown as a player and wouldn't have reached near-professional skill levels."

Jessie drew in a breath. *Professional!?*

"At Springvale, Jessie will be challenged in practice every single day," the headmaster said. "We're *the* defending New England champions, four years running. It's the toughest league in the country, and three of our graduates played on the U.S. Olympic team that won the gold medal in 1960. And let's not forget Tibbetts, a star at Princeton."

In the back of Jessie's mind, he wondered why Coach Stone wasn't saying much. Shouldn't he be the one talking about all those championships, since he'd helped make it happen? Jessie was getting the impression that the coach didn't really want to be there, and that he didn't like Jessie anywhere near as much as the headmaster did. In fact, Jessie was guessing that this coach didn't like him at all.

"We can make Jessie the best player he possibly can be," Mr. Whitney said. "I'm not guaranteeing Jessie will make the NHL someday—none of us knows that. But we can make the most of that impressive ability of his."

Jessie's heart hammered and he looked to his father, whose face showed no emotion.

"This isn't just about hockey," the headmaster continued. "Of the one hundred nine students in last year's graduating class, thirty-four went on to Ivy League schools; that's almost a third of the class. There isn't a prep school in the country with a better record. Springvale could open the doors for Jessie that could help him get into Harvard, Yale or Princeton."

Jessie felt his eyes widen. *Harvard? Him?* His stomach churned, just like it did before a big game. He knew he was smart; his teachers told him so, even if in some cases it came across grudgingly, as in, "You're smart . . . for a Negro." Yet coming from other teachers, the praise felt genuine, compliments based on their true admiration for his work.

But Harvard? He wasn't smart enough for Harvard. Was he?

"Springvale Academy can provide Jessie with an extraordinary opportunity," Mr. Whitney said, "both academically and athletically. It's the best of both worlds."

He leaned forward and went on. "We're offering Jessie a full scholarship. All expenses paid, right down to the last penny."

Mrs. Stackhouse gasped, and her husband sat back in his chair, surprised.

Jessie almost burst out of his seat, ready to shout, *Yes! I'll take it! I'll take it!* He'd only felt this excited just before a game, when he was about to bolt through a locker room door and onto ice. But this time he wasn't on skates or in uniform, so he could only sit and wait for his father to respond. Jessie looked at Pop, wishing he could tell him, *Take it, before they change their minds!*

But a frown creased his father's forehead and he didn't look excited at all. Jessie's eyes widened; what was there to think about? They'd offered him a full scholarship! Pop couldn't be considering saying no, could he?

"Coach Stone," Pop said. "Your headmaster sounds very enthusiastic about Jessie coming to your school, but you've said hardly a word. Why is that?" He leaned forward. "I have a feeling that you're hoping we'll say no."

Coach Stone reddened ever so slightly, then glanced at Mr. Whitney, who glowered at him. "I, uh—" the coach said, shifting in his seat, a sour look on his face. "I support the headmaster," he said and smiled weakly. "I'd welcome the addition of Jessie to the team."

Dr. Stackhouse sat back, his eyes never leaving the coach's; then he said, "Oh, really?"

The room fell silent, the tension thick. Jessie was sure

everyone could hear the hammering of his heart. Why didn't Pop just say they'd accept the offer? Who cared if the coach didn't really like him? Plenty of Jessie's coaches hadn't liked him—at least not until he'd scored goal after goal; after that, they liked him just fine.

Visions of playing in the NHL floated through Jessie's mind. He could imagine hearing the Boston Garden announcer say, "At right wing, Number 42, Jessie Stackhouse," and amidst the wild cheering of the packed house, Jessie envisioned himself skating for the very first time to the blue line in an NHL jersey—a Boston Bruins jersey, of course. He'd stand on the blue line next to Bobby Orr as the National Anthem played, his heart swelling with pride that he'd made it.

Then the referee would drop the puck; it would deflect to an opponent, but Jessie saw himself crushing the guy into the boards, a clean but hard check that rattled the boards almost as much as the guy, then pictured himself scooping up the loose puck. He'd be flying after that; no one could match his speed, and there was no better feeling on Earth. He'd skate around a defenseman and fire a shot— not just any shot—but a rocket-blast that would roar past the helpless goaltender and fly into the net with such force it'd almost rip through to the other side. Then the buzzer would sound and the crowd would roar. His teammates would congratulate him, and someone would fish the puck out of the net so he could treasure it as a souvenir of his first NHL goal, one of many to come.

His father's voice brought Jessie back down to Earth, to their dining room, where he was telling the visitors,

"This isn't something we'd ever considered before," Pop said. "Jessie's only fifteen, and we never expected to lose him so young to school. When he goes off to college, of course; but not at fifteen. He's just so . . . young to be leaving home."

Alarms went off in Jessie's head as he digested the words. Could Pop actually turn down this amazing deal? Jessie felt a sick, sinking feeling in his stomach. He'd turn sixteen in November; then he'd get his learner's permit to drive, and he'd be almost an adult. But Pop was talking like he was still a little kid. Jessie couldn't believe what he was saying.

"This is a difficult decision for most families," Mr. Whitney said. "A boarding school isn't the right choice for everyone. But you could visit Jessie on weekends and he'd come home during the holidays, and even on long weekends if he didn't have a game."

Pop's eyes narrowed. "How do you know Jessie is academically qualified?"

Who cares? Jessie wanted to scream.

The headmaster licked his lips and went on. "I admit that this offer comes very late in the process, later than we'd usually consider an application, so we haven't had access to Jessie's records. We're making an exception in his case because of his talent; we're just guessing about his academic skills."

"But if you're an elite academic institution—" Dr. Stackhouse said.

Just say yes, Jessie thought, wishing he could say it.

"One of Jessie's former teammates, Tommy Simpson,

told us that Jessie is academically gifted. We were interested in Tommy, too, until he decided to go to Canada."

Pop snorted. "In the future, you may want to do a little more homework. I've seen doorknobs smarter than Tommy Simpson."

"Regardless of academic record, we'd have Jessie repeat his freshman year to give him time to adjust to the academic workload."

Jessie frowned. *Stay back? But why?*

The headmaster gestured toward Coach Stone. "That'd also give Jessie four years of eligibility to play hockey. That's very attractive on the athletic side of things, but it's secondary to the academic concerns. We consider it almost mandatory for any student coming from a public school; they generally need the year to be ready for the rigors of a Springvale education. We'd also provide Jessie with tutors."

Anger flashed across Pop's face. "So you expect him to have problems? Why? Because he's black?"

The headmaster flushed. "No, not at all. It's just that most of our students come from private schools. Those who come from public schools, especially those in um—" He waved his hand helplessly, trying to find the right words.

"This is not a ghetto, Mr. Whitney," Pop said, his voice testy. "Lynn may be a grimy, blue-color city with more than its share of problems, and while it may lack the resources of the lily-white suburbs and the private schools your other students come from, it is *not* a ghetto. Do not make assumptions about my son or his education based on his race. If he attends your school, I will insist that his instructors make no assumptions about him because of his color. Is that clear? Do you understand?"

Mr. Whitney turned so red, Jessie thought he might explode. "Mr. Stackhouse, I assure you that I didn't mean anything by it."

Okay, Pop, enough. You proved your point. Now just say, yes, Jessie pleaded silently.

But Pop wasn't done. "Lots of people 'don't mean anything.' But 'not meaning anything' doesn't change their assumptions. The fact is that Jessie is almost a straight-A student; I am a physician and his mother is a teacher. But you've already concluded that he'll need to *stay back* a year and require tutors because—" he pointed to Jessie's face, "—because of the color of his skin."

Mr. Whitney swallowed slowly. "I apologize if I made inappropriate assumptions about the public schools here, Dr. Stackhouse. But I assure you that repeating a year is quite common for most incoming students, and I meant no offense when I mentioned tutors. I only meant to show that tutors will be made available to support Jessie should he need them."

"Which leads me to my next question," Pop said. "Prep schools like yours have hardly led the way as far as integration goes. Exactly how many black students do you have enrolled at Springvale at this point?"

The headmaster glanced at Coach Stone, then took in a deep breath. "None," he said. "We have one black student entering in the fall. Jessie would be the second."

"None," Pop said, then let the silence go on a bit for emphasis. "And how many black students in the past ten years?"

The headmaster cleared his throat. "Sir, please hear me

out. When I came to Springvale Academy last year, no black student had ever attended the school. My predecessor was not on the cutting edge in terms of race relations, and he maintained the previous practice of excluding black people. He also followed a long-standing Jewish quota, and I'm sorry to say that these policies were still in place when I took over. But I'm working hard to change all that."

Out of the corner of his eye, Jessie thought he saw Coach Stone grimace for a split second.

Mr. Whitney continued. "I personally tried to recruit two black students last year, but wasn't successful. That's why I was delighted to recruit our first black student several months ago, and I hope Jessie will join him and make it two. We'll continue recruiting and more will join them next year, and in all the years to come. While I can't excuse the school's past failings, I can change what happens from now on, and I'll personally guarantee your son's well-being when he's enrolled. If he encounters any problem—*any* problem whatsoever—my door will always be open to him, both at the office and at my residence on campus."

He turned to Jessie and said, "Even if you have a problem at three o'clock in the morning, please knock on my door and wake me up. Springvale Academy's greatness has been marred by this one wrong-headed policy, and I *will* remove it. I give you my word on it."

As silence fell over the room, Jessie's hands began to sweat and his mouth went dry.

"Gentlemen, I'm not afraid to put myself in harm's way for a righteous cause," Pop said. "I've marched to Selma with Dr. Martin Luther King; I've joined the sit-ins in Birmingham, and I've been knocked down by Bull Connor's water cannons."

Jessie'd heard these words many times before, but for him, they never got old. He'd always swelled with pride at hearing Pop speak about his bravery in the fight for civil rights. But this day, Jessie almost burst with happiness because he was certain what Pop was leading up to: Pop was going to say yes, that Jessie'd be going to Springvale Academy. And from there, a whole new world of opportunities beckoned—Harvard or Yale, and maybe even the NHL after that. Jessie might just become the second black hockey player to make the big-time after all.

Pop continued talking about his experiences. He pointed to a spot above his right ear and said, "If you look close enough here, you'll see the scar from a Mississippi policeman's billy club that took me down. Almost fractured my skull. I won't even tell you where he kicked me as I lay barely conscious on the ground."

"Oh, my." The headmaster gasped.

"I'd put myself in harm's way again," Pop said, "because I'd be making a better world for Jessie and all the generations to come. I'd take the plunge and enroll *myself* in your school, despite all its bigotry and racist history." The headmaster recoiled at these words, but Pop kept going. "For myself, I'd welcome the challenge."

Euphoria flooded Jessie and he felt all warm inside. He couldn't hold back a huge smile.

Then Pop leaned forward and said, "But I will not sacrifice my only son. I will not throw him into your den of lions."

Jessie couldn't believe what he'd just heard. Pop had said no! Jessie'd been so sure that his pop's speech about going into harm's way would lead to telling their guests that they'd accept the offer and that Jessie, too, would become a groundbreaker in his own small way, like Jackie Robinson, Rosa Parks, and James Meredith.

Jessie shot to his feet "No!" he blurted out. "That isn't fair! You're just a—" Then the right word came to him, something he'd heard in Reverend Roy's sermon last Sunday. "—you're just a hypocrite!"

"*Sit down*, young man!" Momma grabbed him by the elbow and her sharp nails dug into his skin. "Mind your manners before I *hypocrite* your behind."

Feeling numb all over, Jessie sank into his seat.

Pop simply stared at him for a long time. When he finally spoke, he directed his words at the two visitors, but his eyes never left Jessie's. "How long before we have to give you our final decision?" he asked.

The headmaster's eyes darted to the coach, then to Jessie, Momma, and Pop. "We're actually past our deadline. We're making an exception only because—"

"May we have the rest of this week to think it over?" Pop asked. "We'd give you our final answer on Monday."

"Yes, I suppose we could do that."

"Thank you," Pop said, finally turning to face the two guests. "We need to discuss this as a family, and perhaps I need a little more time to think this through myself."

"Certainly," the headmaster said. "If you have any questions, our phone numbers are on the back of the brochure."

A heavy silence descended on the room.

"I suppose we should be going," the headmaster said at last.

That's when Jessie noticed that Coach Stone hadn't taken any of the strawberry shortcake in front of him; in fact, he hadn't even touched the fork.

2

Jessie sat alone on the sofa in the front room, flanked by Momma and Pop sitting in chairs on either side of the sofa. On the coffee table lay the most recent issues of *Newsweek*, *Ebony*, *Sports Illustrated*, and *Down Beat*, and the smell of Pop's coffee filled the room.

"I'm sorry I called you a hypocrite," Jessie said. "I didn't mean to be disrespectful. It just came out."

"It always 'just comes out' with you," Pop said, his jaw line hardening. "How many times are we going to have this conversation before you get the message? There are times you can be a spitfire, but there are times to watch your mouth. I don't ever want to hear you disrespect your Momma or me in public ever again."

Jessie looked down at the magazines. On the cover of *Sports Illustrated*, UCLA's Lew Alcindor was taking a hook shot. Then he said, "I'm sorry."

"Do I need to take your tickets to the James Brown concert on Friday and tear them up? Will that teach you a lesson?" his father asked him.

Jessie's eyes shot up to look at Pop. "No! You can't do that."

"I *what?*" Pop looked at Jessie with his eyebrows raised.

"I mean, you wouldn't do that. Please, Pop. I'm taking Rose." Jessie paused, thinking that this ought to be reason enough, but he noticed that Pop's expression had only softened a little. "Neither one of us has ever seen him before, except on *Soul Train*. But never live, and Rose has been looking forward to this so much! Me, too." Then Jessie held his breath.

Pop glanced at Momma. "Maybe next time you're about to say something you shouldn't, you'll think about this James Brown concert. And how you *almost* missed it."

Jessie breathed a sigh of relief.

"But no TV for the next three days."

Jessie nodded and said, "Okay." He'd figured that would be the best he could hope for.

Pop's eyes glinted. "But your Momma reserves the right to *hypocrite* your behind—" he said, "—whatever that might be." He looked to Momma, and began to chuckle and shake his head. "How you ever come up with those sayings, I'll never know."

Then they all began to laugh, even Momma, who tried to shoo away their merriment at her expense.

Jessie's laughter quickly faded, though, and he felt hollow inside. He waited a few seconds, then said, "It still isn't fair, Pop. If you can march to Selma with Dr. King, I should be able to go away to a white school. Selma was dangerous; cops had guns and attack dogs. At Springvale Academy, nobody's going to have guns or attack dogs. And the head-master promised me his protection." He looked pleadingly at Pop and saw that he was getting nowhere, and the same went for Momma. "I *can* make a difference. Isn't that what you've told me to do, make a difference? Where would we be if Jackie Robinson's parents told him it was too danger-ous for him to play major league baseball on an all-white team? Or if James Meredith's parents told him it was too dangerous to be the first of us to integrate the University of Mississippi? What if Rosa Parks did the easy thing, the safe thing? I can *be* the Jackie Robinson of that school."

Momma and Pop glanced at each other.

"I can do it," Jessie said. "Please let me try. I know I can do it. And I can defend myself."

Momma jumped in. "Against ten boys just as strong as you? Twenty? Young men much stronger than you have been strung up on a tree."

"That's not going to happen to me. This school is in New Hampshire, not Alabama or Mississippi."

"There's more than enough racism up there, too," Pop said, launching into another lecture, just as Jessie knew he would, once *Alabama* and *Mississippi* had slipped out of his big stupid mouth.

Inspiration struck Jessie, just as Pop was winding down on his lecture. He'd insisted on Jessie memorizing speeches and quotes from Dr. Martin Luther King, and one of them fit perfectly here.

Jessie looked Pop in the eye. "Dr. King says, 'He who has not found something to die for isn't fit to live.'"

Pop's jaw dropped. Seconds passed before he spoke.

"Nice try, using my own hero's words against me. Forget it. I'm not letting you die for hockey."

"I'm not going to die." Jessie looked at his parents and felt it all slipping away. Dreams he hadn't even known he'd had, the ones the headmaster had so lovingly described, were now slipping through his fingers; dreams like New England champions, Olympic gold medals, the NHL. Pop didn't understand any of that. He liked sports but didn't love them the way Jessie did.

But suddenly, another wave of inspiration struck him. "It's not just about the hockey. Mr. Whitney said I might be able to go to Harvard."

Pop rolled his eyes. "White men like them can promise you the world, Jessie. They can talk all they want about Harvard and Yale, but the plain fact is that there's never even been a black student at Springvale Academy before—never. You can't get to Harvard if you don't survive Springvale. And tell me something: What did you think of that coach?"

"I don't think he liked me," Jessie said.

"You don't *think* so?"

"I'm sure he didn't," Jessie admitted.

"And was it just you he didn't like?"

Pop had him cornered now, and Jessie had to concede. "No, it wasn't just me. He didn't touch Momma's strawberry shortcake, and after we shook hands, I saw that he wiped his hand off on his pants."

Pop smiled. "Good—you're paying attention." He spread his hands wide and went on. "So, do you see now why we have to say no? It's a school that's almost certainly loaded with racists. It'll be just you and this other young man, against over four hundred white boys. And if your own coach feels the need to wipe his hands off after he touches you, it means he wants no part of you. I'm certain he was only here because the headmaster forced him."

Jessie felt empty inside; he'd used all his arguments and lost.

"It isn't safe for you at that school, dear," Momma said as tears welled up in her eyes. "You're all we've got. We can't risk losing you."

3

Thursday, April 4, 1968

Jessie, still filled with anger and frustration over the Springdale situation, could barely speak to his parents, especially Pop. He made all the decisions, no matter what Jessie had said; it just didn't seem fair to him and his resentment was obvious.

"Watch your attitude, young man," Jessie's mom had warned as he'd picked at his breakfast the next morning. He didn't feel like eating or doing anything else, either. She was just about to scold him again—he could tell—when Pop shook his head and exchanged looks with Momma using that special brand of silent communication they shared.

Jessie trudged off to school, came home, sullenly waded through his homework, and then rode silently in the car with his father on the way to a six o'clock Spring League hockey practice while his mother made dinner. But no matter what he did, Jessie couldn't get Springvale Academy out of his mind.

Even when he stepped on the ice, the one place where he'd almost always been able to leave his troubles behind, that resentment toward his parents festered. A hat trick of lost dreams flashed before his eyes: Harvard, the Olympics, and the NHL. Gone, gone, and gone. All because Pop wouldn't allow anyone else to be a hero in their family. It was fine for Pop to put himself in harm's way from the Ku Klux Klan; but Jessie couldn't even go to a campus filled with white runts half his size. Maybe he shouldn't have said the word aloud with the headmaster and coach right there, but as far as Jessie was concerned, he'd been right about Pop. He was a hypocrite with a capital H. And Momma was almost as bad, horrified at the thought of him going away, no matter where it turned out to be.

"You're still my baby," she'd said, words that made Jessie want to scream. He'd be sixteen years old later this year, and mature for his age. She and Pop told him that all the time, but when it counted, they didn't stand by it.

The whistle blasted. Jessie blinked, felt the rush of cold air over him, and heard the loud hum of the rink's refrigeration system. As his thoughts returned to practice, he heard the whistle blast again and looked around.

Stevie and Ritchie, his line-mates, had taken off on a drill, leaving him behind. Jessie felt his cheeks burn hot with embarrassment and he looked down at his skates. What had he been doing? As Stevie and Ritchie returned to the head of their lines, they stared at him. He almost never got distracted on the ice.

Coach Ralph, short and squat, skated over. "Is there a problem, Jessie?"

"No—I'm sorry. I was just . . . ." He shook his head in frustration, unable to explain himself.

"Let's get it right this time," Coach Ralph said, then blew the whistle.

Jessie cradled the puck on his stick and took off, skating ahead ten feet, then dropping the puck and cutting to the left wing while Stevie crisscrossed behind him to the center, where he picked up the drop pass. The three weaved in and out, and Jessie finished with extra mustard on his shot into the top right corner of the net past Mike, their goalie.

The next time through, Jessie flew, his skates barely touching the ice, and his shot almost ripped a hole in the back of the net. At least that's how it felt, the way it was supposed to be.

And that's how it was the next time through, and the time after that. Sweat poured off Jessie, a good, cleansing sweat, forgiving him after getting caught with his head in the clouds.

That wouldn't happen again.

As Jessie worked out his anger, he fired one shot after another past Mike: blocker side high, blocker side low, glove side high, glove side low, and five hole. Jessie was putting his frustrations behind him and Mike was paying the price. Jessie beat him with dekes, too. But when he deked to the forehand and then to the backhand, then tucked it back around on the forehand, Mike exploded.

"Gimme a break, will ya!" he shouted, skating out of his crease and behind the net. He slammed his stick against the glass in frustration.

A part of Jessie felt bad; he'd been making Mike look foolish without meaning to, something he'd never do during pre-game warm-ups. That was when players deliberately shot into the goalie's pads or glove, or just a little bit off them, so the goalie could make every save, mentally preparing for the game and never once letting the puck get past him. You weren't trying to score before a game; you were warming up the goalie—that was the code. But there was no such code in practices, when every shooter tried to score every single time, building up that habit of taking advantage of every opportunity.

Usually during practices, Jessie would toss a bone every now and then to Mike to keep the goalie's confidence high. But for the past fifteen minutes, he'd clobbered Mike with the bone, the double-deke being the icing on the cake of goaltender humiliation.

To even things up, the next time Jessie skated down the ice, he ignored the opening Mike gave him in the upper right corner, but instead aimed at the post and clanged his shot off it.

"Hah!" Mike yelled.

But as Jessie skated along the boards, he noticed the parents, Pop included, all scrambling out of the stands and rushing out to the lobby. What was that all about?

Jessie got in line and tried to make sense of it; he hadn't seen anything like that since his first tryout with the team three years ago. He could tell that lots of the parents didn't like him, or more accurately, didn't like the color of his skin; he guessed that he made them uncomfortable. But they'd forgotten all about that once he started scoring some

31

goals in every game, and some of them had even begun talking to his parents.

So what was this commotion all about? Jessie waited, paying close attention to the new drill that Coach was describing; he wasn't about to screw up twice in the same practice—messing up even once was bad enough.

Minutes later, the Zamboni operator blasted the siren that signaled the end of practice. Coach blew his whistle and everyone headed off the ice and into the hallway leading to the locker rooms.

"Jessie!" his father called out as he stood alone, looking haunted. He motioned Jessie to his side as the other parents stared at them, obviously alarmed. "Dress as fast as you can," Pop said. "Don't talk to anyone and get back out here—and be quick about it."

Alarm tingled from Jessie's fingertips to the hair on the back of his neck. "What's the matter, Pop?"

"Just do what I say."

Concerned, Jessie grabbed his dad by the elbow. "Is it Momma?"

"Just do—" Then Pop bowed his head. His shoulders began to shake and he said the terrible words. "It's Dr. King. He's been shot."

Jessie shuddered, but he had to ask, "Is he—"

"I don't know, son. Just hurry. I don't want these people to see me if Dr. King—if he—" Then Pop choked back a sob, turned, and rushed outside.

His head spinning, Jessie raced into the locker room, threw his equipment into his bag and quickly pulled on his street clothes.

"What's wrong?" Mike asked.

Jessie shook his head, unable to speak, and charged out of the room.

●

Pop stared ahead, rocking back and forth, as Jessie tossed his bag and sticks in the back of the car. The radio, tuned to news station WBZ, blared, covering most of the rumble from the car's bad exhaust system.

"It's over," Pop said, at first so softly that Jessie couldn't understand him. Then he repeated it a bit louder. "It's over. Dr. King is dead. A man of such peace. Such peace! And they shot him like a dog." He rested his head on the steering wheel and repeated, "Like a *dog*."

Pop turned to Jessie and opened his arms, taking him in a fierce embrace. Pop shuddered as they hugged tighter and tighter, and he kept asking, "Why . . . why . . . why?"

When they sank back in their seats, Jessie felt numb all over and a sharp pain stabbed deep in his gut.

"He was the best of us all," Pop said. "You should've seen him, should've heard him preach. I'd have walked to the North Pole and back for him." He shook his head, then absently turned on the defroster to clear the fogged up windshield and banged the dashboard when it didn't work. Wiping the windshield with his bare hand, he whispered, "I can't believe he's gone."

A sudden sense of loss struck Jessie. He felt like he'd been sucker-punched in the gut, but was barely able to understand why. After all, he hadn't marched with Dr. King like Pop had, and he hadn't really thought much about the Civil Rights Movement. He was just a kid, and that was adult stuff.

But Jessie, too, had his dream—to play in the NHL just like Willie O'Ree. Sitting there in the car, in the aftermath of the shattering news, it occurred to Jessie for the first time that his dreams, just like those of his friends and all the grownups like Pop and Momma, were all tied up in Dr. King. And now, a man with a gun had just taken all that away.

"'I have a dream...'" Jessie said.

Pop looked over, bewildered. He still hadn't shifted the car into gear when he said, "What?"

"'I have a dream,'" Jessie continued, reciting the memorized words of Dr. King, "'that one day this nation will rise up and live out the true meaning of its creed: 'We hold these truths to be self-evident: that all men are created equal.'"

Pop turned off the radio, his eyes filled with tears. His voice shook as he spoke, "'I have a dream that one day on the red hills of Georgia the sons of former slaves and the sons of former slave owners will be able to sit down together at the table of brotherhood.'"

Jessie's father had come up with this back-and-forth recitation with Jessie on long car trips shortly after Dr. King made the speech in 1963. Pop had witnessed it live among the throngs in Washington, D.C., and contended it was the greatest he'd ever heard and worth memorizing—at least in part. So that's what they'd done, even down to Dr. King's rising and falling cadences.

They recited some of those familiar words, ones full of such beauty and power, but they described ideals that seemed so unreachable. Would they ever live to see the day when they *weren't* judged by their color, but instead by their character? It seemed so hard to believe in, especially knowing that this man of principle and peace had been shot *because* of his color.

The words felt empty and hollow as Jessie spoke them and as Pop responded. There was no dream anymore. The dream was dead.

Jessie's voice broke as he recited the final words, "'Free at last! Free at last! Thank God Almighty, we are free at last!'" and then collapsed into his father's arms. Overwhelmed with despair, they both wept.

4

Jessie and his parents sat huddled on the front room sofa, eyes locked on their black-and-white TV. There were no tears left to be cried, no deeper level of grief to endure. Dr. King was gone, apparently shot by a lone gunman.

"He knew they were going to kill him," Pop said. "It was just a matter of time." He shook his head in bitter disbelief. "Just last night . . . it must have been his last speech . . . I saw it on the news. He spoke of getting to the mountaintop and seeing the Promised Land like Moses in the Bible. He said, 'I might not get there . . . but I'm not worried. Mine eyes have seen the glory of the coming of the Lord.'"

Pop drew in a deep, ragged breath. "He was such a great man. I can't believe he's gone." He put his arm around his wife, who sat next to him, then reached out and squeezed Jessie's shoulder. "The cities are going to burn. The Black Panthers will say that nonviolence doesn't work." He shook his head. "Maybe they're right."

"Jordan!" Momma exclaimed. "Surely you don't mean that."

Pop looked at Momma, a faraway, lost look in his eyes. "I don't know what I mean. I don't know what to think anymore."

The images on the TV screen showed riots breaking out in almost every big city across the United States, including Boston, just a half hour's drive away. Buildings burned, and sometimes entire city blocks went up in flames. Sirens wailed everywhere, as helmeted white policemen chased after black men and beat them with their night sticks. Burglar alarms rang out as other black men poured into stores, emerging with their arms loaded with clothing, TVs, and radios.

"This is everything Dr. King opposed," Pop said.

"My dear sweet Jesus," Momma said. "Look at what's happening."

President Johnson called for calm, as did Boston Mayor Kevin White. But the news cameras showed that nobody was listening. Rage seethed in the black inner cities, and nothing anyone was saying seemed to matter.

"You don't think they'll burn down your clinic, do you?" Jessie's mom asked. His father had two medical offices where he saw patients; one was here in Lynn, and the other, a clinic, was located in the center of Roxbury, Boston's impoverished black neighborhood. Jessie had gotten the impression long ago that Pop lost a lot of money on his Roxbury practice, treating most people for free, but knew it as his father's way of helping the community. "Surely they'll leave it alone, won't they?"

Pop stared at the TV screen's images. "That isn't what I see." He said nothing for a while. "All that bottled-up rage is exploding. They're burning their own neighbor-hoods and they don't even care. I can't see that my clinic will be any different."

Jessie could almost feel the heat of the fires and smell the smoke. As they watched the news, a funeral-like gloom fell over the room.

"You don't think rioting will spread here to us, do you?" Momma asked, a nervous quiver in her voice. Lynn, a city of almost one hundred thousand people, was roughly two-thirds white. The Stackhouses lived in one of the bet-ter, predominantly white neighborhoods, although all the houses on their street were modest.

"We'll be fine," Pop said, but he didn't sound con-vinced.

Momma whirled suddenly to face Jessie. "You're not going to that James Brown concert tomorrow night!"

"But—"

"Don't you 'but' me, young man," she said. "You're not going anywhere near the city! Can't you see what's hap-pening? The Lord gave you eyes. Use them!"

Jessie pointed to the TV set and said, "That's in Rox-bury. The Garden is miles away from all that."

"What's wrong with you, child? You think it'll be safe to see James Brown anywhere in the city right now? Who do you think will be going to that concert? Happy white people?"

"But Rose and I—"

"Even more reason. If you think you're taking that sweet little thing into the city, you haven't got a penny's worth of common sense in your head." She shook her head in exasperation. "You are *not* going into the city, and after dark, you're not stepping foot outside this house."

"That isn't fair." Jessie looked to Pop for help.

"Don't look at me. Your Momma's right. It isn't safe."

Jessie felt his face burn hot. He couldn't go away to Springvale Academy because it was too dangerous. He couldn't take Rose to see James Brown because it was too dangerous. This place was getting like a jail.

He got up to leave and was halfway out of the front room when he heard the local newscaster mention James Brown. Jessie stopped. The Boston Garden box office was offering refunds to ticket holders concerned about their safety, and rumors circulated that the city was even considering canceling the event.

Jessie didn't look at Momma; he wouldn't give her the satisfaction of an I-told-you-so raised eyebrow. Instead he just walked away, and although he didn't slam his bedroom door—that would have gotten him in trouble—he closed it very hard.

5

Despite everything, Jessie and Rose got to see the concert after all, although not in person. With the mayor's office and city council terrified of fifteen thousand black youths descending on the Garden, they arranged for WGBH to televise the concert live.

"Your Pop will be working late and I'll stay out of your way," Momma said. "I'll give the two of you your privacy, and after it's over, I'll drive Rose home." She cocked her head. "As long as you promise to behave yourself."

And so, with Momma in another part of the house, Jessie and Rose sank into the front room sofa, a bowl of buttered popcorn on the coffee table. A *Please Stand By* sign filled the TV screen, as if this were some test of the Emergency Broadcast System. Behind the black-and-white TV with its antenna perched on top, a large picture window, its curtains drawn, faced the front lawn and the street.

Some hot date this is turning out to be, Jessie thought. Instead of awaiting James Brown's appearance on stage surrounded by thousands of other screaming and chanting fans, they were sitting on a sofa, eating popcorn, and watching a *Please Stand By* sign.

Jessie felt so disappointed, he'd almost mentioned Springvale Academy and the full scholarship offer, not wanting to hide it and figuring the night couldn't get any more ruined than it already was. But then he thought better of it. He'd tell her, just not now.

An announcer came on and in a pompous voice asked listeners to please be patient while technicians worked on the audio feed, saying that the James Brown concert would be broadcast as soon as possible.

Jessie got up, turned down the TV's volume, and put on James Brown's *Live at the Apollo* album, figuring they'd listen to him one way or another. The music crackled to life, the vinyl's grooves already well worn, and "Soul Brother Number One" began to sing.

"I guess this is better than nothing," Jessie said. "But it ain't gonna be the same."

Rose snuggled close to him. Jessie put his arm around her shoulder and said, "Let's make it the same." She rested her head against him, smelling sweet and clean, her hair the scent of strawberries. He could see the tiny diamond in the necklace he'd given her for her birthday sparkling in the TV's meager light. Looking into Rose's soft brown eyes, he felt all his anger and frustration melt away.

She took his hand and told him, "I love you, Jessie."

"Me, too," he said.

Rose tilted her head, a sly grin on her face. "You love yourself? Is that what you mean? Or do you love me?"

41

He grinned, feeling so much better now. She could do that to him. "I love you."

"You sure now?" Rose teased. "I don't want to be making out with you if you ain't sure whether it's me you love or not."

"I love you, and I'm sure," Jessie told her.

"Me, too," she said and giggled.

Jessie kissed her full on the lips, moist and soft with a hint of mint. His pulse quickened as they wrapped their arms around each other.

That kiss lasted for a very long time.

When they finally came up for air, she asked, "Still think it's not the same as being at the Garden?" Her eyes danced.

"It's better."

Rose stroked his cheek, then said, "Right answer."

They kissed again, this time even longer.

"We'll have to do this until the show starts," Rose said when they stopped.

A half hour later, the show still hadn't started, but Jessie didn't mind at all.

"I thought we're supposed to behave," Rose said with a wicked grin.

"We are. We ain't doing anything wrong."

"Kissing this good gotta be sinful," she told him.

"The Lord forgives," Jessie said, and felt the laughter roll through Rose. Then their lips met again and nobody was laughing.

●

They'd been making out for almost an hour and were almost disappointed when the show started. But they sat up when the introductions began, with Mayor White taking his bows and James Brown dedicating the performance to Dr. King's memory.

Soon, Jessie and Rose were on their feet, dancing to "Soul Brother Number One's" music, not really minding that the tinny sound coming from the TV's speakers was a far cry from hearing it live. It didn't really matter; when James Brown sang "I Feel Good," Jessie and Rose sang along as they moved to the beat. They both laughed when Jessie tried to imitate James Brown's howl, and he felt good, just like the song said, and was sure Rose did, too.

They were having a great time. That is, until the football-sized rock crashed through the picture window.

Shards of glass sprayed everywhere as the rock clipped the top of the TV set, barely missing the rabbit ears antenna, and bounced onto the carpeted floor.

Rose screamed and Jessie froze—the rock had landed close to where they'd been dancing. The picture window now looked like a spider web, but with a huge hole punched in the middle, one the size of a beach ball. A jagged sliver of glass dangled then fell, shattering on the wood floor.

In the darkened room, lighted only by the flickering images on the TV screen, Jessie thought the rock was a bomb. He grabbed Rose and they ran out of the room and down the hallway, then heard a clumping sound coming up from the basement as Momma burst through the basement door, meeting them in the kitchen.

"What happened? What did you do?" Momma asked, breathless, with her eyes darting between Jessie and Rose.

"We didn't do anything," Jessie said. Rose, who'd been clinging to him, pulled away. "Somebody threw something through the window—a bomb or something."

"*A bomb?*" His mother looked horrified.

"Jessie," Rose said, "I think it was just a big rock."

The three looked at each other, then walked cautiously back to the front room, just in case it really was a bomb, not wanting to set it off. They peeked into the room, then Momma went past Jessie and Rose to turn on the light.

It was definitely not a bomb, just a football-shaped rock, chipped on one side. Jessie stared at the rock in disbelief. Who would do that?

Another loose shard of glass fell from the window pane and shattered below. Rose yelped, then covered her mouth and giggled nervously, saying, "Sorry."

James Brown continued to sing, but now no one was watching.

Jessie let go of Rose's hand and stepped closer to the window. Cool air blew into the room and glass crunched beneath his feet. He realized for the first time how heavily he was breathing.

"Get behind me," Momma said.

"I'm all right," Jessie said.

"I said, 'get behind me!' Make me say it again, child, and I'll behind your behind."

Jessie looked at Rose, feeling embarrassed, but she put a hand to her mouth, suppressing a giggle. As Momma crept forward, Rose mouthed the words *behind your be-*

hind? Jessie just shrugged, then had to hold back his own laughter in spite of the situation. That was typical Momma.

"I don't see anybody out there," Momma said. "But we aren't going to find out by ourselves." She strode from the room. "Come with me."

She picked up the telephone from the stand at the end of the hallway. First, she called the police, then Pop. Pop would get there as soon as he could, but he still had two more patients to see.

●

When the police finally arrived, their cruiser's lights flashing, Momma, Rose, and Jessie stepped outside. The porch light cast their shadows onto the walkway as the patrolmen parked along the curb. They got out of their car and stared at the front of the house.

Momma moved down the walkway to get a look, then gasped. "Oh, no," she said; pain covered her face.

Jessie rushed to see for himself, and when he did, all the air rushed out of him. It took all his strength to keep from doubling over as he stared at the message spray-painted across the front of the house. It read:

NIGGERS

GO AWAY

He felt like someone had reached inside him, grabbed hold of his guts, and twisted them. His pulse pounded in his head and Rose clung to him, her body shaking. She was crying.

Rage filled Jessie; he wanted to find whoever had done this and break them in half with his own bare hands.

6

Two days later, the Stackhouse family returned home from a church service in honor of Dr. King that had been filled with tearful tributes. The soulful music had never been finer, and when Nadine Clayton sang the beloved hymn "Precious Lord, Take My Hand," everyone wept.

Now, seeing the boarded-up front window, Momma looked like she was going to start crying all over again. The three walked through the hallway and into the dining room. Pop looked at Jessie somberly, then said, "Sit down, son. We need to talk."

The tablecloth was plain white with a lace trim, and a glass bowl filled with fruit sat in the middle of the table. Pop sat at one end with Momma beside him; Jessie on the opposite side.

"This isn't easy for us," Pop said, and Momma burst into tears.

Jessie wondered what he'd done, and couldn't think of anything, unless they're trying to make him feel guilty about making out with Rose, and that sure wasn't going to happen.

"Your momma and I have talked a lot about this, and I'm still not sure we're making the right decision," his father said, then sighed. Momma sniffed, then dabbed at her eyes with a handkerchief. "We've reconsidered our decision about you going away to school, to Springvale Academy."

Jessie's eyes widened. "I can go?" An electric shock ran through him as he asked, "Really?"

Pop took a long time to respond. He chuckled ruefully and shook his head, then glanced at his wife. "I guess we know where he stands," he said to his wife, who stared down at the tablecloth and said nothing.

Before he went on, Pop drew in a deep breath. "We knew all along that it was a great opportunity. I don't know about this NHL thing, but the academic possibilities at the school are remarkable. There's just no denying it, much as your mother and I would like to."

He drummed his fingers on the table and Jessie held his breath.

"It was your safety we were concerned about," Pop said.

"And we're *still* concerned," Momma added.

"Very concerned," Pop continued. "But there's no longer any safe place left. It's not just Detroit, Chicago, and D.C. that are burning to the ground. Boston hasn't fared quite as badly—James Brown appears to have saved the city from that fate—but . . ." He swallowed. "My clinic is gone—up in smoke."

"No!" Jessie said, not believing his ears. "Why would they—"

"When a mob's rage boils over, it can do the most self-destructive things. But we'll be fine. After all, I lost money running that clinic. Most of my patients couldn't afford to pay. They're the ones I'm most worried about." He tapped the table and said, "I'll work out of my office here in town until we decide what to do next." His look darkened as he waved toward the front room. "We're not safe here, either. That broken window—next time it could be a Molotov cocktail that burns the place to the ground, with us in it." He shook his head. "No, there's no safe place left. Not anymore."

Jessie couldn't find any words.

"Your Momma and I have begun thinking that you may be safest at Springvale Academy, away from all this madness, in the pastoral hills of rural New Hampshire. We hope so. But we may be sending you into the worst part of the storm. We don't know, and God help us if we're wrong. I've spoken with the headmaster, Mr. Whitney, about our concerns. He assures me he's taking personal responsibility for your safety, and that you'll be safer up there than you would be staying here. So if it's what you want, and if you think it's the best thing for your future, we won't stand in your way, no matter how hard—"

"You're still my baby," Momma blurted out.

"Momma, don't say that." Jessie hated it when she talked that way.

"Well, you are," she said. "You're all we've got." She choked on the words. "And now you're going to leave us."

Jessie's dreams flashed through his mind—images of himself skating against the best, playing in the Olympics, and in the NHL. Maybe he'd have a shot at the future he'd hoped to have.

His mother walked around the table and hugged him. "You're going away, aren't you?

For Jessie, there was no question.

●

The following afternoon, Rose looked at him expectantly. She and Jessie sat on the wooden benches in Tony's Pizza & Subs as customers bustled in and out, the phone ringing off the hook with take-out orders. The aroma of tomato sauce and melting cheese wafted over them, mixed with those of the other foods. Aside from the steel grating protecting the front windows, slid back for now, and the earlier closing time, Tony's looked just like it had before other cities began burning. White customers looked nervous, but nothing more; the destruction in Detroit, Chicago, and Washington, D.C., might as well have happened on another planet. Even Boston, only a half hour's drive away, felt like it was on another continent.

Rose flashed a smile of brightest white. "So?" she said. "You said you had something to tell me."

Jessie felt a lump in his throat; this was going to be harder than he'd imagined. She was so pretty, especially when she smiled like that, and it melted something deep inside him. But as he began, in awkward fits and starts, to tell Rose about Springvale Academy, her expectant smile faded. She blinked as if he'd slapped her, then looked away, the pain visible in her soft eyes.

49

"So you're going away," she said when he finished. Her words hung in the air.

"I can't turn down this kind of opportunity," Jessie explained. "My momma and pop hated the idea of me going away, but even they could see the advantages. They're the best in competitive hockey—they win the New England Championship most years. And three of their graduates were on the Olympic hockey team that won the gold medal. Another guy might make the NHL soon, and the academic program is so good, that could get me into an Ivy League school, maybe even Harvard—"

"You don't care about the academics," Rose broke in. "Who are you trying to kid? It's all about hockey. Hockey this, hockey that. That's what you really love." In a soft whisper, she added, "Not me."

Jessie felt paralyzed; he couldn't speak or even think. Rose had never sounded this angry or this hurt, not even when they'd had their worst fights.

"What were you expecting?" Rose said. "That I'd be happy for you as you skate out of my life?" She said the word *skate* with extra venom. "Okay, I'm happy for you. I'm so happy, I could just spit. I'm *overjoyed* that you're leaving me. I'm *in heaven* thinking that we're done." She threw up her hands. "Is that what you expected? Was that what I was supposed to say?"

Jessie struggled for words. He hadn't known what to expect her to say; he hadn't really thought about it that much. He knew now that he should've thought about it a lot more, and figured out the right way to tell her.

Finally, all he could say was, "I'm not leaving you."

"Not now, but in September. It's like what happened to my grandma when I was ten. She got the cancer bad, and they gave her six months to live—she only lasted four. So you and I got five months to live—five months. Probably only last five days instead; we're in our coffins now—we just don't know it. Least *you* don't know it."

"We don't have to break up when I go away. If we love each other enough—"

"If we *love* each other enough?" Rose's voice was loud enough by then to make heads to turn. She noticed, then took a deep breath and said more softly, "You are such a dreamer, Jessie. You gonna be six hours away—three up and three back. You say you coming back for Thanksgiving and Christmas? So I get to see you twice, and then you go back up there until June, except maybe one or two other short vacations. I see you four times in almost a year, and we're supposed to stay together? How we gonna do that?"

Jessie had no answer for her and was silent.

"How much you thought about that?" Rose asked.

Jessie had an answer this time, but he didn't want to tell her.

"I bet last night you were in bed thinking about all the championships you're gonna win, and dreamt about gold medals and the NHL, and what's-his-name—Willie O'Ree." She snorted. "Maybe you even dreamt about becoming a Harvard man. But did you think of us at all?"

Jessie couldn't meet her fiery eyes. "I'm sorry. I was just so excited, I didn't—"

"I *hate* hockey." Rose practically spit the words out. "Why can't you be like everyone else and play hoops, or football, or baseball? Don't you know hockey's for white boys?"

"It's what I—" He stopped himself from finishing the sentence, but the words had almost slipped out—Jessie had meant to say hockey was what he loved.

Rose's lip trembled. "That's what I been saying. It's hockey that you love."

"But I love you, too." Jessie took her hand, but she pulled it away.

"You're so intense about that sport," Rose said, as if Jessie hadn't spoken at all. "It's all you can think about, like you're a little crazy."

Jessie saw an opening and took the shot. "I'm crazy about you."

Rose rolled her eyes. "Oh, brother. Where'd you get that line, from some book?"

"No! I mean it."

A tear trickled down Rose's cheek. "You're only crazy about one thing."

The pizza came, but neither of them touched it.

"Come over here," Jessie said at last, and Rose got up and slid onto the bench beside him. He put his arm around her and told her, "I love you." She rested her head on his shoulder, covered her face, and began to cry.

Helpless, all Jessie could do was hold her, ignoring the disapproving looks of an older white couple.

Rose didn't stop until the wet shoulder of Jessie's shirt clung to his skin.

"I'm sorry if I'm supposed to be happy for you," she said, her voice choked. "But I can't do it. I hate this more than you'll ever know."

7

August 31, 1968, Saturday

Rose came over to the house so she could kiss him
goodbye. They'd made it through the spring and summer,
arguing more than they ever had before, the tension always
between them. But they shared plenty of good times, too,
and she always felt so good in his arms, as if they were two
pieces to a puzzle that clicked perfectly.

But to be fair, he'd told her she could date other boys,
though it'd pained him to say so. He'd be gone almost ten
months with almost no trips back home. A part of him
hoped she'd come up to visit sometimes with his parents,
but he knew he couldn't suggest it.

When they'd talked about it, she'd looked at him with
her sad brown eyes and had said, "You can date other girls
too, if you want—since you be at an all-boys school." Then
her mouth had twisted into a grin as she held back the tears.

Jessie hugged her there in the driveway and kissed her
one last time, long and hard, before he climbed into the
back seat of Pop's Plymouth. As they pulled away, he

turned around and looked out the back window, waving as she blew him a kiss.

The breeze blew in through the open car windows, feeling good against Jessie's face as summer wound down with the temperature still in the eighties. He was going to miss Rose. *A lot*.

●

As they headed out of town, grimy brick buildings gave way to billboard advertisements that lined the route through Boston. On the static-filled AM radio, WILD played James Brown's latest hit, "Say It Loud, I'm Black and I'm Proud," with Jessie bellowing the title to Momma and Pop's amusement. Jessie thought his Afro, which he'd grown out in the last few months, matched the emotion. Black was beautiful, baby.

As soon as they left the range of WILD's shaky signal, Jessie handed Aretha Franklin's latest eight-track tape, *Aretha Now*, to Pop. But when "Soul Sister # 1" began to belt out "Think," it almost seemed as if Rose, not Aretha, was asking Jessie to think about what he was trying to do to her. But he wasn't trying to do anything. Did she think this was easy for him? A Marvin Gaye tape soon replaced *Aretha Now*, followed by more James Brown, the volume not quite as loud as Jessie would like, but all that Momma would allow.

Eventually, Jessie picked up a dog-eared copy of *Sports Illustrated* from a pile on the seat beside him. Already two months old, the cover featured the face of a black athlete wearing sunglasses, with an image superimposed showing him sprinting towards a hurdle, his arms pumping. The title of the cover story was "The Black Athlete— A Shameful Story."

He was mesmerized by the cover. His English teacher, Mrs. MacKenzie, had talked about symbolism in class, but it had gone over his head at the time. He hadn't understood about the boat's mast being a crucifixion symbol in Hemingway's *Old Man and the Sea*. Why bother with symbols? If a writer wanted to say something, then he should just say it outright.

But Jessie got why symbolism was used on this cover. He hadn't gotten it at first, but after reading Jack Olsen's story, it had leaped out at him. The black athlete approaching that hurdle had to get over a lot of other hurdles besides the one in front of him.

As he flipped to the lead story, the first in a series of six, the magazine automatically opened to page twelve. And once again, the quote of one college's athletic director leaped out at Jessie. "In general, the nigger athlete is a little hungrier, and we have been blessed with having some real outstanding ones."

The nigger athlete is a little hungrier. Jessie asked himself again if that was how the Springvale Academy headmaster saw him. Was that why Jessie had gotten a full scholarship? Jessie didn't think so. He could see Coach Stone thinking that for sure, but Mr. Whitney?

Jessie thought about what Rose had said about him, about how intense he was, a little crazy even, and wondered if that was just him being hungry. He didn't like to think of himself in those terms. But what was he supposed to do?

Stop being so hungry, stop being a little bit crazy about hockey?

In a way, Jessie wished he'd never read the articles. They'd taken this dream come true and painted it with ugly colors, tainting it before he even got to the school. He tried to reassure himself that what Jack Olsen had written about wasn't the way it'd be at Springvale Academy. After all, those were colleges Olsen had written about, a lot of them in the South. Springvale was a high school in New Hampshire. You couldn't get much farther North than that. Still, he couldn't shake the fear that he was leaving Rose and his family for something that could turn out to be a nightmare.

Not even five months had passed since the Springvale people's visit, but Jessie felt five *years* older, and more like he was heading to college instead of prep school as a repeating freshman. He had a feeling he'd need to mature even faster in the coming months.

Jessie flipped the pages to another quote, this one even more haunting by Harry Edwards, the former black athlete who'd been advocating a boycott of the upcoming Olympics.

"Black students aren't given athletic scholarships for the purpose of education. Blacks are brought in to perform. Any education they get is incidental to their main job, which is playing sports. In most cases, their college lives are educational blanks."

Was that what they expected Jessie to do at Springvale Academy? Just perform? It could be the case. After all, hadn't the headmaster talked about tutors and repeating Freshman year? The headmaster had beaten a hasty retreat under Pop's withering glare and declaration that Jessie would *excel* in the classroom or not be there at all, but Jessie could read people well enough to know that Harry Edwards was probably right. Jessie had been recruited to score goals and integrate the school. All that talk about Harvard and Yale had been just that and nothing more—talk.

Say it loud, I'm black and I'm proud.

Well, he'd show them.

●

The cracked two-lane road that led from Route 89 twisted and turned for fifteen miles, past scattered farms with barns, silos, and herds of cows. One moment, the air smelled clean and sweet of pine, only to have shifting winds bring them the faint but unpleasant hint of manure in the fields. When the sign announced that they were entering Springvale, only thick clusters of trees lined the roadside, but soon the little town emerged. Palmer's Motel came first, its sickly pink paint peeling, its vacancy sign dangling from only one hook.

"Of course there's vacancy," Momma said. "Who'd stay at that fleabag?"

A two-story, red brick schoolhouse came next, its grassy playground dotted with little kids running and playing on the swings and jungle gym, even though it was Sunday. Then came a gas station, a small supermarket with about a dozen cars in the parking lot, and a post office scarcely larger than Jessie's bedroom. A sign in the darkened window of a small bookstore near the center of town read:

WELCOME SPRINGVALE ACADEMY STUDENTS

Winslow's, a general store with fresh white paint and cloudy windows, offered live bait, freshly made grinders, and homemade pizza.

"I hope they don't mix the three," Momma said.

Pop grunted.

When they drove past the Springvale First Baptist church, its steeple rising to the heavens despite its modest size, Momma clucked her tongue. "Like there'd be a *Second* Baptist church in this cow town?"

Pop eyed her wryly and said, "Now, now."

She shrugged. "I'm just saying."

"I think we knew what you thought of this place before you even got here," Pop said.

"Was I wrong?" she asked.

Pop didn't respond, probably knowing that he had no chance of winning this battle.

After another mile, the trees on the left gave way to a wide, open grassy field, and a white sign in Old English script said:

SPRINGVALE ACADEMY
Established 1842

Tiny American flags around the sign fluttered in the breeze.

Pop turned onto a road leading to a parking lot up ahead. After a hundred yards, a tall, muscular teenager waving a red construction site flag greeted them. He had a thick mop of blond hair poking out from a Boston Red Sox cap, and he wore khakis and a maroon Springvale Academy T-Shirt that showed off his chiseled physique. Using the flag, he motioned them into the parking lot. But then he stopped waving, bent over, and took a closer look at the occupants of the car.

"Hey, you!" He called, shaking his head as if there'd been some mistake.

He walked over to the car, and in a hushed voice, said, "This is for the Springvale freshmen. The service entrance is—" Then he spotted Jessie in the back seat. Looking mystified, he added, "Freshman orientation?"

The muscles in the back of Pop's neck bunched and he gripped the steering wheel so hard, it looked like it might snap.

"That's right," Pop said.

The young man nodded slowly. "Oh." He looked from Pop back to Jessie. "Okay."

"Unless," Pop said, voice dripping with sarcasm, "you have a separate parking lot for coloreds."

The young man's face turned red. Pursing his lips, he waved them through, his eyes fixed on Jessie as if he was memorizing his face. Stitched on the sleeve of his T-shirt was the name Dirk. Jessie didn't look away, swiveling his body around to look through the rear windshield even as the boy's eyes blazed.

Whether this was the right way to start here or not, the righteous rage of Harry Edwards's words burned in Jessie. If boys like Dirk thought Jessie was going to "know his place," they had another thing coming.

Say it loud, I'm black and I'm proud.

59

"What are you doing, Jordan, talking like that?" Momma scolded, snapping Jessie out of his reverie. She stared at Pop and said, "We're not here for thirty seconds, and you're shooting your mouth off. What's wrong with you?"

Pop's mouth tightened and he didn't say a word; he just pulled into a parking spot between two Cadillacs, both polished and spotless, their chrome gleaming in the midday sun.

Momma spun around to face Jessie. "And what about you, young man? You're as bad as your father."

"I didn't say—"

"You didn't need to say a word. How long you think you're gonna last here in Crackerville if you go staring down every boy who looks at you cross-eyed?" She shook her head and glanced at Pop. "What am I going to do with the two of you?"

Jessie felt his face grow hot. He didn't care what Momma said. He wasn't going to the back seat of anybody's bus.

"Lord have mercy!" Momma said. "He gave me the two most stubborn men on the face of his creation."

The words flew out of Jessie's mouth. "Momma, I'm not gonna be their Uncle Tom."

Her eyes widened. "What did you say?"

"I'm black and I'm proud," Jessie said, and to him, it was as if James Brown had performed the introduction to the call-and-response, challenging him with, "Say it loud—" then holding the microphone out for his response. Jessie added, "Like James Brown says, 'I'd rather be dead on my feet than live on my knees.'"

Momma's voice went up an octave when she said, "What are you *saying*?" Then she spun on Pop. "Jordan, will you speak to the boy? Talk some sense into him." Without waiting, she whirled back to Jessie. "What has come over you, child?"

Only seconds before, words had flown out of his mouth before he could stop them. But now words failed him.

"I've just been . . ." He shrugged; he'd talked to Momma and Pop only a bit about the *Sports Illustrated* series because he hadn't wanted to give them an excuse to back out of agreeing to let him go to Springvale and make him stay home. But he needed to be honest with them now, so he told them, "I've been reading about things." And he meant he'd read not just Jack Olsen's series, but also the writing of Langston Hughes, James Baldwin, and even Eldridge Cleaver.

"I'm not gonna sacrifice my *dignity* here just to get by," he explained. "I'm black and I'm proud, and I don't care who hears it. If they don't like it, that's their problem."

"Lord have mercy. You're gonna get yourself killed, talking like that." Tears welled in Momma's eyes when she asked him, "How long you been thinking like this?"

"I don't know," Jessie said. "A while, I guess."

"And you just decided to tell us now?" Momma asked.

Jessie swallowed. He'd changed a lot this past summer. He liked to think he'd become a man. His eyes had opened to a lot of things beyond the hockey rink, such as what it meant to be a young black man in this changing world. He'd come to realize that there was more to life than making the NHL. But there were also plenty of times when he didn't even know what to think.

Jessie shrugged. The car suddenly felt unbearably hot; with only a light breeze blowing through the windows, the air had grown heavy and humid, its smell musty. Sweat beaded on Jessie's forehead. When he leaned forward, his shirt clung to his back. He plucked it loose.

"Can we get out?" Jessie suggested.

"No!" Momma snapped. "Jordan, talk to the boy."

Pop's shoulders rose and fell. His eyes met Jessie's in the rearview mirror.

Pop turned around slowly and frowned. "Son, I shouldn't have said what I said to that boy back there. I was thinking he was just some kid from town who needed a verbal slap in the face, a wakeup call. I didn't notice the school T-shirt. I wasn't thinking." He sighed. "I'm hoping he isn't one of your classmates. If he's an upperclassman who came early to help with freshman orientation—and something tells me that's exactly what he is—then I've made you an enemy before you even stepped out of the car. And for that, I'm sorry. That was foolish of me. Irresponsible."

"Pop," Jessie said. "Only way he was gonna like me is if I looked like Casper the friendly ghost."

Pop chuckled ruefully for a moment before his face again turned grave. "That may be true, but—" he took in a deep, wheezing breath—"I do share your Momma's concerns. You need to be Jackie Robinson here, not Stokely Carmichael or Rap Brown. You're going to be outnumbered here, and not just by a little. It'll be an overwhelming number, more than a hundred to one. You can't be militant in an environment like that."

Jessie's father took a breath and went on: "You're going to have to show restraint here. You can't be fighting every racist you see. Otherwise, you'll be fighting all the time. And if you're surrounded by fifty of them, you may have right on your side, but after you throw one punch, they're gonna beat you senseless, and maybe worse."

Even as Jessie's shirt clung to him and he wiped beads of sweat off his forehead, a chilling fear came over him, seeping into his bones and filling him with dread. It drove away the haunting words of Harry Edwards and Jessie suddenly felt certain that he wasn't the right person to be a groundbreaker. He'd open his big mouth or get angry at the wrong person, and then, who knew what would happen to him.

"It's like when we were organizing down in Mississippi," Pop said. "Trying to register people to vote."

The car felt like a furnace by now, and Jessie had heard this story many times before, but you couldn't stop Pop at a time like this. It'd just mean they'd stay there even longer if he tried to change the subject.

"We were meeting at the church," Pop said, "and they drove up in their cars and stood in front of their grills, holding their shotguns. Now the Lord might have been on our side, but it was those rednecks who held the shotguns.

"Was that the time to flaunt our pride? 'Say it loud — I'm black and I'm proud?' I don't think so. We all linked arms, bowed our heads, and began singing, 'Amazing Grace' as we filed out of the church. We kept singing all the way down that dusty road.

"Now, do you think I'd be sitting here today, if I'd

smart-mouthed those rednecks like I did to that boy today? Or glowered at them like you did?"

Jessie didn't respond.

"I asked you a question," Pop demanded.

"No," Jessie answered.

"That's right. Sometimes you need to have enough wisdom to hold your peace. There's a time to speak, and times when God help you if you don't. I know it isn't easy for you to hold your tongue." He glanced at his wife. "You've got your momma's gift of gab."

Momma slapped at his arm in a way that might have been playful in a less sobering conversation, but not this time.

"We are going to overcome some day," Pop said. "I know it, and you know it. They can kill Medgar Evers and they can kill James Chaney and they can kill Dr. King, but they can't kill our spirit. We surely will overcome." He grasped Jessie's shoulder and went on, "But you best pick your fights when they're numbering four hundred and you're only one of two. Use your wisdom, Jessie. Wisdom. We're counting on you to be wise while you're up here breaking new ground."

Jessie's head spun. When he listened to Pop talk like this, it made sense. When he listened to James Brown, dying on your feet made more sense than living on your knees. When he read the words of Harry Edwards, he felt he'd rather die than be Springvale Academy's Uncle Tom.

"Sometimes I feel so confused," Jessie said. "Everybody seems to know how I should act . . . except me."

"You've got a head on your shoulders, son, and a heart

to match. You're going to win them over here. I don't know how hard they're going to make it for you, but you're going to win."

Jessie nodded without meaning it. Five minutes ago, he'd felt the same way. No one could keep him down. He'd show them all. But now, thinking about his father's advice, he wasn't so sure.

8

A succession of signs in bright red letters that read "Freshman Orientation" directed them on concrete walkways surrounded by vast expanses of the thickest, greenest grass Jessie'd ever seen. And although the air smelled of freshly cut grass, there wasn't a loose blade to be seen. Raucous bird calls filled the air.

The last sign led to Grayson Field House, an immense red brick building that appeared to be only a couple years old. No surface of dirt or grime coated the bricks; they still looked new. The windows were trimmed in white and an American flag beside the entrance rippled softly in the light breeze. The Stackhouses walked up the concrete steps and opened the heavy oaken doors.

Inside, Momma gasped and Jessie's jaw dropped. The immense foyer, brightly lit by two glittering chandeliers, reeked of money. Ornate latticework circled the room, and photographs of athletic teams in polished, gold frames covered the walls. Beneath the photos stood marble trophy cases, each displaying an array of trophies and memorabilia. Jessie's eyes were drawn to an ancient-looking football. The lettering read:

1936 New England Champions
Springvale 48, Cushing 6

The three gawked like tourists who were seeing New York City skyscrapers for the first time.

"Oh, my," Momma whispered.

Pop shook his head. "If this is what the gym looks like . . ."

Laughing, Jessie began to strut like a peacock. "Momma," he said, "Eastern Junior High had a gymnasium." Looking down his nose at her, he said, "This—is a *field house*. We don't have anything so common as—" he turned up his nose as if getting a whiff of ripe garbage on a summer day. "—as a common *gymnasium*."

"Okay, Jessie Rockefeller," Momma said, and they all laughed.

Despite his clowning, Jessie felt a twinge of doubt, wondering how he could possibly fit in with all these rich kids, but he pushed it away as they advanced through the doors to the basketball court. Four large tables were spread out across the court in front of the signs: A-G, H-N, O-S, and T-Z, each one lettered in Old English script. Hanging in front of each table was a banner bearing the Springvale Academy logo in maroon and gold, the school's colors. Behind each table sat two women serving lines that were only one or two families deep.

As the Stackhouses walked toward the tables, the soft buzz of conversation dwindled to silence as one by one, heads turned to face them. It was just like a row of dominos falling.

●

Pop and Jessie carried two suitcases and two boxes up the stairs to his room in Williams Hall while Momma carried his few clothes on hangers: a suit, five dress shirts, and three pair of dress pants. Pop slid the key for room 317 out of the orientation packet, but before opening the oaken door, he gave it a solid rap. The Beatles song "Back in the USSR" blared from the room next door, and a faint smell of incense wafted through the air.

When no one answered Pop's knock, he unlocked the door and they all stepped inside a surprisingly spacious room. It was divided into two mirror images of matching desks, beds, and dressers running along two walls. Beside the door stood an oak closet also divided into halves. Dozens of empty hangers hung on both sides.

Jessie walked to the large window set into the far wall. With its shades up, the window looked out on an expanse of thick green woods just fifty yards away. A bird darted from a tree and pecked at the grassy ground.

When the music next door paused between songs, Jessie could hear a woodpecker hammering away at some distant, unseen tree, giving off a rapid knocking sound.

"This is beautiful," Momma said; she'd criticized everything about the town since they entered it, but she had to acknowledge this. "You *are* going to keep this place neat, aren't you?"

Jessie rolled his eyes. "No."

"It would be a sin not to, Jessie."

Pop grinned. "Son, if you know what's best for you, you'll clean up every time you know your Momma's coming for a visit."

●

A knock on the door came just as Jessie was sliding an Otis Redding album onto the platter of the Sears stereo system Momma and Pop had bought for him. Maybe it didn't look like much, but it was the first one he could call his own. At home, if he wanted to listen to his albums, he'd had to use the family stereo in the front room, which wasn't possible if someone else was watching the TV there. Here in his room, he'd be able to listen to his records whenever he wanted, and it just added to the luxury of the room.

Momma, who'd hung up his clothes and rearranged everything he and Pop had transferred from the suitcases to the dresser drawers, bustled to the door.

Jessie slid the stereo's knob into the Up position so the needle wouldn't drop down onto the record, knowing it'd be rude to greet his roommate with a blast of music instead of a handshake.

Momma opened the door and a short white boy with curly black hair stood there. He was wearing dress slacks, a white shirt, and a tie. "Hello, I'm Preston," he said. "Preston Bradford."

Jessie stepped forward and introduced himself, and they shook hands. Jessie couldn't help but feel disappointed; he'd hoped to room with the other black kid. Preston not only had the pasty white skin of someone who hadn't stepped outside all summer; he also looked like he'd be as much fun as a dictionary. *A white shirt and a tie?* Jessie knew they had to wear blazers and ties to classes, but a white shirt and tie for moving in? It just wasn't natural.

"So you're Jessie's roommate?" Momma asked, then she looked about for luggage or Preston's parents.

"No, I'm next door," he said, pointing to where the music had been coming from, and it was only then that Jessie noticed the music had stopped. "I just came by to say hi."

"Jessie?" Momma asked.

He turned to her.

She tilted her head and gave him the eye.

"What?" he asked.

His mother rolled her eyes and said, "Did you forget to pack your manners?"

Forget to pack . . .?

"Oh, I'm sorry," Jessie said, realizing what she'd meant. He nodded to his mother and said, "Preston, this is my momma," then turned to his father and said, "And this is my pop."

They all shook hands.

"Where are you from?" Momma asked.

"Upstate New York, near Albany," Preston said. "But my father works in Washington, D.C. He's a congressman."

Jessie's ears perked up, not only because of what Preston had said, but also for the nonchalant way he'd said it.

"A congressman?" Momma said. "Really? Are your parents still here? I'd love to meet them."

"They were supposed to move me in, but there was some emergency in D.C., so my father couldn't come and my mother had to stay home with my little sister and brother. My brother's ten. He could've come along, but my sister is three and it would have been—" He shrugged and went on. "You know three-year-olds. So our driver moved me in and headed right back home."

Momma's eyebrow arched and Pop looked surprised, too. Jessie figured they were thinking the same thing he was. *Our driver?*

The three Stackhouses were speechless.

"Would you like to see my room?" Preston asked.

It seemed an odd question. "Isn't it the same as this one?" Jessie asked.

"Well . . . in some ways, yes; in other ways, no."

When he stepped inside Preston's room and the blast of cool air hit him, Jessie understood. The two rooms had the same physical dimensions and furniture, but their similarities ended there. Here in Preston's room, an air-conditioning unit sunk into the far wall below the large window hummed away and a television sat on a stand at the foot of Preston's bed. But what really caught Jessie's eye were the bookshelves. Whereas Jessie's bookcase held the compact Sears stereo, a handful of books and notebooks, thirty or forty record albums, and a stack of *Sports Illustrated* magazines, Preston's screamed wealth, with leather-bound books, hundreds of albums, and glittering stereo components, including a separate tuner, amplifier, pre-amplifier, and turntable that must have cost thousands. The walnut-colored speakers were larger than Jessie's stereo.

"Listen to this," Preston said. He pulled an album out of its sleeve and put it on the turntable. He adjusted chrome knobs on the amplifier and said, "Special effects." The sound of a bird chirping came out of the speakers so clearly that Jessie looked about the room expecting to see the bird.

Preston grinned. "Pretty good, eh? Close your eyes."

The sound of glass breaking made Jessie jump, then he laughed at his own reaction. Cats meowed, dogs barked, and finally, a jet took off. It sounded so lifelike that Jessie could almost feel the force as the jet roared past.

What am I doing here? Jessie wondered. He didn't mean Preston's room, but Springvale Academy. *These people are going to laugh at me. I don't belong here,* he thought.

Jessie shook his head, banishing that thought, but he knew he could never again feel the same way about that cheap stereo Momma and Pop had given him, the one he'd been so proud of just minutes before.

"My roommate's name is Franklin Stoddard," Preston said, pulling Jessie out of his reverie. He waved at the empty half of the room and said, "I hope he's neat. I'm sure he is. His father is one of the top editors at *The New York Times*."

"Is everyone here from rich or famous families?" Jessie asked, hoping it wasn't true.

"Not everyone. Not your roommate," Preston said. "His name is Charles Jones."

"Yeah, that's what it said in my orientation packet," Jessie said. "I wonder what he's like."

Now it was Preston's turn to look surprised. "You don't know?"

"Know what?"

"He's the other Negro."

9

Jessie left a note for Charles on his desk, asking him to join them, and the four walked over to the giant tent that had been erected over the soccer and lacrosse fields behind the field house. Long before they reached even the fringe of the assembled crowd, the smells of spicy barbeque, onions, peppers, beef, and sausage wafted to them.

"Whoa! That smells great," Jessie said. "I love a barbecue. Gets my stomach to growling."

Momma glanced at Preston and told him, "Jessie has a healthy appetite—a very healthy appetite. Only time he slows down is when he's with a girl."

Thoughts of Rose flitted through Jessie's mind, but he pushed them away. He didn't want to get all moody in front of his first friend.

A black waiter dressed in a black vest and white bowtie approached, carrying a tray of appetizers. Eyes fixed on Jessie, he smiled. "Scallops wrapped in bacon? Stuffed mushrooms? Shrimp cocktail?"

Jessie said, "Yes, yes, and yes."

"Absolutely, sir," said the waiter, whose smile broadened as he handed Jessie a small china plate.

"But please take care of my parents first," Jessie quickly added. "And my friend, Preston."

"That's the only way we're going to get anything to eat," Momma said, a sparkle in her eyes, the earlier disagreement apparently forgotten. "This school can throw away its garbage disposal units now that Jessie Stackhouse is on the scene."

Even before Jessie bit into the bacon-wrapped scallops, he groaned with delight. The mere smell of the hickory-smoked bacon sent his salivary glands into overdrive. He couldn't imagine anything tasting better.

"Excuse me!" he said as the waiter turned to leave. "Could I get a couple more of those?"

"Jessie Stackhouse!" Momma exclaimed. "You'd think I never fed you. Leave some for everyone else."

"Momma, they have plenty." Jessie loaded three more scallops onto his plate. He wished he'd skipped the stuffed mushrooms to leave more room for the other good stuff. He'd never tasted stuffed mushrooms before and decided he'd leave those for last, just in case.

"You can see what the phrase 'eat his parents out of house and home' means," Pop said to Preston. "After a year with Jessie, this place will have to raise tuition."

They continued to move through the great tent, heading toward the array of grills where marinated steak tips, jumbo shrimp, ribs, barbequed chicken, and cheeseburgers sizzled.

Classical music resonated from a stand where four

tuxedoed students played string instruments; Jessie guessed they were juniors or seniors.

"I believe that's the school's chamber music quartet," Preston said. "It's legendary. Competition for those spots is supposed to be fierce, especially for violin and cello."

Jessie recognized the violin, or at least he thought he did, but it looked like there were two of them, even though they looked different.

"Which one is the cello?" he asked.

Preston launched into a lecture about stringed instruments and classical music, and Jessie soon wished he hadn't asked. He had no interest in the difference between a violin and a viola, or how Beethoven compared with Mozart. But there was no stopping Preston.

"Do you play an instrument?" Momma asked Preston.

"Yes. The piano." He smiled and added, "I'm pretty good, if I may say so myself."

"Can you play rhythm and blues?" Jessie asked. "How about Little Richard?"

"My father would break my knuckles if he caught me playing anything like that," Preston said. "I'm only allowed to play serious music."

"What about Duke Ellington or Thelonious Monk?" Pop asked with an edge in his voice that Preston seemed to miss.

"They're jazz, right?" Preston asked.

When Pop nodded, Preston shook his head. "No jazz for me. Like I said, only serious music."

Pop pursed his lips and his face clouded, but rather than engage in a debate, he simply excused himself to get a drink.

Preston resumed his chamber music lecture for a bit longer. Then he brightened and turned to Jessie, saying, "But enough about music. This is quite a place, isn't it? What do you think?"

"It's real nice," Jessie said.

"Beautiful," Momma said. "I'm sure Jessie will get a wonderful education here."

Preston leaned close to them and said, conspiratorially, "It probably seems even better, coming from the ghetto, right?"

Jessie froze, and so did Momma's smile.

"I'm not coming from the ghetto," Jessie said.

Preston looked first stunned, then disappointed. "You're not?"

"No," Jessie said. "It may surprise you to hear this, but not all black people live in the ghetto."

Preston flushed. Just seconds later, he excused himself.

●

Jessie and his roommate Charles spotted each other at the same time and made a beeline for each other.

"Charles?" Jessie asked when he got within twenty feet.

"The name's 'Stick,'" he said. "Nobody calls me Charles." Jessie could see where the nickname came from; Stick stood little more than five-foot tall and couldn't weigh much more than a hundred pounds. He was indeed a stick. A toothpick also protruded from the corner of his mouth, and even his nametag read *Stick Jones*.

"Man, you a sight for sore eyes," Stick said.

"You got that right," Jessie said.

"I almost as happy to see you as to see my lady."

"I ain't *that* happy to see you," Jessie said, and they both laughed.

Jessie introduced Momma and Pop, this time without prodding, and Stick followed suit with his momma, a short, tired-looking woman with a beaming smile.

"Did I hear you play *hockey*?" Stick asked, a disbelieving look on his face. "A brother your size should be playing hoop."

Jessie often got tired of hearing this, but his delight at finally meeting the one other brother on campus deflected any irritation about it. "Best black man on skates since Willie O'Ree."

"Who's Willie O'Ree?"

"Who's Willie O'Ree?" Jessie repeated, shaking his head and pushing Stick playfully. "What's wrong with you? He's the only black man ever to play in the National Hockey League." Jessie leaned close. "I'm gonna be the next."

Momma shook her head and rolled her eyes.

"A hockey player," Stick said in a tone that made it sound like the most disappointing thing in the world. "The one black cat I can hang with here's a *hockey player*." He broke into high-pitched laughter. "What's this world coming to? I gotta talk to you 'bout slapshots and— and—man, I don't even know what else. Some kind of line? Red lines and—"

"There's a red line and two blue lines."

"What for?"

"They're so you can't just wait behind everyone else, then get a long pass and an easy goal."

Stick shook his head, still mystified. "Whatever you say, man."

"What you play?"

"Football. Basketball. Baseball." He grinned. "*Normal* sports. The ones black people play."

Stick's mother spoke up. "Basketball's why he's here, how he got the scholarship. Nobody can stop him. But nobody can stop him on the football field, too. He's fast as lightning."

"You best be fast as lightning at your size," Momma said to Stick. "Some of those big boys, they'll break you in two if they hit you."

"I'm five-nothin' tall, and weigh a hundred-nothin' pounds. But I'm something. Them big boys can't hit what they can't catch. I work my black magic on 'em." He chuckled and said, "I'm black magic, baby."

"It's the truth," Stick's momma said. "Only one who can stop him is his coach."

"Why, that's just like my Jessie," Momma said, puffing up with pride. "Other teams have a player following him around. They call it shadowing."

Jessie rolled his eyes. Momma had trouble telling the difference between the blue line and a clothesline, but here she was, talking about shadowing, just like she was some kind of expert.

"Other teams play him dirty," she continued. "Try to get him into the penalty box so he can't score goals. That's the only way they can stop him."

"Penalty box?" Stick asked with a sly grin. "That like a jail?"

●

They made their way to Wexler Auditorium for Mr. Whitney's orientation address, along with all the other students and their families. Inside, three great chandeliers hung from an ornately painted ceiling. The five of them—Jessie, Pop, Momma, Stick, and his mother—filed into a middle row, the two boys beside each other. They sank into their seats, so plush and comfortable that Jessie wondered if the audience would fall asleep.

A film depicted Springvale Academy's illustrious history, closing with its most famous alumni: a United States president, five senators, and four governors; a Nobel Prize winner in chemistry; fifteen Olympic medalists, including six in hockey; and sixty-two corporate CEOs.

"I'm their next president," Stick whispered when the film was over. He laughed and Jessie joined in.

Then the headmaster moved to the podium.

"I'd like to welcome all of you to Springvale Academy, one of the finest—we think the very finest—institutions of its kind in the country," he said. He pointed to the audience. "All of you will be our most valuable asset. You come from all parts of the world and have many differing backgrounds, but you all share in one thing."

The headmaster paused and silence fell over the hall.

"You share excellence," Mr. Whitney finally said. "You are the cream of the crop, and this country's elite."

He smiled. "And to prove my point, I'd like all of you to do something for me."

Everyone waited, and then the headmaster continued.

"I'd like you to stand up," Mr. Whitney began, "if you expect to finish in the top half of the class."

The sound of nearly all the students getting to their feet filled the auditorium. Laughter broke out, followed by applause. Jessie glanced down at Stick, who'd remained seated.

With an embarrassed shrug, Stick stood. Ducking his head, he said to Jessie, "Who you kiddin', man?"

Jessie had been surprised and amused that almost every student except Stick had stood, all of them assuming, based on their previous successes, that they'd finish in the top half. Mr. Whitney's exercise illustrated just how difficult the competition would be, how hard they'd all have to work, and the expectations they'd set for themselves.

But Stick's assumption that neither one of them would finish in the top half also surprised and disappointed Jessie.

"I'm a good student," Jessie said. "Really good."

"Yeah?" Stick said. "Einstein on skates?"

"I'm serious," Jessie told him.

Stick shrugged and said, "Okay."

After telling the assembled students to sit down again, the headmaster underlined what they'd all realized immediately, that the bar was set high and that not everyone could finish in the top half.

"Man, at least I know who I am," Stick whispered as the headmaster rambled on.

Jessie locked eyes with Stick and told him, "So do I."

●

After the orientation speech ended, Jessie headed toward the family car with his parents. This was the designated time for parents to leave so the incoming boys could continue with orientation activities without them.

Momma's eyes predictably welled with tears, and one after another trickled down her cheeks. "You're still my baby, Jessie. I know you hate it when I say that, but I can't help it. You're so young to be away from home."

"I'll be fine, Momma. I can take care of myself."

She nodded and gave him such a long bear hug that he wondered if his clothes would take on her lilac scent. Sniffling, she whispered, "I love you so much!" Then her body began to shake and she repeated, "So much."

Jessie held his mother tight, at first embarrassed that other students might see, but then deciding he didn't really care what anyone thought.

When they finally released each other, Pop put his hands on Jessie's shoulders and told him, "You're going to have to be a man now, and maybe before your time. But I know you've got what it takes. You're a very mature young man." He squeezed Jessie's shoulders and said, "I'm so proud of you, Jessie. You've got greatness in you."

Then his father gave him a bear hug, too. "Call us each weekend," Pop said, his voice choking. "More often if you need to." He pressed some bills into Jessie's hand. "This is a little extra cash, just in case you need it."

Jessie took a quick peek at the twenties, then said, "Wow. Thanks."

It didn't seem real that Momma and Pop were actually leaving until the car doors slammed and the engine turned over.

Jessie moved away from the car, suddenly overwhelmed with loneliness. Part of him wanted to tell them not to go. But they smiled and waved, and so did Jessie.

And then they were gone.

10

That night at eight o'clock, all the freshmen of Williams Hall packed into the first-floor common room. It didn't look as though anyone was missing; freshmen slouched in the common room's easy chairs, some sitting on the floor, and others leaning against the wall. A gentle breeze wafted through the open windows, cooling the forty or so tightly packed young men.

As Mr. Richardson, their "dorm parent," made his way to the center of the room, the buzz of conversation fell silent and he introduced himself. Thin and wiry, and about thirty years old, he lived in a first-floor apartment in the dorm. He also taught English and coached the swim team.

"Okay," he said, "you should all be able to guess the rules," he said. "No drugs of any kind; He slowly turned and added, "No alcohol," and grinned. "That is, unless you buy enough for me, too."

Everyone laughed.

"No girls in the rooms," he said, wiggling his eyebrows like Groucho Marx. "Unless you set me up with their older sisters."

More laughter.

Jessie liked Richardson; he was cool, funny, natural and at ease. That definitely put him in the "plus" column at Springvale.

"So that we can all get to know each other, I'm going to ask each of you to tell us three things about yourself that the rest of us wouldn't already know. We'll go around the room three times, so you only have to come up with one thing at a time."

Jessie puzzled over what he'd say and hoped Mr. Richardson started on the other side of the room.

Still pivoting slowly so he could see everyone, Mr. Richardson said, "For example, I could tell you that on Tuesday nights, I like to dress up in my mother's lingerie."

Jessie felt his jaw drop, and all around the room, eyes widened.

Then Mr. Richardson broke into uproarious laughter. "You should see the looks on your faces. Check it out and look at each other! I was just kidding about that to see if you were paying attention," he said.

Everyone began to laugh. This guy was good; he'd really gotten them going.

"Okay, I'll tell you a real fact—no punch line this time. My favorite thing to do is listen to the Rolling Stones and eat brownies hot out of the oven topped with ice cream."

Yeah, Jessie thought, *brownies with ice cream. Not bad.*

And to Jessie's relief, Mr. Richardson picked someone on the other side of the room to tell a fact about himself, beginning with a red-haired kid with freckles.

"My name is Jimmy Duvall and I come from Los Angeles, where the most beautiful women in the world live." A dreamlike look came over his face. "They all want to be movie stars, and my favorite thing is to watch them sunbathing on the beach in their bikinis."

The room erupted with applause and wolf whistles.

When the noise finally died down, Mr. Richardson commented, "That's a good one. You gotta love starlets in bikinis—almost as much as starlets without bikinis."

Stunned uproarious laughter filled the room. *Could a teacher really say that?* Jessie glanced at Stick and Preston, who were laughing and had to be thinking the same thing. They'd gotten the coolest dorm parent in history.

"Hey guys, don't tell anybody I said that," Mr. Richardson said. "Don't get me in trouble! Oh, and by the way, that reminds me of a rule I forgot to mention: no girlie magazines in your rooms." A somber air filled the place as Mr. Richardson looked at them sternly and warned, "And if you have any, don't let me find them." Then his stern look gave way to a playful one. "Because if I do, I'll have to confiscate them—and my closet doesn't have room for any more."

They all roared again. *Man, this guy was the coolest.*

Jessie racked his brain for what to say about himself. He'd talk about hockey, of course, but he needed *three* things and wanted to start off with something else.

So when it became his turn, he said, "My name is Jessie Stackhouse. What you probably don't know about me is that my father is a doctor and he marched to Selma with Dr. Martin Luther King."

"No good, no good," Mr. Richardson interrupted. "That's about your father, not about you."

"Oh, okay," Jessie said, thinking that others had made reference to their families, though maybe not as directly. It would have to be hockey, then.

"When I was seven years old, my pop took me to see a Boston Bruins game. Willie O'Ree scored a goal for the Bruins that night and I fell in love with hockey. He's the only black man to ever play in the NHL." Jessie looked about the room. "I want to be the second one."

A few heads nodded, but a lot more had looked uncomfortable as soon as Jessie mentioned race. He'd seen that look so many times; it was the one that said, "Would you please just go away? We'd rather pretend you didn't exist." Well, that was just too bad. He *did* exist, and he was at Springvale to prove it.

The self-introductions continued around the room with a lot of Boston Red Sox baseball fans being quick to say so, a couple New York Yankees fans getting good-natured boos, a tall kid with a Southern drawl saying he loved 'Bama Crimson Tide football, Stick mumbling about being a basketball player, and Preston talking about music.

By the time the third round got underway, it seemed that all the guys were talking about what kind of girls they liked.

Jimmy Duvall, the sunbathing fan from California, said, "I like blondes. Can't get enough of them. Blondes, blondes, blondes."

Another countered, "I like redheads. They're hot."

Soon everyone was talking girls. Jessie mentioned

Rose's big brown eyes and her pretty smile when his turn came.

"Italian girls!" someone said.

"Cheerleaders!"

That one drew loud cheers.

"Chunky girls, with some meat on them."

"Skinny, but with big boobs."

Then it was Stick's turn. He said, "I like white women."

A shocked silence filled the room, as guys stopped chewing their gum in mid-chew. Jaws hung open and boys shifted uncomfortably in their seats.

Stick bellowed with laughter and said, "You should see your faces!" He hooted. "It's like I just dropped a turd in your punchbowl." Jessie joined in, seeing the looks on their faces. It was priceless. A few boys joined in with nervous laughter, but the humor appeared to be lost on most of them.

"Where I come from, we hang Nigras for sayin' that," said the tall boy with the thick Southern drawl.

Jessie felt as though he'd been slapped. No, it was worse than that—a lot worse. He shot to his feet, fists clenched, with Stick at his side.

The tall kid stood up, too, as Mr. Richardson rushed into the middle of the circle, holding his hands out. "Okay, okay. Cool it. This isn't how we're going to start the year."

Under his breath, Jessie muttered, "Stupid redneck."

"Sit down!" Mr. Richardson shouted. "All of you."

Jessie waited for the peckerwood to sit down first.

Neither moved.

"Now!" Mr. Richardson ordered. He didn't seem so cool anymore.

Jessie waited the extra split second, satisfied at seeing the redneck back down first.

●

While Preston's stereo next door blasted the Beatles and the Rolling Stones, Jessie and Stick lay sprawled on their beds listening to Aretha Franklin.

"What concerns me isn't the one redneck," Jessie said. "It's everyone else. I could see it on their faces, plain as day. They just want us to go away so they can talk about their Red Sox and their blondes and their cheerleaders."

Stick grinned. "Ain't nothin' wrong with blondes and cheerleaders."

"Will you stop that?" Jessie shook his head. "Jeez."

"Jus' sayin'."

"Did you see their faces?" Jessie asked.

Stick looked him in the eye. "I ain't blind."

"So what do we do next?"

"Ain't nothin' we can do," Stick said.

Jessie had to agree.

11

Early the next day, Jessie headed over to the field house, a hockey stick in one hand and a workout bag slung over his shoulder. In the lobby, he gawked again at the extravagant chandeliers and marble trophy cases, wondering if that would ever grow old for him, and then headed to the weight training area. Roughly the size of a football field, it housed both free weights and a Universal machine. A running track circled it on the outside. Only a lone figure cycling through the Universal prevented Jessie from being alone.

He got to work, taking a dumbbell and, resting a knee and one hand on a bench, began to work his biceps, starting slow, warming up his muscles, but then pushing himself harder. When he thought he'd pushed as far as he could go, Jessie coaxed another rep or two as he thought about the redneck's cruel words. *You can't hurt me, peckerwood. You're only making me stronger.*

Soon Jessie's T-shirt dripped with sweat, its salty tang on his lips. He focused for an entire hour on his upper body, working it until he felt satisfied that he'd done enough.

Then he changed T-shirts, moved to the circular track surrounding the weight area, and began 30-yard sprints. The distance didn't matter much; the key was acceleration and having that powerful burst of speed that shot him ahead of the next guy. He sprinted and recovered repeatedly, then switched to sprints that changed direction with quick pivots.

No one would ever outwork him—no one. If he pushed himself now, even as his legs felt heavier and heavier, then they'd feel light and as powerful as pistons when he needed it—on the ice.

Jessie'd begun lifting weights only in the past year and a half, but he'd been sprinting all his life, racing one friend after another to the next hydrant, or to the street corner, or to see who could get to the ice cream truck first.

Jessie always won.

He intended to keep it that way.

He changed shirts again, using a towel to wipe the sweat that poured off his face. Then he gathered his stick and bag, and headed down the corridor that connected the field house with the hockey rink. He wasn't sure if he'd be able to get on the ice, but he figured it didn't hurt to try.

He walked through the lobby and opened one of the doors to the rink. A blast of cold air hit him and he stepped back into the lobby to put on his sweats. That done, he reentered the chilly rink, and in the dim light, moved through the stands.

He stopped, stunned at the sight of all the maroon and gold championship banners that hung from the ceiling. *Did Springvale ever lose?* There were three rows of them, dating from before World War II to the present, with banners hung for every year this decade except 1961 and 1964. There wasn't one yet for this past spring's title, but that would certainly change on the season's opening night, when the 1968 banner would be hoisted to the rafters with all the others.

Jessie took it all in: the dark wood paneling, the banners of all the league's teams, the familiar background hum of the refrigeration system, but most of all, he stared at the overhead scoreboard, one comparable to the one he'd seen at the Boston Garden. He wondered how much it had cost. He'd never played in a facility where a four-sided electronic scoreboard hung above the ice, displaying the score in every direction. He guessed that when the score almost always conveyed good news, everyone should see it.

Shaking his head in amazement, Jessie sat on a bench and put on his skates. Then he took out his still stiff but already sweat-stained new gloves, and picked up his stick. After fishing three pucks out of his bag, he tossed them over the glass and opened the door to the ice. It was such a luxury having new ice all to himself—something that would never happen back home, where the rink was booked every hour, from four in the morning until midnight. If Bobby Orr and the Bruins got any more popular, rinks soon would be running twenty-four hours a day.

Jessie dug his skate blades into the ice, feeling that wonderful sense of freedom as he glided around, from one side to the next. He crossed over his stride, picking up speed in the turn, then accelerated to full speed as he picked up a puck. He stickhandled, cradling the puck with soft hands as if it were as fragile as a raw egg; he crossed the blue line, pivoted, and drew his stick back. Then with a grunt, he drove the stick violently against the puck, hitting the ice just behind it so the stick would bend ever so slightly and give the slapshot its full force. The puck rang off the inside of the post, up near the crossbar, and caromed into the net.

A perfect shot.

Jessie smiled. He liked the finesse moves: the faking and the stickhandling, the perfectly placed pass, and especially the speed. But most of all, Jessie loved the power moves—slapshots, bone-crunching checks, and racing into the corners to outmuscle his opponent for the puck.

All alone in the dim light and feeling a total sense of peace, Jessie fished the puck out of the net and headed back up ice. He continued for another twenty minutes, then practiced quick-release wrist shots from the slot, that most prime of all scoring areas, fifteen or twenty feet in front of the net. He worked on his backhand, the toughest of all shots to control because the curve of the stick bent in the other direction. Next, he sprinted from blue line to blue line, stopping hard, spraying ice chips into the air, then crossing over and racing back to the other blue line.

Speed. Acceleration. Quick pivots.

Jessie didn't ever want to lose a race to a loose puck. To him, each one was his, had his name on it. And if an opponent thought he could take it away, well, good luck to him. The guy better take his best shot because Jessie intended to come out of every corner with the puck on his stick.

Winning those battles would be his ticket to the NHL,

make him the next Willie O'Ree. Jessie picked up a loose puck and ripped off another rocket. He imagined taking a hit just as he followed through, but in his mind, it'd be the opponent who fell to the ice.

The overhead lights suddenly brightened, not all the way, but more than twice the dim glow they'd been giving off.

Jessie glanced up, heard them hum, then looked to the stands. There, once his eyes adjusted to the light, he spotted a man at the far end, standing behind the top row with his arms folded.

"Stackhouse?" the man called out. "That you?"

It was Coach Stone.

"Yeah," Jessie hollered and waved tentatively, unsure of what else to do.

Coach Stone nodded. Even from a distance, he looked grim. "Come to my office when you're done."

He turned and left.

Jessie glided to the nearest loose puck, cradled it in his stick, rotating his wrists. Should he quit right away and hustle up to the office? Coach Stone didn't look happy, but Jessie couldn't recall seeing him look happy back home, either.

What was the problem? He knew Coach didn't like him, but wasn't it all right for him to be here now? The letter Coach sent out over the summer said the ice was being put down even before freshman orientation to make it available for captain's practices and extra work. Jessie couldn't imagine that he'd overstepped his bounds by skating today.

He half-heartedly tried a couple more drills, but was

only going through the motions and he knew it. To him, if he wasn't wiping sweat off his forehead, he was wasting his time.

With a resigned sigh, he gathered the pucks and changed back into his sneakers. Should he take a shower first? No, he didn't want to keep Coach Stone waiting. He also wanted to find out what he wanted.

He made his way up the stairs to Coach's office and knocked on the open door.

"Did you want me to shower first?" Jessie asked from the doorway.

Coach Stone sat behind his desk, wearing a bulky gray Springvale Academy sweatshirt with a whistle around his neck. He exhaled a cloud of smoke and put his cigarette on a maroon-and-gold Springvale Academy ashtray, and his fleshy, pockmarked jowls moved as he slowly chewed a piece of gum. He looked Jessie up and down.

"Sit down," Stone said, then wrinkled his bulbous nose with all its broken blood vessels. "I've smelled worse."

The office resembled a gallery, with black-and-white photographs of all his Springvale Academy championship teams, seventeen in all, adorning two walls. In each photo, the players huddled behind a trophy, holding their index fingers aloft in the number one sign. Beside them stood Coach Stone, his hands behind his back and a tight grin on his face.

Jessie's eyes widened when they turned to the wall behind the coach, where autographed photos showed him huddled with the likes of Gordie Howe, Bobby Hull, Jacques Plante, and, yes, Bobby Orr.

"Pretty impressive, huh?" Coach Stone said.

Jessie reacted with a start and blinked. "Yeah. Wow."

Coach grinned a self-satisfied smile in spite of himself.

"I don't think you realize what a privilege it is to play for this school," Coach said, the smile gone now. "There's no greater privilege for a hockey player your age." He narrowed his eyes, implying that Jessie didn't deserve it.

"I appreciate it, sir," Jessie said, gulping and feeling unreasonably nervous. "I do."

"No, you don't," Coach Stone said, his voice cold and hard.

Jessie tried to figure out why Coach would say that. What had he done wrong? He was already working hard, had beaten everyone onto the ice as far as he could tell. The upperclassmen were just arriving today, but not one other freshman had taken the ice yet.

"If you appreciated this opportunity—" Coach Stone leaned close, "—then you wouldn't show up here looking like that." He pointed to Jessie's head. "Looking like one of them Black Panthers."

Jessie froze. *What was that supposed to mean?* He didn't have on a black leather jacket or black beret, the official uniform of the Panthers.

"If you want to play on this team," Coach Stone growled, "get your hair cut. Maybe your friend, the other colored boy—"

Jessie's blood ran cold at that phrase, but he fought to stay calm.

"—maybe he'll get away with it, but no Negro on my team is going to wear an Afro. You got that?"

95

Jessie swallowed, his heart pounding. His hands shook when he said, "Yes, sir."

"You'll look like a Springvale Academy Warrior and you'll act like a Springvale Academy Warrior. Do you understand me?"

Conflicting thoughts raced through Jessie's head. What would Harry Edwards say about this man? What would he say about Jessie if he lay down to Stone like some whipped dog? That in only a day at Springvale Academy, he'd willingly become an Uncle Tom?

And yet Jessie saw his future flashing before his eyes. This was his shot, his shot at maybe someday making the NHL, his shot at a Harvard or Yale education. *Everything* was riding on this. He couldn't blow it.

"Yes, sir," Jessie heard himself say.

"Okay," Stone said, nodding his head, as if they'd gotten *that* matter settled and now it was on to the next item. He puffed on his cigarette and blew a plume of smoke in Jessie's direction. Then he said, "I heard there was trouble last night."

All this was coming at Jessie too fast. No Afros and . . . trouble? There'd been that little shouting match with the redneck last night, but Stone couldn't have heard of that, could he? But what else could he be referring to?

"Trouble?" Jessie asked.

An exasperated look came over Stone's face. He pursed his lips as if he'd just sucked on a lemon. "Don't play dumb with me. I know everything that goes on in this place. *Everything*."

Jessie cleared his throat. "You mean the argument during the orientation session?"

Palms spread out, Stone shot him a look that said, *of course, what else?*

"Sir," Jessie began in his most respectful voice. "My roommate, his name is Stick—he's the other black student. He made a joke and this red—um, this Southern boy started talking about lynching us back where he comes from."

Stone nodded but said nothing.

The room felt like a furnace, especially compared to the ice below. Sweat poured down Jessie's face, stinging his eyes. Blinking, he wiped it away.

"Of course there's gonna be some angry words after something like that," Jessie said defensively. He didn't add what he'd felt like doing to the redneck to make sure those words never were spoken again.

"What was the joke?" Stone asked, a smug look on his face, as if he already knew the answer.

"It was, um—" Jessie fumbled for words. "You see, everyone was talking about girls and stuff. What kind of girls they liked. You know, blondes and cheerleaders, and one guy said he liked 'em with some meat on their bones. Just goofing around, you know? So then Stick said he liked white women."

Coach Stone just glared.

"It was a joke," Jessie said, not really sure Stick meant it entirely that way but not concerned himself about that detail at the moment. "Stick laughed really loud and everything, then said that the look on everyone's faces was the funniest thing he'd ever seen."

Coach Stone's jaw set and his eyes narrowed. "I—"

Jessie jumped in. "It was just like Mr. Richardson's joke about wearing his mother's lingerie."

Coach's eyebrows arched. "His *what*?"

"It was a joke. To get us to loosen up and talk to each other. He didn't really mean it. Just like Stick."

Coach shook his head. "I don't see the humor. Not in any of it." He took a long drag from his cigarette, then stubbed it out. "Especially not in interracial dating. That's a very serious matter, and we're going to nip that one right in the bud, you understand? Right this minute."

Jessie swallowed.

"There *will* be some dances, about one each month, and a formal at the end of the year," Coach said. Then he pointed a finger at Jessie. "Don't ever let me catch you once with a white girl. If I do, you can pack up your equipment and go home that day. *No white girls!*"

Jessie's mouth felt as dry as cotton.

Coach's face flushed. "Do you understand me?"

Jessie nodded.

Coach Stone leaned forward. "You coming here wasn't my idea. It was that do-gooder Whitney, thinks he knows everything." He narrowed his eyes. "I didn't want you then, and I don't want you now. You got that?"

Jessie didn't move.

"I'm just looking for a reason to cut your 'Little Black Sambo' ass," Coach said. A slight grin came to his face. "And I'm sure you're gonna give it to me. Ain't that right? You couldn't even keep your mouth shut with your own father. Called him a hypocrite right to his face. That's how it is with you people. No respect at all."

Jessie sat there, frozen.

"Ain't that right, boy?"

"Yes, sir." Jessie forced the words out of his mouth, his voice cracking. When Stone's grin broadened, Jessie realized his mistake. "I mean, no, sir."

Stone licked his upper lip. "I think you were right the first time." Then he nodded toward the door and said, "Now get going."

His head swimming, Jessie stood.

"Now don't you go running to the headmaster," Stone said, shaking his head. "Don't even think about it. It'd be the worst mistake you ever made. You may be Whitney's Black Puppy, but if he hears you yip even once—" Stone drew his index finger across his throat. "—you're a goner." He flicked his hand in a shooing gesture and said, "Get out of here."

Jessie staggered out the door.

●

When Jessie got back to his room, Stick was stretched out on his chair, a toothpick in his mouth. When he heard what had happened with the coach, he said, "How we supposed to stay away from white girls when there ain't no black ones within a hundred miles?" He snorted. "They gonna ship some up from the city?"

"It gets worse," Jessie said, still in shellshock. "Stick, I'm only on the team because Mr. Whitney forced Stone to take me. Stone called me the Headmaster's 'black puppy,' said he didn't want me, and was just looking for an excuse to get rid of me."

Stick closed his eyes and shook his head.

"I knew he didn't like me," Jessie said bitterly, "but I didn't think it was this bad."

After a long silence, Stick asked, "So what you gonna do?"

Jessie shook his head in frustration. "Not much I can do, is there?" He drew in a deep breath and exhaled loudly. "Guess I gotta somehow *make* him want me. Score so many goals, he's got no choice."

Stick nodded. "And stay away from the white girls."

That part Jessie wasn't worried about. Everything else, though, made his stomach churn.

12

After a fitful night's sleep, Jessie groaned at the clanging of his alarm clock and rolled over. A second later, his eyes shot open and he jumped out of bed. Classes started today and he didn't want to be late.

Stick leaned back in his chair, his legs resting atop his desk. "Morning, Sleeping Beauty."

Jessie yawned. "I had trouble getting to sleep last night."

"You eating breakfast?"

Jessie gave a mock flex of his muscles. "Do I look like I skip meals?"

"Get dressed and I'll go over with you."

Jessie stretched. "How 'bout I go back to bed and you wake me up in ten minutes?"

"Get going."

"Why you in such a hurry?"

"Already been up for an hour, and I'm tired of sittin' here waiting for you."

Jessie stepped over to the closet where a mirror hung

inside the door. He looked at himself and groaned. "I'm gonna hop in the shower. I'll be fast."

"You got ten minutes."

Jessie grabbed a towel, toilet kit and clothes, then ran down the hallway to the floor's common bathroom, shared by eight rooms. Four sinks, their porcelain spotless and chrome glistening, separated two toilet stalls and urinals to the left and two shower stalls to the right. Jessie started the hot water in the closest shower, rushed over to the urinal, and figured he was down to eight and a half minutes by the time he ducked into the shower. He'd brought shampoo and a fresh bar of soap but was surprised to see a dispenser mounted on the wall labeled "Shampoo" and "Bath Soap." He gave it a pump, shampooed his hair quickly, lathered up, enjoying the blue liquid's lemon smell, and rinsed off. He toweled dry with what he figured was four minutes to go, threw on his clothes, fixed his hair, and brushed his teeth. He thought he looked ridiculous in the mandatory blazer and tie, but knew everyone else would, too. As he dashed back down the hall, he figured he had a minute or so to spare.

But the door to his room was shut. He turned the knob—locked.

He knocked. No answer.

Panic shot through him; he hadn't brought his key and he'd trusted Stick to wait for him. Now he was locked out on the first day of classes. He needed his notebooks from inside the room and couldn't show up for math carrying a towel, a toothbrush, and all the rest of his things.

Jessie jostled with the knob again and pounded on the

door. "Stick!" He looked both ways down the hall. No one. He'd have to go to Mr. Richardson to get back in the room, and he already seemed to dislike Jessie.

Jessie couldn't believe this could happen on the first day. Could he make any worse impression than getting locked out of his room? And if Mr. Richardson wasn't there, who knew how long it might take to get in? He might have to miss breakfast, and when that happened, he got a headache and spent the morning so hungry he couldn't focus on classwork.

Even though he knew it was pointless, Jessie pounded on the door again. "Stick!"

Stick had left without him. What a jerk. Jessie pounded one last time in frustration and turned to head for Mr. Richardson's room.

Suddenly the door swung open. Stick, wearing his blazer and tie but glaring, hissed. "Can you keep it down? I'm trying to sleep."

Jessie opened his mouth to respond and Stick whooped with laughter. After a split second, Jessie joined in.

"Man, I thought you was gonna bust the door down," Stick told him.

Jessie gave him a playful shove. For the first time, Jessie felt like he had a little brother.

●

After a breakfast of eggs, bacon, and pancakes, Jessie and Stick met up with Preston and his bookish-looking roommate, Franklin Stoddard, as they were leaving the dining hall and they headed for math class together. Jessie thought they all looked silly in their blazers and ties. Although Jessie and Preston hadn't spent time together since their clash at the barbeque, when Jessie told their neighbors about Stick's prank, they all had a good laugh and everything was cool.

As they got closer to class, Jessie stopped and pointed off to the left. "I thought Andrews Hall was over there."

"Andrews Hall? Algebra is in McKillip," Preston said and pulled out his schedule. At nine o'clock, it showed Algebra in McKillip Hall, Room 117.

Jessie looked again at his schedule. He was sure it had said Andrews, and it did. Nine o'clock, Mathematics, Andrews Hall, Room 102.

"We're not in the same math class?" Jessie asked.

Preston looked at Jessie's and Stick's schedules. "Your class is General Math," Preston said. "We're taking Algebra."

"But I was supposed to be taking Algebra," Jessie said. "I thought they'd just listed it on the schedule as Math."

Preston shook his head. "There are two tracks. The school calls them Gold and Silver, but everyone else calls them Ivies and States." When he saw Jessie's confusion, he explained, "That's for what kind of college it prepares you for, the Ivies or the state schools. The Ivies track includes Algebra. The States is Basic Mathematics."

Jessie felt astonished as they compared schedules. He'd known about the two tracks, though not about the nicknames for them, but his schedule didn't match what he'd requested.

He and Stick were taking basic math, Earth science, English fundamentals, French, and history, compared to Preston's and Franklin's Algebra, biology, English literature, French III, and advanced world history. Preston's added an additional class in introductory Spanish.

"They put me in all the lower track classes!" Jessie couldn't believe it. "Both of us," he said, glancing at Stick.

"S'okay by me," Stick said. "What's your problem?"

Jessie stared at the paper, but his hands shook so much that he couldn't read it.

"You got the form the school sent over the summer?" Franklin asked, pushing his glasses up on the bridge of his nose. "And you sent it back?"

"Yes! I went over it with my parents," Jessie said. "We spent a lot of time talking about the classes to pick 'cause we heard this place was really tough. We thought I shouldn't sign up for more than I could handle. So we asked for regular French and English, and didn't even think about a sixth course. But I was supposed to get Algebra, biology, and advanced world history."

Stick looked at Jessie like he was crazy. "You didn't ask for the easiest courses?"

"No. I got all A's in those courses last year. I mean, not those courses, you know, not Algebra. I mean math and—" Jessie was so angry he couldn't even talk straight "—math and science and . . . and history. Straight A's! And they're gonna stick me in the lower track? Why?"

"What school did you go to?" Franklin asked.

"Not one of your fancy private schools," Jessie snapped. "But a decent one."

Franklin gave him a look that told him that fact explained it all.

"They *talked* to me about Harvard," Jessie said. "They talked about Yale." He was shouting now, but he didn't care. Three boys approaching from the opposite direction gave him strange looks. He wanted to scream, "What're you looking at?" But he held his tongue, waiting for them to pass by, his rage boiling.

Seething, he said in an angry whisper, "You think Harvard takes *anybody* from the bottom track? How 'bout Yale? Princeton? *Any* of the Ivies?"

Nobody answered.

"Of course not! They were just blowing smoke. Sayin' whatever they thought I wanted . . . whatever my family wanted to hear. *Harvard!*" Jessie spit the word out.

Harry Edwards's words from the *Sports Illustrated* article came back to Jessie:

Black students aren't given athletic scholarships for the purpose of education. Blacks are brought in to perform. Any education they get is incidental to their main job, which is playing sports.

That was it, wasn't it? Harry Edwards might as well have been talking about Jessie Stackhouse and not about black college athletes. Jessie hadn't been brought to Springvale Academy to get the kind of education that would get him into Harvard or Yale. *Black students aren't given athletic scholarships for the purpose of education.* No Algebra, biology, or advanced world history, or any other Gold or Ivy track courses. *Any education they get is incidental to their main job, which is playing sports.*

Jessie felt like he was about to explode.

13

Jessie burst into the headmaster's office, feeling like he did just before delivering a bone-crushing check on the ice, his body tensed and adrenaline rushing through him. All day he'd become angrier about being put into the less demanding track. He wasn't going to let them do this to him.

The headmaster rose from behind an immense mahogany desk. Behind him, a large picture window looked out over the athletic fields. Matching bookshelves lined the two adjacent walls, filled with expensive looking leather-bound books. The room had an air of age and tradition, from the old polished wood that had been there for decades, and everything sparkled, from the gleaming brass light fixtures to the furniture with its faint lemon smell.

Mr. Whitney smiled and pointed to an armchair bearing the Springvale logo. "Have a seat, Jessie. I have an appointment soon, but what can I do for you in the meantime?"

"My courses are all wrong," Jessie said, struggling to stay calm. "I didn't realize at first when I got my schedule.

I requested Algebra, biology, and advanced world history, but all my classes are the lower track ones." He pointed to the reception area outside the door. "I asked Mrs. Saltonstall to change them, but she looked up my records and said I'm where I'm supposed to be." Jessie's voice raised. "But I know I'm not."

Mr. Whitney cleared his throat. "Placing students in the right classes is a difficult undertaking. The school doesn't always view things in the same light as the students or their parents might."

"But I got straight A's in all those subjects. I shouldn't be in lower track classes."

Mr. Whitney nodded. "Keep in mind that almost all of our student body comes from private schools. You may find that the lower track here is comparable to the highest track coursework at public schools like the one you went to."

Jessie dug in his heels. "But they're not going to get me into Harvard or Yale, are they?"

Mr. Whitney winced. "What you have to understand, Jessie, is that we made an exception when we offered you a position here at Springvale Academy." He picked up an expensive looking pen and rolled it between his fingers. "Prospective students have to take examinations that measure their knowledge and aptitude before we even consider their application. But in your case, we waived the testing because the last exam dates had already passed when we became aware of your talents. That left us quite in the dark when it came to assessing your abilities and where to place you. We had to extrapolate the scores you might have achieved on the examinations. Since you come from a school system that is . . . well, inferior, to those of the rest of our students, we need to help you adjust to our more rigorous standards."

"I don't need help adjusting," Jessie said, his anger building. "Better change it now than next year, or the one after that. By that time, it'll be too late. Give me the challenges now."

"I don't think you're taking everything—"

"I'm taking *everything* into consideration," Jessie said, unable to hold back his frustration any longer. "My entire future rests on what track you put me in, and somebody based that decision not on me getting straight A's in math and science, but on some extrapolation just because I didn't go to a private school. If you insist on putting me in dumbed-down classes—"

"They are not dumbed-down—"

"—if you insist on putting me in the lower tracks, I'll pack my bags and leave as soon as my parents can get back up here to get me."

Anger flashed across Mr. Whitney's face and he turned red. "Do you have any idea the risks I've taken to bring you into this school? Do you have *any* idea?"

Jessie shook his head.

Mr. Whitney pointed his index finger at his own chest. "I've put my career on the line for you and Stick. And that's the thanks I get? Having you come in here and issue ultimatums? Let me tell you something, Jessie. I have many enemies here who're hoping you'll fall on your face and take me right down with you." Then the headmaster froze, obviously regretting letting those words slip out.

"Sir, I appreciate what you've done," Jessie said and took a deep breath. "But my mother is a teacher, and she says that if you don't start out in the top track, it gets harder and harder to get up there. I'm not going to settle for a second-best education. I can't do that to myself, not even to help you out. You give me the courses I need, the courses a straight-A student deserves, and I won't let you down."

Mr. Whitney blinked, looking flustered. "You have no idea how difficult the upper track courses are, Jessie—especially for an athlete. The physical demands of your training. . . the time commitment . . . the traveling to away games."

The gleaming silver clock atop Mr. Whitney's desk *tick-tocked* louder and louder. Jessie's mouth felt dry, and his hands wet and clammy.

"Sir, are you familiar with the name Harry Edwards?"

Mr. Whitney furrowed his brow and frowned. "It sounds familiar, though I can't quite place it. What does he have to do with this discussion?"

"He's a former black athlete who's been involved in the proposed Olympic boycott."

Mr. Whitney's face hardened and his eyes narrowed.

"I was reading some of the things Harry Edwards has been saying about the treatment of black athletes—"

"Jessie," Mr. Whitney interrupted, his voice filled with anger. "We've given you a full scholarship to one of the most expensive and prestigious private schools in the nation. I would say that's mighty fine treatment, something many white people wish they were blessed with."

Jessie plunged ahead. "Harry Edwards said, and I've

got this memorized, 'Black students aren't given athletic scholarships for the purpose of education. Blacks are brought in to perform. Any education they get is incidental to their main job, which is playing sports. In most cases, their college lives are educational blanks.' "

The headmaster's face turned pale, but Jessie kept going. "This isn't college, but it's the same thing. If you're going to put a straight-A student—straight A's in math and science, I mean—in the lower track, then you're not doing me any favors, even if you mean well. You're doing exactly what Harry Edwards said; you're using me." Jessie gritted his teeth. "And I won't be used."

Silence fell over the room, interrupted only by the ticking clock. Jessie's heart hammered; he bit his lower lip and brushed a bead of sweat off his temple. After what felt like hours, Mr. Whitney nodded.

"You are a very persuasive young man," he said with a sigh and shook his head. "It isn't often that a student is able to convince me to change my mind. Some day, you might want to consider becoming a lawyer."

Jessie smiled.

A sour look came over Mr. Whitney's face and he tapped an index finger on his desk. "Coach Stone and I have an agreement that he'll be consulted over any of his players' curriculum changes. He's not going to be happy about this. Unless—" He shook his head and didn't finish the thought. Instead he muttered, "Imagine that. A hockey coach unhappy with the headmaster. What a strange place this is."

Then he remembered he wasn't alone and turned his

focus back to Jessie. "So you want top track in math and science?"

"I'd like it in history, too, but math and science are the subjects I'm most upset about." When Mr. Whitney didn't respond right away, Jessie added, "I have no problem staying lower track in English and French." He grinned. "I ain't so good in languages."

Mr. Whitney's eyes twinkled before a nervous look returned to his face. "I'll talk to Coach Stone. I'll *tell* him that you're moving up in math, science, and history, too."

Jessie felt his smile broaden from ear to ear, as if he'd just scored the game-winning goal in overtime. He wanted to whoop and pump his fist.

"You have to promise me that if you start having problems in these courses, you'll come to me right away. If we have to make adjustments, we'll make them." A somber look came over him. "We're taking a chance here, Jessie. Not that I don't believe in you because you've made me a believer. But we're taking a chance and we can't lose on this. If it blows up in your face, it blows up in mine, too."

●

Steppenwolf's "Born to Be Wild" blared next door, so Jessie went over as soon as he saw that Stick wasn't around.

"That's great," Preston said, after Jessie gave him the news. "You won an argument with the headmaster. I'm impressed." Preston rummaged through a neat stack of papers atop his desk. One at a time, he pulled out three pages and handed them to Jessie. "Here's the syllabus for Algebra, Biology, and World History. You can use my textbooks tonight until you get your own tomorrow." He rummaged some more, frowning.

"Thanks," Jessie said, "but I'll just wait until tomorrow and exchange the ones I've got for the right ones."

Preston gave him the eye, resumed his rummaging, then spotted what he was looking for on the other side of the desk. He handed two more sheets of paper to Jessie. "These are the assignments for Algebra and Biology. They're due tomorrow."

"Tomorrow?" Jessie repeated, surprised.

Preston nodded.

Jessie scanned the top page and then the next. Homework on the first night. And not just a little—twenty Algebra problems and twenty-five biology definitions to memorize—plus reading in both textbooks. What had he gotten himself into?

"It looks worse than it is," Preston said.

Jessie rubbed the papers between his fingertips, not sure they really existed and said, "Jeez."

"No training wheels in these courses. Just pedal, steer, and hope you don't crash," Preston told him.

Jessie couldn't take his eyes off the assignments. This wasn't like his old school. He already had homework— hours of it!—on the first night. He wondered if he should have been a little less cocky with Mr. Whitney.

"Hey, Einstein," Preston said, launching a book into the air. Jessie caught it: *Principles of Algebra*, a thick one, with maybe six hundred pages. It smelled new, which it was, unlike the old, battered copies handed out back at his former high school.

"I'm working on Bio right now," Preston said. "So you start with Algebra and then we'll switch."

Jessie nodded, still numb. He'd never gotten homework on the first day of classes before. In fact, he'd always been able to get most of any homework done during study hall, which they didn't have here.

No training wheels? Preston wasn't kidding.

Jessie returned to his room, sank into his chair, and opened *Principles of Algebra*.

What had Mr. Whitney said? *If this blows up in your face, it blows up in mine, too.*

Uh-oh, Jessie thought.

14

Jessie got started on the Algebra problems, which weren't as hard as he'd originally thought, but they'd take awhile. Then Stick came back to the room.

"Wanna go downtown after dinner?" Stick asked. "Look around?"

"Can't. Too much homework."

"What're you talkin' about? We ain't got homework tonight."

Jessie pointed to Preston's Algebra textbook and the problem set. "I do *now*. I talked to Mr. Whitney—well, argued is more like it—and he's moved me to the three upper track courses I requested. Man, have I got the silver tongue."

Jessie's smile faded when he saw a look of shocked betrayal on Stick's face.

"What you do that for?"

"I told you," Jessie said, surprised at the reaction. "You know, straight A's and all that. I only wanted to be placed where I belonged."

"But . . . I was counting on you, man."

"Counting on me for what?"

"To, you know, hang with me. We could help each other out. Stick together. Ain't that what brothers're supposed to do?"

"Help each other out? What're you talking about? Did you think I was gonna do your homework? Were you gonna help me out in class?"

"Stick together, man. That's what I mean."

"Man, I'll help you out. But don't expect me to . . . to sacrifice my—my future."

Stick gave him a sour look. "Future," he said, almost spitting the word out.

"Yeah, *future*." Jessie slammed his pencil down on his desk. *Did everything have to be an argument?* He was getting tired of having to fight for everything. "I need to get the best education I can here. And so should you. I'm not lettin' them use me to play hockey for them and then graduate no smarter than a shoe-shine boy."

Stick's eyes narrowed. "That what you sayin' *I* am?"

Jessie sighed. "No. Course not. You're smarter than you think you are."

Although Jessie did wonder; Stick hadn't seemed to pay much attention in any of the classes they'd shared that day, and if it wasn't just the first-day blues, then he truly might be in over his head.

He went on. "You just . . . well, it seems like the school you came from wasn't very good."

Stick snorted.

"The headmaster said I didn't go to private school like most of these guys," Jessie said. "But my school wasn't bad. I got a chance. If you work, maybe you can move up, too, next year."

"Yeah, right."

"I can't hold myself back just to stay in the same classes with you. You can't expect that. You ain't that pretty," Jessie added, trying to lighten things.

But Stick fell silent.

"I'm still gonna be in your English and French classes," Jessie said.

"Good for you," Stick said bitterly.

An awkward silence hung in the air.

"Listen, bro," Jessie said. "You need help, I'll help as much as I can."

Stick nodded sullenly.

"You can't expect more than that."

"Yeah, we're stickin' together, all right." Stick lifted his hand with his index and middle fingers extended right next to each other. "Just like this, man." He turned his hand around and lowered the index finger so that only his middle finger was extended. "We real tight, bro."

●

Stick made a point of not going to dinner with Jessie. *Well*, Jessie thought, *be that way. I can't help it*. Since Preston and Franklin had eaten earlier, Jessie went by himself, the Algebra book his only company.

Preston had been right. Jessie had gotten eleven of the Algebra problems done in an hour, but still, Jessie wondered about the time commitment. Once the season started, with its practices and road trips, he'd have to cram an awful lot of studying with an awful lot of hockey into a very little amount of available time.

Well, Einstein, he told himself, *that's what you're here for*. You're gonna score goals and check opponents into the cheap seats, and maybe there's a roster spot waiting for you in the NHL. But you're not gonna get used; you're gonna get an education that sets you up for life.

Even if it kills you.

●

By Friday morning, Stick was acting as though nothing disagreeable had happened between them. Jessie was happy to follow suit, and was relieved. He didn't think they could afford to be feuding, not with the way the rest of the dorm was treating them. Other than Preston and Franklin, no one had been even remotely friendly. Every day, wary glances or looks of outright hatred greeted Jessie and Stick.

Even Preston's apparent friendliness was tinged with more than a hint of patronizing superiority, probably treating him and Stick the way his congressman father acted toward voters seeking a favor. Jessie wondered if Preston'd been showing off his stereo or if he'd deliberately tried to make Jessie feel bad about his own. And Franklin seemed to be following Preston's lead.

Considering their lack of social connection to the other boys, Jessie suggested he and Stick go into town that night to see a movie. When Stick said he didn't have the money, Jessie offered to pay. If there had been any lingering resentment from earlier in the week, Stick's broad smile showed there were no hard feelings.

The theatre was large, with a huge lighted marquee, but inside it was old and very plain, without any ornate furnishings. The lights were just ordinary lights, the refreshment stand nothing more than functional.

Struck by the contrast, Jessie realized he'd already stopped noticing Springvale Academy's opulence. The chandeliers, the polished brass, and the marble staircases had become part of the backdrop, and now felt as normal as the grime on the brick buildings back home in Lynn.

The movie playing was *The Odd Couple* starring Walter Matthau and Jack Lemmon. It would have felt good to get away from the campus no matter how lousy the movie, but *The Odd Couple* was anything but lousy. It was very funny, and Jessie and Stick were still laughing about some of the lines as they began the mile-long walk back to the campus.

"Thanks, man," Stick said.

"Forget it."

Stick worked his toothpick. "I think that girl behind the popcorn counter liked me. Might ask for her phone number next time."

Jessie rolled his eyes. "She didn't even look at you."

"She was tryin' to cover it up."

"And doin' a mighty fine job."

"White girls can't get enough of me."

"Stop it."

"Nothin' finer than The Stick."

"So now you're *The Stick*? It ain't enough to be just *Stick*. Like you're royalty or something?"

"Yeah, royalty. King Stick and his Black Magic. Man, that do sound good. King of the white women."

"You're gonna get in trouble, you keep talking like that."

Stick laughed. "I just messin' with you. Why you always gotta be so serious? You a lot like Felix in the movie."

"Felix? I'm nothing like him. And I'm not always serious. Where'd you get that?"

"When's the last time you messed with someone, or told a joke, or . . ." Stick laughed again, and said, "Or locked someone out of their room?"

Jessie couldn't think of a time.

"See what I mean?" Stick said. "Judge Stick do pronounce you guilty. This year's gonna be a jail sentence if you don't lighten up. All you'll be doin' is studyin' and workin' out. You gotta relax, man."

Jessie shrugged. He didn't think he had time to relax.

A cool breeze wafted through the air. The streetlights ended as Jessie and Stick continued along the cracked two-lane road back to school, walking along the shoulder, Jessie on the inside. The gravel crunched beneath their feet and a half-moon lighted the otherwise darkened fields beside them. The stars shone bright in the black sky, so much brighter than at home. What sounded like millions of crickets chirped, and in the distance an owl hooted.

"Sure don't smell like the city," Stick said. "I do miss the smell of rotting garbage."

A car rumbled past. For a brief moment its exhaust fouled the clean, pine-scented air and its noisy muffler interrupted the chirping.

"Guess we better see lots of movies before the snow hits," Jessie said. "I don't mind long walks, but not in the winter."

"Yeah, you're right. Wanna go again tomorrow?"

"I got too much studying."

Stick gave him the eye. "A year of jail, I'm tellin' you, man."

"How about when they get a new movie in?"

Stick shrugged.

"Okay, next Friday, then," Jessie said.

"That's more like it."

It struck Jessie that Rose had probably gone to the movies, too, maybe even seen the same show. He wondered who she'd gone with. Just thinking about her with someone else—probably that lousy creep Leroy—got Jessie's blood boiling.

"What's the matter?" Stick asked.

"Nothing."

"Yeah, right."

Jessie went to kick an egg-sized stone and in the moonlight almost missed. "It's just . . . that was the first movie I've seen without my girl in a long time. Her name's Rose and she's real nice. That's all." After a while, he added, "I wish this place weren't so far from home."

"She still your girl?"

"Well . . . sort of."

Stick looked at Jessie like he was crazy. "Sort of? Who you foolin'? There only be two answers to that question. Yes and no. And if you up here until June, the answer's no. Just like with the girl who *used* to be my girl. So stop thinkin' about her. She ain't your girl no more. My girl ain't mine no more. Nothin' we can do about it."

Jessie felt both glum and angry. "That makes me feel a *lot* better."

"I'm just sayin'."

"You don't have to rub my nose in it."

"I'm rubbin' both our noses in it, so we stay away from it next time."

"I guess so."

"Unless you hurtin' so bad you want me to pretend."

"Pretend what?"

"Next time pretend I'm Rose. In that dark theatre, you can hold my hand. Maybe I can even wear some perfume for you. And when you go to kiss me, I'll slap your face and call you a nasty boy, just like Rose."

Jessie blinked, shocked at first, and then began to roar with laughter.

Eyes twinkling, Stick kept going. "I'll complain about you eatin' all the popcorn, too, just like Rose."

It felt good to be laughing, *so good*.

Until the pickup truck rumbled up beside them.

"Where you two jigs going?" boomed a deep voice from inside the truck's darkened cab.

Jessie tried to keep his voice calm, even as his heart jack-hammered and his mouth went dry. "Back to school," he said.

The pickup inched along, matching their speed, and the voice boomed out again. "There ain't no jigs at the Academy."

Jessie wondered how to respond. That there never used

to be jigs, but there were now? After what felt like forever, he said, "We're new. This is our first year." Jessie began walking faster and so did Stick, but the pickup picked up its pace, too.

"Come on, tell the truth. You was robbing somebody's house, wasn't you?"

Jessie knew this wasn't going to end well. It was only a question of how bad. Out of the corner of his mouth, he whispered to Stick, "Get ready to run." He faced the truck. "We went to the movies. We saw *The Odd Couple*." He turned so that even in the moonlight they could see how big he was. He didn't think he could scare them away, but it didn't hurt to try. "We don't want any trouble."

"Oh, you don't, do you?" the voice said, and higher pitched laughter from inside the cab chimed in. "What if *we* want some trouble?"

Jessie couldn't believe what flashed through his head. *Then you're gonna get it.* Where had *that* come from? The words never formed on his lips, but what crazed part of his mind had thought that? Nervous sweat broke out across his forehead and he sucked in short, quick breaths of air.

The pickup truck stopped and a door clicked open behind them. Jessie and Stick took off. Stick veered off down the shoulder and into the moonlit fields, his short legs churning with blinding speed. Jessie sprinted straight ahead so the rednecks—he'd already begun to think of them that way—would have to split up.

"Get 'em boys," the deep voice said.

Jessie glanced back and saw the outlines of two men— he assumed they were men, though they could have been tall boys. One took after Stick and the other came right at Jessie.

The pickup shot ahead and then screeched to a halt. The driver's side door flew open, and in the pool of light coming from inside the cab, Jessie saw a mountain of a man jump out. He had to be close to seven feet tall and weigh three hundred pounds. A ski mask covered his face.

Trapped between the two rednecks, Jessie started across the street but then spotted fencing running along the opposite side. He reversed and sprinted for the fields. With a grunt and a shout, the rednecks chased after him. Stick was out there in the darkness somewhere and Jessie didn't want to lead them to Stick, but what choice was there?

Jessie glanced over his shoulder. He was pulling away, as he thought he would. The mountain of a man was almost as slow as a mountain, lumbering and grunting, and the other man wasn't much faster.

Jessie never saw the third redneck until just before he slammed his shoulder into Jessie's gut and drove him into the ground. The back of Jessie's head crashed against a small rock and a multitude of stars suddenly flashed before his eyes. A knee slammed up into Jessie's crotch and he screamed as blinding pain shot through him.

"Get the other one," shouted the man who was closest to Jessie. His breath stank of onions and beer, and his body reeked of sour sweat.

Jessie punched at the back of the man's head, but he could do little more than flail away, unable to put any weight behind it. Even as his midsection cramped in agony, Jessie tried to wrestle the man off him, but he'd only gotten him turned partway when the steel toe of a boot crashed into the side of Jessie's head.

Grunting, the mountain of a man dropped to his knees beside Jessie, and punched him hard in the head.

For an instant, Jessie tasted the sharp bite of his own blood and his ears rang.

Then everything went black.

15

Jessie drifted in and out of consciousness while the ambulance bounced along the back roads, its siren wailing. He couldn't stop moaning. He hurt so bad all over. His head rang and his stomach roiled. And then darkness overtook him again, giving him relief, at least for a while.

When he finally came to, he couldn't think straight; his mind was in a fog. It took—how long, seconds? Minutes?—to realize that he couldn't see a thing—only blackness.

In a wild panic, Jessie tried to sit up, but pain bolted through every muscle. He gasped and lay back down, but not all the way down. He was propped up, and in a bed.

He moaned; he hurt all over. But none of that mattered compared to being—surely he couldn't be—*blind*.

He fumbled around him: a metal bed rail, a tray table. The room smelled of antiseptic and Lysol. A soft beeping noise interrupted the laugh track of a TV, and something was stuck in his arm, strapped in place by adhesive wrap.

This was a hospital, it had to be.

Pain pierced his head like the tip of an icicle and again he groaned.

He touched his eyelids, and then recoiled at the sharp jab of pain his touch had set off.

Maybe he wasn't blind after all; but he could tell that both of his eyes were swollen. He tried to open the left one and couldn't. Then he tried the other.

It opened a crack and light pierced the back of his skull.

Jessie groaned, but whooped with joy at the same time. He could barely make out shapes through the slit of his eyelids.

He wasn't blind!

He touched his teeth: all there. He tried to take a deep breath, but that gave him another sharp stab of pain.

Then footsteps approached and he heard muffled whispers.

He tilted his head up, forced an eye open and made out the form of a nurse carrying a clipboard. She was a big tank of a woman, and she stepped to his side.

Jessie tried to mumble something, but his mouth was so dry, he couldn't manage anything intelligible. He licked his cracked lips; they were another part of his body that stung, and he tasted blood.

"Where am I?" Jessie asked.

The nurse held a fingertip to his wrist and counted, then jotted down a number on her clipboard.

"This is St. Jude's Hospital," she said and strapped a blood pressure cuff on his arm, pumped it up, and slid a stethoscope beneath it. She nodded and wrote down another number, and said, "Somebody did quite a job on you."

The fog in Jessie's brain cleared and the memories began flooding back. The movie. The pickup truck. *Stick*.

"Am I the only one here?" Jessie managed through his battered lips.

"Your parents are on the way."

Jessie winced. He couldn't even begin to think of what they'd have to say about this. But that wasn't what he'd wanted to know. "No, I mean another student—my friend. He was with me walking back to school."

"There's another Negro." She frowned. "He's in almost as bad shape as you."

●

"My dear sweet Jesus," Momma said as she rushed into the room a few hours later. She rounded the bed with Pop following on her heels.

She stopped, gasped, and put her hand to her mouth. "Oh, no, my baby. What have they done to you?"

Kneeling by the bed, she brushed a hand across his forehead.

Jessie flinched, expecting her touch to hurt worse than it did.

She pulled her hand away, saying, "I'm sorry, Jessie. I didn't mean to hurt you."

"It's okay," he said, tasting blood again as his lips split open. "It didn't hurt. Just be careful."

Tears poured down his mother's face as she kept repeating, "My poor baby."

"Who did this?" Pop asked, his voice shaking with emotion.

"I don't know," Jessie said. "They were wearing ski masks."

"How many?"

"Three. Got Stick and me coming back from the movies."

Pop's shoulders slumped.

Shaking her head, Momma said, "Lord help us."

"Any broken bones?" Pop asked. "Other than your nose, I mean."

"No, the doctor said—" Jessie wet his lips, "—busted nose, bad concussion. That's all."

Momma's eyes went vacant. "That's all? "

"Have the police been here yet?" Pop asked.

"No."

A grim look came over him. "They will be."

Momma dabbed at her eyes with a handkerchief, then stroked his arm. "After you fall asleep, your Pop and I will go pack your things. Then we'll get you out of this awful place."

"No." Jessie seized her wrist. "I'm not quitting."

"But you can't stay—" She looked to Pop for help. "Good, Lord. Jordan, talk some sense into this boy."

Pop closed his eyes and rubbed his forehead. "We hadn't thought you'd want to stay. We were just so upset, and we just assumed you'd . . ." As his voice trailed off, his eyes took on a vacant look.

"It isn't the school's fault." It hurt to talk, but Jessie

wasn't going to lose this fight. "It was just three rednecks from town. Could've happened anywhere." Jessie shifted and winced as the pain shot through him. But he set his jaw and said, "I'm not gonna let them win. They're gonna have to kill me."

"Oh, Lord," Momma said. "My dear, sweet Jesus, help us."

Jessie realized he hadn't said the right thing, but there was no changing that now. Besides, it was true.

"I'm not running," he said.

●

When he returned two days later to his dorm room, that angry boast mocked him. He could barely sleep, and even when he did, he awoke with stabbing pain behind his eyes. He jumped at every sound, and couldn't concentrate on his studies, no matter how hard he tried. He recoiled whenever he looked in the mirror and saw his battered, swollen face staring back. He could barely recognize himself.

The rednecks had gotten Stick, too, but only after he'd come back to help Jessie. That made it worse; Stick had gotten away clean, but Jessie's screams, mixed with the rednecks' gleeful, savage cries, had brought Stick back. They'd made him pay, beating him senseless, too.

The nightmare hadn't ended on that night; it just kept coming back in Jessie's mind.

Jessie lay sweating on his bed, the dorm room's walls closing in on him like a coffin, musty and humid, and airless. The throbbing in his head flared hot red, intense and blinding. His heart raced and he couldn't breathe. It felt like there was no oxygen in the room, and his nostrils stung with the remembered odor of his attacker's sour sweat and his foul breath of onions and beer.

Jessie bolted out of bed, not caring if he woke Stick, and dashed to the window, shut tight and locked at his insistence. He steadied himself until the room stopped spinning and the flash of nausea subsided. As the stars above twinkled in the dark, cloudless sky, Jessie looked out over the fields illuminated in the half-moon's meager light. He could see no one, and he knew the fields were empty, but he couldn't keep himself from straining to see any movement in the shadows.

None. Of course not.

Even so, he looked beyond the fields and toward the woods. He saw no one there, either, but that didn't mean they weren't out there, hidden in the darkness, waiting until he fell asleep to strike. He couldn't even make out the white birch trees; how would he see the skin tones of his attackers or their black ski masks in that darkness?

This is silly, he told himself; he was acting like a little kid afraid of the bogeyman under the bed.

Silly, except for one difference. There really was no bogeyman; the only thing that haunted little kids was their vivid imagination. But Jessie's bogeyman was real. In fact, *he'd* had more than one.

After reliving that horrible night for a while, Jessie finally blinked and remembered he was in his room in the dorm and not back out on that road. There wasn't anything outside that would hurt him, he told himself. He pushed the window up and clean, cool air wafted over his moist skin.

Behind him, Stick groaned in his bed, no doubt reliving his own nightmare, then he turned over to face the wall.

Jessie gulped in the fresh air and tried to calm the hammering in his chest that the memories had provoked.

Get a grip, he told himself.

He rubbed his throbbing temples and thought of his boast to Momma and Pop: *I'm not running*.

Those words mocked Jessie; yeah, he was quite the tough guy. He'd only been running ever since, seeing huge bogeymen with rock-hard ham-sized fists around every corner, afraid to go to bed with the window open.

The breeze tickled his chin and Jessie shuddered. The clean scents of pine, roses and freshly cut grass wafted into the room. He hoped that they might purify his mind of those odors that lived inside his head, like bogeymen of the — what was the term they'd just learned in Biology? — of the olfactory nerves. Maybe he'd never get rid of that smell.

Jessie went to the door on wobbly legs and checked that the chair he'd brought from the common room was still propped under the doorknob. It was silly, he knew, because the rooms were all locked. But he could never be too sure — not anymore.

Then he sank back down on his bed, sitting with his feet touching the floor.

Although the cool breeze felt so soothing, he knew he had to close that window; he couldn't leave it open and make himself vulnerable. But his words still haunted him: *I'm not running*.

He laughed to himself, seeing no humor in it, but unable to stop as he thought of his false bravado and foolishness. *No, not me. Not running at all.*

He put his head in his hands. So this was what it felt like to go mad.

Jessie toppled back onto the bed and stretched his cramped legs out, then curled into a fetal position. He was soon asleep, and before long all of Jessie's bogeymen came climbing through the window into his nightmares. In his dream, they didn't even need a ladder; they just pulled themselves inside somehow in the blue glow of the moonlight. The mountain of a man came first, grunting and exhaling loudly, the sill creaking beneath his weight. His black ski mask covered his face, but a yellow, leering grin showed through the red-outlined hole for his mouth. The second and third thugs followed, their faces blurred. "The only good jig is a dead jig," the mountain said, and the others laughed. Jessie tried to cry out but couldn't; he was paralyzed in his dream, and a sweaty hand covered his mouth. He tried to crawl out of bed but couldn't with the massive body straddling his torso. He tried to put up his hands to protect himself, but couldn't with those legs as thick as tree trunks pinning him down. Then the huge fist came down at his face. Jessie screamed.

Awake now, he sat up gasping for breath. He tasted salt on his lips and wiped his palm across his face, then wiped it off on the sweat-drenched sheets.

He licked his lips: salt, not blood, from sweat? tears? Only then did he realize the thugs weren't there. Nobody was, except for him and Stick, who was sitting up in bed, wide-eyed with terror, his back against the wall.

"I'm sorry," Jessie gasped. He'd done it again—he'd wakened Stick with his recurring nightmare.

16

A few weeks later, Jessie's heart hammered even before he adjusted the seat to the stationary bike, climbed on, and opened his History textbook. The smell of sweat filled the air, but none of it was his. Grunts of exertion echoed off the field house walls, but they came from others. He felt like a stranger in this most familiar of places, with his hands shaking and his mouth dry.

The bruises and cuts on his face had healed, but headaches had wracked him since the attack. "You have a brain bruise," Pop had told him before prescribing a regimen to begin, once the headaches had been gone for three full days—and not a minute sooner. "You *must* let it heal before you do anything else, Jessie. Absolutely no contact sports. *After* the symptoms are gone, and only then, you can slowly build up the physical activity. Stop as soon as your body tells you—you'll feel it. *Do not rush back.*"

But cabin fever set in on day three, and by day seven it was driving Jessie crazy not to be active. He just couldn't help himself, so ignoring his headaches and Pop's advice, Jessie climbed on a stationary bike, one angled toward the corridor that led to the arena—his true destination, as if he could somehow pedal himself back onto the ice if he worked at it. He'd lasted all of thirty seconds before the nausea overcame him. The vomit erupted up into his mouth, sour and acidic, even as he stumbled off the bike and staggered toward a trash container. Then he retched and retched, the pain stabbing him so hard in the eyes, he saw bright lights flashing across his field of vision, a truly scary sight. The rancid, raw smell of the vomit kept him retching long after nothing remained, until his knees wobbled and his head spun. Then he'd cleaned his hands and face, his mouth puckering until he sipped some cold water and rinsed out, the sour taste still lingering.

After that reminder not to rush his recovery, Jessie gave it three more days, doubting that he could restrain himself beyond that. He'd always like to push, push, push, believing that if he pushed himself harder than the next guy, when the two of them met, he'd win.

But he couldn't push now. He had to sit and wait.

And wait. Even after the tenth day, even after the twelfth, even though he couldn't remember the last time he'd been inactive for even *two* consecutive days. A couple times, he'd almost given in, pulling himself back only when he recalled the awful results when he pushed himself too soon. So, as hard as it was, Jessie waited and listened to his body's advice.

In the end, it took fifteen days before Jessie could get back to practice and workouts. The aftereffects of the concussion would take as long they had to, and if he didn't like it, too bad. All he could do while he waited was feel powerless and frustrated as his scrambled brains healed.

Now, as Jessie climbed back onto the bike on Day Eighteen, three days into his resumed workouts, he felt the tension he'd feel in an overtime game, imagining the puck on his stick and his team's fate resting on his shoulders. Setting the bike on level one, the setting with so little re-sistance it almost felt like he was pedaling only air, he slowly began to move his legs.

Jessie fought back the temptation to ratchet the setting up to his usual level, even though he thought using this lit-tle resistance was a waste of time. Little old ladies could do level one. But he waited until he got through an entire minute before bumping it up to level two.

"What an athlete!" came a sarcastic voice behind him.

Jessie whirled around and felt the slightest sensation of his brain jiggling, but then it disappeared so fast, he wondered if he'd imagined it. He waited for the stab of nausea he'd felt before, but none came. And why had this guy with blond hair down to his shoulders chosen him to pick on?

"You probably know me," the guy said, moving in front of the stationary bike. He waited for an acknowledg-ment and pursed his lips when Jessie looked at him blankly. "I'm Dirk Stapleton."

The first name was enough to jar Jessie's memory; Dirk had been the kid who'd directed Pop to the service entrance when they first arrived for freshman orientation. Jessie couldn't help remembering their stare-down as they drove away.

"Senior captain of the hockey team." Dirk offered no hand to shake. "Three-time All-New England defenseman."

"Glad to meet you," Jessie said, unsure of what else to say.

"I'm supposed to tell you about captain's practices."

Supposed to tell you? Jessie wondered what that meant.

"Coach Stone says you did the same as the rest of the team. You chose working out as your fall sport so you could focus on hockey." A tight sneer formed at the corners of Dirk's mouth. "Level two—you're a workout champion."

"I—"

Dirk waved him off. "Be as lazy as you want. I don't care." Jessie again tried to explain, but Dirk ignored him and kept talking. "I run captain's practices for everyone who isn't playing a competitive sport in the fall. Mostly we do a few drills to warm up, and then we scrimmage. It gives us a chance to start skating now, so when the official practices begin, we'll all be at top speed."

"I can't—"

"That's all right," Dirk said, his hand raised in a stopping gesture. "They're optional; they have to be, or else it's a violation under the league's bylaws. Nobody *has to* attend. Stone isn't even allowed to watch, so feel free to skip them all." He began walking away, but then turned back and said, "Nobody really wants you there anyway."

Then Dirk trotted off.

Him, too? Coach Stone didn't want Jessie around, and now, neither did Mr. "Three-time All-New England." Jessie wondered if *all* his teammates would be lined up against him—before he even had the chance to put on Springvale's maroon-and-gold.

As he considered this possibility, a crushing depression blanketed him. He could be the best teammate they ever had, if only they'd give him the chance. But somehow, that didn't seem too likely.

Only when he looked at the clock on the wall did Jessie's mood brighten: six minutes and counting. No headache, no nausea. He bumped the level up two more times before quitting.

Then, pushing away the sting of rejection, Jessie smiled just a little.

He'd show them. Every last one.

●

"How you doing?" Jessie asked, anxious to tell Stick the good news about his side-effect-free workout.

Stick sat angled in his chair, a leg draped over one of the chair's arms, an elbow propped against the other. Stick manipulated his ever-present toothpick in the corner of his mouth and shrugged. "Got a headache, myself."

Stick, too, had suffered a concussion in the attack. But football was a fall sport with games to be played, headaches and nausea or not, so he'd rushed back to practice and play. And, while returning a punt in Saturday's game, he'd taken a hit that knocked him out cold.

Even though he felt a bit guilty about sharing his good news, Jessie told Stick about the workout, leaving out Dirk Stapleton's poisonous message.

"That's good, man," Stick said.

"Listen," Jessie said. "I talked to my pop yesterday and told him about you getting knocked out. He says you got to wait for your brain to heal before you play again."

Stick rolled his eyes.

"I know you don't wanna hear it," Jessie said, "cause you ignored me last week. But he said it's even more important to let it heal after getting knocked out like that. He said you could suffer major brain damage otherwise."

Stick eyed him. "Musta already happened."

"What do you mean?"

"When I was little." He looked away. " 'Cause I'm already brain damaged."

Jessie sighed. He hated when Stick talked like this.

"You're not brain damaged," Jessie said. "Not yet, at least."

"Easy for you to say. You be Einstein on skates. I'm the one with the brain damage."

"Take any of these rich white boys and send them to your old school, they wouldn't know any more than you," Jessie said.

"C'mon," Stick said. "They all smarter than us, 'specially me. They make me look like a dope. But they smarter than you too, bro, so stop pretending they ain't."

"I ain't pretending."

Stick shrugged. "Whatever." He sat up. "So you gonna help me with my math homework or what?"

"I got a lot of studying to do myself," Jessie said. That was no exaggeration. The top-track courses demanded almost every spare minute for assignments. "But I can spare half an hour tonight."

"Thanks, man."

"You got your English paper written?" Jessie asked. English and French were the two classes they still shared.

Stick gave an amused snort. "Football team got me a tutor for English—a scholarship student like us. Needs the bread." Stick grinned broadly. "He's writing my paper in the library right now."

Jessie felt his jaw drop. He was speechless.

Stick chuckled. "Times like this, you one funny-lookin' cat." He imitated Jessie, opening his mouth wide, bugging out his eyes and throwing his arms wide in mock surprise. In a squeaky falsetto voice, Stick said, "Why, Stick, whatever are you doing? You're . . . *cheating*! You should be ashamed of yourself!"

Jessie fumbled for words. What could he say? Stick's mocking words weren't far from what he'd have said.

"But . . . how long do you think you can get away with that?" Jessie asked.

Stick shrugged. "Long as I need to, I guess. I ain't worried about it."

It felt all wrong to Jessie, but he couldn't say why. It wasn't just a matter of whether Stick got caught. But then all the pieces fell into place in his mind and he knew why it bothered him so much.

"You know those *Sports Illustrated* articles I told you about," Jessie said. "Did you read any of them?"

"Nah," Stick said. "Sorry, man. I ain't much for reading. Got too much to do for all these classes. No time to read your magazines."

"That's not the point," Jessie said. "Those articles are all about *you*."

"Whatcha mean, me? I'm famous?" Stick grinned uncomfortably.

"If you don't get an education here, a real one, where *you* do the work and *you* learn what you're supposed to learn, not just having some tutor writing your papers, or me doing your math problems, where are you gonna be four years from now?"

Stick shrugged. "I'll find me some college to take me. They always need a good point guard." He raised his hands in the motion of taking a shot. "Or a wide receiver."

"And then what?"

"Take my shot at the pros."

"You know the odds. There're only a couple hundred jobs in the NBA."

Stick shrugged again. "I'll take my shot. That's all I can do."

"What if you don't make it?"

"Then I didn't make it." Stick's voice cut through the air with an edge in it. "What's your point, man?"

"My point is that if you don't get an education, a *real* education, here and at college, then the schools are just using you. You'll win them championships, fill their stands with fans, maybe put them on TV. But what are they doing for *you*, if you're not even getting a real education? Nothing! That's what Harry Edwards says. They're using you, and unless you hit the million-to-one chance of playing in the pros, you got nothing when it's over."

Stick shifted in his chair, looking angry beneath his cool demeanor. "Ain't a million-to-one. Not for me."

"Okay, a hundred-thousand-to-one. Make you feel better?"

Stick glared.

"Here's a math problem I'll solve for you," Jessie said, angry now, too. "That means for every time you make the NBA or the NFL, the other 99,999 times, you spend the rest of your life being nothing more than a janitor, cleaning someone else's toilets, or picking up white people's garbage and bringing it to the dump, or shining their shoes. That's your future, if you're gonna let someone else do your homework."

Stick snapped his toothpick into two, then spit the pieces on the floor. "Easy for you to say. *You* be Black Einstein." Stick flicked at a loose sliver of toothpick with his tongue, then spit out the fragment, too. "Your daddy's a Doc-tor," Stick said angrily, making Pop's profession sound like two words. "He a smart man; makes you smart, too. Me?" Stick snorted. "I don't even *know* who my daddy is. But I'm sure he wasn't no Doc-tor. He probably some pimp, or a janitor or garbage collector. I ain't got no Doc-tor's brains in my head; I got janitor's brains, so if I don't make the pros, then I gonna be a janitor. So don't you worry 'bout me. You gonna be a Doc-tor like your daddy? Then I'll clean the toilets in your pretty Doc-tor's office. Or I'll shine your shoes or cut your lawn. Or maybe I'll wash your Cadillac."

Stick put a fresh toothpick in his mouth and leaned back in his chair, his cool veneer back. "Don't you worry none 'bout The Stick."

●

After dinner, Jessie tried to help Stick with his math homework, but he soon became frustrated. The more he tried to show Stick how to solve the problems, the more Stick expected Jessie to work through them for him. Jessie sensed that Stick felt hopelessly lost, but when he tried to explain *why* some value was the correct answer, Stick just scribbled it down, nodded his head, and said, "Got it." Then he'd point to the next problem, even though Jessie suspected Stick didn't understand what they'd done on the last one.

But Jessie wasn't about to argue anymore—he didn't have time and he was worried about his own homework. Instead, he added more explanation to each problem and hoped that when Stick nodded his head, he actually got it.

●

That night in his dreams, the mountain of a man came after Jessie again. The nightmares had become less frequent, but they remained so vivid. This time, the huge man played field goal kicker with his steel-tipped boot, using Jessie's head as a football. Waking, Jessie sat up, once more drenched in his own sweat. But this time he didn't cry out and wake Stick. Instead, Jessie calmed his breathing and walked on shaky legs to the window, where he watched sheets of rain pelting down.

At least he hadn't woken Stick. That was progress.

●

After classes the next day, Jessie headed for the field house where he worked out again, studying while he pedaled the bike, increasing the previous day's workout. The next day, he added light weights and sprints, and the day after, he got up early to skate before breakfast.

No headaches or nausea. The next step was captain's practice. He'd try it that night.

So after classes, Jessie raced back to the dorm, finished his Algebra homework before an early dinner, then plowed through most of his Biology homework before it was time for practice.

He was ready—more than ready. He couldn't wait! It felt like forever since he'd gone one-on-one with a defenseman and beaten him, or rifled a puck past a goaltender.

As he stepped outside the dorm, Jessie felt the competitive juices pumping again. His fingers tingled, and each step toward the field house came with a light bounce, almost as if he was on a trampoline.

It was cool out that evening; the air had begun to bite with autumn's chill, especially now that the sun had set. The crickets chirped their chorus and the stars twinkled so much brighter than back home. With that thought, a pang of homesickness blindsided Jessie. Only seconds before, he'd been so happy, eagerly looking forward to his first real hockey action. But now, seemingly out of nowhere, a melancholy cloud had descended on him. Jessie's most vulnerable times came at moments like this when he least expected it; and, like a hit from behind into the boards, he was powerless to defend himself. The predictable times for homesickness, such as when he called his parents or got a letter or a package, didn't seem to bother him much at all. When he talked to his mother, she sometimes seemed hurt that he didn't sound more homesick, so last time he'd worked himself into a funk before he called—just so she wouldn't feel bad.

He missed his parents. He missed Momma's cooking, even though he'd just eaten a heaping plateful of lasagna and steak tips. It'd tasted great, but it wasn't like Momma's. And he was surprised to admit to himself that he missed her embarrassing, smothering hugs and he'd love her kiss on his cheek right now. He even missed the never-ending supply of Pop's lectures about everything from what it meant to be a man to the sacrifices of civil rights leaders and the greatness of Dr. Martin Luther King. Jessie even felt nostalgic about Pop's annoying, mile-long list of rules: no more than two hours of TV, eat your vegetables, wear a suit and tie to church. Do this. Don't do that.

But most of all, he missed Rose. Those big brown eyes. That pretty smile. Those soft lips. Who were those soft lips kissing now? Who was she dating? Would they ever get together again?

Jessie shook himself. He couldn't think that way or he'd go insane. For what felt like the millionth time, he reminded himself what a beautiful campus this was and what a great opportunity it offered.

But he wasn't sure he believed it anymore.

17

Jessie entered the field house feeling lonely, despite being surrounded by students working out. As he headed down the connecting corridor to the rink, he could hear the catcalls, boisterous talk, and laughter echoing from the locker room.

He took a deep breath, opened the door, and stepped inside.

All heads turned toward him and silence fell over the room.

Jessie nodded and moved to an empty bench, feeling eyes still locked on him. He pulled out his equipment and began to dress, noticing the locker-room smell of thick sweat and Lysol, mixed with the familiar layers of hatred and mistrust.

"Look who's here," a voice called out. Jessie looked up, trying to manage a slight smile and noticed the captain, Dirk Stapleton, who stood near the opposite wall. "Thirteen captain's practices and he finally shows up. That's what I call true commitment and hard work." A few boys laughed and others snorted in derision.

There had to be close to a dozen other guys in the room—most of them tall, muscular, and long-haired—but Jessie doubted he had a single friend there. No one in the group would play Pee Wee Reese to his Jackie Robinson by standing up for him when opponents turned vicious.

Jessie had seen these same looks from other teammates before this, looks that said, *What are you doing here? You don't belong.* But he'd always been able to turn them around, at least partially, by carrying the lion's share of the scoring burden for the team. Okay, none of them would set him up for dates with their sisters, and not many of them had considered him an equal in *all* ways, but as long as he was a superman on the ice and winning game after game for them, his past teammates had been happy enough having him around.

Could he do it again? Jessie wasn't sure. This was no ragtag collection of kids who'd be easily impressed. This was the home of championship after championship, its roster loaded with All-New England picks like Dirk. Jessie didn't know if he could win over this crowd, but he'd have to if he wanted to fulfill his dreams.

"I wanted to come back sooner," he explained, trying to keep his voice even while looking around the room. "But I couldn't even work out for almost three weeks."

"Tough as nails," Dirk said with a smirk. "Maybe we should put a skirt on you and make you into a figure skater." He wiggled his butt, then flicked his long hair back with a feminine gesture.

Everyone laughed but Jessie, and only then did he begin to wonder why the captain's long hair and that of his teammates met Coach Stone's standards but Jessie's Afro didn't.

"I had a bad concussion," Jessie said, hating the defensive tone in his voice. "It gave me really bad headaches." He knew those words were a mistake as soon as he said them.

"Oooooooo!" Dirk said, wide-eyed in mock horror. "Headaches!"

The laughter grew even louder.

Jessie felt his anger burn as his face grew hot. Hadn't any of them ever gotten a concussion? This wasn't fair and they all knew it.

But he couldn't think of anything else to say so he silently bent over, felt the blood rush to his head, and laced up his skates. He'd just have to answer them on the ice.

When they were dressed, half the team put on the yellow fishnet pullovers and the other half put on red ones. By the time everyone showed up, each side had three substitutes who'd rotate through either forward or defense, depending on which skater came off the ice for a breather. Having only three backups worked well in pickup games like this, since the forwards coasted when the other team had the puck, giving them a chance to catch their breath.

Except no one caught their breath when Jessie got the puck along the left wing boards. As soon as it touched his stick, Rocco lined him up for a big hit, elbows high. Jessie slid the puck to the nearest teammate wearing a red fishnet and sidestepped the hit. He skated up the ice looking for a return pass, and when he got it, Dirk converged.

Jessie faked to the middle, then accelerated wide to the

outside around Dirk, carrying the puck out of the defenseman's reach. As he cut to the net, a stick rapped him on the back of the head. The rubber helmet cushioned the blow, but it would have been an obvious penalty in an officiated game. Ignoring the cheap shot, Jessie bore in on the goaltender, picked an opening high to the short side, and ripped a shot into the back of the net. As he raised his hands to celebrate, Dirk slammed him into the boards.

"Don't you ever do that again," Dirk snarled under his breath.

Jessie pushed him away. "What's wrong with you?"

Players from both sides quickly surrounded them, but no one tried to separate them.

"I don't like *prima donnas*," Dirk said. "Freshmen need to know their place."

Know their place? Jessie was pretty sure his being a freshman had nothing to do with this.

"You just didn't like me faking you outta your jock strap," Jessie said.

"Watch your mouth," Dirk said and gave him a half-hearted shove, then turned to skate away.

But Jessie's anger got the best of him. "You didn't look like no All-New England to me."

Dirk's eyes narrowed, and without dropping his gloves, he threw a wild haymaker that Jessie easily blocked.

The other players quickly moved in to separate the two.

"Knock it off, guys," someone said.

Jessie pushed a flap of his shoulder pads back under his jersey and skated for the bench. It seemed like a good time for a breather.

Dirk skated to the other bench and Jessie wondered if this would be like one of those pro game fights, where two antagonists came off the bench and went right back at each other, dropping their gloves and swinging away. That happened in some Bruins games he'd watched, but it'd never happened to him. Amateur hockey banned fighting, and violating that ban resulted in quick suspensions. Jessie had never even been in a fight in a real game; only down on the ponds, playing far from the oversight of referees. After his first knockout of a bigger kid, no one challenged him again.

As Jessie sipped from a water bottle, he scolded himself for his big mouth. At his first practice, he'd tangled with the team captain.

How dumb had that been? *Keep your mouth shut next time*, Jessie told himself.

Still, Dirk's phrase came back to him. "Freshmen need to know their place." Jessie's blood boiled anew. *Know my place? I don't wanna fight everyone here. But if you make me, I will.*

Jessie returned to the ice before Dirk did, so there was no chance to skate right at each other and go at it. Jessie had no intention of continuing the grudge, but he wasn't going to skate away, either. If Dirk Stapleton wanted a fight, they'd fight. Jessie knew this was the last thing he should be thinking about his first time back on the ice, but Harry Edwards's words kept ringing in his head. No way was Jessie going to be Dirk's good little Tom.

It took several minutes before Jessie and Dirk clashed again, but for any teammates hoping for more excitement, it was worth the wait. A player wearing the red fired a shot that the goalie blocked. When the rebound caromed into the corner just out of Jessie's reach, he raced after it, his back turned to Dirk, but feeling him on his heels. Just as Jessie was about to scoop the puck and turn out of the corner, a cross-check sent him flying face-first into the boards.

Face down on the ice, Jessie blacked out for a split second before returning to stars twinkling across his field of vision. His head pounded; pain shot behind his eyes. Clenching his eyes shut, he tilted his head back, making sure he could move his neck. He got to his knees, trembling with rage.

A hit from behind into the boards was the dirtiest of plays, one that could break a player's neck and end in paralysis. It was also one of the worst hits someone recovering from a head injury could sustain.

Jessie staggered to his feet, tasting blood in his mouth. He glared at Dirk, who returned a grinning smirk. Blood trickling down his chin, Jessie dropped his gloves.

"You wanna go?" he said, not feeling all that solid on his skates. He doubted that a fight would be a good move for him after blacking out, but he couldn't allow a cheap shot like that to go unchallenged.

"Nah," Dirk said with a sneer. "I'd get your *ugly* on my fists and it might not come off." He looked around for approval and got a few chuckles.

Jessie still couldn't believe it—hitting from behind wasn't allowed; it just wasn't done—ever. If you could see a guy's number, you had to pull up. Coaches taught that from day one. You never took the chance of paralyzing someone in the heat of action, not even your most bitter rival. Nobody hit from behind, especially with an intentional cross-check that advertised you'd done it on purpose.

Jessie spit blood onto the ice and said, "Bad enough you'd cheap-shot anybody like that," he said, clenching his fists with rage. "But your own teammate?"

Dirk snorted. "You really don't get it, do you?" He tapped his helmet. "Not too bright, are you? Well, I'll spell it out for you, so clear, even *you* can understand." He leaned forward and through clenched teeth said, "You don't belong here. You are *not* my teammate. Your kind can put on the same jersey as me, but you ain't never gonna be *my* teammate."

Jessie blinked in disbelief and a volcano of rage erupted inside him. He wanted to beat Dirk into a bloody pulp. He wanted to see blood streaming down his face and broken teeth falling out of his mouth.

Feeling like he really wanted to kill Dirk, Jessie tried counting to ten to calm down.

One. *I want to kill him.* Two. *I want to kill him.*

No, that wasn't helping.

Jessie knew he wouldn't *really* kill Dirk; at least he didn't think so, despite the powerful urge to try. But then, from somewhere deep in his memory, Jessie recalled Pop telling him about Jackie Robinson enduring racial taunts, and that he was somehow able to deflect them so he wouldn't absorb the poison and have it contaminate him, too.

Jessie tried to think of Jackie Robinson, then he answered Dirk.

"Well, the school says I'm on this team," Jessie said. "The school says I have as much of a right to this jersey as you do. So you better get used to me, 'cause I ain't going nowhere."

13

After a restless night's sleep, Jessie awoke in the early morning light to another pounding headache stabbing him right behind the eyeballs. Even his ears rang.

Jessie cursed Dirk and his gang of bigots, the hatred welling hot in his heart. And not just for Dirk, but for all of them for standing aside and letting it happen. No one had said a word in his defense. No one had lifted a finger. *No one.*

Jessie thought of a phrase Pop often used: *No snowflake in an avalanche feels responsible.* He hated all of them, every snowflake on the hockey team.

Yet he couldn't very well give up, could he? Doing that would rob him of his dreams and give them what they wanted. No, giving up was not an option.

But how could he play with teammates he hated? Hockey wasn't like track and field, where each man runs his own race. It wasn't even like baseball, where almost every play was based on an individual's effort. Yes, infielders might cooperate for a double play, but pitchers threw pitches, batters took swings, and fielders caught the

153

ball. In hockey, you had to work with your teammates: pass to the open man, read your line mates to know where an opening would develop, cover defensively for each other. You had to read and react.

All of that and also make any opponent pay who cheap-shot your teammate. You got his number, and when the opportunity arose, you drove him *through* the boards and blasted him into the cheap seats. You did whatever it took to make sure that cheap shot never happened again.

The problem this time was that the guys who Jessie should be ready to defend had become his attackers, if only by inaction. *One of your kind can put on the same jersey as me, but he ain't never gonna be my teammate*, Dirk had said. And that meant those guys weren't going to pass Jessie the puck, even if he was wide open with no defender in sight. They hated him for the color of his skin, and now he hated them for it. Jessie crawled out of bed, wincing at the stabbing pain in his head, and rubbed his temples. His stomach roiled, and he puckered his parched mouth to try and produce some saliva.

He tiptoed out of the room to avoid waking Stick, who snored softly in his bed, eased the door shut, then made his way down the hallway to the bathroom, thinking that he'd go to Stick's football game that afternoon. He'd been pretty sure a couple days earlier, when Stick mentioned that after two away games, this one would be at home. Jessie could take the hint; he knew Stick wanted him there.

Jessie worried about the ringing in his ears. That was new, and a possible sign that he'd entered an even more dangerous position than before—a bit like Stick. Dirk had set him back to square one: total inactivity until the headaches went away. With Jessie's workout time reset to zero, he couldn't claim to be too busy to go to Stick's game. He hoped the raucous cheering wouldn't send slivers of pain reverberating inside his skull.

When he got back to the room, Stick was awake, but since he'd be having breakfast with the football team, Jessie left and ate alone. By the time he returned, Stick was gone.

Jessie tried to study, but with his brains turned to mush from his injury, he couldn't concentrate. He kept reading the same paragraphs over and over, remembering nothing.

●

Hours later at the game, the football floated down to Stick at the ten-yard line. Wearing number seven, he caught the ball and darted upfield, smaller but quicker than everyone else. He cut left, faked back inside, freezing one defender, then cut back outside again, his legs a blur as he raced past guys who looked stationary by comparison. One by one, opponents lunged at Stick and missed, or else dove too late, after he'd already blown past them.

The roar of the crowd got louder as Stick crossed the forty, thirty, twenty, and ten yard lines, and then into the end zone.

Jessie had been holding his breath—something he did whenever Stick was involved in a play—forgetting that this would make his temples throb. If Dirk's cheap shot had set Jessie back to square one, he hated to think of what another concussion might do to Stick. End his career? Turn him into a vegetable?

Jessie'd never understood why his mother became so nervous whenever he played. Sometimes it was so bad, she had to leave the stands and wait in the lobby of his school, pacing back and forth until the game ended and he was safe. It had seemed foolish, like one of those things mothers did that left their sons scratching their heads. But now he understood, at least a little.

It was scary watching Stick, knowing the dangers he faced. Given the chance between playing and being a spectator, Jessie would always rather play, and despite his fears for his roommate, he whooped when Stick reached the end zone. It was Stick's third touchdown of the game, two on long passes and this one on a kick return. Apparently, Jessie's worries had been overblown.

Jessie wondered if he'd been wrong after all about Stick's chances in the pros. The odds might be long, but Stick was electric—Black Magic. Every time he touched the ball, amazing things happened. No wonder *The Springvale Record*, the school newspaper, compared his moves to Gale Sayers and O.J. Simpson. No wonder the football coach had gotten Stick a tutor.

And he was even better at basketball.

●

Jessie called home that night at eight, following the schedule his parents had requested. He was to call every Saturday night, as well as in emergencies or when he felt especially homesick. And though pangs of homesickness had struck at times, Jessie hadn't felt a sufficiently overwhelming urge to call. As a result, the Saturday night calls became the only time Jessie talked to his family, a time he both looked forward to and dreaded. The attack had set both his parents on edge and they hung on every word, anxious to learn that no other danger lurked.

Jessie greeted his parents, who were each on an extension at home. They exchanged brief pleasantries, and then Momma got right to the point.

"How are your courses going?"

"Fine."

"Are you studying hard?"

"Yes." He could almost hear over the line her frustration with his short answers, but what else could he say? Still, he added, "I'm working real hard. Probably six hours yesterday."

But it was an exaggeration; between working out in the morning and the disastrous captain's practice at night, there hadn't been six hours left when he could have studied. And Jessie had already decided he wasn't going to tell his parents about the captain's practice. In fact, he'd resolved not to tell them anything bad, now or in the future. That attack had shaken them badly, Momma more visibly and vocally, but Jessie thought it had hit Pop even harder. In his grim silence, Jessie could tell that his father had been rocked to the core. Since there wasn't anything to be gained by worrying them further, he'd handle the situation on his own and not go running to his parents with his troubles.

"How about algebra?" Momma asked.

"It's hard. There's lots of homework in all the top-track courses. The teachers expect a lot of us."

157

Pop spoke up. "We do, too."

No kidding, Jessie thought.

"How are your grades?" Pop asked. "Going to a great school isn't going to get you into Harvard. You need the grades, too."

Tell me something I don't already know. "I know, Pop. I'm trying hard."

"Have you had any tests yet?" his mom asked.

Jessie ran down the list of minor quizzes, pointing out that the big exams would come later in the semester.

"No headaches?" Pop asked.

Jessie licked his lips. "Right," he said. It would have been the truth, until last night.

"No symptoms at all?" his father prompted.

"I'm fine," Jessie said, exhaling slowly and softly, sure they could hear the lie in his voice. Something churned inside Jessie's stomach. He hated lying to his parents, and the hundred fifty miles that separated them made it seem even worse.

"Good," Pop said. "You had me a little concerned there for a while."

"Have you heard anything more about the police investigation?" Momma asked.

Jessie tensed; he'd known this was coming, just like it did in every other call. And the answer was always the same: "No." Jessie just wanted to forget about it.

"How long is it going to take them?" his mother asked, her voice becoming somewhat shrill. "How many three-hundred pound, seven-foot white boys live out there? What is wrong with those police?"

Jessie didn't reply. He'd grown tired of asking himself that same question, and knew the answer as well as his parents did: if Jessie had been white, those suspects would have been arrested weeks ago, alibis or not.

The silence on the line lasted so long that Jessie wondered if they'd been disconnected.

Finally, his mother spoke up. "They aren't gonna do a thing, are they?"

"No, Momma. I don't think so."

When Jessie hung up a few minutes later, his head hurt worse than ever before.

19

Not long after Jessie's phone call, there was a knock on his door. Alone in the room, Jessie asked, "Who is it?"

After a moment's pause, an accented voice said, "Frenchie—I mean, Jacques."

Jessie opened the door to find a tall, muscular boy with flaming red hair. His black jacket was zipped all the way up, and Jessie recognized him from his English class and possibly somewhere else, maybe freshman orientation.

The boy looked nervous and uncomfortable. "My name is Jacques Desjardins, but people here call me Frenchie. I come from Quebec, outside of Montreal. I was wondering if I could speak to you," he asked in a heavy French Canadian accent.

"Sure," Jessie said and introduced himself. They shook hands.

Frenchie stared down at the floor. "I came by . . . to, um—" he drew in a deep breath, "—to apologize."

Jessie waited to hear why.

"I was there for the practice last night," Frenchie said. "What Dirk did was . . . awful. Terrible! In my league back home, he would have been suspended for a long time. To do that to a teammate on purpose?" Frenchie shook his head. "I apologize because I saw what Dirk did, but I said nothing. He is the captain and I am only a freshman. I didn't want to make him angry."

Frenchie looked pained, but then he gave Jessie an odd smile and said, "My father is a farmer. He has sayings for everything, and he would say that if I don't defend you next time, I should no longer wear a cup while playing hockey. Why wear a cup if you have no balls?"

Jessie grinned and extended a hand. "Your father would be wrong about that. Your apology proves you need a cup." Jessie's grin broadened. "A big one."

Frenchie broke into a grin, too, and pumped Jessie's hand again. But then his grin faded. "You were not at practice tonight. Are you all right?"

"Just some headaches." Jessie shrugged as they both sat down. "I'll be all right in a few days." He silently added, *I hope*.

"There is something else," Frenchie said and averted his eyes. "At practice tonight, Dirk was, ah—he was making fun of you in the locker room. I don't like to, how do you say it, tattle? But I thought you should know."

"I'm not surprised," Jessie said. He'd been relaxed, slouched in his chair. Now he sat up straight and gripped the armrests of his chair. He didn't think he wanted to hear Dirk's words, but his curiosity got the best of him. "What did he say?"

"He was calling you names, saying you're gutless. That the only reason you are in this school is because you're the headmaster's pet." Frenchie looked uncomfortable. "He called you the headmaster's pet gorilla."

Jessie winced, but instead of his familiar rage, he felt only exhaustion. *Was it ever going to stop?*

Frenchie continued. "When I tried to say something, he began to make fun of me. He called me . . ." Clearly uncomfortable, Frenchie didn't finish.

"Go ahead." Jessie could pretty much guess what was coming next.

"You are *not* going to like this. Maybe it would be better if I didn't tell you."

"I'm sure I can guess. Dirk's not exactly an original thinker."

Frenchie tilted his head sideways and gave Jessie a look that said, 'Okay, you asked for it,' Then said, "He called me . . . a Negro-loving frog. Only he didn't use the word *Negro*."

Jessie nodded. It was exactly what he'd expected.

"Frog is because I'm French-Canadian."

"Got it," Jessie said with a grin, amused that Frenchie assumed the only epithets he'd know were the ones used for Black people.

"There is something else," Frenchie said.

"What?"

"Dirk said if you try to come back to one of his captain's practices, he won't let you."

Jessie stared. "But—"

"Dirk said that Coach Stone has to take you once the season starts, but captain's practices are different. He said he can do anything he wants."

The league prohibited official practices until the end of fall sports, but captain's practices gave those players a two-month head start.

Jessie figured he was at least a week away from trying to take the ice again, but he never imagined that when he was ready, he'd have to fight for the chance to return to his rightful place.

"He can't do that," Jessie said. "Can he? The school provides the ice so we can get a head start on the season. It's kind of like having us take 'Working Out' as our fall sport. If the school does this to help the team, it can't let Dirk ban me."

Frenchie looked bewildered. "I don't know."

Jessie groaned. Only one person could overrule Dirk Stapleton—Coach Stone.

●

As Jessie entered Coach Stone's office the next day, he immediately noticed the new black-and-white photograph hanging on the wall behind the coach's desk. It showcased the stern face of George Wallace. When Jessie saw it, his heart sank. Then he saw the "Wallace for President" bumper sticker plastered on a filing cabinet in the corner.

As head of one of the most racist states in the country, Alabama governor George Wallace had fought Dr. King's efforts to both break segregation and allow black voter registration. Wallace's most famous speech included the words, "I say segregation now, segregation tomorrow, segregation forever." In some Alabama counties, the Klan had so intimidated potential voters that not a single black person was registered. Jessie could still recall his father's pain and anger when he talked about what had happened before he joined Dr. King's march to Selma.

As a third-party Presidential candidate, Wallace had no chance to win, but his very candidacy was an insult to every black man and woman. And now, to have that hateful face of segregation looking down on him made Jessie's skin crawl. Coach Stone might as well be flying the Confederate flag and dividing his office into two sides, one for Whites and the other for Coloreds.

Jessie tore his eyes away from George Wallace and looked on the florid face of Coach Stone. Then he asked, "Can Dirk ban me from captain's practices?"

Stone gave Jessie a disinterested shrug. "He's the captain. They're called captain's practices, so he calls the shots."

Feeling helpless, Jessie plunged ahead anyway. "But Dirk doesn't pay for the ice, Coach. The school does, and it's for all of us."

"I'm not interested in arguing semantics with you, Stackhouse. I'm a busy man."

"But the school makes the ice available to give the team a head start. The whole team—not just the captain's favorites. No player, not even the captain, should be able to deny anyone else on the team the chance to get ready for the season."

Stone chewed on a piece of gum, his ruddy jowls moving up and down. "It's my understanding that Dirk has a very solid reason for kicking you out of the practices."

Jessie couldn't believe it. "Because he hates blacks? That's a solid reason?"

"That ain't what I said." Stone gave Jessie the eye, seeming to say that he'd heard enough and wouldn't listen to any more. "What I heard, and this is from multiple sources, is that *you*—" Stone pointed a finger at Jessie "—dropped the gloves and Dirk showed remarkable restraint in not doing the same."

Jessie's jaw dropped.

Stone hunched forward. "A *freshman* drops his gloves, looking to fight the senior captain, and the *freshman* thinks he's the victim?" Stone shook his head. "I don't think so. What *I* think is that Dirk's admirable restraint, in the spirit of team unity after your hotheaded behavior, is exactly why I expect him to be one of the best captains in the history of this program. Dirk put team first, something *you people* never do."

You people? His hotheaded behavior? *Dirk's* admirable restraint? This was outrageous on every level. The truth had been turned upside down and inside out. It was insane!

Jessie didn't know where to begin. "He cross-checked me from behind into the boards," Jessie said, struggling not to shout. "Dirk could have broken my neck. I was lucky he didn't. But I sure wasn't lucky hitting my head again. The headaches, nausea, and dizziness are back and I'm not sure when I'll be able to return to the ice."

Stone rested his elbows on the desktop and steepled his fingers. "So you couldn't attend a captain's practice right now, even if Dirk let you. That makes your complaint one big hypothetical."

"It's a matter of principle!" Jessie said. "When I'm ready to return, I should be allowed to come back."

Stone leaned forward conspiratorially and lowered his voice. "You know, just between you and me . . . we never had these problems with white players."

Jessie almost exploded. "Oh, yeah? Well, I'll bet none of them ever heard their redneck captain say, 'One of your kind can put on the same jersey as me, but he ain't never gonna be my teammate.' "

"Stackhouse, I've heard enough. I have work to do. Dirk's the captain and he makes the rules. I'm not going to change them, especially not for some hypothetical situation." Stone motioned for Jessie to get up. "Now, I don't want to see you again until the first day of practice."

A smirk crossed the coach's lips. "And if you're still injured by then and can't take the ice, we'll just have to do without you. I hope you know how brokenhearted I'll be."

20

Jessie bounced back quicker from his injuries this time. Only two weeks later, Jessie completed his entire circuit of workouts at full speed: the stationary bike for endurance, sprints for explosive speed, and free weights for strength. He'd done them all without a problem—no headaches, no nausea, no dizziness. But also, no captain's practices.

He'd dismissed any thought of seeing Stone again and requesting his intervention. If Jessie were dying of thirst, Stone wouldn't even hack up a ball of spit to save him. Jessie wondered, though, if he should sit down with Dirk and try to work things out man-to-man, even if Dirk didn't consider Jessie a man, and maybe not even human. Dirk would probably refuse to talk about it, but what could it hurt?

So Jessie made a point of intercepting Dirk and two of his friends, Rocco and Sully, on their way from the field house to the rink.

"Dirk, can we talk?" Jessie said.

"Get lost," Dirk growled.

"I want to come to your practices," Jessie said. "I can help this team if you'll let me."

Dirk glanced at Rocco and then Sully, then grinned. "We ain't letting you."

●

The next day, Jessie skipped his workout, rushed through homework and dinner, then headed for the common room with Stick. Most nights, Jessie avoided the common room. Why try to socialize with people who didn't like you? More often than not, there were arguments over what shows to watch, and when Jessie did watch something, he often felt accusing eyes on him. It was okay for everyone else to ogle Goldie Hawn on *Laugh-In* or Peggy Lipton on *Mod Squad*, but not him or Stick; a lot of the guys looked uncomfortable if they did. And if hoots and catcalls erupted when Goldie was showing lots of skin and gyrating her hips while saying, "Sock it to me!" the room fell uncomfortably silent if he or Stick joined in.

So Jessie and Stick stayed away, hanging out in their room and studying, talking, or listening to records. They stayed there by themselves even after they overheard people call it Little Harlem. Jessie and Stick ventured into the common room only when something particularly compelling came on TV, like the World Series between the St. Louis Cardinals and Detroit Tigers; college football games involving USC and its star running back, O.J. Simpson; or pro football on Sunday.

Tonight was one of those nights. The Summer

Olympics had begun and the 100- and 200-meter dashes were Stick's and Jessie's favorite events.

"When you gonna get your homework done?" Jessie asked Stick as they headed for the common room. Stick had gone straight from football practice to the dining hall where they met, and had scarcely cracked a book while Jessie finished up his English paper.

"Don't worry 'bout me, Einstein," Stick said before giving him a look that closed off further questions.

Jessie hoped Stick wasn't dumping even more homework on his tutor, but he'd given up trying to play parent. Much as he felt that, as a friend, it was at least some of his business, in the end, he suspected it wasn't. And Stick wasn't going to listen to him anyway.

Jessie felt even guiltier that he'd rushed through his own homework. He knew he'd cut some corners. And he'd skipped his workout. Maybe Stick was right. He needed to take care of his own business before he started nosing into Stick's.

But the 100-meter dash—man, the ten seconds it took could light up a big city. The 200-meter race could be even more dramatic, not to mention the mile run, and all the other events in between. To Jessie they offered an almost hypnotic attraction, like the most addicting of drugs.

Apparently, a lot of the other guys felt the same way because the common room was packed. Every chair was taken and guys sat on the floor cross-legged, their eyes glued to the TV set, barely glancing Jessie and Stick's way. The two stepped past clusters of bodies and sat down in the middle of the floor.

"Hey, how am I supposed to see?" Jimmy Duvall complained from his spot on the floor behind Jessie. Jessie understood and got up to move, realizing that no one would be able to see past him. He was over six-feet tall now, and though he'd trimmed his Afro a bit after Coach Stone insisted, he'd let it grow ever since, planning to cut it again only when the season was about to start.

Hearing Jimmy's comment, Stick frowned and said, "I ain't movin'."

"That's okay." Jessie grinned. "You a midget. A big man's got to move."

Jessie waded through the bodies clustered about and in front of the common room's seven leather chairs and stepped back against the wall. There'd be no room to sit, but he didn't mind standing.

"How come the Summer Olympics are being held in October?" Jimmy Duvall asked during a commercial. "Since when is October in the summer? Was it because of that Negro boycott everyone was worried about?"

"No," Jessie said, keeping his tone even. "Four years ago it was the exact same thing. The Summer Olympics were held in October then, too, so it's nothing new." He left unsaid that the boycott threats had had nothing to do with it.

The room fell silent, as if everyone were suddenly focused on the aftershave commercial. Jessie wondered if he'd been expected to remain silent. If so, too bad.

When it came time for the finals of the 200-meter dash, he said, "It's gonna be John Carlos all the way." No one responded so he added, "Tommie Smith pulled his groin a little in the semifinals, you could see him reach for it." The two Americans had run away from the field in their semifinal races. If not for Smith's injury, Jessie couldn't see anyone touching either of them; they'd finish neck-and-neck in the third and fourth lanes. But a bad groin and the third lane's tight turn was a bad combination. Jessie was afraid Smith would pull up lame and not get a medal at all, a cruel blow for an athlete who'd trained so hard.

Again, no one responded, so Jessie kept quiet after that.

For the first half of the race, Jessie's prediction was dead-on. Carlos came out of the turn clearly in the lead and accelerated into the straightaway.

But then—

Tommie Smith flew right past Carlos, making Jessie's favorite look like he was standing still. He was already a yard ahead—then two. So strong, Jessie thought. Look at those legs flying.

And then it was over: Tommie Smith had tied the world record and Carlos had fallen apart, losing his technique as he'd watched Smith roar past, allowing a white guy from Australia to catch him.

Jessie saw himself running like Tommie Smith when he trained tomorrow, arms pumping, legs pistoning up and down with such power. But Jessie's sprints never went more than forty meters, let alone a hundred or two hundred meters. That's because in hockey, the straight-ahead bursts didn't last any longer than that; the key was acceleration.

But tomorrow, he'd be like Tommie Smith. He'd try 200-meter dashes just for the one day. He'd fly like the fastest man in the world. *Taste my dust, baby.*

Jessie lost himself in his reverie until the opening strains of the National Anthem came from the black-and-white television, the sound typically tinny and laced with static.

But what Jessie saw made his jaw drop and his heart hammer in amazement and admiration.

"Oh, my God," muttered someone up front.

There on the victory stand, Tommie Smith stood on the center podium, his head bowed and his gloved right fist raised in the Black Power salute. To his left stood John Carlos, his gloved left fist raised in the same salute.

A shiver quivered through Jessie in something like the religious fervor he usually felt at church revival meetings with people whooping, crying, and praising the Lord.

Just seeing that salute made Jessie want to whoop and cry.

"What are they *doing*?" one boy said.

"Look at them!"

"That's a disgrace!"

"Send 'em back to Africa."

As the clamor around him grew louder, Jessie closed his eyes, bowed his head, and, just like Tommie Smith, lifted his fist in the air.

The familiar voice of Mr. Richardson cut through the others. "Put your hand down!" he commanded.

Jessie slowly opened his eyes and met Mr. Richardson's, but he kept his fist held high. This defiance left the dorm parent, so cool and suave little more than a month ago, trembling with rage. His chest heaving, his face red, and his teeth bared, Richardson screamed, "I said put your hand down!"

The anthem played on but Jessie didn't move. He glanced at Stick, who'd gotten to his feet looking worried.

As a voice off to the left yelled out the N-word, someone shoved Jessie and everyone seemed to be shouting.

Mr. Richardson got up in Jessie's face, his nose only inches away from Jessie's. He snarled, "Get it down or I'll tear it down."

Jessie didn't answer him directly. Instead, he simply joined in the anthem instead, singing loud and strong: ". . . *bombs bursting in air, gave proof through the night* . . ." His voice, never that good to begin with, slipped off-key and then was drowned out by the jeers from his housemates.

"Stop him!"

"What does he think he's doing?"

"We hate you, too!"

"He should be expelled."

Even while both sides jostled him, Jessie stayed strong on his feet. ". . .*Oh say does that Star Spangled Banner* . . ."

Furious, Mr. Richardson grabbed Jessie's elbow and tried to pull his arm down.

But Jessie pushed him away and kept singing. "... *O'er the land of the free. And the home of the brave*."

Only then did Jessie lower his arm and unclench his fist. But he was ready to do more than just show his fist if anyone so much as pushed him again; that's how filled he was with righteous rage.

"Are you trying to cause a riot?" Mr. Richardson shouted, his face red and spittle on his lips. The difference between the suave comedian he'd first appeared to be and his hateful, unmasked sneer made Jessie think of Dr. Jekyll and Mr. Hyde. This man had never been his friend, no matter how he'd claimed to be, and that hateful truth was now exposed for all to see.

"You like to cause trouble, don't you?" he asked Jessie.

"I stand up for my beliefs, *sir*," Jessie said, emphasizing the term of respect to make it sound almost sarcastic. "Even if they're not popular around this lynch mob."

The words "lynch mob" were like an open-handed slap across Mr. Richardson's face. Jessie could almost see the red, stinging blotch and the watering eyes, just as if he'd hit the man.

"Don't try that on me." Richardson pointed to the TV behind him. "That was a *shameful* display. By those two . . . by those two—" It looked like Richardson could only think of the most forbidden racial slur in his current state of rage and not being able to use it was tongue-tying him. He finally managed to say, ". . . those two Negroes." Then he added, "Imagine the *ingratitude* after what this country has done for them! If not for this opportunity, those two would probably still be picking cotton."

But Jessie didn't back down. He pointed to the TV set, saying, "They're supposed to represent this country, but if they lived in parts of Alabama, would they be allowed to vote? No. Would they be served if they sat down to eat in an all-white restaurant? No. Would their children be allowed to go to the all-white schools? No."

"That's Alabama."

"Mississippi, Georgia—"

"That's the South."

"What happens up here in the *enlightened North*?"

Jessie asked, making no secret of his sarcasm now. Molten anger poured out of him. "If Tommie Smith tries to buy a house in the lily white suburbs, what happens to him?"

"He—"

Jessie cut Mr. Richardson off. "I'll tell you what happens. The house suddenly goes off the market and the neighbors have paid off the seller." Then Jessie pointed to Mr. Richardson. "How many blacks were there in the neighborhood *you* grew up in?"

"That's beside the point."

"That's because when the Tommie Smiths of the *enlightened* North try to rent an apartment in your neighborhood, it's not available." Jessie thrust out hands. "Here's what happens: poof! It's gone!" His voice shaking with rage, Jessie said, "Tommie Smith has every right to protest this country's treatment of black people. It's a national disgrace."

"It's a disgrace to shame this country with a gesture like that," Mr. Richardson said, but in a faltering tone, as if trying to muster the lost forcefulness of his earlier words.

"He made that gesture because this country's shamed itself."

"Then go back to Africa," a voice called out.

Jessie wondered how someone so dumb had gotten into Springvale Academy. "My ancestors didn't come here by choice. They came here in chains. We only want what's fair." Jessie looked for Stick but couldn't see him in the cluster of bodies that was crowding around him. Frustrated, Jessie turned up the volume and intensity. "We demand the civil rights guaranteed by the Constitution where it says that *all* men are created equal."

A look of smug superiority came over Mr. Richardson's face. "Equal my ass," he said.

"Yes, equal," Jessie said. "And unless this country is prepared to go beyond *talking* about it, then black men of courage and conviction like Tommie Smith and John Carlos will speak up and not look the other way at bigotry and injustice."

"That's enough!" Mr. Richardson said, gripping Jessie tightly by the elbow. "Quiet down, now."

"No, I won't be quiet," Jessie said and gasps erupted all about the room. "Freedom of Speech means *all* speech, not just the words *you* want to hear."

Mr. Richardson's eyes blazed. "Mr. Stackhouse, I *demand* your respect."

Jessie didn't back down. "Respect has to be earned. You *had* my respect." He shook his head. "But not anymore."

Mr. Richardson looked like he was going to hit Jessie. But instead, Jessie felt a hand tugging at his arm. He was about to fling it away when he realized it was Stick.

"C'mon, man. Let's go," Stick said. He leaned close and whispered. "You just gonna get us beat up again."

Jessie didn't want to give an inch. If Stick wouldn't stand beside him, he'd take them all on by himself. Mr. Richardson could be first for all he cared. Jessie glared into the man's dark, hate-filled eyes.

But Stick pulled on his arm again and said, "C'mon, Einstein, think!" Jessie could see the fear in his eyes.

After glaring at Mr. Richardson one last time, Jessie ducked his head and began to shoulder his way through the

Cracking the Ice

crowd. The catcalls and jeers grew louder as he and Stick
made their way through the gauntlet and on both sides, boys
jostled them, either deliberately or because of the pressure
from outside the circle.

Jessie and Stick broke through the crowd and headed
for the stairwell to the third floor. Hearing the angry voices
behind them, Jessie felt two opposing urges inside him. Part
of him wanted to sprint up the stairs, taking them two or
three at a time to get away from this powder keg as quickly
as possible. But he felt an even stronger urge to raise his
fist and hold it high all the way to their room. Only Stick's
obvious fear kept Jessie's fist at his side.

Jessie walked slowly and deliberately, his head held
high and his shoulders back. He wondered if this was how
it felt when Pop had marched with Dr. King; they'd braved
snarling dogs, policemen's billy clubs, and shotguns in the
trigger-happy hands of men whose faces showed only hatred. Jessie thought so.

And so, even though he was still angry, he smiled.

21

Stick slammed the door behind them. "Are you *outta your mind*? They wanted to kill us down there."

"I'm not backing down," Jessie said.

"You got a death wish—fine. Just don't include me. You gonna make those flowery speeches? Let me know so I can get away from you. 'Cause right now I just want to play ball. I ain't gonna be on no crusade."

"Maybe you ought to be."

Stick glared. "Easy for you to say—you the son of a Doc-tor. You be Black Einstein. You can afford crusades. All I got is ball. I can't afford to get suspended for fightin'. I can't miss no more games. Coach still mad at me for missin' the one when we was in the hospital."

Jessie's anger flared yet again. "You should have told him you'd try harder not to get attacked by the local version of the Klan."

"That'd go over real good—Coach's a big fan of sarcasm." Stick shook his head. "You'd actually say that to the man, wouldn't you?"

"Maybe." Jessie thought back to his first meeting with

Coach Stone and how intimidated he'd felt. "Maybe I'd also bow my head and say, 'Yes, massah.'"

"Yeah, easy to be tough inside your head," Stick said. "Outside, it be tougher. Coach carries a big stick and he like to use it." Stick sat down on his bed. "So don't get me suspended or nothin' like that."

"Why would they suspend us? We didn't throw any punches. They were the ones pushing and shoving me around."

Stick looked at Jessie like he was from another planet. "You kiddin' me, bro? Soon as one of them throws a punch, you fight back. By the time it be over, they say you give the Black Power salute, then we both spit on the flag, messed with those boys' mommas, and threw the first five punches. They just defending themselves and the U.S. of A. Who you think everyone's gonna believe?"

Jessie couldn't think of what to say. Stick was right.

"There something else, too." Stick looked away. "I can't be havin' no white-bread sucker-punching me. In that room, there be two of us and how many of them? Twenty? Thirty?" He toed the carpet. "I still get headaches. Having trouble concentrating in class and doin' my homework. If I didn't have that tutor . . ." Stick's voice trailed off. "I gotta make it through football season without another big hit to the head. I be okay once football over and hoop starts."

Alarm shot through Jessie, but before he could respond, Stick added, "So don't go gettin' my head kicked in 'cause you tryin' to be the next Martin Luther King."

"Stick, you can't keep playing if you're having headaches. My pop says—"

Stick held his hand up. "You already told me what your pop says. I'd like to listen, but Coach talks louder." He chuckled ruefully. "Coach yells louder. And you know it ain't the same if a black player gets hurt. If he don't play, he just a lazy, loafin' you-know-what."

●

That Saturday, the air was cool and crisp beneath a cloudless blue sky. The leaves in the trees had turned into a bright mix of yellow, red, and all the shades in between. Students, parents, and a few townies filed into the stands at Emersen Stadium in greater numbers than for any other game this season. The Warriors remained undefeated and were facing Avon Old Farms, their rival in many sports.

In the stands behind the thirty-yard line, Jessie and Frenchie stood huddled in thick jackets, hands in their pants pockets as they bounced on the balls of their sneakered feet, trying to keep warm.

"How are the captain's practices going?" Jessie asked.

"Okay," Frenchie said, looking uncomfortable. "I told you I would stop going if—"

"Don't apologize, and please, keep going. You have to be my spy."

"I'm just saying—"

"Stop saying," Jessie said. "Besides, the real practices start next week. I'll be fine." But Jessie wished he really felt that way. He'd gone for a private skate every morning that week, but it wasn't the same as playing with team-

180

mates. He hadn't passed a puck to a live person in four weeks and was anxious for the official practices to begin.

The kickoff dropped to Stick at the ten-yard line. He darted up the middle, faked one tackler, then cut to an open seam on the right. But then, just as he was about to burst through, an arm reached out and clipped his foot, tripping him and sending him falling forward into a sprawl.

A collective sigh of disappointment erupted from the stands and Jessie exhaled, only then realizing he'd been holding his breath. He was disappointed that Stick hadn't broken off a long gainer or even a touchdown, but he'd been holding his breath out of fear for Stick's safety. Jessie mouthed a silent prayer: *Nothing to the head. Please, nothing to the head.*

On the next play, the Springvale quarterback missed Stick badly on a pass down the right side. It should have gone for a touchdown, but instead the ball flew out of bounds. Stick had beaten his man by a good ten yards. He was like bottled lightning.

The boys watched the game awhile, then Frenchie said, "There's an initiation for all the freshmen trying out for the team. Next Saturday night."

"When did you hear that?"

"Captain's practice. Last night. It sounds, well . . . the seniors laughed and said we would have to eat worms and . . . and do stuff." Frenchie gulped. "I think they were just trying to scare us, but—"

Jessie nodded. "Looks like they succeeded."

"Yeah, well, I'm not really scared. Just . . ."

"Nervous."

"Yeah."

Great, Jessie thought. *Another roadblock that had nothing to do with hockey*. At least this one would be nothing more than a little nonsense, nothing compared to dealing with a team captain and a coach who seemed to hate him. He looked forward to the day when all he'd have to beat was a defenseman and a goalie. That would feel like a power play by comparison.

"I'm sure it'll be nothing," Jessie said.

At least his worries over another head injury for Stick were unfounded. Before the game ended, Stick had scored two touchdowns—one on a punt return that had everyone turning to the person next to them, saying, "Did you see that?" and the other on a short five-yard pass that he turned into a sixty-yard score.

Lightning in a bottle, Jessie thought. They couldn't hit what they couldn't catch.

●

That Saturday, Jessie called home earlier than usual because the freshman initiation was scheduled for seven p.m.—not that he told his parents anything about it. He found that the more he hid from them, the harder it became to tell them anything. The conversations had initially run ten or fifteen minutes long, but lately they'd gotten down to five minutes of mostly awkward silences, punctuated by Momma's attempts to get him to talk, and his five- or six-word replies. Jessie hated freezing them out like that, but what else could he do? Every topic was a potential land mine just waiting to blow up if he said that wrong thing. At least he was saving them money on the phone bill.

When he hung up after a heartfelt "I love you" to both parents, Jessie flopped back on his bed feeling about as depressed as he'd ever felt since starting at Springvale Academy. And who wouldn't in his shoes? Out of a school of six hundred boys, he could claim only two friends—Stick and Frenchie. Even Preston next door had become more distant. Jessie figured he'd just been a curiosity that Preston had grown tired of after his initial interest.

Two friends, and everyone else either hated him, feared him, or felt only indifferent toward him. It was like the most impenetrable goaltender was blocking him from any other friendly contact at Springvale.

Jessie felt so lonely. His parents seemed so far away, they might as well be twinkling with the stars. Rose, too. Actually it was worse with Rose, and thinking of her was far more painful for him. He didn't have to think of anyone taking his place with his parents, but whenever he thought of Rose, he wondered who she was with. Who was she holding hands with? Who was putting his arm around her, and who was kissing those beautiful lips? Jessie couldn't stand it so he pushed her out of his mind. He knew he was stuck at Springvale and he might as well make the best of it.

But just two friends? *Two?* Was it all his fault? Maybe so, maybe he was delusional thinking it was everyone else's fault, but he didn't think so. He knew he'd been judged by almost all his classmates based solely on the color of his skin even if his outspoken approach hadn't helped.

Stick had teased him about it, saying, "Man, you sure your pop ain't a preacher? Don't he give a sermon on Sundays? 'Cause, man, if he does, you take after him. You don't ever shut up."

Well, Jessie thought, if it was a crime to speak up, he was guilty. *Put them handcuffs on me, 'cause I ain't learnin' my place.*

Was that what had happened to him? Was he in social handcuffs now, in restraints he'd willingly slipped into? *No*, Jessie thought. He wasn't taking the blame for this isolation. It wasn't his fault, and it was their loss if they shut him out—his teammates, classmates, and everyone else there who'd prejudged him and turned their backs on him.

Yeah—their loss. Keep trying to convince yourself, Jessie thought. But it didn't feel like their loss to him; it felt more like his own.

Jessie got up and went to his bookcase, then slipped the James Brown record from its cover and set the vinyl disk onto the turntable. A crackling hiss came out of the speakers; he'd been wearing the grooves out of this song and it had the snap, crackle, and pop to prove it.

Say it loud, I'm black and I'm proud.

He stood there, singing along, and when the song was over, he switched to an Aretha album. Soon she was belting out R-E-S-P-E-C-T and Jessie made it a duet.

He felt a little better now after his sing-along. It wasn't a lot, but it was better than nothing.

22

As he walked with Frenchie to the ball field where all the freshmen had been told to congregate, Jessie thought of Stick's surprising refusal to talk about his own initiation with the football team.

"That's the thing," he'd said, glancing up from reading an article about himself in the school newspaper. "It's the code. You don't tell nobody outside the team. Not even your best friend."

Jessie was taken aback. "Not even me?"

Stick rolled his eyes. "What I just say?" Then, speaking very slowly, he said, "Not. Even. To. Your. Best. Friend." The corners of his lips curled up with the hint of a smile and he added, "Or don't Black Einstein speak English no more?"

"Yeah, but we're brothers," Jessie said.

"That ain't how it works. It's a team thing. Team bonding. It make you feel closer to your teammates—even the rednecks."

Jessie frowned. He couldn't imagine anything bringing him closer to Dirk, Rocco, or Sully. He also couldn't imagine Stick sharing a secret with some of the bigots on the football team and not letting Jessie in on it.

"I'll tell you this much," Stick said. "Some of it be dumb and some of it silly. But some of it was kinda fun."

Jessie wondered if it involved drinking. He'd never tasted alcohol before and knew plenty of kids his age had tried it, but it was a mortal sin as far as his mom was concerned. To hear her tell the story, her brother Samuel had wasted his life in an alcoholic stupor and she would not allow it to happen to anyone else she loved. Not a drop of alcohol was allowed back home and Jessie didn't dare try sneaking out to go drinking like some other kids for fear of incurring his mother's wrath, which would be severe if she so much as smelled it on him.

"Did they get you drunk?" Jessie asked.

"What'd I just tell you? I can't say."

"Frenchie said they were gonna make us eat worms and stuff like that."

Stick laughed. "And you believed it? C'mon, Einstein. They just messing with you. Ain't you smart enough to see that?"

But Jessie knew there was a huge difference between their situations. Stick's teammates respected his talent and his team's leaders didn't hate him. In Jessie's case, they didn't just dislike him; their hatred felt so intense, he was sure they'd do anything to drive him off the team and out of the school.

"You ain't met Dirk," Jessie said. "He'd love to make me eat worms—or worse."

"He probably not as bad as you say," Stick said. "Least

not after you show him how good you are. That's what happened with me. The captain, a guy they called Buster, didn't like me so much at first. Soon as I scored my first touchdown, he changed. After my fifth touchdown, he was about ready to cut the throat of the first white boy who called me names."

"No kidding?" Jessie said, wishing they'd talked more about the football team before this. It might've made him feel better.

"Well, he's not really ready to cut some boy's throat," Stick said. "That was a . . . what you call it, a metaphor?"

"It's called hyperbole—an exaggeration."

"Yeah, right. Whatever. But Buster be ready to fight for me now—like a sinner found Jesus."

"Now *that* was a simile." Jessie grinned. "How about that! Hyperbole and a simile, back-to-back. There's hope for you yet, Stick."

"Don't tell nobody," Stick said. "Don't wanna ruin my rep."

"We gonna get your butt to Harvard."

"Yeah, right. And you gonna be president."

They'd both laughed for a while, but Stick had gotten serious when Jessie tried again to get him to talk about his initiation. "Stop worryin'," he'd said, closing out the subject. "It ain't so bad."

And that's what Jessie kept telling himself all the way to the ball field. He suspected Frenchie was doing the same thing, but neither said a word.

●

The wind whistled through the trees just beyond the outfield fence and the field smelled of damp earth and everything growing that was green, especially all the evergreens surrounding them on the other side of the fence. Jessie shivered and tugged on his jacket's zipper, making sure it was snug to his chin. This was a night to be back in his dorm room, warm and listening to his records, or else watching TV in the common room, even with the barely submerged tension he often felt there. He'd be glad to be anywhere but outside, waiting with the nine other freshmen so the upperclassmen could have fun with this stupid initiation.

It ain't so bad, Stick had said. Jessie hoped his friend was right.

Looking at the other faces, Jessie saw that most showed the same unease he felt—he could almost smell the fear. And some of these boys wouldn't even be making the team; unless the upper classes had few team members, the odds of all ten freshmen surviving the final cut weren't good. Jessie tried to pick out who'd be the least likely to make it, starting with the smaller, frailer looking boys. Then he reminded himself that Stick wasn't even five-foot-six and changed his mind.

"When are they going to get here?" a squat boy with freckles asked. Jessie had him pegged as a defenseman for sure, or maybe a goaltender. No way could he be quick enough to be a forward.

"Maybe the joke's to make us stand out here all night," another said. "Make us miss lights out while we freeze our butts off."

Jessie hoped that'd be all it turned out to be, but somehow he didn't believe Stick's reassurances. He couldn't imagine Dirk settling for some harmless fun when the opportunity for abuse was within his grasp.

Jessie jumped when an owl hooted nearby; so did most of the others. Then they all broke into a nervous laugh.

Finally, distant voices cut through the night, their yelling and laughing getting louder as they got closer. A large pack of boys squeezed through the gate beside the first base dugout, emerging two or three at a time. Flashlight beams sliced through the darkness and the boys sauntered across the first base line, Dirk in the lead, with Rocco and Sully on either side, and the rest trailing. Their wide grins became visible in the dim moonlight as they crossed second base, still laughing and hooting.

"Fresh meat!" yelled one voice in the back.

"Ready to eat worms, boys?" called out another.

Slowly they encircled the ten freshmen.

"Who's wet their pants?"

"Anybody crying for their mommy?"

"You will be soon enough."

The older boys all laughed and the three captains stepped forward. Dirk raised his hand for silence, and then he looked directly at Jessie with a hard gleam in his eyes and an evil grin on his face.

Jessie felt a chill go down his spine.

"Okay, all you rookies," Dirk said. "For some of you, this is going to be one of the most fun nights of your life." He scanned the freshmen. "But for some others, it's going to be one of your worst." As the older boys laughed, Dirk locked eyes with Jessie.

"You're going to learn a few things tonight," Dirk said. "First, that you're all a bunch of rookies who don't know anything. And these guys—" Dirk gestured to all the upper-class boys encircling the freshmen, "—are all your superiors. You're going to learn to obey them, whatever they tell you to do. Respect them, above all the seniors."

Dirk glared at Jessie. "Some of you think you're better than everyone else. We're going to take care of that tonight. You're going to learn your place." Dirk kept his eyes on Jessie for a couple seconds, then looked around at the older kids. "Ain't that right, boys?"

They all cheered, then a few began chanting, "Dirk! Dirk! Dirk!" while pumping their fists. Dirk smiled, obviously basking in the glow. Then his face clouded over and his features grew hard. "Before we go any further, there's something important we need to talk about. What happens tonight goes no further than us. It's nobody's business but our own, and it's private. That means you tell no one about it. Not your roommate, not your girlfriend back home, or your mommy or your daddy. Not even your priest. No one! Do you useless rookies hear me?"

A few nodded and others mumbled words of agreement.

"I can't hear you!" Dirk shouted.

"Yes!" the freshmen called out in unison.

"Yes, what?" Dirk challenged.

"Yes, sir!" the freshmen yelled, Jessie with them, even though he only mouthed *sir*.

"You *never* tell anyone! Is that clear?"

The freshmen called out their agreement.

Then Dirk put his hands on his hips and leaned forward. "If there's anyone here who won't swear they'll take this secret initiation to their graves—"

Take this to their graves? Was Dirk just trying to scare them some more?

"—now is the time to go back to your rooms."

Jessie's ears perked up. He'd happily go back to his room, if all it cost him was some embarrassment. His bad feelings about tonight were growing stronger by the minute.

Dirk's next words clarified what Jessie had guessed. "You can go back to your nice, comfortable rooms and call your mommy and daddy—" he paused and looked around him with a glint in his eyes, "—and tell them that you quit the team." He leaned forward. "That's because you have two choices: pledge your silence and become part of this amazing team, or else leave us now and don't ever come back."

No one said a word.

"Everybody swear it?"

Jessie mouthed a silent word of false agreement as others nodded.

"I can't hear you!" Dirk bellowed.

"Yes, sir!" the freshmen yelled—even Jessie.

23

"Why did you separate me from the others?" Jessie asked, not even trying to disguise his concern. Dirk, Sully, and Rocco had led him away from all the other freshmen, hopping the shoulder-high outfield fence and heading for the thick forest beyond.

"'Cause you're different," Dirk said.

Now Jessie was really scared.

They reached the edge of the forest and Dirk told Jessie to put out his hands.

"What are you going to do?" Jessie asked.

Anger flared on Dirk's face. "You don't get it, do you?"

But the problem was, Jessie very much got it. Dirk hated him and would do almost anything to drive him off the team. Jessie wasn't sure what Dirk's limits were, or if there even were limits. He only knew that the fiery gleam in Dirk's eyes hinted of madness. Maybe he'd just imagined it, but he didn't think so.

Dirk leaned in close until their noses were only six inches apart. His breath, warm and moist, smelled of onions and garlic. When Jessie shrank back, Dirk stepped forward and got back in his face.

"You don't ask questions," Dirk said. "You do what we say. Or weren't you listening?"

Jessie wondered if he should make a run for it. Get away from whatever this maniac had in store for him. But one of them would probably catch him, and then . . . then he'd be in even worse shape than he was now. And if he got away? Any hope that he'd eventually be accepted on the team would be lost. He'd be the chicken who ran back to the dorm room, afraid of his own teammates—even if he had good reason to fear at least some of them.

Jessie gave in and put his hands out.

"That's better." Dirk looked at Rocco and told him, "Tie him up."

Terror shot through Jessie and he looked over his shoulder to run, not caring what anybody said to him. But Rocco looped one muscle-bound arm around Jessie's neck and held him tight.

When Jessie tried to pull away, other unseen hands grabbed hold of him. Rocco, grunting, tightened his grip until Jessie began to choke and by reflex, Jessie reached up to move Rocco's arm away.

"Trust us," Rocco hissed in a moist growl.

The coarse sleeves of his wool jacket smelled faintly of mothballs and made Jessie's neck itch. He tried to wriggle free but couldn't—Rocco's powerful vice-like arm held him tight. Jessie gagged until Rocco, grunting, eased his grip just a little.

"Trust us, nigger," Dirk said and howled with deranged sounding laughter.

Despite his panic, the madness of Dirk's words registered and a feeling of icy dread flooded over Jessie. What were they going to do to him? Why had they taken him away from everyone else? He heard raucous laughter and catcalls back on the other side of the outfield fence, without any cries of pain or humiliation. Everyone else sounded like they were having a good time. And that was when he realized it wasn't likely anyone in the other group would be able to hear him, or they might assume that he was having a good time, too.

Rough hands grabbed his wrists and tied them together with a coarse, thick rope that tore at his skin. Then they bound his feet, looping the rope tight about both ankles. Unable to separate his legs, Jessie could barely keep his balance and stay on his feet.

"What's the problem, hot shot?" Dirk asked in a sneering, sarcastic tone. "Ready to wet your pants?"

Jessie fought back the panic that was overtaking him as his heart hammered and sweat beaded on his forehead, then ran into his eyes, making them sting. His legs began to wobble and he told himself, *They aren't going to kill you. They aren't even going to hurt you. It's all a game to see how much they can scare you.*

But Jessie wasn't convinced. Dirk's brutality at the captain's practice made it clear that Dirk wouldn't hesitate to hurt him, maybe even cripple him.

Jessie wondered if he should call out for help while he still could, or if that was what Dirk and his crew were waiting for, just so they could mock him? Suddenly a thick piece of cloth was shoved into Jessie's mouth and tied behind his head, ending any chance of shouting for help.

Then someone planted a boot against the small of Jessie's back and shoved him; with his feet tied together, Jessie could manage only a short hop before toppling over, turning to the side as he fell to avoid hitting the ground face first.

Dirk dropped down and lowered his face close to Jessie's.

"Ready to drop your gloves again, hot shot?" Dirk bared his teeth, looking like an animal ready to tear his victim's throat out. "Ready to fight *your captain*?"

Dirk clenched his fist and drew it back; when it came at his face, Jessie flinched, expecting the blow, but Dirk's fist stopped an inch away from Jessie's nose, knuckles white and shaking with rage.

"I ought to mess your face up good," Dirk said. "Teach you your place."

"Dirk?" Rocco asked, a nervous tone in his voice.

"*What?*" Dirk snapped. He got up and stood toe-to-toe with Rocco. "You got something to say?"

Rocco shrugged and shuffled his feet.

"I didn't think so," Dirk said.

Then he yanked Jessie to his feet and gave him a little shove. Jessie toppled over again, and Dirk repeated the process, this time shoving him harder.

Jessie rolled onto his back and avoided looking at Dirk but stared up at the other two boys. Rocco's face was hard and impassive, but his eyes darted nervously toward Dirk. Sully stood motionless, his eyes wide.

Their expressions confirmed Jessie's suspicions. This

was Dirk's show and they were just going along for the ride, like uncomfortable little boys trapped by a lunatic driver playing chicken.

"I think he's thirsty," Dirk said.

He motioned to Rocco, who disappeared for a moment and then returned with a can of Budweiser. Dirk popped open the can and guzzled down several gulps, his Adam's apple bobbing up and down. He belched, then stared at Jessie. Deliberately, he hocked up a wad of phlegm and spit it in the can.

Dirk dropped to one knee, tilted Jessie's head forward, and put the can against his gag-filled mouth.

As the smell of beer filled his nostrils, Jessie thrashed his head from side to side. Not because of his mother's warnings, either. The thought of Dirk's phlegm floating in the beer got Jessie's stomach churning. He gagged and the sour taste of bile filled his throat and turned it raw.

Dirk tilted the can and beer seeped past the cloth and into Jessie's mouth, splashing his face and going up his nose. The bubbling and sizzling made him gag again.

Jessie sat up coughing, the sour aftertaste in his mouth; he tried to spit, even with the gag in the way, but had no luck.

"I can't believe it," Dirk said. "I think I missed that big mouth of his. Get me another one."

Dirk took one gulp, then spit it all on Jessie's face. It stung Jessie's eyes and felt sticky on his face.

"Ready to quit the team yet?" Dirk asked.

Without waiting for an answer, he poured the rest of the can out all over Jessie's face.

Suddenly, he jerked Jessie to his feet. But with his ankles still bound together, Jessie fell back to the ground again.

"The boy can't stand up straight," Dirk said in mock surprise. "I think he might be drunk."

The next beer went down Jessie's back.

●

Dirk and his henchmen put a pillowcase over Jessie's head and carried him deeper into the woods. Jessie didn't try to resist, even though he wanted to; but bound and gagged, he could barely move. If he thrashed, they'd end up dropping him. Jessie's panic was growing but wasn't quite full blown—yet.

Shivering as the cold wind buffeted his clothes, Jessie also shook with fear. He'd seen the looks on Rocco's and Sully's faces. Neither of them would have taken things anywhere near this far, and he could see they were as afraid of Dirk as Jessie was. But he also knew neither of them would be likely to lift a finger if Dirk crossed over whatever line existed between humiliation and torture.

When they set him down, Jessie stood for only a second before he fell again, snapping small twigs beneath him and landing in a bed of dry leaves.

"Look at him," Dirk cried with glee. "He's drunk!"

Rocco and Sully laughed nervously.

Though the sharp taste of the beer remained in Jessie's mouth, still pungent in the soggy gag, he knew he wasn't drunk. He hadn't swallowed much beer, but not being able to see, he was disoriented. And with his feet tied tightly together, he had no way to balance himself.

"Look at him," Dirk said. "He can't handle a few sips of beer. He's like a little girl. Too bad we didn't bring a dress and some girlie underwear. We could dress him up."

Beneath the pillowcase, all Jessie could smell was beer. And he itched from the sticky layer of dried beer.

"This is gonna be good," Dirk said with glee.

Jessie tried to calm himself, but his hands shook and his heart pounded.

"Start the fire," Dirk commanded.

Jessie waited, panicking more by the second and trying not to think about what Dirk intended to do with a fire. Soon he could smell smoke, then heard the crackling flames.

Suddenly *a rope* slipped over Jessie's head and fell around neck. Jessie tried to pull away, but strong hands held him. Then off came the pillowcase.

Jessie gasped and terror shot through him.

Dirk, Rocco, and Sully surrounded him, their heads covered with the white hoods and robes of the Ku Klux Klan.

That meant the rope around his neck wasn't just a rope—*it was a noose*.

Jessie's legs went weak. He began to tremble.

Dirk pulled the noose tight around Jessie's neck, but not so tight that he couldn't breathe. The coarse rope dug into his neck and tore at his skin.

Now Jessie's panic overtook him. He tried to scream but choked on the gag. He brought his bound hands up to his neck, trying to get his fingers under the noose to loosen it. But it was too tight and he only gouged himself trying.

Jessie looked at the three boys in their KKK robes and hoods as the firelight flickered in their masked faces. Then he spotted it—in a circle of stones, a burning cross rose from the fire—it was another KKK symbol.

Were these boys secret members of the Klan? He'd hoped they might just be goofing around by wearing the robes, but this had gone way past playing around.

"Doesn't look so tough now, does he?" the leading hooded figure said. It was Dirk's voice—of course. "Looks like he's ready to cry for Momma," Dirk added.

Jessie told himself they were just trying to scare him. They couldn't get away with actually doing more, and it was just an initiation. Sick, nothing more. . .

But then Dirk grabbed the rope dangling from a tree. Jessie saw that it was looped over a heavy branch—one thick enough to bear his weight—and ended with the noose around his neck.

Dirk began to pull on the rope, taking up the slack. He leaned close then pulled off his white hood. Eyes gleaming, he asked, "You ready to give your *all* for the team?" then he gave the rope another tug and laughed.

Beneath their hoods, the other two boys glanced at each other. Jessie thought it might be Rocco who reached out as if to grab Dirk but then stopped.

Jessie shook violently now as Dirk, grinning, pulled gently on the rope.

Jessie began to choke. He rose up on his toes, gasping for air.

"Sully, cut his legs free," Dirk said. "When we hang him, I want to see them nigger legs kick."

One of the hooded figures hesitated, then stepped forward and took the butcher knife that Dirk handed him. Then he steadied one of Jessie's trembling legs and said, "Don't move," his voice cracking. "I don't want to cut you." It was Sully.

"Isn't that sweet!" Dirk sneered. "Why don't you give him a kiss?"

Sully glanced back, then cut through the rope that bound Jessie's ankles together.

When his legs broke free, Jessie jumped on weak, leaden legs, getting a brief gasp of air before the noose cut hard into his neck and raised him up a bit more.

His head swam. His heart jack-hammered. He thought of his mother, who hadn't wanted him to come to school here.

She'd been so fearful, so nervous.

She'd been so right!

He thought of Pop and—

Dirk whooped with laughter. "Trust us, you uppity, no-good—"

"Dirk," Rocco said in a pleading tone. "I think—"

"*What?*" He bared his teeth and glared at Rocco. "What do you think?" He pulled on the rope just the slightest bit more and the noose tightened around Jessie's windpipe.

Jessie gagged and choked. Panic flooded over him. *They're really going to do it*. Wrists still bound together, Jessie dug his fingernails into the flesh of his neck, trying to burrow beneath the noose.

He had to pull it loose—he couldn't breathe.

Dig. Dig even into your skin. Pull it free—was all that raced through his mind. He felt spittle run out of his mouth.

"Please!" he tried to cry out through the soggy cloth.

Wasn't anyone going to help him?

"Please!"

Oh my God, I'm gonna die.

"Please!"

Jessie felt his bladder let loose. Warm liquid ran down his legs. Crazily, he thought of how Momma would react when she heard that the last thing he'd done was piss his pants. Still clawing at the noose about his neck, he choked at the smell of the urine soaking his pants.

"He did it!" Dirk cried out gleefully. "Little Piss-boy did it!"

The voice seemed a million miles away.

Jessie tried to stand higher on tiptoes, like a ballerina. But legs trembling, he sank back down an inch.

Air! He needed air! Even as his body shook, he tried to get back that lost inch and got it for a few seconds. But then he couldn't stay on his toes any longer and sank.

The noose bit hard into Jessie's neck, choking off all air. He felt everything turning black; then the tension on the rope gave way.

Dirk threw his arms out to his side, as if looking to hug a long-lost relative. "Free at last," he cried, "Free at last. Thank God Almighty, I'm free at last."

Jessie crumpled to his knees, understanding only in the deepest recesses of his mind that Dirk was mocking Dr. King.

Jessie toppled face forward and he felt hands on him turning him over as he drew in wracking gasps of air into his lungs. His chest spasmed and bright flashes shot across his field of vision.

"God, Dirk—" Rocco said behind him. "You could have killed him."

Unseen hands, rough and shaking, slipped the noose from Jessie's neck, then untied the gag.

Jessie spit it out, then repeatedly choked and gasped for air.

"Look at that! Piss-boy peed himself!" Dirk said, a fiery madness in his eyes.

Jessie got on all fours as his chest heaved. Bolts of white pain shot through his temples; it felt like his head would explode as every muscle trembled. He swallowed, trying to rid his mouth of the sour taste of vomit, and still could smell piss and beer.

Murderous rage surged through him. Shaking uncontrollably, he glared at Dirk.

Then Jessie flew out of his crouch and lowered his shoulder like a middle linebacker, driving himself straight into Dirk's chest.

Dirk made an *ooof* sound as he fell with his arms splayed.

Jessie lifted the captain off his feet, then slammed him hard into the ground. It was like he was trying to drive him all the way to Hell.

Now it was Dirk's turn to groan in pain with the wind knocked out of him. He lay there wheezing, unable to speak.

Jessie got to his feet, towering over the writhing bigot lying on the ground before him. Fists clenched and shaking, he took a step and waited for one of Dirk's goons to come after him, but to his surprise, the only movement was Dirk's as he thrashed in the dirt.

"He's got the wind knocked out of him," Rocco said. Rocco and Sully looked at each other.

"What do we do?" Sully asked.

"I think you gotta give him mouth-to-mouth," Rocco said and stepped back.

"I'm not giving him mouth-to-mouth," Sully said.

A flash of humor cut through Jessie's rage. He didn't think Dirk could die from getting the wind knocked out him, but it sounded like his friends were willing to risk it rather than put their mouth to his.

Jessie bent over Dirk, whose eyes went wide, perhaps in anticipation of another hit or else getting mouth-to-mouth from a black man. Jessie grabbed the front of Dirk's KKK robe and picked up the captain until his chest was thigh-high, then dropped him. Dirk landed on his back with a grunt and a wheeze.

Alarmed, Sully, standing behind Jessie, said, "What are you doing?"

Though the urge to slam Dirk into the ground again was almost overpowering, Jessie once again lifted him up and dropped him on his back.

Dirk sucked in one loud gasp of air after another.

"You don't have to give mouth-to-mouth," Jessie heard himself say as he stepped back.

The urge to kill Dirk—or at least to pound his face into a bloody pulp—returned and Jessie clenched his fists and prepared to take on Rocco and Sully. Checking behind him for an escape route, he realized there was none, only a path deeper into the woods, and he didn't want to get any farther out of earshot. And at the moment, Rocco and Sully blocked his way back to the ball field and beyond that, to the dorm.

Dirk staggered to his feet, madness in his eyes. Hissing, he wound up and threw a wild roundhouse hook. Jessie stepped back and to the side, thinking of Muhammad Ali always circling his prey.

"Hold him!" Dirk screamed, his spittle flying.

"No," Rocco said, stepping between Dirk and Jessie. "This has gone on far enough—too far. *Way* too far."

"*Hold him!*" Dirk screamed again.

But no one moved.

Dirk brushed past Rocco and glared at Jessie. "We shoulda lynched you, not just made you piss your pants. We shoulda done it!"

Jessie knew he couldn't just step back this time. He'd make Dirk pay, no matter what the consequences.

Dirk swung wildly and Jessie took one step back, easily avoiding the punch. Then, letting loose all of his pent-up rage, he smashed his fist into Dirk's face.

He squarely hit Dirk's nose, crushing bone and cartilage with a crunch that should have sickened him. Although a tiny part of him was revolted, he mostly considered that sound the most pleasing thing he'd ever heard.

Dirk howled as blood gushed from his nose. He reached up to stanch the flow and Jessie gloated inwardly at Dirk's wide-eyed reaction to his own blood-covered hand.

Not waiting for his tormentors to recover, Jessie raced for the path back to the ball field, twigs snapping beneath his feet. Sure they were right behind him, he was too scared to check, his lungs burning as he left the forest behind and sped onto the field.

Only then did Jessie glance behind him, where, to his surprise, no one followed. Then, from deep in the woods, he heard angry shouts that made him race for the dorm. He didn't slow down until he stepped inside Williams Hall, taking the stairs three at a time to the third floor and his room.

24

Bolting inside, Jessie slammed the door behind him. He dropped the room key to the floor and bent over, gasping for breath. He shook with rage, fear, and exhaustion.

The hot room felt like a furnace, but he made no move to take off his sodden jacket or other foul-smelling clothes. His T-shirt clung to him.

Sweat stung the raw, bruised skin of his neck and he could again feel the noose tightening, pulling him upward, choking him. Panic flooded him and though his chest heaved, he somehow couldn't breathe.

The room spun and Jessie staggered, toppling to the floor, in wracking sobs. Then, he crawled to the telephone and fumbled with the receiver, his hand shaking so violently that he knocked the phone to the floor. Sprawling, Jessie held the receiver to his ear, listened for the dial tone, then called home.

Was it too late for Momma and Pop to drive up tonight? Jessie hoped not. He wasn't sure he could last until morning. What if Dirk and his boys came after him tonight?

Jessie shuddered, putting his hand to his neck, clawing at the invisible fibers of a rope that wasn't there.

The phone rang a second time and his heart quickened. Could they have gone out for the evening? *Please, not tonight.* He needed them to come now and not waste a minute. He had to get out of there.

The phone rang a third time and Jessie pleaded, *Please pick up! Get me out of here.*

A fourth ring and Jessie's heart sank. *Pick up the phone!*

The phone rang a fifth and sixth time. *No! Where are they?*

Despite knowing it was futile, Jessie held on until the tenth ring, then clumsily hung up. He'd never felt so scared or alone in his whole life.

●

Jessie didn't know how long he'd lain there, the cold sweat pouring out of him, before his own stench got to him. His clothes clung to his skin and he had to get them off, their foul odors all too vivid reminders of the scene he'd just fled. And he desperately needed a shower.

Jessie staggered to his feet on wobbly legs, then grabbed clean clothes and a towel, and started toward the door but then froze. What was he thinking? His locked door was his only protection from Dirk and his buddies. He couldn't step outside and be safe, certain they wouldn't come after him to silence him for good.

Jessie began to shake all over once more. Teeth chattering, he leaned against his desk, closed his eyes, and tried to steady himself. He'd wait for Stick to get back; then Stick could guard the bathroom door while he showered. Fearful, Jessie looked out the window but saw no one—not Stick, but not Dirk, Rocco or Sully either.

But then the pungent odor of his filthy clothes hit Jessie once again and he was ashamed. He didn't want Stick to see—or smell him—like this. It was too humiliating, and Jessie's stomach churned at the thought.

The sour taste of vomit rising in his throat got Jessie moving and he flew through the door and down the hallway, fighting the inevitable eruption. He burst into the bathroom, slamming the door against the wall, then bolted into a toilet stall.

After he'd thrown up and flushed, the sour taste remained. He spat several times, then got to his feet, and turned on the cold water at the nearest sink. He washed his hands, then drank clean water from his cupped hands. He swished the cold water in his mouth and spat, rinsing until the sour taste faded.

Down the hall Jessie could hear a door open and he ran for the shower stalls, ducking inside the farthest just as the bathroom door opened. He held his breath and waited until the urinal flushed and, after a quick splash of water at the sink, the door opened, then closed, and he was alone once more.

Hearing a door slam shut down the hall, Jessie finally started to breathe normally. With no other sounds audible of people moving elsewhere on his floor, Jessie pulled off his clothes and dumped them outside the shower stall. He turned on the water almost hot enough to scald, then ducked under the powerful spray.

When the water hit his rope burns, Jessie sucked in a sharp breath and hissed. Cuts stung all over his body, especially on his neck, wrists, and ankles. He wondered if he'd have permanent scars, but then fell quickly into a sinking depression.

All his dreams had been wrapped up in this place. Here the scouts would see him play, and at the New England Championships. If he could have impressed them—and he was sure he could have—that would've been his ticket to Harvard or Yale, or even the NHL.

But now Jessie felt all of those dreams washing down the drain, along with the soap suds and hot water. Gone, all because of bigots like Dirk and Coach Stone. They were like his own personal versions of George Wallace, and just as that racist governor had blocked the entrance to the University of Alabama, preventing two black students from registering for classes, Dirk and Coach Stone blocked his own entrance to his future—all because of the color of his skin.

Jessie knew he couldn't stay at Springvale. Sooner or later, Dirk and his buddies would find a way to kill him. Dirk's insane hatred would never be controlled. Jessie again felt that noose and shuddered. And without realizing he was doing it, he stood on his tiptoes again, right there in the shower, stretching his neck so he could breathe.

Taking a deep breath, Jessie tried to fight off the panic.

Focusing on the job at hand, he scrubbed away the remains of the horrible evening, trying not to think about it. But despite the lather and no matter how much he scrubbed, the smells still lingered in his nostrils. He wasn't sure if it rose from his soggy clothes on the floor outside the shower stall or was just stuck in his head, and he didn't actually care.

●

"What happened to you?" Stick asked when Jessie came back to their room. Sprawled out on his bed, Stick sniffed the air and, with a sly grin, said, "They get you drunk? Sure smells like it." He nodded to the open window, saying, "Figured I'd air it out in here 'fore Richardson got a whiff of your 'initiation.' Told you it was no big deal." But then Stick's grin disappeared as he looked more at Jessie. "What's that on your neck?"

"*No big deal?*" Jessie sat on the edge of his bed. "I had a great time. I can't wait till the next time I almost get lynched." He glared at Stick, knowing he wasn't being fair to his friend, but unable to stop himself.

"Lynched? What you talkin' about?"

As Jessie told the story, Stick made no effort to hide his shock. His jaw dropped and he shook his head. When Jessie finished talking, Stick lay on his bed in stunned silence. "I don't believe it," he finally said.

"I ain't making this up," Jessie said.

"Oh, I know you're not," Stick said. "I just can't believe it! At my initiation, they didn't do nothin' like that.

210

And there be some bad rednecks on the team." Then he asked, "Is it 'cause hockey don't have black players?"

"It ain't hockey. It's Dirk. He's insane," Jessie said, then reconsidered. "Maybe part of it's because of the sport being so white. These guys ain't never played with black teammates. They don't know how to handle it—maybe they're afraid of me. At least the rednecks on your team have seen black football players before. They ain't seeing nothing new with you out there."

"What you gonna do?" Stick finally asked.

That's when the crushing reality hit Jessie: there really wasn't anything he could do. The bad guys had won. Jessie got up off his bed and slid out his luggage from beneath it. Opening the first suitcase, he said, "I'm giving up. I can't do this anymore." Palms up, Jessie said, "If I stay here, Dirk's gonna kill me."

"You just quittin' the team?" Stick worked his toothpick furiously. "Or you leavin' school altogether?"

"I'm leaving," Jessie said without a moment's hesitation. "I gotta get out of here—now." But then Stick's question sank in and Jessie thought about it. He hadn't considered staying at Springvale without playing hockey— that'd been his reason for coming here—that and the education.

Ever since Jessie'd first strapped on skates, he'd never considered not playing hockey. It was in his blood, a big part of what made him who he was. He couldn't conceive of not playing. He and the sport were like a team that he couldn't break up. Jessie rubbed his temples, trying to clear his muddled mind. Then it came to him why he couldn't quit hockey and stay here, even if he could do the unimaginable and stay off the ice for a whole year. He couldn't stay because he had a full scholarship to play hockey.

But Jessie knew he couldn't play hockey here, not with Dirk and his supporters, not after having a noose around his neck, haunting him.

"I'm calling my parents tomorrow morning," Jessie said. "It's too late to call now and I wouldn't want them driving all night, which they would if they knew. But tomorrow, I'm gonna call them and—and tell them to come get me. I'll admit defeat." Jessie said, staring at the floor. "I quit."

Stick nodded, his hangdog expression making him appear very lonely.

●

Jessie sat bolt upright in the darkness, drenched in cold sweat and gasping for breath as he clawed at his throat, trying to pull away an unseen noose. Panting, he closed his eyes and lowered himself back onto the bed, his sheets damp to his touch. Then his shame from the night before washed over him. But as the sweat dripped off him, he flipped the pillow to the dry side and remembered where he was.

He climbed out of bed, took off his sweaty T-shirt, and dropped it to the floor. Shaking, he grabbed a dry one from a drawer and put it on, wincing as it slid over the rope burns on his neck. His mouth felt as dry as cotton.

Walking to the window, he stared down at the floodlit

entrance below, empty but for the shadows. He looked out into the distance where somewhere in that darkness, a tree had dangled that noose. Under that tree, Dirk had stripped him not only of his dignity, but also of his hopes and dreams.

This school was supposed to be his ticket to a brighter future, and Dirk had robbed him of all of it.

Jessie clenched and unclenched his fists. He took a deep breath and thought of Pop braving the brutality of the Alabama police as he marched with Dr. King to Selma. He thought of the Freedom Riders braving the Klan. He thought of Jackie Robinson and Muhammad Ali, of Willie O'Ree and Harry Edwards, and of Tommie Smith and John Carlos.

There in the darkness, Jessie gritted his teeth, raised his clenched fist, and bowed his head in the Black Power salute.

Dirk Stapleton might think he won, but he had another thing coming to him. Jessie stood there feeling triumphant for all of ten seconds before it hit him. *Who am I kidding?* He dropped his fist feeling foolish.

Black Power? At a school where the two blacks were outnumbered a couple hundred to one? Dirk had another thing coming to him? From who? Big, bad Jessie Stackhouse? That was a joke—a real knee-slapper. He was completely powerless, with no friend or ally to stand behind him and make a difference. Other than Stick and maybe Frenchie, Jessie didn't have a friend in the whole place.

But then the sudden realization hit Jessie—he *did* have an ally! What had he been thinking? Mr. Whitney was the headmaster and he'd stood up for Jessie before. He'd even told Jessie that they were in this together; he had no doubt Whitney would protect him from Dirk.

As he pondered that, a troubling thought hit Jessie. Would going to the headmaster be like tattling? Would he be a snitch, whining about his plight, trying to get someone else in trouble? But then he thought of Pop on the Selma march and other civil rights battles; had it been tattling when Pop and the others spoke to reporters? Had it been snitching when Dr. King begged for federal protection for black people trying to register to vote? Of course not; that was common sense. When the Klan and racist Selma police chief Bull Connor incurred public outrage for their brutality against the marchers, that was simply justice, not tattling.

If Jessie went to Mr. Whitney, he'd simply be after justice, and demanding only what had been stolen from him—his dreams for the future.

He decided to get dressed and go to the Headmaster's Quarters and talk to Mr. Whitney first thing in the morning and tell him everything that Dirk had done at the initiation.

25

Mr. Whitney's face clouded with anger as he sat opposite Jessie, Dirk, Rocco, Sully, and Coach Stone, who sat in a semicircle before him. Rocco and Sully shifted uncomfortably, a real contrast to Dirk's casual, nonchalant attitude—so out of place on someone with two black eyes and an obviously broken nose.

"Mr. Stapleton," Mr. Whitney said in clipped words. "What do you have to say for yourself?" The headmaster had just summarized the events Jessie had recounted for him earlier.

Dirk shrugged. "Every team here has freshman initiations," he said in a nasal tone. "This one just got a little out of hand."

Mr. Whitney's tone was pure ice when he said, "Did it now?"

"Yeah," Dirk answered. "It did for both of us. Maybe we both got a little carried away."

"Maybe?" Mr. Whitney challenged. "*A little?* You simulated a lynching on a black student. That's a *little* over the line? What exactly would you call a lot over the line?"

215

"I dunno."

"You could have ruptured his larynx if you'd gone any further. You would have killed him!"

Coach Stone leaned forward and said, "There are two sides to every story."

"Are there? I'd be interested to hear how there can be *any* other side to a story involving the near lynching of a black student."

"They didn't lynch him," Coach Stone said in a condescending tone. "It was faked."

The headmaster pointed angrily at the coach, saying, "Don't you dare patronize me. This young man had a noose pulled tightly enough around his neck to give him *rope burns!* There is nothing *fake* about that! You insult the intelligence of everyone here, except perhaps Mr. Stapleton," he turned his icy glare on Dirk, "to even suggest otherwise."

Dirk recoiled at the headmaster's words as if he'd been slapped.

"Mr. Whitney, what you're overlooking," Coach Stone said, "is that Dirk Stapleton was provoked."

Provoked? Jessie couldn't believe he'd heard right—did Coach Stone really say that?

"I want to hear this," Mr. Whitney said, icy sarcasm in his tone.

"Dirk admits to going over the line," Stone began, "but only after the Negro—"

"Excuse me," Mr. Whitney interrupted. "This young man has a name. I suggest you not only learn it, but also use it. His name is Jessie, not 'the Negro'."

A sour look came over Coach Stone's face and he all

but rolled his eyes in disgust. Then, in short, clipped words, he restated his point. "Dirk went over the line only after Jessie Stackhouse sucker-punched him."

"*What?*" Jessie blurted out. He was astonished by the bald-faced lie.

Stone pointed to Dirk. "You can see the damage Jessie Stackhouse inflicted on his own team captain. The boys were only going to taunt him with the noose, dangle it in front of his face and stuff like that. Tasteless, I agree." He shrugged. "But boys will be boys. It only turned ugly after the sucker punch. Dirk got angry, but I think most of us would overreact in those circumstances." He shook his head. "I can't say that I blame him."

Mr. Whitney looked dumbfounded. "I can't believe what I'm hearing."

Neither could Jessie. "That's a lie!" he shouted. He knew he sounded hysterical but by that point, any sense of calm had left him. All he felt was a powerless rage.

He went on. "I fell to the ground after Dirk dropped the rope. And after they took the noose off me and untied my hands, I got to my knees." Jessie waved a hand toward Rocco and Sully. "Dirk started laughing at me and calling me . . ." He stopped, mortified, not having told the headmaster about pissing in his pants. He looked down at the floor and felt his face grow hot, then went on. "He called me Piss-Boy because—" Jessie took a deep breath. "—because when Dirk put the noose around my neck and pulled up the slack, I-I peed my pants. So he called me 'Piss-Boy.' That's when, after everything that happened, I just exploded. I tackled him and slammed him to the ground, hard.

Then he took a swing at me and missed." He glared at Dirk. "But *I* didn't miss."

"No way a freshman does this to me," Dirk said and pointed to his nose. "Not without it being a cheap shot. The nig—" He stopped and swallowed. "He may be big, but he ain't Cassius Clay."

Jessie was annoyed by Dirk's use of Muhammad Ali's former name but didn't let it distract him.

"He's lying!" Jessie said, motioning in Rocco's direction. "Rocco tried to say something to stop him but Dirk wouldn't listen; and he wouldn't stop. And that was all be-*fore* any punches got thrown."

Mr. Whitney leaned forward and turned to Sully and Rocco. "Mr. Sullivan, Mr. Antonelli, what do you have to say about this?"

Sully and Rocco looked at each other, then at Dirk, and finally at Coach Stone. The silence hung heavy in the room.

Rocco wet his lips. "I, um . . . I agree with Dirk." He averted his eyes. "It's Stackhouse who's lying."

"Yeah, that's it," Sully said.

"That isn't true!" Jessie said, his breath quickening and his hands, clenched in tight fists, shaking.

"That's three-to-one," Coach Stone announced. He shook his head. "I know these boys. I've never once heard them tell a lie."

The headmaster whirled on Sully and Rocco, then said, "Tell the truth or I'll have you expelled!" he thundered. "What happened first?"

Sully glanced nervously at Coach Stone.

"Don't you dare look at him!" Mr. Whitney shouted,

making everyone jump. "Keep your eyes on me, and you'd better tell me the truth."

Sully's eyes got very wide and, ignoring the headmaster's command, he glanced first at the coach and then at Dirk.

Rocco squirmed in his seat, then, averting his eyes, said, "I was telling the truth. Stackhouse sucker-punched Dirk."

Jessie felt the air go out of him as Sully chimed in. His shoulders slumped and he thought about the story of *Alice in Wonderland*. Right now, he felt like he too had fallen into a world where nothing made sense. Vermin like Dirk could do whatever they wanted, then tell lies to cover up. It almost defied belief.

Hearing Sully's words, a triumphant gleam shone in Coach Stone's eyes and a smile curled on his lips.

The headmaster stared at the three boys, his chest heaving with each breath. Then he told them, "I don't believe you."

"They all agree," Stone said, pointing in their direction.

"I didn't ask your opinion!" Mr. Whitney snapped at the coach. "This entire situation reeks of a cover-up."

Mr. Whitney glared from Coach Stone to Dirk to Rocco, and finally to Sully, then he said, "Even if I believed that Jessie punched Dirk first—which I don't for a minute—it doesn't excuse their behavior, which is beyond outrageous. It's reprehensible and repugnant, and I fully intend to punish all three of these boys."

By now, the headmaster's face was a stormy red.

"Oh, come on, Louis," Coach Stone said.

"Excuse me? What did you call me?" The headmaster asked the coach.

"I mean, 'Mr. Whitney.' " Stone said, waving dismissively. "This kind of hazing goes on all the time. It happened when I was on the team, and it'll happen when these kids' grandchildren are on the team. It's a form of team-building. It breeds unity."

Mr. Whitney turned to Stone looking incredulous. "Pretending to lynch a black student breeds unity? Please explain that, if you will."

Coach Stone nodded to Dirk, who cleared his throat before he began speaking. "See, the idea is to build trust. Put the freshmen in what seems like a dangerous situation and prove to them that you'll be there for them. Let them know they can trust you."

Jessie snorted. He recalled Dirk's words about trust and doubted he could ever forget them. He shook his head in disbelief.

"It's done all the time," Stone said, "at every school, on every team."

Mr. Whitney glared at the coach.

"It may sound weird," Dirk said.

"More than that," Mr. Whitney said.

"We *could* have killed him," Dirk said, his eyes flickering for just an instant. "I could have pulled harder on that rope and he couldn't have done anything about it. He'd have just swayed up there in that tree. But I didn't do that. It was all about team-building, just like Coach said."

Stone jumped in. "The boys did take it too far, I admit.

But it was just horseplay designed to prove a point—that they could be trusted by their teammates."

Jessie felt like he was trapped in a bizarre dream. *Trust?* He would *never* trust Dirk—or Rocco or Sully for that matter. How stupid did they think he was?

"Let's not make a federal case out of this," Stone said, spreading his palms. "If Stackhouse had cooperated, he'd have gotten the same benefits as the rest of the freshmen: trust, unity. He'd know he could rely on the team's leaders. Instead, he cheap-shot his captain and it all got messy."

Jessie got to his feet, seething. "You have got to be—"

With that, the headmaster put his hand on Jessie's elbow, silencing him. "Sit down, Jessie," he said. "Let me handle this."

But Jessie didn't want to sit down, and he sure didn't want anyone else to handle this.

He wanted to rip Stone and Dirk into pieces, along with the rest of them. He wanted to pummel Dirk's nose again, this time even harder.

Breathing in ragged gulps of air, Jessie tried to calm down as he slowly lowered himself back into his chair.

Stone gestured in Jessie's direction. "See what I mean? He's like a keg of dynamite ready to blow up." Then he added pointedly, "I told you this wasn't going to work."

Mr. Whitney leveled a finger. "You'll be quiet or I'll have your head. I don't care how many donating alumni you have in your back pocket."

Stone gritted his teeth at that, but said nothing.

"I've made my decision," Mr. Whitney said, his voice shaking with emotion. "Nothing anyone can say will matter now. So let's get down to the bottom line: Mr. Antonelli and Mr. Sullivan, both of you are suspended for the first five games of the season."

Rocco winced and shook his head and Sully blanched.

"You can't do that!" Stone's face flushed.

"Oh, yes I can." The headmaster turned to Dirk next and said, "Mr. Stapleton, it's a ten-game suspension for you."

"Ten games? *Ten?*" Dirk's eyes grew wide in shock. "But that's right when the colleges do most of their scouting."

"You should have thought of that last night when you were tightening the noose around Mr. Stackhouse's neck. Consider yourself lucky that I haven't expelled you."

"You can't do this!" Stone said, seething.

"I can and I have," Mr. Whitney told him.

"Are you going to start coaching next, call out the line shifts, too?" Stone asked.

"I will if I have to," Mr. Whitney replied.

Stone fixed Jessie with a look of pure hatred.

Mr. Whitney's back went rigid and he held his head high. "This is a school of dignity. I won't have it turned into a haven for the Ku Klux Klan."

Coach Stone rose and Mr. Whitney did, too. They glowered at each other, standing toe-to-toe, their chests heaving, for what felt like a long time.

Then Stone's eyes narrowed and he said, "I told you the boy would be a cancer."

26

Two days after that tense meeting in the headmaster's office, Halloween decorations hung everywhere in the gymnasium. Orange and black crepe paper streamers dangled from the ceiling; Jack-O' Lanterns guarded every doorway; and fake ghosts, skeletons, and witches on broomsticks adorned the walls. The music of the Beatles and the Rolling Stones rocked the place, and the air carried the faint scent of sweat and talcum powder, masked by the overpowering scents worn by the two hundred teenage girls in attendance, not one of them black. Conversation and laughter, loud enough to be heard over the pounding music, echoed off the walls.

When they weren't dancing, most of the boys had grouped together based on their sports team. The soccer team stood at the far end; beside them were the swimmers, and the football team had gathered off to the left. And although the hockey team hadn't yet held its first official practice, it held court off to the right, well aware of its status as the school's marquee sport. Groups of giggling girls eyed Dirk, Rocco, Sully, and the others, all but pleading for one of them to ask them to dance, each holding her breath as a boy approached.

Jessie and Stick stood isolated in a corner, outcasts much like the scattered geeks who, mindful of the so-called Wallflower Rule, counted the minutes until they reached the one-hour mark, when they'd finally be allowed to leave.

Earlier, the captain of the football team, a beefy lineman with bad acne, who everyone called Buster, had approached Stick and complimented him, saying, "Great game today."

"Thanks." Stick had scored another three touchdowns that afternoon, sending Springvale Academy into next Saturday's season finale with an undefeated record. "You, too."

Buster shrugged. "You in much pain?"

"Not too bad." Stick grinned. "They can't hit what they can't catch."

"That's what I like about you," Buster said. "Your humility."

Stick laughed. "Can't have everything."

Busted nodded his head in the direction of the football team and said, "Why don't you come over with the rest of the guys?"

Stick gestured toward Jessie. "What about my friend? This is Jessie Stackhouse."

Buster made a face like he'd just tasted sour milk. "No offense, but . . . he's hockey." It was no secret that many football players, expecting to be the biggest men on campus, resented the hockey team and all the attention it got as the school's marquee sport. "We're trying to stick together as a team," he said and grinned awkwardly. "No pun intended."

"Gotcha," Stick said. "Thanks anyway, but I think I'll stay here."

The sour look returned to Buster's face and he said, "Suit yourself." Then he walked away.

"You didn't have to do that," Jessie said.

Stick looked at Jessie like he'd said something unbelievably stupid. "There's teams, my man," he said. "And there's *TEAMS*."

Jessie felt a feeling of warmth spread through him. A lot had gone wrong in his two months here, but he could see Stick and him staying thick long after they graduated—friends for life.

"'Sides, I can't leave you standing here," Stick said, "defenseless against all these white women."

Jessie laughed. *Definitely friends for life*.

The DJ put on the Beatles song "Get Back," and boys and girls stepped onto the dance floor. Soon the room vibrated with teenage bodies in motion.

"Too bad our girls ain't here," Stick said. He and Jessie had talked about the girlfriends they'd left behind, admitting to each other that when they went home for the holidays, their girls would most likely be involved with someone new. Long-distance phone calls were too expensive, and letters . . . well, Jessie had gotten one from Rose that first week and had responded, but there hadn't been another. And he'd gotten one more than Stick. But they'd stuck to the illusion by calling them "their girls."

"Rose sure can dance," Jessie said. He thought about their last dance together, and her bright smile.

"Man, if they were here, we'd show these peckerwoods how to move," Stick said.

Jessie sipped his punch. "You got that right." But then he got thinking about the dances Rose had gone to since he'd been gone, and about who she'd probably been dancing with. That was a bad place to go and his spirits sank.

The guitar riffs started off the next song, one Jessie didn't recognize, but its blues chords perfectly matched his mood.

"Bet you a quarter that this is as black as the music gets," Stick said.

Jessie didn't feel like small talk, but figured he'd play along. "They gotta do some Motown, even this place."

"Put your money where your mouth is," Stick said.

"Deal," Jessie told him.

The seconds ticked by slowly. Both had been told by their coaches to stay away from the white girls, but there wasn't even a single black girl for them to dance with, or even talk to. Yet they had to stay for the full Wallflower Hour. It was so unfair.

"Man, if the ugliest black girl in the world showed up, she'd look like Tina Turner to me right now," Stick said.

"Really? Tell me more."

"She could weigh three hundred pounds and it wouldn't matter."

"Three hundred pounds?"

"Well," Stick said. "Okay, two-fifty."

They both laughed.

Another song began and still no Motown. New pairs of boys and girls made their way onto the dance floor and the required hour slowly dragged by. Twenty-seven minutes to go.

"Whoa," Stick said. "Check out that girl over there in the white miniskirt." He groaned as he watched her, "Mmm, mmm, mmm."

Jessie tried not to stare, but her miniskirt barely covered her behind, which she moved to the beat of the music, making her luscious legs flash. "Wow," Jessie said and sipped his punch, shaking his head.

"I could make her one happy woman." Stick chuckled. "After I show her what a real man be like, she'd never be satisfied by no white boy again."

"Watch it," Jessie warned.

"That's what I'm doing, man—watchin' it. And likin' it."

They both laughed.

"She got moves almost as good as me," Stick said.

Jessie grinned. "Sorry, but I like her moves a lot better."

But Jessie's grin froze as he saw Dirk walking toward them with Rocco and Sully in his wake. Jessie's every muscle tightened and his stomach churned.

The three hockey players formed a semicircle around Jessie and Stick.

Dirk folded his arms across his chest and asked, "What do you two think you're looking at?"

The sound of Jessie's hammering pulse pounded in his ears like a bass drum and his breath quickened.

"That's what I thought," Dirk said. "You boys are looking at something you can't have, at something you shouldn't even be *looking* at, if you know what's good for you." He looked to Rocco and Sully, then said, "Ain't that right, boys?"

They nodded, but Rocco looked uneasy.

"So don't let us catch you two staring at Cindy like that again," Dirk said. "Not at her, and not at any of the other girls, either. You understand me?"

Jessie kept his eyes locked on Dirk's.

"You understand?" Dirk hissed. "Nobody in this town's gonna send their daughters to this dance anymore if they find out you people are gonna be looking them over, wanting to talk to them. Wanting to do a lot more, like your kind of jungle stuff."

Jessie looked at Dirk's mangled nose and wanted to crumple it again and hear that crunch of bone, along with Dirk's howl of pain. He clenched and unclenched his fists, then, realizing he'd been holding his breath, he forced himself to inhale slowly.

"Answer me, or do I have to explain it to you in Swahili?" Dirk said and glanced at Rocco and Sully for approval. They laughed, though Rocco seemed nervous and his laugh forced. Dirk's grin broadened. "I might even have to go back to my room for my English to Swahili dictionary."

Breathe in and breathe out, Jessie told himself. *Ignore what he's saying.* But Jessie couldn't ignore it and his hands shook with rage.

"What's the matter?" Dirk said. "Can't talk? Cat got your black tongue?"

Jessie clenched his fist tighter, imagining driving it into Dirk's face with all his might.

"Don't do it, man." Stick's voice, so soft it was little more than a whisper, startled Jessie.

Jessie swallowed and drew in a deep breath. He tried to calm the fire that coursed in his veins all the way to his tingling fingertips. He looked away, trying to find something else to focus on, something to douse the flame within, but instead his glance caught one of the ghosts tacked to the wall. Now, its white-sheeted form reminded him of the Klan robes the boys had worn to torment him only two nights ago.

Jessie touched his neck, almost expecting to feel again the coarse rope. His throat constricted and he could almost smell the stench of beer and urine.

Dirk laughed. "Will you look at that! Piss-Boy's about to wet his pants again."

The memory, so vivid when mixed with those two smells, made Jessie glance down at his pants, which of course were dry.

But seeing Jessie's reaction made his three tormentors howl with laughter. Jessie hated himself for reacting to Dirk's taunts.

"Hey, tell me, Piss-Boy," Dirk said. "There's something I've always wondered about your kind. When you were a baby and your momma nursed you, was the milk chocolate?"

The boys shrieked with laughter yet again, then they turned and walked away.

Jessie and Stick stood there not looking at each other, waiting for the hour to be over, when they could at last leave this nightmare of a dance.

Before the hour was up, Jessie won his bet with Stick when Sly & The Family Stone broke the musical color line with their hit song "Dance to the Music."

Jessie didn't have the heart to collect.

27

The chill autumn air gusted through Emerson Stadium, carrying with it the smells of hamburgers, hot dogs, and sausages grilled by tailgaters, along with the large quantities of beer they guzzled. Townspeople, alumni, and students packed the stands, looking like three different species. The townspeople came arrayed in their sensible winter jackets, some still carrying the faint smell of mothballs, along with work boots and woolen hats. The rich alumni sported tweed jackets, scarves from Gucci, and fedora hats. The townies smoked cigarettes, primarily Winstons and Camels, while the alumni puffed on aromatic-smelling pipes. The students almost all wore their maroon-and-gold school jackets with the Springvale Academy logo—the figure of a Warrior holding a tomahawk aloft—emblazoned on the back.

Springvale Academy's football team would finish the season with a perfect 9-0 record, with a win over their archrival, St. Sebastian's. Stick had already broken every school record, some dating back four decades, for overall touchdowns, punt return touchdowns, and kickoff return touchdowns. The stadium buzzed with nervous anticipation.

The opening kickoff floated towards Stick and a brief hush fell over the crowd, which held its collective breath. As the football landed in Stick's waiting hands, the expectant silence gave way to cheers, almost as if someone had flipped an unseen electric switch.

Stick headed straight up the field carrying the ball, then faked to the right, and cut left into an opening. He broke past one tackler, froze another with a fake back to the inside, and was gone.

Jessie yelled, "Go, Stick!" but his voice was lost in the crowd's jubilant cheers. Stick streaked down the far sideline, first ten yards in the clear, then fifteen, then twenty. He could have made the last ten yards doing handstands with the ball tucked in his jersey and no St. Sebastian's player would have caught him.

Jessie turned to his parents, who'd driven up that morning to celebrate his sixteenth birthday, and grinning from ear to ear, said, "See what I mean about Stick?"

"My goodness, that boy is *fast*," Momma exclaimed.

Pop and Jessie eyed each other and laughed. Momma didn't follow sports much, except when Jessie was playing. Her penchant for stating the obvious had become a private joke between father and son. According to Momma, Muhammad Ali was awfully quick and nimble, Bill Russell sure could block shots, and now Stick was *fast*.

Jessie's heart sank when he thought back to Momma's shock and fear in the parking lot when she saw the rope burns on his neck. She'd cried out. "My Lord, what happened to you?"

Before they'd come up, Jessie had tried to gently suggest that a future weekend might make for a better trip, what with official hockey practices starting on Monday and the first scrimmage next Saturday. But Momma would have none of it.

"Child, it's your *birthday*!" she'd said, sounding wounded that he'd even suggest they skip coming up for his big day. "Besides, I haven't seen you in three weeks! I don't care if a blizzard comes, we're driving up. Don't you worry; we'll be there for your scrimmage next week, too, Lord willing. Your Pop's Plymouth is going to put on lots of mileage this year."

Jessie had considered borrowing a scarf to cover his neck, but that would've only postponed the inevitable.

"What have they done to you?" his mother had asked as Pop's eyes bore in on him.

That was how Jessie came to tell them an edited version of what he'd gone through, hating himself as he downplayed the incident as *horseplay* that had got out of hand, using Stone's dismissive word to describe what had happened. Jessie kept quiet about his recurring nightmares about that terrible night.

"Mr. Whitney, the headmaster, gave out harsh punishments," Jessie explained as quickly as he could, trying to erase the horror-struck look on his parents' faces. "Dirk is going to miss almost half the season for his part in what happened."

"I should think so," Momma said.

"He should have expelled all of them," Pop said, his voice shaking. "That was no prank."

"It's harsher than you think," Jessie said. "Dirk will be suspended while many of the colleges are making recruiting decisions, so this hurts him a lot." Jessie felt his stomach churn and he mused that this must be how defense lawyers felt with clients who were mass murderers.

But Pop said, "This is utterly unacceptable. I want to speak to the headmaster about this."

"We're taking you home with us tonight," his mother said, her voice shaking with emotion. The words felt like cold daggers in Jessie's heart and the fear he could see in her eyes nearly tore Jessie apart. She hugged him tight and when she pulled away, she said, "No one is going to do that to my son and get away with it."

"Momma, he didn't get away with it," Jessie pleaded. "The headmaster punished him and even told Coach Stone he'd be watching his every move. Mr. Whitney said he'd fire him if something like this ever happened again." Jessie's stomach churned once more, realizing he shouldn't have exaggerated that last part, but what else could he do? He couldn't leave the school, not now. He wouldn't give up on his dreams and he wouldn't let his parents make him.

Jessie hardened his jaw and told them, "I'm not leaving." He watched his parents exchange glances and went on. "Pop faced dangers far worse than this marching with Dr. King. And Jackie Robinson had to put up with death threats." Jessie almost reminded them about the dangers Dr. King had coped with before his assassination, but then realized that would have only confirmed their worst fears.

Momma's chest heaved with a big sigh and said, "Enough with the speeches."

But Jessie went on. "You're the ones always telling me that life isn't fair. Well, if life was fair, then I'd be free to pursue my dreams—the NHL, getting into Harvard or Yale—without this . . . this kind of crap. But we all know life isn't fair. I don't like it either, but I'm not gonna let them steal my dreams and I'm not gonna quit. I'm gonna force them to accept me, whether they like it or not."

Then Jessie held his breath and waited as Momma looked at Pop, her shoulders sagging in defeat.

"I'm *still* going to have a talk with that headmaster," Pop said.

But Jessie took that as surrender. He'd won.

●

Springvale led 21-7 in the third quarter when it happened. St. Sebastian's had kicked away from Stick after the opening return for a touchdown, aiming all their punts out of bounds and squib-kicking their one other kick-off, bouncing it along the ground to Stick's blockers. The crowd had booed St. Sebastian's cowardly moves to avoid Stick's lightning returns.

Jessie was struck by the fact that on the football field, Stick was the hero everyone loved, but they didn't want him even looking at their daughters when the game was over. Harry Edwards had nailed it and Springvale Academy was no exception. They'd brought in Stick to perform and he'd truly succeeded. But they expected him to be a good little Negro the rest of the time, especially staying away from white girls and keeping his mouth shut. Jessie's gut just churned as he thought about it.

As Jessie watched the game, Stick caught a short pass over the middle and was quickly surrounded, then slammed to the ground. His friend sprang to his feet as if they hadn't touched him, something he'd told Jessie he always tried to do just because he liked to see the frustration in his opponents' eyes.

"What do your classmates say about the results of the presidential election?" Pop asked as they watched the team huddle. On Tuesday, Richard Nixon had defeated Hubert Humphrey in a close Presidential election. George Wallace, the segregationist Alabama governor who'd run as a third party candidate, had won five states, getting almost ten million votes.

"Most of them were for Nixon," Jessie said. "It's almost all Republicans up here." He didn't tell his father that more had supported Wallace here than Humphrey.

The Springvale quarterback faded back to pass but he missed Stick, who'd gotten past his double coverage. It was third down and five yards to go.

"Nixon scares me," Pop said. "When a candidate runs on 'law and order,' that usually means 'lock up the Negroes.' I'll always wonder what would have happened if Bobby Kennedy hadn't been assassinated."

Jessie muttered his agreement, but he didn't really feel like talking politics right now. Pop always seemed to do this at sports events, as though the sport itself didn't interest him, but rather was only a venue for discussing more important topics. When he brought up the War in Vietnam, Jessie nodded politely but mostly tuned out his father.

On the field, the quarterback rolled to the right but then pitched back to Stick, running a reverse. Stick dodged one tackler, gave ground to avoid another, and needed to beat only two other defenders to turn the corner. But as he planted his foot to fake one way, a tackler dove right at his legs.

Stick's knee buckled, and though it had to be impossible over the roar of the crowd, Jessie was sure he heard Stick scream. His friend whip-lashed back in obvious pain, then landed face up on the ground.

A hush fell over the crowd.

Jump up, Jessie hoped, knowing that it wasn't going to happen this time. Icy shivers ran down his spine as he sent a mental message to his friend: *Jump up, Stick. See the frustration in their eyes. C'mon, Stick. Jump up!*

But Stick wasn't going to be jumping anywhere any time soon.

●

The preliminary diagnosis of severely torn knee ligaments was confirmed at the hospital. Mr. McCafferty, the football coach, got the news from the doctors and, grim-faced, conveyed it to the Stackhouses before heading back to school.

"What does it mean?" Mrs. Stackhouse asked as they sat in the waiting room, surrounded by stacks of well-worn magazines.

Pop looked somber. "Depends on how bad the damage is. It could mean he has surgery and, after a year of rehab, he comes back." He pursed his lips. "He won't be as quick as before, and he'll always be one hit or awkward cut away from a re-injury that finishes him off." He shook his head in obvious dismay. "Or it could be that his playing days are already over."

Jessie felt like he'd been punched in the gut. Stick's playing days over? Sports was all Stick had. He lived to play football and basketball.

"Twenty, thirty years from now, maybe it'd be a different outcome," Pop added, though Jessie barely heard him. "If we can transplant a heart like Dr. Barnard did last year, we should be able to do better with knee injuries." He sighed. "But not right now; I'm afraid Stick's days of lightning quickness and elusive moves are over."

A pall fell over the room and it felt like a funeral. The more Jessie thought about it, the more appropriate that was. If Stick couldn't run . . . . Well, Jessie couldn't even bear to finish the thought.

"I'm surprised his momma wasn't here to see his final game," Momma said. She stiffened and added, "His final football game, I mean." Flustered, she added, "This year, at least."

In her own awkward way, Momma had expressed what Jessie, and no doubt his father, were both thinking.

"Stick told me she went to all his basketball games but never watched him play football," Jessie told his mother. The next words nearly caught in his throat. "She was too afraid . . . too afraid he'd get hurt."

"Oh, my," Momma gasped. "That poor woman!"

Jessie supposed she was right, a mother naturally sympathizing with another mother's plight, but he couldn't think about Stick's mother. All he could think about was Stick. *Aw, man*, he thought. *This sure isn't fair*.

●

His parents gave him his birthday presents before they left—two nice sweaters and a trophy to hold the puck from his first Springvale Academy goal, a gold plate at the base to be inscribed with the date of the game.

They were really cool gifts, but it was hard to get excited after what had happened to Stick. It just didn't feel like a birthday anymore. Momma had even argued with Pop over giving him the trophy, saying he shouldn't stay at Springvale at all, never mind score goals because Jessie needed to go home with them, and not spend another day there before anything worse happened.

Jessie's mother sobbed great shuddering tears when she hugged him beside the Plymouth, the cool wind blowing leaves around their feet. Jessie hated it when she cried like this; it tore him up inside. But this time, he felt even more disturbed at the fear in his father's eyes. Pop had spoken with Mr. Whitney and stated his concerns, and he'd heard the same reassurances as Jessie, but still, that haunted fear remained.

When they finally drove off, clouds of dust rising in their wake, Jessie waved once and watched until they were out of sight.

A part of him wished that they'd forced him to leave with them.

28

When Jessie walked into the locker room for the official start of the hockey season, it felt like the captain's practice all over again. All eyes turned to him and a hush fell over the half-empty room, where seconds earlier, the loud buzz of conversation had been filled with hoots and wisecracks.

Lockers ran along all four walls in the large rectangular room, with wooden benches before them where boys sat. Dark wood paneling extended from the tops of the lockers to the ceiling, with the maroon-and-gold school crest centered on each wall. The room smelled of musty socks and jerseys, menthol pain liniment, and the stale sweat accumulated in layers upon the equipment.

In so many ways, Jessie loved those smells, an admission that had caused his mother to wrinkle her nose in disgust. But it was true. Putting on the equipment, even when it was ripe and overdue for washing, then strapping on his skates, excited Jessie like almost nothing else. His pulse quickened and his breath deepened. The *thwick-thwick* sound of wrapping tape around leggings to hold knee pads in place, or taping a stick blade filled him with joy. Even using a blowtorch to bend a more exaggerated curve to the blade of his stick made him happy.

And yet, here there was also that churning in his gut that, even though this felt like home, many of his teammates—and others—considered him a trespasser. In that respect, Dirk wasn't wrong when he'd said nobody wanted him there.

"Go ahead, guys," Dirk said to the fifteen or so other boys sitting on the benches. "We're not gonna let Piss-Boy ruin this for us." He got up from the bench where he'd been sitting, acting like he was inviting Jessie to take him on as he stood there, bare-chested, with the straps of his hockey pants slung over his shoulders.

A sour taste filled Jessie's mouth as he looked into Dirk's eyes.

"Negroes and rookies go to the far end," Dirk said.

But Jessie didn't move. He tried to hold back his anger, as he said in as even a tone as he could manage, "That isn't necessary."

"You knew where to dress?" Dirk asked.

"You *know* what I mean," Jessie said.

"Maybe I think it *is* necessary," Dirk told him.

Between gritted teeth, Jessie said, "I can help this team, but only if you'll let me."

"We don't want you. But you just won't take the hint."

"Well, you've got me, whether you want me or not. And if you're half the leader you pretend to be, you'll knock it off."

Dirk snorted and looked around the room. "He's telling *me* how to be a leader. This nigger troublemaker—"

"*No more!*" Jessie snapped. The words tumbled out before he could stop them. "Don't ever use that word on me again, unless you want me to break your nose in a couple more places."

Dirk took a step toward Jessie, who dropped his bag and stick on the rubber floor. Was this how it was going to go all season long? Or was this how it was going to end? There were fifteen of them and only one of him—an equation that he probably should have considered before opening his big mouth.

"You're a cancer," Dirk said, pointing his finger as he advanced towards Jessie. "You're gonna ruin this team. Look at what you've already done!" Dirk didn't stop until he stood toe-to-toe with Jessie, his raw, meaty breath in Jessie's face.

But Jessie didn't flinch. "You wanna see the cancer? Go look in the mirror."

Dirk shoved him, but Jessie'd planted his feet and didn't move.

"That one's free," Jessie said. "The next one you'll pay for."

Dirk glared at Jessie, his breath ragged and stark hatred all over his face. He snorted and, as he turned to walk away, he gave Jessie the slightest of shoves in the chest, barely touching him but letting him know that he'd taken that next one after all.

Jessie clenched and unclenched his fists. It wasn't until Dirk sat down and pulled a roll of tape out of his bag that Jessie picked up his own gear and moved to the far end of the locker room, barely noticing the squishing of the rubber mat beneath his feet.

●

Coach Stone blew the whistle nonstop. It hung from a cord around his neck, but it rarely left his lips, and then only so he could bark out instructions or shout reprimands at the players. With the hum of the refrigeration system as a backdrop, the whistle's shrill cry started a drill, stopped it, and interrupted it when anyone made a mistake.

"What are you doing?" Stone screamed red-faced time after time, directing his wrath almost exclusively at the twenty or so newcomers trying out for the team, their status underlined by the plain white jerseys they wore in stark contrast to the maroon-and-gold jerseys of the returning players.

"Move your feet, move your feet!" Stone shouted.

Jessie moved his feet, flying up and down the ice, sending a spray of ice chips into the air when he slammed on the brakes. He drove his legs like pistons, outracing every player in and out of the orange cones set out to force direction changes, not once reaching the end line behind another skater. He blew away everyone but Rocco, Frenchie, and a senior from Wisconsin called Cheesie.

This, Jessie thought, was what he was here for. Being on the ice shoved all the harassment and abuse into the background. He could skate, stickhandle, and shoot, and no one could stop him from giving his best.

Or so he thought, until the individual drills ended and Stone began two-on-ones and three-on-twos, followed by two-on-twos. Time after time, the older players' passes to him weren't on the tape of his stick but in his feet. Sometimes he recovered, slowing enough so he could kick the puck up onto his stick where it belonged, but by that point, the timing was off just enough to make a difference. Other times, no amount of lower-body dexterity could rescue the play.

Coach Stone seemed not to notice the reason for the failure of the play, but only that Jessie was involved. A sour look came to Stone's face and he shook his head.

Even the one time Jessie turned their mean-spirited sabotage into pure gold somehow worked against him. Rocco's pass came well behind him, so Jessie turned sideways, reached back with one hand on his stick, and caught it on the tip of the blade. He pulled it up to his skates, kicked it forward, then spun around to avoid the defenseman and beat him to the outside. The return pass to Rocco, all alone on the far post, so startled him that he didn't even have time to mishandle it and he quickly tapped it into the open side almost by reflex.

The play drew hoots and cheers from several freshmen, along with what sounded like gasps from many veterans. But then came the long, shrieking whistle from Coach Stone.

"Stackhouse, quit showboating!" Stone hollered. "What do you think this is, the Harlem Globetrotters?"

Jessie stood there dumbfounded.

"If there's anything I can't stand," Stone said, "it's a hotdog. Now gimme four suicides."

Before Jessie took off on the four back-and-forth lengthwise sprints, he saw a smirk on Rocco's face that confirmed what Jessie had guessed. One or two bad passes might be part of the game, but when they happened repeatedly, it was a sign of sabotage.

By the end of the practice, the veterans had given up all pretense of subtlety. Ray Charles and Stevie Wonder could have seen what was going on, even though Coach Stone pretended not to. It took all his restraint for Jessie not to drop his gloves and take on the entire group of veterans and Coach Stone with them.

Jessie hated them all and seethed with pent-up rage. But he knew exploding would have worse consequences for him than for his enemies. If he ever gave these peckerwoods what they deserved, he'd be destroying his own future, as satisfying as it might be for the moment.

Keep your eyes on the prize, he told himself over and over, remembering the folk song used during civil rights marches.

When the coach blew the final whistle, Jessie felt none of the disappointment that usually came with leaving the ice. He felt only relief that practice was over, his only satisfaction coming from the fact that he hadn't punched out anyone's lights.

But relief wasn't as close at hand as Jessie'd wished.

"Stackhouse," Stone yelled as Jessie stepped through the door onto the rubber mat. "Get over here."

Jessie raced over to where Coach Stone stood along the far bench, stopping on a dime.

Stone tugged at the baseball-style Springvale Academy cap on his head, his eyes narrowed.

"You think you're quite the hotshot, don't you?" the coach said.

Jessie didn't know what to say so he said nothing. What was the right response to such a question?

Stone glared at him and Jessie could smell stale cigarettes with the hint of whiskey breath on the coach.

"Don't be so sure you're going to make this team," Stone said.

Jessie froze, his eyes widening as his jaw dropped. *Not make the team?* But he'd done everything he could, despite what the others had done to make him look bad.

"Go get changed," Stone said. "You smell like a gorilla in heat." Then he skated away.

●

Jessie ignored the glowering stares in the locker room. He showered and dressed quickly, then rushed back to the dorm. Though the swirling icy winds bit his ears and nose, and his wet hair began to freeze, Jessie preferred it to what he'd faced in the locker room.

He'd ask Stick if his teammates had ever treated him like this, and if so, he wanted to know how long had it taken for them to come around. Was it one touchdown? Two? Stick's captain had, after all, gone out of his way to invite Stick to be with his teammates at the dance. Jessie couldn't imagine Dirk ever doing that.

But then it hit Jessie. Stick didn't need to hear about his problems. Not now, not with far worse problems of his own. Stick's career now hinged on tattered knee ligaments that might be mangled beyond repair, and Jessie couldn't go to him now, whining about mistreatment at the hands of redneck, mean-spirited fools.

Jessie couldn't tell his parents either; he couldn't give them any more reason to pull him out of school. They were just itching to do that if given the excuse.

There was no one to talk to, no one to ask for advice or even a sympathetic ear.

Jessie was now totally on his own.

29

In the team's first scrimmage that Saturday, Coach Stone played Jessie on the fourth line with two rookies, Larry and Adam, who could skate okay but whose hands were made of stone. Every pass he fed them hit their stick and hopped away, as one golden scoring opportunity after another went by the boards.

Jessie had always tried to break the ice with new teammates by passing them the puck, giving them great chances that earned their respect and appreciation for the easy goals they scored, but when Larry and Adam fumbled all those chances, it almost seemed to embarrass them.

Jessie began shooting more, but after turning down a pass to Adam in the slot, choosing instead to skate from behind the net and stuff the puck just inside the post for a goal, Jessie heard Stone scream from the bench. "Pass the puck, Stackhouse!"

As Jessie skated alongside the bench where teammates normally offered congratulations after a goal, not one of them extended a hand. Instead, Stone continued to give him an earful.

"I won't have selfish players on my team!" Stone barked. "Go take a seat!"

Jessie trudged to the back bench and sat down as Stone continued to yell at him, but Jessie had stopped listening. Stone was either insane or an idiot, and maybe both.

●

As badly as the scrimmage had gone, it was no match for what happened in the opening game. Although Jessie hadn't joined rookie hopefuls like Larry and Adam on the list of roster cuts, he also wasn't on the list of players dressing for the home opener. With Rocco and Sully, both forwards, suspended along with Dirk, a defenseman, Jessie never considered the possibility that he wouldn't be on the ice for the game.

Instead, he sat in the same section as Dirk, Rocco, and all the other players who were sidelined. But being in the stands wasn't the worst of it. When he'd taken his seat, the rest of the boys got up, shooting poisonous glances his way as they moved ten seats down from him. Jessie didn't budge at the insult—he could take a hint.

But sitting there, Jessie couldn't help wondering, was all this worth it? It made no sense for him not to dress. Even as a rookie, he belonged on one of the top two lines, based on what he'd seen at practice. He wasn't being egotistical; it was simply the truth. To not be one of the twelve forwards who dressed on any game night boggled his mind. To not dress with two of the best forwards suspended defied all logic.

His call home to tell his parents not to bother driving up for the game had been as bitter as it had been unexpected. After he dropped the bomb and the three exchanged bewildered comments, he'd hung up as quickly as he could. This slap had hurt so bad, he couldn't even talk to his family about it.

After Northland scored five minutes into the game, one of Jessie's sidelined teammates sidled over and sat down beside him. A rookie, the boy had dirty blond hair and peach fuzz skin that made him look ten years old with no hope of ever shaving.

Jessie tensed up and waited.

"Mind if I sit here?" the boy asked.

Jessie recalled that the kid's name was Will Butler and they were in the same Algebra and Biology classes. "Sure, have a seat," Jessie said and moved his elbow off the armrest between their two seats.

Filled with anger, frustration, and lingering shock, Jessie couldn't help but ask. "What happened? Those guys kick you out?"

Will glanced over at the others and said, "No." Then he looked at Jessie, sizing him up. "You're pretty tough, you know that?" he said.

Jessie didn't respond. He didn't feel very tough right now. He might feel tougher if he could bust Dirk's nose again, but right now, reduced to spectator status, he felt about as tough as a marshmallow.

"I mean," Will said, "How do you stand it? It's like it never stops. It's not fair what they're doing to you."

Jessie felt something soften inside him. *Somebody* had

noticed. Based on what he'd seen, this kid had been lucky to even survive the cuts. It wasn't like one of the stars or Coach Stone had said this. But *someone* had noticed and actually had the courage to say so.

"Thanks," Jessie said.

"It's a joke that you're not dressing. You should be on the top line and the power play if you ask me."

Jessie felt himself smile. "Thanks." He tried to think of what to say about Will and couldn't very well repeat the boy's words. It'd be phony and would probably sound like sarcasm. All Jessie could come up with was, "Too bad you're not dressing."

Will shrugged. "To tell you the truth, I thought I was going to get cut. I'd love to play, but for now, I'm happy I made the team."

"Don't get too satisfied with sitting here," Jessie said. "If you do, you'll never get down there." He nodded toward the ice.

"Yeah," Will said, looking as though he understood the truth of what Jessie had said but was unable to dispel his own doubts.

●

As the game progressed, Cheesie scored twice to give the Warriors a 2-1 lead. Each time, the players all stood and clapped, but only Dirk seemed to be into it. It was tough to get enthused about someone else doing what should be your role.

"Why are they doing this to you?" Will asked after they sat down.

Jessie gave him a wry look. "You blind?"

"But that's so . . . so dumb. And . . ."

"Evil?"

"Yeah."

"Welcome to my world."

Springvale Academy won 5-2, but after Jessie, Will, and the others walked down to the locker room to join the team, everyone looked glum and Stone breathed fire with every word. Northland was a cupcake to open the schedule, a tune-up before the real games began. Even though Springvale had outshot its opponent 53-11, requiring Northland's goaltender to stand on his head, any winning margin that was less than ten goals wasn't much better than defeat, and Stone let them know it.

●

The next day, Jessie and Will talked between classes about everything from going home for Thanksgiving to their homework that night, to how it sure would be nice if the school was coed. They lingered on that last topic for a while.

But on Wednesday when they were sitting together again in the stands while the team played St. James, Jessie was in no mood for talking. He watched, livid, while Springvale again struggled to put the puck in the net, this time losing to a team that had no business being on the same ice with the Warriors. If this was the best Springvale Academy could muster without the suspended players, then Saturday's match against Deerfield Academy was going to be a blowout.

"Sooner or later, Stone has got to play you," Will said.

Jessie's eyes never left the ice. He was way too angry to speak.

That was more than could be said for Coach Stone after the game. The locker room echoed with his profanity-laced tirade that lasted well after the sweat stopped dripping off the players. When he finally finished, Jessie headed for the door, eager to get away.

Instead, Mr. Whitney grabbed him as soon as he exited the locker room. Impeccably groomed, the headmaster wore a tweed suit with brown suede elbow patches. He smelled of pipe tobacco, cologne, and mint mouthwash.

"I'm glad I caught you," he said.

Jessie stopped and looked around, unsure what he'd done wrong this time.

Mr. Whitney smiled in a reassuring way. "I'm sure you're frustrated with how things are developing with the team."

Jessie nodded.

"So am I," Mr. Whitney said. "I want you in my office tomorrow morning at eight. We're going to confront Coach Stone and get to the bottom of this."

"Really?" Jessie said.

Mr. Whitney nodded, his smile giving way to a grave, determined look, his jaw set and his eyes faraway.

Jessie felt all the anger, frustration, and humiliation lift off him. "Thank you, sir." He held out his hand, and when Mr. Whitney shook it, Jessie pumped so hard, the headmaster winced.

"Don't break it off," he said. "I'm going to need it."

"Sorry, sir."

Mr. Whitney gripped Jessie's shoulder and squeezed. "Don't you be sorry about a thing."

●

The next morning in the headmaster's office, Coach Stone's face grew redder and redder until Jessie thought he might explode. The two of them sat opposite Mr. Whitney in his elegant office.

"I'll brook no meddling from you about how I run my team," Stone said. "You may be the headmaster, but it's *my* team. You may find that many alumni consider my job more important than yours."

Mr. Whitney leaned forward, his elbows on his desk. "I don't care what the alumni say—"

"You might want to reconsider," Stone said. "The last headmaster who talked like that got tossed on his can before he knew what hit him. It's time you get with the program."

"*Wrong!*" Mr. Whitney glared. "*You* report to *me*. It's high time *you* remember that."

Stone squinted, fire in his eyes, and pointed a yellowed finger at the headmaster. With his voice dripping sarcasm, the coach asked, "Shall I consult you for my line combinations, oh exalted one? Perhaps you'd prefer a two-man forecheck over our one-man? Maybe you can demonstrate some skating drills at the practice." Stone smiled wickedly. "That's hockey skates, by the way—not figure skates."

Mr. Whitney flushed.

"How many championships have you won?" Stone

asked with a sneer. "Oh, I believe that would be—*none*! How many have I won? Stackhouse, how many have I won?"

Jessie knew the answer—seventeen—but wasn't about to help Stone.

Mr. Whitney took in a deep, noisy breath and his nostrils dilated. "Frank, I believe we all know the answer to that question."

Stone began to say something, but the headmaster held up his hand, stopping him.

"I wouldn't presume to tell you how to run your team, but we have extraordinary circumstances here," Mr. Whitney said. "I've watched some of your practices and went to both games. It's clear to me that you're blatantly discriminating against Jessie, as are most of his teammates, all because of the color of his skin. I cannot tolerate or condone that, and as headmaster of this school, I will not allow it."

"You couldn't tell the difference between a blue line and a clothesline," Stone sneered.

"I don't need to be a hockey expert to know what's going on. It's so blatant, anyone can see it."

"I don't see any discrimination at all," Stone said and leaned back in his chair.

Jessie shook his head in amazement at Stone's audacity. The coach noticed and turned to glare at him. Jessie froze.

"Anyone who isn't blinded by the same hatred you've shown can see," Mr. Whitney countered. "Jessie is clearly one of the most talented forwards on our team. He's faster and has a harder shot—"

"There's more to hockey than that," Stone snapped.

"You're telling me that every player you dressed on the third or fourth line is a better player than Jessie."

"There are intangibles—"

"Like the color of Jessie's skin?"

"He's not a team player!"

Mr. Whitney slammed his fist on his desk. "I think it's *you* who isn't a team player. You'd rather lose games than play a black man."

"I'm the hockey coach. I make the decisions."

"Not this time! I've committed to integrating this school and I don't care if you like it or not. You will do your part to implement this integration or I will have your head!"

The two men locked eyes, fury firing from one to the other.

"For the next five games, you will play Jessie," Mr. Whitney said. "And not on the fourth line. You will give him enough ice time to prove himself. And you will tell your posse of rednecks that they will stop tormenting him." The headmaster's voice rose. "They will pass him the puck on his stick and not into his skates. They will *try to win* instead of focusing on driving Jessie off the team. If they don't, I will fire you. I don't care how many championships you have. *Do you understand me?*"

Stone stood, his face almost purple. Then he pointed a shaking finger at Mr. Whitney. "You picked the wrong guy to mess with. Do-good-ers don't last long here," Stone said, then turned and stomped out the door, slamming it behind him.

Jessie's heart hammered so hard he thought his chest would explode.

"Five games, Jessie," Mr. Whitney said. "Coach Stone is going to have a bee in his bonnet and he's not going to be easy to play for, but I'm sure you already knew that. But at least this gives you a chance."

"Thank you, sir." Jessie, thunderstruck at what he'd just seen, got to his feet. "I won't disappoint you."

A faraway look came to Mr. Whitney's eyes. "Don't thank me just yet. You may end up wishing I'd kept my mouth shut."

●

As Jessie was about to enter the locker room the next afternoon, Will emerged, carrying his bag and three sticks. Jessie smiled and was about to say hello when Will turned his way, a pained look in his eyes.

"What's the matter?" Jessie asked.

"I got . . ." Will's voice choked with emotion. "I got cut."

"When?"

"Just now. Coach just told me."

"What did he say?"

Will swallowed, met Jessie's eyes for a second, then looked away. "He said that he didn't think I fit in."

Jessie knew exactly what that meant.

30

Adrenaline surged through Jessie as he stood on the blue line, the National Anthem blaring from the speakers above. His heart pounded and his palms felt moist inside his hockey gloves. This was his chance, his first game. Third line with Johnnie Stewart and Matt Templeton. On the bus ride down to Greenfield, he'd sat alone near the front, thinking about this moment and visualizing how it would look.

Arrayed on the opposite blue line were the Greenfield Raiders, always a powerhouse just like Springvale Academy. Last year, Springvale had defeated them in the semi-finals, but not without a struggle. It had been a 2-1 game until the final minute, when the Raiders had pulled their goalie for an extra skater. After Shep made one big save, Rocco had scored from center ice into the empty net.

Dressed now in their home white jerseys, the Raiders consisted primarily of hulking players who were at least six feet tall and close to two hundred pounds. The size advantage Jessie had known back home would be lost here. He'd be just another redwood, towering and strong, but imposing to no one. He'd have to use speed to beat this group of defensemen.

When Jessie hopped over the boards for his first shift, his fingers tingled and his ears echoed with the pounding of his heart. He raced over to the far wing, and when the puck squirted loose, he poked it over to the boards and scooped it up. In one stride, a hulking defender crashed him into the boards and the puck squirted free.

This wasn't going to be like back home, Jessie knew in a flash. No one was big enough there to body him off the puck. But here, everyone was big. He'd known that from the practices, but there was no substitute for game action.

A Raider skated up ice with the puck, carrying it into the offensive zone, and ripping a slapshot. Shep made the save and held on for the whistle. Jessie moved to take his position on the face-off, only to see the first line hop over the boards.

How long had his shift been? Ten seconds? Fifteen? He glanced at the scoreboard and saw the time remaining in the period: *12:21*. He'd snuck a quick look just before taking the ice so he'd know the exact moment his Springvale career had started, so he knew for sure now that his shift had been all of twelve seconds.

Keeping his face neutral, Jessie sat on the back bench. At least, he told himself, he'd gotten his feet wet. He'd taken that first hit and touched the puck for the first time. Next time, he'd make a difference.

From behind, Stone ducked his head next to Jessie's, smelling of cigarettes and Rolaids. "Ain't so easy, is it hotshot?"

Jessie said nothing.

"Next time, hold onto the puck."

Stone disappeared for the far end of the bench.

On Jessie's next shift, his line took over just as the Raiders dumped the puck into the Springvale end for a line change of their own. A defenseman, Nick Caldwell, corralled the puck behind the net, fed it up the left boards, and Jessie's line spent the rest of the shift in the Raiders end, working the puck along the boards and in the corners, tiring out the defenders. When Taylor Hodges scored less than thirty seconds later, Jessie felt a sense of satisfaction and gave himself a sliver of credit.

In the second period, however, the 1-0 lead evaporated when the Raiders scored three goals, all against the first line, one of them while Springvale was on the power play. It didn't matter much that Jessie twice set Matt up in front for great scoring changes. Matt shot wide on the first and right into the goalie's chest on the second. All that mattered was the disaster on the scoreboard.

In the intermission between the second and third periods, Coach Stone read them the riot act, ranting and raving for several minutes before picking up the trash barrel, loaded with used tape and broken sticks, and hurled it against the far lockers before stomping out and slamming the door behind him.

Cheesie, filling in for Dirk as team captain, yelled, "C'mon guys! Who's the champions, them or us?"

Several other upperclassmen joined in, and though the words sounded a trifle forced and lacking in the absolute certainty of champions who *knew* they would somehow win every game, soon everyone else joined in, even Jessie.

With Stone sticking with the top two lines until the third period was almost half over, Jessie felt his muscles stiffen as he continued to sit on the bench. He shook his legs and flexed his knees to try to stay loose as the minutes ticked by. The players on the top two lines were showing their fatigue, huffing and puffing a little more each time they came to the bench. Even worse, they were losing races to the loose pucks during their shifts, their legs now heavy and robbed of their usual quickness.

After a whistle stopped play, Stone finally barked out, "Matt," signifying the third line. Jessie stood, shook both legs, and sprang over the boards. His legs felt wooden. He'd been sitting too long, so he raced to the face-off circle in the defensive zone to get his blood pumping.

Matt won the face-off back to Nick Caldwell, who rimmed the puck along the boards as Jessie raced to reach it before the Raider defenseman. Jessie won the race and chipped the puck off the boards and around the defender. Matt picked up the indirect pass and carried the puck through center ice with Jessie and Johnnie racing up the wings.

Jessie took the return pass, crossed into the offensive zone, and spotted the goalie off his angle just a bit, giving up too much of the far side. Jessie took two strides, wound up for a slapshot, and blasted it for the far side. It rang off the inside of the post, just below where the post and crossbar met, and caromed into the net.

When the red goal light when on, Jessie jumped into the air and threw his hands high.

Gooooooal!

Jessie let out a whoop. "Yes!" he roared. All his pent-up frustrations gushed out like a geyser. "Take that!" It had been a perfect shot, a huge goal to put the Warriors within one. The other four skaters on the ice surrounded him, all seemingly about to give him the celebratory hug that follows all big goals, but instead they pulled up and just pounded gloved fists together and patted him on the helmet.

Jessie didn't care. He'd been in this position before at home. Some guys eventually warmed up, a least a little, while others kept their distance. It didn't matter. He'd shown that he could play. He'd done it and no one could deny him that. Maybe the team could come back now and at least salvage a tie. This goal gave them a shot.

Jessie beamed as he skated to the bench, holding the puck he'd gotten from the referee. It would look nice nestled in the trophy he'd gotten for his birthday, real nice.

The crowd was suddenly quiet, perhaps fearful that Springvale Academy would do to them once again what they'd done so often in the past. But out of the soft buzz of the crowd, one young male voice rang out: "Go back to Alabama and pick some cotton!"

Jessie spun to look in that direction even before he realized he was doing it.

"Yeah, you," the voice hollered. "You heard me."

Gasps and nervous laughter rippled through the arena.

Ears burning as the rage surged within him, Jessie took his seat on the bench. A player's first goal at any level was always a special moment, but with all he'd been through, this had become the biggest goal of his life. And it figured that one stupid racist had sucked all the joy out of it.

"Stackhouse," Stone growled. Jessie turned, expecting some sort of congratulations. But instead, Coach said, "Don't be such a damned rabbit ears."

Hands shaking, Jessie squirted water from the nearest bottle into his mouth.

●

The Warriors lost, 3-2, with Greenfield's lead holding up. The team, sullen, with their heads down, trudged into the locker room. Sweat dripped onto the rubber matting on the floor as curses rang out.

Stone walked into the room flanked by Mr. Chase, who acted as both assistant coach and trainer. Stone's glare went around the room and everyone froze, even boys in the middle of pulling off their wet, smelly jerseys.

Stone spat on the floor. "That was a disgraceful effort." All around the room, shoulders sagged and heads drooped, all eyes now focused on the ground. "That wasn't Springvale hockey. This season hasn't been Springvale hockey."

Stone sucked in a loud gulp of air. "We've got some people in this locker room who're putting themselves before the team. They think they're special." Jessie's ears perked up. "Well, they ain't special—not one little bit."

"We're only half a team right now, because some individuals have put themselves above the team." Stone's eyes locked on Jessie, who could scarcely believe his ears. He stared right back at the coach. "We're missing our three best players right now because of that. It's just pure selfishness."

Jessie wondered what Stone meant. Was he criticizing

Dirk, Rocco, and Sully for their actions? Had that been the selfishness? Or could Stone possibly be blaming Jessie? Surely that wasn't the case, Jessie thought. But if not, then why was Stone glaring at him? Deep in his gut, Jessie knew what Stone meant. He'd known it from the instant the words came out of Stone's mouth.

"Selfishness!" Stone barked. "This team ain't gonna be worth a damn until we get rid of it."

What did *that* mean?

Stone spat again on the floor. "Change up. No showers. If your parents are outside waiting for you, or if any of you pansies got girlfriends who came just so they can give you a kiss, forget it. You don't talk to parents or girlfriends after a loss. Bus leaves in fifteen minutes. If you're not on it, we leave without you." He glanced at Jessie. "Trust me, there's some of you I hope don't make it."

Jessie threw his equipment into his bag, toweled off as best he could, and got dressed in under six minutes. He rushed out to the bus, blinking the snowflakes out of his eyes, then threw his bag and sticks into its undercarriage. He was about to board when he heard a familiar voice call out.

"Jessie!" From about a hundred yards away, his mother waved to him. She trotted in his direction, snow kicking up with every step as Pop walked briskly behind her.

Jessie shook his head. "I can't talk," he yelled. "I gotta go." He turned to step onto the bus.

"Wait," his mother called and broke into a run. Jessie looked around nervously but didn't see Stone or Chase. He winced, knowing this was going to end badly.

"Just one minute," his mother said, her arms outstretched as she got to within twenty yards.

"Momma, I can't talk."

"But we drove three hours to see you play," she said, confusion flooding her face. "Can't we talk to you for just a minute?"

Jessie looked around. "Coach's rule—'cause we lost."

"But I saw one of your teammates talking to his parents in the lobby. I'm sure they were his parents. He's a spitting image of his father."

"Momma," Jessie said, a sinking feeling in his gut. "It's different. Stone hates me."

"Jessie, your manners," Momma said. "You don't call an adult by his last name. It's Mr. Stone or Coach Stone."

A parade of boys was now heading for the bus.

"He's looking for an excuse to cut me. Please don't—"

Jessie heart jumped as he saw Coach Chase step out of the arena and head toward the bus.

"Just give me a hug," Momma said and stepped toward him.

"I gotta go," Jessie said and ducked into the bus, stumbling as he tripped up the stairs. He didn't look back, praying only that his mother didn't get really headstrong and follow him onto the bus.

He plunked down in a seat and, looking out the window, waved.

On the long ride back to the campus, the stench of the other sweaty athletes was overpowering. Jessie tried to read his Algebra book but couldn't concentrate. All he could see was the hurt look on his mother's face as he left her.

31

The Warriors lost their next game too, this time, 2-1. Stone ranted and raved, but that just made things worse. Everyone played tight, holding their sticks in a white-knuckle grip, their confidence shaken. Playing in a bewildered haze, they seemed to be marking time until their three leaders returned. No one could remember the last time Springvale Academy lost three of its first four games.

Jessie had played well, nothing spectacular, but he was adjusting to the size and speed of the game at this level, feeling more comfortable with each shift. He couldn't take over and dominate like he was used to doing back home; he had no switch to flick when the team needed another goal or two. But it felt like he was close, just a split second away from making his presence felt in a bigger way.

He closed that gap in the next game. Stone put him on a line with Frenchie and Taylor and the trio clicked right away, especially Jessie and Frenchie. Matt had been a good passer, but he couldn't throw a puck in the ocean. Johnnie was the opposite. If you tried a give-and-go with him, it was just a give. Jessie had thought it was personal at first, until he saw Johnnie do it to Matt, too. Between Matt's inability to score and Johnnie's inability to work with his linemates, the former line had been doomed to mediocrity at best. Frenchie, Taylor, and Jessie scored on their first shift, igniting a spark, and they finished with four of the team's five goals in a 5-2 win.

"That was a big win," Frenchie said to Jessie afterward in the locker room, a big smile on his face.

"Huge," Jessie said as he pulled off his sweat-drenched jersey. No one wanted to say it aloud, but if they'd lost that game and fallen to 1-4, they might never have recovered, at least not enough to make the postseason tournament. Only four teams qualified, and every year, at least one very good team got left out.

●

Even with Rocco and Sully coming back to rejoin Cheesie on the first line, Stone kept Jessie, Frenchie, and Taylor together as the second line, bumping Chris Johnson and Nick Sizemore, two seniors, all the way down to third. They both gave him and Frenchie dirty looks, as if the two rookies had taken away something they'd earned, but Jessie didn't mind. No one else joined in, recognizing how ineffective the two seniors had been with Cheesie. And with Frenchie getting the dirty looks as much as he did, Jessie didn't feel singled out.

Springvale Academy won the next three games easily, winning by scores of 9-2, 5-3, and 6-1. Rocco, Sully, and Cheesie picked up where they'd left off the previous year as the league's most feared combination, but Jessie, Frenchie, and Taylor matched them goal for goal. In his first six games, Jessie scored eight goals and assisted on ten others. In the 9-2 rout, he recorded his first hat trick with the Warriors.

With every practice and every game, Jessie felt the frozen attitude toward him slowly thawing. He knew he'd never break through with the hard-core guys like Dirk, though the captain had at least stopped calling him Piss-Boy. But the hostile looks and stares from the other guys were giving way to grudging acceptance, and in a few cases, apparent admiration for what he'd added to the team. Although this thaw seemed to melt at glacier-like speeds, it was there, at least in the locker room and on the ice. Defensemen who'd instinctively passed to one of the other forwards no matter how open Jessie had been were now beginning to treat him as an on-ice equal.

Not that anyone would be inviting him to join them for a pizza downtown anytime soon; Jessie knew that day might never come. He suspected he'd remain a social pariah until the day he left Springvale, but any level of acceptance, even limited to the locker room and the ice amounted to progress.

Soon, exams were starting and it seemed that every second of Jessie's time was spent on studying or hockey, but he felt a weary sense of satisfaction. The team kept winning, including a dramatic victory 4-3, over a major rival, Exeter, with Jessie scoring twice. The locker room, previously tense, now echoed with the laughter and boisterous storytelling of a winning team. Not even Stone's criticisms after seemingly every shift could dampen Jessie's mood.

He boarded the bus for the away game against Oak Ridge, Springvale's most bitter rival, his Algebra and Biology textbooks under his arm. Exams loomed next week, but Jessie felt as confident about them as he did about hockey. He studied most of the way, setting the books aside only when the bus driver shouted that it would be only another ten or fifteen minutes until they arrived.

Jessie leaned his head back and closed his eyes. He shut out the banter in the back of the bus, the creaking of a nearby seat cushion, and the hum of the tires outside. He pushed away the bus's musty smell and the scent of some boys' aftershave. He cleared out his mind, and though he'd never been to the Oak Ridge rink, he tried to visualize the ice surface and Oak Ridge's towering defensemen, especially Corey Simonton, their first team All-New England selection last year. He and Dirk had been named New England's top defensemen as juniors and he'd be tough to beat.

Jessie saw himself trying to take Simonton to the outside and beat him with speed. He saw himself fake a slapshot, freezing Simonton, then blasting past him. Jessie saw himself faking to the outside, then cutting back inside as soon as Simonton committed.

Jessie ran through all the moves in his mind, and when he couldn't think of any more, he ran through them again, even as the bus took one turn after another. He didn't open his eyes until the bus lurched to a halt.

Stone stood over him, staring down. "Glad to see Sleeping Beauty has gotten her beauty sleep."

Jessie blinked. "I was—"

"Save it for the headmaster. I'm sure he'll buy it."

Stone shook his head. "That's the problem with you people. You've got all the athletic ability in the world but no discipline. Million-dollar talent, but spit for brains."

An acidic steam built inside, but Jessie held his tongue, even while the raw acid taste began to rise in his throat. Stone's attitude never changed. Sure, he'd played Jessie after he'd been forced to do so and then elevated him to second line only when the season teetered on the brink. But his words never changed. Nothing Jessie did was good enough for the man. Stone was a disciple of George Wallace and nothing Jessie could do would ever change that.

Jessie imagined all the things he couldn't do: spitting in Stone's face and challenging him to a fight; skipping all that and just cold-cocking the guy; taking a hockey stick and cross-checking him right in the nose, enjoying the crunch of bone and spurting blood. Jessie knew he'd never do any of those things, but the acid steam inside him grew and grew.

He walked off the bus, knowing that as soon as the opening buzzer sounded, someone on Oak Ridge was going to pay. Jessie would see Stone's face beneath the Oak Ridge helmet and check him so hard into the boards that the building would rattle.

An hour and a half later, after walking around to get the kinks out from the bus ride and going through the team's pre-game rituals and warm-ups, Jessie got his chance. He came flying off the bench on a line change just as an Oak Ridge defenseman sent a soft "buddy pass" to a forward who was looking back for it and didn't see Jessie coming until it was too late. The Oak Ridge forward never had a chance. That's because Jessie saw only the hideous sneer of his coach's face under that helmet, along with his hatred for all things Black.

Jessie lowered his shoulder and drove it into the forward's chest with all the force his coiled legs could deliver. He flattened the forward, who'd been moving in one direction and in the next instant was laid out horizontally in midair, his stick flying toward the rafters as the air in his lungs was knocked out of him.

It was the hardest Jessie had ever hit anyone in his life, but it was clean and legal. The fault lay at the feet of the defenseman for giving him the buddy pass—short for "Sorry, buddy"—one that all but painted the bull's-eye on the guy's chest.

As the crowd gasped, Jessie felt a tingle of the impact in his own head, instantly setting off alarm bells. It was only a tingle, but it flashed him back to where he'd been only two months earlier, unable to even ride the stationary bike without throwing up. He'd better back off hitting on the next shift or two just in case he told himself. He'd better be sure that tingle didn't mean anything.

Jessie raced for the loose puck, cradled it with his stick, and—

A shrill whistle blew. Jessie turned and saw the referee, wearing the usual striped shirt and orange armband, pointing at him and holding his arm aloft, signifying a penalty. As the crowd booed, an Oak Ridge skater came at Jessie and threw a punch. Jessie turned his head and the fist caught only helmet. Then another Oak Ridge player blind-sided Jessie with a cross-check to the back, the stick feeling as though it had broken his ribs. Another stick chopped him between the legs and Jessie's cup rang hollowly as the bolt of white pain shot through his abdomen and he doubled over.

The whistles sounded loud and long in the cold air. The crowd's boos turned to cheers. *Where is everyone?* All Jessie saw were Oak Ridge white and blue jerseys. One punch caught him in the nose, another in the back of the neck. But all he felt was the searing agony radiating upwards from his crotch.

Where are you guys? he wondered. Where was his team?

Above his own groans, Jessie heard swearing in French and knew that at least Frenchie had joined the fray. Then came Nick and Taylor, followed last by Joey Hightower.

By the time the linemen pulled them all apart, sticky blood covered the lower half of Jessie's face. On reflex, he licked it off his lips, revolted by its sharp and bitter taste.

Boos from all about the arena cascaded down on them. As the linesman led Jessie to the penalty box, the catcalls began, growing in intensity and hatred, ranging from the usual "Throw him out!" and "Cheap shot!" all the way to a bloodcurdling, "Kill him!"

Jessie sat in the penalty box and rocked back and forth. He felt a lot more than a tingle now. Stars danced before his field of vision and his head rang like a dinner bell. The pain in his crotch continued to spasm.

Then he heard it—a booming male voice shouted "*Nigger!*"

The crowd fell silent for a split second, shocked and unsure how to react.

271

Another voice echoed it, followed by another, this time shrill and female.

Soon an entire section had joined in, and Jessie closed his eyes, wishing he could also close his ears.

Minutes later, after the referee and linesmen finally sorted out the penalties, the referee skated back to the penalty box where Jessie had been joined by Frenchie, Nick, and Taylor.

"You two," the referee said, pointing to Jessie and Frenchie, and giving their numbers. "You're gone."

Jessie didn't understand. "Gone?"

"You're out of the game. Let's go."

Jessie couldn't believe it. He'd delivered a huge check, but a legal one, and then he'd gotten the snot kicked out him.

"For what? Getting hit by too many punches?"

"Shut up and move it," the ref said.

Jessie stood and stepped through the door to the penalty box. "It was a legal check."

"Then consider it for starting a riot."

As Jessie and Frenchie began to cross the ice, popcorn boxes and cardboard soda containers rained down on them, some far from empty. The racial chants grew louder, echoing off the low ceiling.

Halfway across the ice, Jessie's pride welled up from deep within him. He would not take this like a whipped dog. They could only take away his dignity if they let him.

Jessie bowed his head and raised one clenched fist in the symbol of Black Power. Though his hockey glove was quite unlike Tommy Smith's and John Carlos's, the rednecks caught the meaning fast enough.

"*Go back to Africa!*" one man screamed, his face twisted in cold hatred. The venom came from all sides now and in the form of every possible epithet.

Jessie ducked as a shoe flew by his head and more popcorn boxes littered the ice. Something hard caught him on the side of his helmet, then bounced and rolled away — a souvenir puck.

Jessie turned to warn Frenchie to cover his eyes, but then his jaw dropped and his heart soared. It was the most astonishing thing he'd ever seen. Like Jessie, Frenchie held one clenched fist aloft with his head bowed.

Choked with emotion, Jessie stepped off the ice and passed through the gate that led to the locker room. He didn't even care when a cold, sticky liquid doused his face, its ice cubes pinging down on the rubber floor.

Jessie had at last found his first real Springvale teammate.

●

Frenchie stood next to Jessie as the team filed into the locker room for the first intermission. The players sat down on the benches behind their bags that lay strewn on the floor, then took off their helmets and tossed them on their bags.

"I have to say something," Frenchie said as Coach Stone entered the room.

Stone blinked, looking stunned at hearing the normally silent Frenchie speak, and nodded for the boy to go on.

"I am only a freshman and my English is not so good,

but I cannot stay quiet," Frenchie said. "If we are going to be a team, we must stand up for each other." He grabbed the jersey Jessie still wore. "Jessie is one of us. You may not understand him, and you may not like him. *But he is one of us*." He pointed outside the locker room and his voice shook with rage. "We don't let *anyone* do what they did to Jessie out there. They did it to him, so they did it to all of us. We either stand together, or we lose."

Stone's eyes narrowed and his nostrils flared. He seemed to be weighing what to do next. Finally he nodded, then turned and left the room.

The Warriors, who'd been trailing 2-1, scored three goals in the second period and never looked back. They wouldn't lose another game for some time.

32

Jessie opened the door to his room and shrugged off his winter coat, bursting with the news about Frenchie. Stick looked up quickly, a guilty look on his face, and shuffled the papers on his desk under a notebook. His crutches lay propped against the side of his desk and James Brown boomed from the stereo.

"Cute nose," Stick said.

Jessie touched it gingerly. "I got in a fight." He frowned. "What're you hiding, man?"

Stick leaned back and tried to look casual. "Nothin'."

Jessie stood beside Stick's desk. "Who you kidding?" Stacked on the far side of the desk, back near the lamp, were Stick's textbooks. On the near side, the notebook sat on top of sheets of paper sticking out at odd angles. "You got something there you don't want me to see. Come on, Stick. Don't lie."

Stick shrugged. "Okay. But you can't say nothin'. I been sworn to secrecy."

Jessie felt offended. "Even from me?"

"'Specially from you." Stick shifted uncomfortably.

"You the Black Einstein, and your momma be a teacher. So they told me not to let you know."

"Who's *they*?"

"*They*," Stick said. He put a fresh toothpick in his mouth and leaned back. "People in the Athletic Department—I can't say who. They help out star athletes who have trouble with their grades. You know, make sure they stay academically eligible." Stick smiled. "And I be a star." His gaze dropped to the cast on his knee and his smile faded. He took a deep breath. "I in trouble with my grades, so they helpin' me."

"Your tutor writing your papers again?"

Stick didn't answer.

Jessie was pretty sure the tutor had never stopped. "Is that some paper you're supposed to look at so you can at least *pretend* you wrote it?"

"Nah," Stick said. "But listen to yo'self, all high and mighty. Black Einstein be above all that stuff 'cause he don't need no help."

Jessie wasn't so sure about that. Black Einstein had better get down to studying or he was gonna flunk math, just like the White Einstein had. But his mind just couldn't let go of what Stick was hiding. "What you got there, man? Don't make me beat it out of you. You're a midget and a cripple, so don't think I can't do it."

"You gotta promise not to tell."

"Have I told on you so far?"

"That's not an answer."

Jessie folded his arms. "I won't tell. What you doin'?"

Stick eyed him for a few seconds. "Lots of my teachers give the same tests year after year. Maybe that don't happen in your Einstein track, but they do for dummies like me."

"You're not a—"

Stick waved him away. "I don't wanna hear that speech again. Point is, if a teacher is gonna give the same exams, then guys like me can get special help gettin' ready." He pulled the pages out from beneath the notebook and waved them in the air. The top page read:

Fall Semester, 1967

Final Examination

English

"That's cheating!" Jessie said. "That's even worse than getting your tutor to write your paper."

"I be doing the studyin'."

"But . . ." Words failed Jessie. How could Stick not see that this was wrong, and even more than that, self-destructive? He couldn't do this forever.

"I just takin' what the defense be givin' me," Stick said. "In hoop, if a guy guard me tight, I blow past him. If a guy back off, I hit the outside shot. Same thing in football. Guard me tight, I'm going past you, sucker. See . . . you . . . later. Goodbye." Stick said with a wave. "Back off, and I beat you underneath." He shrugged. "Now if a teacher's gonna give the same exam every year, I'd be a fool not to take what he be givin' me."

Jessie was stunned at the logic. "How long do you think you're gonna get away with that?"

"'Til I graduate?"

"And what then? What happens at college?"

"Same thing, I hope."

Jessie shook his head and bit his lower lip. "What if somebody here finds out?"

Anger flashed across Stick's face. "You promised not to tell."

"I'm not gonna tell anyone. I'm just saying." Jessie searched for words. "What if for some reason—I don't know why—there's no more tutor to write your papers and no more old final exams to cheat off? What's gonna happen to you then?"

Stick was quiet for what felt like a long time.

"Then I guess I'll flunk out." He waved at his stack of unopened textbooks. "I ain't you, man. I can't do this stuff."

●

Jessie poured himself into his books, studying every extra minute. When he walked out of the last exam, he drew in a deep breath and exhaled with satisfaction. He was pretty sure he'd done well. He could go into the Christmas break feeling good about himself.

That afternoon, he said goodbye to Stick and wished him a Merry Christmas and Happy New Year, then boarded the team bus for the holiday tournament at Lawrence Academy. The schedule called for a Friday night game, two on Saturday, and potentially two on Sunday—the semifinals and finals.

Jessie had been relieved to suffer no after effects from the fight, other than a headache the next day, which was an off day anyway. The day after, he'd stayed away from contact in practice, and by the day after that, he'd forgotten all about it.

Springvale breezed through the tournament's opening rounds with Jessie scoring four goals in the first three games, then beat Cushing 5-2 in the Sunday morning semi-finals. Jessie scored once and assisted on two by Frenchie.

When Springvale defeated the hosts 4-2 without incident in the championship game, Jessie headed into the holiday break convinced the worst was behind him.

33

When they got home, Jessie helped his mother trim the Christmas tree before he went to bed. It was already December 22, but she'd left the tree bare for him since it had been their tradition since he was old enough to walk that they'd decorate it together each year.

Every five minutes, Momma hugged him and told him how much she'd missed him.

"Really?" he asked after what felt like the hundredth time. "I didn't know that."

Then she hugged him tight once more and he felt the wetness of a teardrop on his shoulder. But Jessie knew it was a tear of happiness, and everything felt just right.

For this week and a half of vacation, Jessie didn't want to think at all. He'd escaped all that, even if for only the holidays. He was going to have fun and take it easy while he was home.

So he called Rose the next day. She'd been out the night before when he called, and had been away visiting relatives when he'd come home briefly for Thanksgiving. He couldn't wait to see her, even though the certainty that she was going out with someone else filled Jessie with dread.

"Let's go for a greasy pizza at Fauci's," he suggested after he finally got her on the phone.

"Jessie," Rose said tentatively in that silky voice that still made his heart skip a beat, even though he hadn't seen her in four months. "I'm going out with someone else now, and I don't think—"

"I know," he said, annoyed but not knowing why. "It's not a date. I'm not gonna come on to you. I just want to see some of my old friends."

"Can Leroy join us? Him and me, we goin' out now."

This wasn't at all what Jessie had in mind, but he wasn't sure what he'd actually planned.

"Otherwise," Rose said, "if he can't come along, he gonna think we having a date."

"Why you going with *him*? He's no good—"

"*Jess-ie!*"

"Okay, okay. Bring him along. See you in an hour."

Jessie wondered if not seeing Rose at all would have been better than seeing her with her new boyfriend.

When she walked into the pizza place, she took his breath away. She looked so beautiful, her hair in a full Afro, her brown eyes making him melt, just like they always had before, maybe even more.

She wore jeans and a stylish leather jacket that wasn't warm enough for a really cold day, but sure accentuated her figure. Jessie stumbled to his feet from one of the booth-style tables where he'd been waiting, his heart pounding. Rose smiled shyly and took off her jacket. Beneath it, she wore a light blue blouse.

"You look like you've never seen a girl before," she said, her radiant smile broadening.

"It's-it's been a while."

She laughed and sat down across from him. "Notice anything different?" she asked.

"You're gorgeous," Jessie said. He hadn't meant for it to come out quite that way, but he couldn't help himself; he felt smitten with her all over again.

She slapped playfully at his arm in response. "Don't be silly."

But he wasn't being silly. She was drop-dead gorgeous.

In a tone usually reserved for talking to kids in grade school, she asked, "What am I missing?"

Jessie wracked his brain. She'd never worn braces—she'd always had a perfect, bright smile—so it wasn't that. It's not like she'd lost weight either. Her figure had always been trim.

She widened her eyes and spread her palms out as if he were being stupid. "For a smart guy, you sure can be—"

"I know you're even more beautiful than I remembered. So if something's missing, it isn't that I haven't noticed. I just can't figure out what—"

Rose clamped her palm over his mouth. "Silly—Leroy is missing." She laughed. "He couldn't make it after all."

"Oh." Jessie felt foolish. "Of course. It's just—all I could think of was you."

"I thought you weren't going to put the moves on me."

"I'm, uh . . ." Jessie wasn't really putting the moves on her, at least not intentionally. She just—well—he was just being natural and regretting making that promise now.

"Let's get some food," she said.

They ordered Cokes and a large cheese pizza, knowing from past experience that she'd eat only two of the many squares Fauci's cut their pizzas into, and that Jessie would eat the rest.

"So what do you do for girls up there?" Rose asked.

Jessie snorted. "They have dances and lots of girls come from the town, but—"

"But what?" When Jessie didn't answer right away, she asked, "What's the problem?"

"All the girls are white." Understanding dawned on Rose's face as Jessie continued. "They have a problem with blacks even talking to white girls—a big problem." He forced a grin. "It's like they know black men are the best lovers and white boys can't compete."

Rose batted her eyelashes. "Oh really?"

Jessie's grin became genuine. "It's a fact."

"I didn't know that," she said, flirting.

"I tried to tell you, girl, when we was going out," Jessie said. "But you wouldn't listen."

"You were a great kisser."

"I kind of thought so myself."

Rose burst out laughing. "That ain't what you're supposed to say. You was supposed to tell me I was a great kisser too."

Jessie smirked. "You were okay. I put up with you."

Rose swatted at his arm. "Best kisser you ever had."

Jessie smiled broadly and stared into those brown eyes so filled with laughter, and he never wanted to leave. *If time would only freeze*, Jessie wished. They'd never walk out the door, never go back to their separate houses, and he'd never go back to Springvale Academy.

"Why you lookin' so sad?" Rose asked.

"'Cause I can't stay here forever with you."

"Ain't you the charmer."

"No, I mean it. Sometimes up there I feel so lonely. If you were there . . ." Jessie shook his head. "I think of you during the dances. I'd give anything to have you around, 'specially during the slow numbers."

"It's three hours away. I can't—" Rose shook her head. "What am I saying? We ain't even going out anymore. If Leroy heard me talking like this—"

"Does he treat you good?"

"He's okay."

"But?"

A bittersweet smile came over her face. "He ain't nothing like you. You were my Romeo, my one and only."

Jessie felt a stab in his heart. "I'll be back this summer. Maybe I won't even go back after New Year's and just stay here with you." He stopped, his eyes widening. That had slipped out before he'd even realized he was thinking it.

"You go back," she said, her eyes pooling with tears. "You got to. It's your whole future that's waiting for you."

But Jessie didn't care about his future just then. Not about the NHL or Harvard or Yale, or anything but right now and those beautiful deep brown eyes staring at him.

"If it's meant to be," Rose said, "we'll get back together some day."

Jessie nodded but he sure didn't feel it. Somewhere

deep inside he knew they were going in separate directions. Maybe before he left, they'd been meant to be. But not now, not anymore.

Rose bolted out of her seat, took his face in her hands and kissed him long and hard.

Then she pulled away, said, "I have to go," and ran out the door.

Jessie called Rose's house the next day and every day after that until he left for school. Each time, her mother said that she was out, but in a tone that told him quite the opposite.

But Jessie didn't blame Rose one bit.

●

Jessie's parents drove him back to school on New Year's Day, arriving at a campus so empty and quiet that their every footstep echoed. Only the hockey and basketball teams, playing in holiday tournaments, had returned early. Stick, at least a year away from contributing to the basketball team—if ever—wouldn't be back until everyone else returned.

The hockey team looked rusty in its one warm-up practice, but they sprang into high gear in the first tournament game, winning 7-1 and stretching its undefeated streak to thirteen by the time it won the tourney's championship game. Over the course of the five games in three days, Jessie scored four goals and assisted on another five, three by Frenchie. The two had clicked right from the start, each seeming to know where the other was going to be before he even got there. Dirk, having completed his ten-game suspension, returned and showed why he'd earned his All-New England honors for the past three years. He also left Jessie alone.

Jessie could tell that Coach Stone, Dirk, Rocco, and a dozen or so others still hated him, but they were keeping quiet about it because he had taken over the team lead in scoring. Dirk didn't speak a word to Jessie, but his eyes still smoldered with hatred and distaste, same as Coach Stone.

The rest of the team seemed to have tentatively accepted Jessie, like they'd put their toes in a lake and decided the water was warm enough to keep going. But he didn't fool himself. He knew it wouldn't take much to lose them, and that only Frenchie stood solidly in his corner.

At night, visions flashed through Jessie's mind of Rose in her light blue blouse, so pretty he could barely stand it. He felt her lips on his and wondered what he was doing here at Springvale, so far from home, so far from Rose, so far from his parents and all his friends.

It took stepping on the ice to remind him of why he was there.

Jessie's first semester report card had brightened his parents' faces when it arrived two days after Christmas. He'd gotten A's in Algebra and Biology, A– in U.S. History, and a B+ in both English and French. For all of fifteen minutes, they'd been so proud of what he'd accomplished at such a prestigious school. Then they'd begun talking about what it would take to pull up those two B+ grades, even though they knew English and French were his weakest subjects.

But now, a week into the second semester, Jessie was worried he wouldn't be able to match his first semester's results, much less get straight A's. A mountain of homework waited for him every night after practice, and tonight he had a problem set in Algebra that looked a mile long, plus a ton of Biology definitions to memorize for tomorrow's quiz. The deadlines for his term papers in U.S. History and English were rapidly approaching.

Ready to pounce on his homework without a second of delay, he opened the door to the dorm room.

"Hey," he said to Stick.

Jessie walked straight to his desk and sat down.

"Man, you got a second?"

"One second, Stick. That's about it." Jessie reached for his Algebra textbook. "I got homework coming outta my ears."

Stick didn't say anything.

Jessie looked up.

A look of panicked desperation covered Stick's face. "You gotta help me, man."

Red alarms went off in Jessie's head. "What do you need?"

Stick swallowed. "Help with my homework."

"What's the problem?"

"I can't do it."

A feeling of dread crept over Jessie. "What subject?"

Stick looked out the window. "All of 'em."

"All of 'em? I can't . . . I mean, I got so much to do—" Jessie shook his head. "What happened to your tutor?"

"He gone."

"He left school?"

"No. He still here." Stick sucked in a deep breath. "He just not tutoring me anymore."

"Why not?"

"Athletic department ain't payin' him anymore. Some football fan in town—they call him a booster—paid for my tutorin' last semester. Another guy, a basketball booster, was supposed to pay this semester, but now that I got hurt, he ain't payin'. He say he ain't never seen me play, and I ain't gonna play this year, maybe never, so why should he pay? That's what he say."

Jessie thought back to when Stick had hobbled into the room a week earlier, ready to start the new semester. His momma had come in behind him.

"Hi, Jessie," she'd said and chuckled. "Or should I call you Black Einstein?"

Jessie grinned. "Stick exaggerates."

"Well, you must be a good influence on my boy. He say he's studyin' all the time." She nodded. "And he got the grades to prove it. I was afraid when his report card come in the mail, but he did *fine*. For a school like this, he did *amazing*. All B's and C's!"

Jessie just nodded.

"I mean," she continued, "he's no Black Einstein, but grades like that at a place like this?"

"I told you I been studyin' hard," Stick said, giving Jessie the eye.

"Yeah," Jessie said. Unable to resist, he said, "You should've seen him get ready for final exams. He studied so hard, he practically knew the answers before the teachers even handed out the questions."

Stick shot him a warning look and Jessie kept a straight face while fighting back a grin at Stick's discomfort.

"I never thought—" Stick's momma began and then stopped, choked up. Her eyes welled with tears. "I never thought I'd see the day when my boy could get an education like this." She dabbed at her eyes with a handkerchief. "He's not gonna have to be no janitor or garbage man or nothin' like that. He's gonna be the first one in our family to go to college. Then he can do anything!"

Jessie had felt suddenly sick to his stomach, knowing

the poor woman's hopes were all an illusion. He'd looked at Stick, who had forced a sick grin, just like now.

"You gotta help me, man," Stick said again. "I can't do this stuff by myself."

Jessie pulled his chair up to Stick's desk, knowing he didn't have a minute to spare himself, but unable to ignore Stick's plea for help.

"I gotta be fast," Jessie said. "You wouldn't believe how much homework *I* got."

"Thanks, man."

As Jessie cracked open a math book that showed remarkably little wear, he could only think of Harry Edwards and how that angry man had gotten it all so right. Stick's usefulness to the athletic department had ended, so they'd discarded him like a used rag.

●

That weekend, Jessie returned from a road trip to find Stick's half of the room empty. His bed was stripped and all his clothes were gone, along with the record albums from his bookshelves. Only a pile of textbooks remained on his desk, with a single sheet of paper on top.

Jessie's heart sank. He walked slowly to Stick's desk and with a trembling hand picked up the sheet of paper.

Einstein,
I may be dumb but I ain't stupid. I drowning, man, and I be taking you down with me. No matter how hard I try to

swim, I still going down. No sense pulling you under with me.

Ain't that one of them metaphors or similes? See? I been trying.

But I ain't never catching up. You know it. I know it. Everybody know it.

Hope you make the NHL, man. Show all them white folk a little of your Black magic, if you know what I mean. Just like the old Stick.

Black magic, man. Use your Black magic.
Your friend,
Stick

PS When you a millionaire, come see me and I help you spend it. Ha ha.

●

Jessie couldn't get Stick out of his mind. He could see the sly grin and the toothpick bobbing, could hear the hearty chuckle and the constant stream of Motown records. He thought about Stick's sense of humor, and how he'd pretended to lock Jessie out while he showered on that first day rooming together. He saw again how Stick nearly set off a riot when he'd said, "I like white women." And of course, Stick's famous Black Magic.

The room felt like a funeral home without him. Time after time, Jessie walked to the telephone, ready to call Stick and tell him he'd made a mistake, that he should come back before it was too late, that he'd help him get by.

But had it been a mistake? Did Stick stand any chance of catching up to everyone else without extensive help, far more help than any one student could offer? It was one thing to dash off a lower-track English paper or scribble down answers to math problems like Stick's tutor had done, but it was quite another thing to teach someone without the basic skills on how to do it themselves.

Stick didn't have a chance. He'd never had a chance since he'd gotten here. He was too far behind to ever catch up, and pretending otherwise didn't change that sad reality.

So each time Jessie got up to make the call, he returned to his chair and slunk down in it without having dialed the number. With a hollow feeling in his gut, Jessie tried to focus on the term papers due on Monday, papers he'd let slide while he'd been helping Stick.

Eventually, the panic of that deadline kicked in and turned his concentration from Stick's plight to his own. If he didn't get words onto the page and fast, he'd be in big trouble. Pushing all other thoughts aside, Jessie took a deep breath and cleared his mind to write.

By lights-out time on Sunday night, he'd finished both terms papers and his Algebra problem set. Exhausted but relieved, he closed his books and set them aside.

Then, shoulders slumping and tears welling in his eyes, Jessie also closed the book on Stick, just as society had done to him years ago.

35

The winning streak hit nineteen games and showed no signs of ending anytime soon. Though racial slurs hurtled out of the crowd every now and then during road games and plenty of opponents had tried to get Jessie off his game with similar tactics, there'd been no repeat of the Oak Ridge episode.

Jessie and Frenchie continued to fill the net, working so well together, but they made for an odd pairing off the ice. They'd sit together on the bus, and if the team had to stay over between Friday and Saturday night road games, they always roomed together. But Frenchie never seemed to talk much and the only thing they had in common was hockey. It was nothing like how it'd been rooming with Stick.

Loneliness covered Jessie like a thick fog. He missed Stick, the empty room hollow with his absence. Jessie missed Rose, too, often falling asleep with the memory of her tearful kiss at Fauci's Pizza. He missed his parents, too. The end of the semester seemed very far away.

But he'd get there, Jessie told himself. Study, then play hockey, then more studying.

•

With a dozen games remaining before the New England Championships, Springvale Academy appeared destined to enter as the number-one seed and odds-on favorite, at least that's how it'd looked until the game against Canterbury.

Late in the second period, it seemed no different from the games that had preceded it. Springvale led 4-1, with both Jessie and Frenchie scoring goals. The game was all but won, when Shep made a routine save and directed the puck to Nick on the left side. As Nick passed up to Frenchie along boards, Jessie cut toward the middle at center ice. Frenchie hit him with a perfect pass, Jessie caught it in stride and was off to the races. With a half a step lead on the nearest defender, no one was going to catch him.

He flew over the blue line, his head up, reading the goaltender who'd come out of his crease to cut down the angle. With the defender whacking at his legs from behind, Jessie bore in on the net. If the goalie backed in to the crease too fast, he'd shoot at whatever opening was available. If the goalie challenged him, he'd deke.

Almost on top of the crease, Jessie deked to his forehand, not just with his head but with his head, shoulders, and the puck. The goalie moved, and, never slowing down, Jessie shifted the puck to his backhand and stuffed it into the open net. As it slid across the line, a stick yanked

Jessie's legs out from under him and he flew face-first into the crossbar, his forehead slamming against the cold iron.

The sound of the impact echoed inside his head. Blinding white light flashed and pain stabbed behind his eyes.

Then everything went black.

●

When Jessie came to, cold, white needles of pain shot through his forehead and eyes. He groaned and muffled crowd noise echoed in his head, each reverberation setting off sharp new spasms of pain. He tried to sit up, but something held him down like a giant's hand on his chest. Jessie groaned again, then winced at the painful sound of his own voice.

He opened his eyes, but all he could see was blinding, bright white light. Terror gripped him and he wondered, *Was he blind?* He closed his eyes in panic, then slowly and fearfully he opened them again. As the lights flashed across his field of vision, he made out the gray lockers, each one obscured by the brightness that covered everything like a thick, sparkling fog. Above the lockers, depending on how he cocked his head, he could detect fragments of the Warriors' logo, able to see an eye or the nose or the mouth, but none of the rest of the face and none at the same time.

The locker room's familiar sweat-laden, musty odors came to him, along with an even stronger, more pungent disinfectant smell. He groaned as nausea wracked his stomach.

He couldn't lift his arms. Panic washed over him. *Was*

he paralyzed? Icy chills ran down his spine. Was he paralyzed? He wanted to scream but couldn't.

In the midst of his blinding terror and shock, Jessie tried to thrash, to do anything just to try and move. He felt a rocking sensation and heard a creaking noise, and even as that set off new waves of nausea, he let out a relieved breath.

So he could move after all—he wasn't paralyzed. Jessie probed around him with his fingers and discovered that he was lying on something—a stretcher. He was strapped down on a stretcher—now it all made sense. That was why he couldn't sit up or lift his hands.

Jessie wished they hadn't strapped him down. His forehead itched and felt wet and sticky. Was that blood? He wanted to reach up and touch it.

A door opened. "Over here," a familiar voice said, loud enough to set off new waves of pain inside Jessie's skull. The distant crowd noise, no longer muffled by the door, grew louder. He groaned.

Four strangers surrounded him, their faces awash in the streaks of bright white light that persisted in Jessie's field of vision. He only recognized Mr. Chase, the assistant coach and trainer. Jessie tensed.

"Don't worry," one of the strangers said with a kind smile. Jessie cocked his head this way and that, like a bird looking for a worm, so he could see past the white flashes. The stranger was a middle-aged white man with salt-and-pepper hair, big jowls, and a pronounced beer belly. "We're just going to get you to the hospital. You took a good hit to the head, but we're going to take care of you."

Jessie thought the man's smile was meant to be reassuring, but Jessie didn't feel comforted at all. He couldn't see right, and he felt as if someone had crushed his head with a sledge hammer.

Mr. Chase bent over, a look of grave concern on his face. "Is there anything I can do for you, Jessie?"

Jessie licked his lips; his mouth felt so dry. "Call my parents, please." They drove up for almost all his weekend games, sometimes arriving late on Friday, but the Wednesday games, like today's, were almost impossible for them because of their work. Jessie was sure they'd be at his bedside as soon as Pop's Plymouth Fury could carry them. "My Pop is a doctor—please tell him what happened." Jessie winced; enough talking. Anything more wasn't worth it.

The stranger and Mr. Chase exchanged glances and Mr. Chase nodded.

"Okay, we're going to pick you up now," the stranger said. "We'll carry you out to the ambulance."

Jessie flashed back to his last trip to the hospital, when he was sent there by the hooded thugs from the town who'd beaten him senseless. He wondered if the unmasked face of one of those thugs would match one of these strangers. He tensed as the four men lifted him up. If there was a match, what were the chances of them dropping him?

●

The strangers got him to the hospital without dropping him once, either intentionally or accidentally. Three hours later, Momma and Pop were hovering over his bed. The smell of disinfectant filled the room and equipment around his bed beeped. Nurses squeaked up and down the hall in their rubber-soled shoes.

An intravenous drip provided Jessie with fluids and medications and his vision had returned to normal, all the flashing lights gone. He could speak now without spasms of pain boring through his head.

Momma, smelling of lilac perfume and talcum powder, bent over and kissed him on the cheek. "My poor boy," she said. "What am I going to do with you?"

Pop, standing beside the bed, patted Jessie's leg. "They were concerned about a fractured skull," Pop said. His frown deepened and he pursed his lips. "That would have been very dangerous. I can't tell you how concerned I was when they told me about it over the phone." He drew air in through his nose. "But you were very lucky."

"I don't understand why they don't have better helmets," Momma said. "Those things are so flimsy."

"The helmet wasn't the problem," Jessie said. "It doesn't cover the forehead."

"Why not?" his mother asked. "It should cover your whole face—the forehead, your eyes, and your mouth. I don't understand it. You have such a nice smile, and I just know that sooner or later you're going to get your teeth knocked out. Or, Lord forbid, an eye."

"In the NHL, most of the players don't wear a helmet at all," Jessie said, preparing to argue that he was doing all he could to protect himself.

But Momma would have none of it. "Look at them— all their teeth are knocked out. Stitches all over their faces, and what about that poor fellow who died? What was his name?"

Jessie winced. "Bill Masterson." Just a year earlier, Masterson had died of head injuries so severe that doctors hadn't even been able to operate on him. Nothing that bad had ever happened before in the NHL—the guy had died!—but it had been an eye-opener for Jessie, who'd always played on the ponds back home without his helmet.

It had been an even bigger eye-opener for Jessie's mother. She'd fixated on the injury and told him she'd sell all his equipment if she ever caught him without a helmet again. That reminder spooked Jessie. How close had he just come to suffering the same fate as Masterson?

"We have a decision to make here," Pop said.

Jessie's heart fluttered. "What decision is that?"

"You were lucky to suffer only a concussion, but it was a major one. You were unconscious for something like five minutes this time."

Jessie sat up and winced, then tried to cover it up. He knew what Pop was going to say.

"Sit back, son," Pop said. "We're not going to arm wrestle to decide."

"But—"

"Two major concussions in the span of a couple months is a concern. In fact, it's a major issue. But I'm not going to tell you to give up hockey."

"*I* would," Momma interrupted.

Alarm bells went off in Jessie's head. He hadn't thought this would ever be a topic of discussion. He could no more envision giving up hockey than he could give up breathing. Jessie couldn't believe his ears.

Momma continued, "I'll have you know that we argued about this almost all the way up here. I can't see that any sport is worth this kind of a risk, no matter how much you enjoy it."

"Momma," Jessie pleaded. "You don't understand. I don't just *enjoy* hockey like I might enjoy spaghetti and meatballs, or watching a TV show." He fumbled for words to describe how he felt. "Hockey is part of me. It's in my blood and I could *never* give it up."

Momma cocked her head. "You will if we say so, young man."

Pop touched a hand to her elbow. "We aren't saying so, Jessie." Momma gave Pop a disgusted look, but he continued as if he hadn't noticed. "If something like this happens again, we'll have grave concerns and might have to—"

"It was a freak accident," Jessie protested.

"We understand that," Pop said. "This kind of injury might never happen to you again. But if it does, we'll cross that bridge when we come to it. What we do have to decide right now is whether you'll play again this year."

"I've got to," Jessie blurted out. He'd known this was where Pop had been heading all along. "This is too important to me. I've worked so hard for this. I've gone through so much to get here." Realizing that the last thing he wanted to do was bring up the lynching episode, Jessie quickly moved on. "We're gonna be the number-one seed and I could be part of winning the New England Championships. Do you have any idea what that means?"

"We know, Jessie, but—"

"I don't think you do. I work and I work and I work to

make myself better. Now I have a chance to win a championship, one that really means something, not like the little ones back home. This is special." He wracked his brain for the right angle. "I owe it to my teammates. I'm the top scorer and they're depending on me." Jessie's words felt false somehow and they sounded that way, too. He didn't really care about most of his teammates. He'd go to war for Frenchie, and Taylor wasn't bad, and neither were the guys who'd accepted him once he'd shown how strong of a player he was. But close to half the team still disliked him just because he was black, and almost all the rest of them had changed their attitudes only because he dominated game after game. If he'd been mediocre, those guys would've stood with Dirk and the rest of his clan.

Jessie had to be honest. He wasn't playing for his teammates. He didn't owe it to them to come back. He was playing for Frenchie and for himself, and for his love of the game. All the rest of them could go take a hike.

Pop cleared his throat. "I don't think—"

Suddenly inspiration hit Jessie. "The playoffs is when all the college recruiters will be watching," Jessie said. And he knew instantly he'd scored a bull's-eye.

"If I can get their attention as a freshman, they're definitely gonna start thinking about me. But if I'm the guy who lets his team down, that only makes me look bad."

Jessie let that last part sink in; he knew his mother was probably a lost cause, but he could tell it was working with Pop.

"I won't come back too fast," Jessie said. "I promise. I did exactly what you said last time, didn't I?"

Pop breathed deeply. "Yes, I believe you did."

"If I'm not having headaches or any other symptoms, and if I can do full workouts without getting dizzy or anything, I should play. *Please*. I promise not to do anything until I'm ready."

Momma shook her head. "I can't believe what I'm hearing." She glared at Pop. "I might as well not be here at all, for all it matters what I say. You two are going to make your decisions and ignore me, just like always."

"We don't ignore you," Pop said.

"How about right now?" she said.

"Momma, we're just going by majority rule. It's a democracy."

Momma fixed him with a glare. "I'll democracy your behind if I hear another word out of you."

Jessie held his tongue. The only way he could lose now was by opening his big mouth and saying the wrong thing. He'd just clamp his hand over it if that's what it took.

Pop breathed in loudly and said, "We're going to give this a try." Jessie almost burst with glee, but restrained himself when he looked at Momma's burning anger.

His father continued. "You'll come back only if you meet all the medical conditions I lay out for you, and not one minute sooner. Do you understand?"

"Yes," Jessie said.

Momma pursed her lips and shook her head. "Child, if you get killed, don't come cryin' to me." And with that, she stomped out of the room.

Jessie couldn't wipe the huge smile off his face. "Thanks, Pop. I won't let you down."

"If you cut any corners . . ." Pop's eyes twinkled. "I swear, I'll have your momma democracy your behind."

36

The headaches wouldn't go away. Jessie could only walk to practice and stand on the bench in his street clothes, glum and forlorn as he watched everyone else go through the paces. In Biology, Mr. Nordstrom had described how a scientist named Pavlov had rung a bell every time he was about to feed his dogs. Soon, the ringing of that bell would be enough to get the dogs salivating. In the same way, when Jessie heard the familiar sounds of the rink, his body responded. The loud *thwack* of a hard shot hitting the glass behind the net made his fingertips tingle with the urge to rip off a shot that echoed even louder. Two players crashing into the boards made Jessie's shoulders tense as he thought of delivering an even harder, more bone-crushing check himself.

Even Coach Stone's shrill whistle that on bad days seemed to drive pinpricks into Jessie's skull, made his legs tense for a quick takeoff on the next drill. He felt like one of Pavlov's dogs who could only salivate. There'd be no meat for him to sink his teeth into as long as he still had the headaches.

Game days were the worst of all. As he sat in the locker room, smelling the sweat and liniment, his equipment still hanging behind him from its hooks, adrenaline surged in Jessie that had no release. He wanted to scream in frustration.

Though Frenchie would offer a "hang in there," and for a while, Taylor asked how he was doing, the rest of the team began to treat him like a leper. He heard the whispers, such as *He isn't tough. They don't gut it out like us. They're lazy. They won't pay the price.* Sometimes he overheard the whispers accidentally, coming back from the bathroom and hearing a few words before the conversation ceased. At other times, the words were spoken just loud enough so he'd be sure to hear them. *I don't care how many goals he's scored, he's ruined this team. He's a prima donna. They all are. It's all about them, not the team.* With every game Jessie missed, the more the resentful looks hardened.

It didn't help that Sully kept separating his shoulder and popping it back in. He shaved his chest and shoulder so that the yards of tape could be used to try and hold him together until the season was over and he could have surgery. Guys would look from Sully to Jessie and make the obvious connection. Sully would suck it up for the team, while Jessie, the *prima donna*, the self-centered Negro, would not, as if injuring a shoulder and a brain were equally serious.

Jessie called home frequently, speaking to Pop and hearing the same words. "You can't even think about coming back until the headaches, dizziness, and nausea are gone. Then you have to be able to exercise without any of those symptoms returning. Don't you *dare* get on the ice before then."

"I won't," Jessie promised. "I won't."

But Jessie couldn't help thinking about it, especially after Rocco tore up his knee and was gone for the season. The offense had dropped off when Jessie left the lineup; the team lost not only his own goals, but Frenchie's effectiveness had plummeted as well. Now, with Rocco on crutches and Sully hampered by his shoulder, the team couldn't put the puck in the net.

●

After a loss to Belmont Hill put Springvale's playoff hopes in doubt, Mr. Chase took Jessie aside. Standing in a hallway outside the locker room, he said, "Jessie, I know your father's a doctor, so I've stayed out of this, but we're in trouble. We might not make the playoffs and that *never* happens here. So as the team trainer, it's my responsibility to take charge. Whether you play or not is my call, not your father's."

Jessie blinked. "Excuse me?"

"The trainer decides whether a player is healthy enough to compete," Mr. Chase said. "It's that way in every sport."

Jessie was stunned. It didn't take ESP to guess what was going to happen next.

"You've been without headaches and dizziness for a few days now," Mr. Chase said. "Your motor skills appear to be fine."

"But I can't ride the stationary bike for more than three minutes without having to puke. My pop says—"

"Your pop isn't making the decisions anymore. I am," Mr. Chase said, his jaw set. "I've spoken with Coach Stone about this and the new plan of action is for you to suit up for practice tomorrow. Take it easy and just skate around—no contact. You'll wear a red jersey to signal you're not to be hit. Then we'll see how that goes."

The familiar acid steam burned inside Jessie, building pressure and eating away at his gut.

"No," was all Jessie said.

Mr. Chase's eyes widened and his eyebrows shot up. "No? Jessie, this isn't a request. I'm in charge here and I've been patient with you long enough. This is an order."

"My pop says—"

"Your pop is not making the decisions!"

Jessie glared. "Okay, you're right—he isn't. I am."

Mr. Chase reddened.

Jessie swallowed. "And I'm listening to my pop. I trust him a lot more than you or anyone else in this place."

Mr. Chase's eyes narrowed. "You will dress for practice tomorrow as I've directed you or your athletic scholarship will be revoked."

●

Jessie headed straight for the headmaster's office. He hated to run to Mr. Whitney again, but he had no choice. He walked into the foyer outside the office, saw no one there, and stepped inside the open door.

Mr. Whitney looked up from where he stood behind his desk, his face pale. A box sat before him on his desk and, with hands visibly shaking, he picked up the photograph of his family that had always sat next to the phone. He placed it in the box.

"How did you find out?" he asked.

A sense of dread came over Jessie. He'd never seen this confident man looking so shaken.

"Find out what?" Jessie asked.

Mr. Whitney looked down at the floor and blinked rapidly, then drew in a deep breath. "I suppose you'll find out soon enough."

"Find out what?" Jessie asked, but he knew the answer.

Tight-lipped, Mr. Whitney said, "The board of trustees has fired me, effective immediately."

"How could they do that?"

"They can and they did."

"But why?"

Mr. Whitney's shoulders sagged. "At a school like this, you have to choose your friends carefully and your enemies wisely. I made the wrong enemies, Jessie. Powerful ones." He snorted. "The board let me know who's really running things around here."

"But I thought the headmaster ran everything. I thought you were the boss."

"Yes and no." Mr. Whitney looked away and suddenly the ticking grandfather clock sounded like a banging drum. The lights from the chandelier seemed to flicker, giving the polished brass fixtures a tarnished look.

"I run the school on a day-to-day basis, but the Board of Trustees hired me and they can fire me. Some alumni, especially those who've made large donations, have a great deal of influence with the board, as do a very few select individuals working here." Mr. Whitney gave Jessie a knowing look.

"You mean Coach Stone?"

Mr. Whitney nodded. "He wasn't the only one, but he was the biggest one—my number-one enemy." Mr. Whitney closed his eyes and shook his head. "I knew I was taking a chance when I locked horns with him."

A chill ran down Jessie's spine. "So I got you fired."

Startled, Mr. Whitney returned from whatever distant place his thoughts had taken him. "No." He looked away for an instant before his eyes returned to Jessie's. "You had *nothing* to do with this."

Guilt crushed Jessie as he realized that Mr. Whitney was lying to protect him, to keep him from feeling exactly what he felt now. If Mr. Whitney had admitted that Jessie was a part of his downfall, Jessie would have believed him. But to admit that Stone had been his number-one enemy, and at the same time say that his fights to defend Jessie had nothing to do with his firing, didn't make any sense.

"I'm so sorry," Jessie said. "I feel awful."

Seeming to sense that Jessie had figured out the deception, Mr. Whitney said, "Okay, you had something to do with this. But you shouldn't feel guilty about it anymore than I feel guilty about what I've done here. You were in the right and I was in the right. But righteousness doesn't always win out, at least not in the beginning. I can still hold my head high, and I will. This school can step back into the Dark Ages if it wants to, but I did the right thing and so did you. You keep holding your head high, Jessie, no matter what happens."

Jessie searched for words. "What will you do now?"

"Search for another job. I'll be fine." His face darkened. "But I'm concerned about you. The old headmaster will be returning on an interim basis while a search is conducted for my replacement. I'm afraid he's not a supporter of equality and integration. In fact, he's just the opposite. He'll only be here for the rest of this school year, but I'd expect that the board will name someone who thinks like he does. It's the way this school has operated for close to a century." He shook his head. "If you think Springvale Academy has treated you poorly at times . . . it's only going to get worse."

Jessie swallowed hard.

Mr. Whitney lifted a memo pad out of the box and waved it. "I've got your parents' phone number and address written down. I'll talk to them about possible options you might want to consider if you decide not to return here next year."

He gestured feebly. "If the changes take place that I expect, you'll probably want to go elsewhere." He shook his head. "What am I saying? If those changes take place, you'll definitely want to go elsewhere. Life here will become hell for you. It might not be safe."

Jessie had to sit down, his thoughts darting in a thousand different directions. *Not safe. Life here will become hell. Go elsewhere. It's only going to get worse.* This was all his fault. The weight of it pressed down on him and he put his head in his hands.

A hand rested on his shoulder. "Don't feel bad about this."

Jessie looked up through teary eyes.

"You did what was right," Mr. Whitney said. "I'll repeat that until you promise me you won't *ever* feel bad about doing what's right. Feel guilt only when you've done something wrong or failed to do what was right.

"You've got a bright future ahead of you, Jessie. Promise me that you'll make the most of it."

Jessie nodded.

"If you want to think that I've sacrificed something for you, make sure that my sacrifice wasn't in vain."

Jessie's voice was choked with emotion. "I will, sir."

A funeral-like silence fell between them and after a while, Jessie got up to leave.

"I'm sorry," Mr. Whitney said. "Why did you come to see me?" He waved his hands helplessly. "Not that I can do anything for you now."

Jessie described his conversation with Mr. Chase, then said, "I was going to ask you about my athletic scholarship."

Mr. Whitney snorted. "Ironic, isn't it? The same people who wanted to keep you off the ice are now threatening to force you back on it faster than is safe for you."

Jessie hadn't thought about it that way; it made about as much sense as a lot of racist thinking.

Mr. Whitney pondered the problem for a while, then finally said, "The payments have already gone in for this semester. It's too late for them to take that away from you. But they can cancel next year's scholarship." He smiled sourly. "I guess they've given you yet another reason to look elsewhere."

Jessie nodded somberly.

"In the meantime," Mr. Whitney said, "listen to your father and stay off the ice."

37

Coach Stone's cigarette tip glowed as he drew in one last, long drag. He exhaled a big cloud of smoke in Jessie's direction, then stubbed the cigarette out. Jessie's nose twitched and he stifled a cough.

Stone rested his elbows on his large oak desk and leaned forward. He pointed to Mr. Chase, sitting off to the side. "Coach Chase here has cleared you to play. He says you should be practicing. So why am I not seeing you out there?"

Jessie had decided beforehand that he'd be as respectful as possible, filling every sentence with a "sir," even though he didn't respect either of the coaches. Stone was evil and Chase a pathetic, slobbering yes-man, unable to do anything without Stone's approval.

"I'm not ready, sir," Jessie said. "I'm dying to get out there and play, but I can't do it yet."

"Doesn't look to me like you're dying to play. You look plenty comfortable, sitting in the stands and taking it easy. In my day we were tough. I got knocked out cold many times. As soon as the smelling salts revived me, I'd be right back out there."

Jessie resisted the impulse to say, "I guess that explains why you're crazy."

Stone opened his mouth and pulled out bridgework that included his eight front teeth. He waved it around like a flag, then opened his mouth to show a wide, toothless gap. He pushed the teeth back in, then ran his tongue across them. "Lost all of those diving in front of a shot. Hurt like hell, but I never missed a shift."

He slammed a fist down on the table, making both Jessie and Mr. Chase jump. "So I don't want to hear any excuses about how you're not ready to play. You suck it up and get ready to play, or else face the consequences."

"With all due respect, sir, I can't. I need to be able to exercise for an extended period without any of the symptoms returning. The headaches and dizziness are gone, but the nausea is still hitting me hard and I need more time."

"Nausea?" Stone practically spit the words out. He looked at Mr. Chase. "Nausea? A poor little unsettled stomach is keeping a hockey player out of the lineup? What is this, a little girls' team? Chase, is this a girls' team?"

"No, sir," Chase said.

"When I was here, my coach didn't think his drills were tough enough if he didn't have half the team puking by the end of every practice." Stone looked at Jessie with disgust. "That's the problem with you people. Some of you are great athletes, I've got to give you that much. But you've got none of this." Stone pounded his chest. "You've got no heart. If you had even half a heart, you'd be out there on the ice."

Jessie fought to stay cool, the acid inside him simmering as his stomach churned. "With all due respect, sir—"

Stone waved a hand dismissively. "Knock off the *sir* this and the *sir* that. We both know that you hate me and I hate you, but you need me and unfortunately I need you." Stone shifted in his chair. "So stop pretending to respect me—it just ticks me off."

Fair enough, Jessie thought, damping down the acid steam. "I don't mind puking. I've had games before I got here that I played with the flu. After every shift I threw up into a bag until I didn't have anything left inside me. One shift, I didn't quite make it back to the bench and someone had to scrape the vomit off the ice." Jessie's cheeks puckered up as he recalled the sour taste. "Puking isn't the problem. My pop says—"

Mr. Chase jumped in. "Your pop—"

But Stone waved his objection aside.

Jessie continued. "My pop says that it's an indication that the brain hasn't healed yet and until it heals, it isn't safe to play. The risk of brain damage is too great."

Stone exhaled loudly. He gritted his teeth, his huge jowls bulging. "I think you're forgetting something. You're the reason we're in this position, and it's high time you take responsibility for it. If you hadn't gone running to the headmaster"—the hint of a smile formed at the corner of his lips—"we wouldn't find ourselves in this position. Those suspensions over something that hadn't left you with so much as a scratch may have cost us the season. We've never started a season 1-3, at least not since World War II." He pointed at Jessie and squinted his eyes. "And that's *your* fault."

"With all due—" Jessie stopped himself, then said, "That's crap and you know it."

Stone's eyes widened in surprise. Chase looked to Stone, as if awaiting instructions.

Jessie pointed at Stone. "Dirk and his buddies were taking their orders from you. I don't know whether you actually told him what to do or if he came up with it by himself, but *you* set the tone. *You* made it clear I was to be driven out if at all possible. So if you want someone to blame for those suspensions, take a look in the mirror."

Stone's face had turned bright red.

But Jessie wasn't done. "You didn't even play me those first two games. That's how much of a genius you are." Jessie regretted those words as soon as they slipped out. But there was no taking them back. Stone rose to his feet, fists clenched even as Jessie added one more line. "If you'd told the team to accept me right from the beginning, we just might be undefeated right now."

"Go clean out your locker and don't ever come back," Stone bellowed. "Leave your jersey behind." He turned to Chase. "Have that locker fumigated. I don't want his replacement to catch even a hint of nigger left behind."

Jessie stood, burning with rage.

But Stone wasn't done. "Your athletic scholarship has been revoked. Tell your beloved *Pop*" — Stone spoke the word as if it were a fatal disease — "that he'll be getting a bill for the second semester."

Jessie wanted to hit the man and his mind screamed with everything he wanted to say, but he forced himself to stay as calm as he could manage.

"That's another lie," Jessie said. "You and I both know that all the payments and credits have already been processed for this semester. There's no bill to send any-where."

Stone's face turned so red, Jessie thought he'd explode. The coach pointed at the door with a shaking hand and said, "Get out of here."

●

Jessie opened his locker, the benches empty around him, the echoes of that afternoon's practice long gone. His eyes blurred with tears, not because he felt nostalgic over his times in this room, but rather because of the unfairness of it all. Sure, he should have kept his mouth shut. How many times had he told himself that? He wondered if he'd ever learn to shut up; no matter how hard he bit his tongue, sooner or later something slipped out that he regretted.

But was anything he'd said actually wrong? To keep him out of those early games, Stone had either been an idiot or a racist. Jessie suspected just the latter, but knew it could easily be both.

He tossed one piece of equipment after another into his bag, each one feeling like a piece of his tattered dreams being tossed away. He bit his lower lip and wondered if he should just pack the rest of his belongings and leave immediately.

The knock came on his door directly after dinner. Jessie got up from his desk, leaving his Biology textbook open, and walked to the door. He'd called home with the news, a depressing call that got Momma crying, just a day after the other depressing call about Mr. Whitney's firing. It seemed that these days, only the telephone company was happy.

"Who is it?"

"Franklin."

Franklin? From next door? What could he possibly want? Franklin was the least likely of people to knock on his door, especially since the novelty of black people living nearby had worn off for Preston. Neither he nor Franklin had spent a minute with either Jessie or Stick since the first week at Springvale and they'd seen each other only in passing, without sharing a single word or nod of acknowledgment.

But Jessie opened the door.

"Hello," Franklin said, his hair slicked back and his teeth still covered with braces.

"Hi."

An uncomfortable silence lasted for seconds that felt like minutes.

"May I come in?" Franklin asked. His glasses slid half an inch down his nose. With an index finger, he pushed them back up.

Jessie couldn't figure out why Franklin would *want* to come in or why he should let him, but Jessie shrugged and said, "Suit yourself." He pointed to Stick's chair, then realized it was covered with his own papers. When no one had moved into the other half of the room, Jessie had taken it over, laying clothes on what had been Stick's bed and spreading papers and books on his desk and chair. Jessie scooped the pile of papers off the chair and moved them to the bed.

"You didn't need to do that," Franklin said.

"It's okay," Jessie said. He didn't feel at all like talking to Franklin but didn't want to seem rude.

"How are things?" Franklin asked.

"Fine," Jessie said as he looked at his neighbor. His posture was as rigid as if an iron bar ran through his spine; his aristocratic nose held high, he was still wearing his blazer and tie, the only student he knew who didn't change into more casual clothes the instant classes were over for the day.

What did he want?

"Listen, I've got a lot of studying to do, so if you don't mind . . ."

"I've heard that things actually aren't fine for you, not at all. How's the concussion?"

317

"Fine."

"Really? Then why aren't you playing?"

Since when did he care? "Okay, I'm not fine," Jessie said. "Not really."

"But you just said—"

"I didn't want to talk about it," Jessie said, annoyed. "So I said I was fine."

Franklin gave a baffled look but said, "Fair enough."

"Listen, I've got a lot of studying—"

"Did I hear correctly that you've been kicked off the team?"

Jessie blinked. So the word was out. News traveled fast in this place. "Who told you?"

Franklin smiled, every tooth looking perfectly aligned, those braces soon to become a thing of the past. "I have my sources." The smile faded and an eyebrow arched. "Accurate sources, obviously."

Jessie said nothing.

"I heard it was disciplinary, for insubordination."

Jessie felt irritation creeping through him. "No, that's not true." Although in a way it was, Jessie realized. He just hadn't thought of it that way. "Stone and I disagreed over whether I was ready to return to the game after my concussion. My father is a doctor and I trust that he has my best interests at heart, surely more than a trainer who reports to Stone."

"Coach Stone?"

"Yeah."

"You don't show him the respect of his title?"

Jessie wanted to say that respect had to be earned, but

this time he kept his mouth shut. Which, of course, made no sense. He was locking the barn now that the horse had gotten out.

"You haven't seemed very happy here."

Jessie eyed Franklin, trying to weigh whether he should throw this odd intruder out or release all the venom that had built up inside him until Franklin ran for cover.

Jessie went with the venom.

"Not happy here?" Jessie asked, the anger in his voice already mounting. "Not happy in this miserable cesspool? Not happy? God, why wouldn't I be happy living here with New Hampshire's own chapter of the Ku Klux Klan? Why wouldn't I be happy playing for a coach whose large mounted photograph of George Wallace tells me exactly what he thinks of me and my people?

"I go to school dances where there isn't a black girl in sight, but God forbid I even look at a white one. The captain of my team and his buddies make me think they're going to lynch me, and when they're punished for it, somehow it's my fault.

"There may only be a dozen people in this whole school who are worth more than a bucket of warm spit. And one of those just got fired. The rest of them can all go to hell as far as I'm concerned."

Jessie was shouting now and didn't even care. Anger coursed through his veins and he went on. "Look at what this school did to Stick. They used him to get their undefeated football season, and then, when he tore up his knee, suddenly all his tutors were gone. They used him like . . . like toilet paper, then they flushed him away. Just like they'd do to me—if I let them."

319

Jessie paused for a moment, confused by Franklin's blank, emotionless stare, but then continued on. "He and I walked downtown once when we first got here—once. We never went back and you know why? We got the living crap beat out of us and the local Huckleberry Hound of a police chief just shrugged his shoulders. Good old boys, I guess, will be good old boys, even several hundred miles north of the Mason-Dixon line. I tell you, the only thing missing from this redneck town is enough sun for the peckerwoods to get a sunburn."

Heart pounding as he clenched and unclenched his fists, Jessie poured out his venom onto Franklin, who took it all in.

Within days, Franklin poured it back out for everyone to see.

●

Talking about Stick had reopened wounds, the scars of which had never healed. The book would never be fully closed on him and Stick. Even if they never saw each other again, Jessie suspected that the fleeting thought of what might have been and even worse, what never could have been, would pass his mind in the years and decades to come. If long distance didn't cost so much, Jessie would call him right now.

But what was there to say? *Hey man, I'm gone now, too. Springvale's Negro Experiment went 0-for-2. Oh, and by the way, how's your knee? Yeah, I was afraid of that.*

Jessie realized he'd just reread the same paragraph in

his Biology textbook five times and still had no idea what it said. Maybe he should switch to Algebra until he got his head together. That was easier to focus on.

Jessie had just opened the Algebra text when another knock came on his door. Again? Since Stick left, the room might as well been in Antarctica for all the visitors Jessie got. Now, two in one night?

"Who is it?"

Jessie had the sudden thought that Franklin might have returned for a follow-up to their bizarre conversation. If so, he wasn't getting into the room. Jessie would tell him in no uncertain terms that he had too much homework to talk anymore.

"It's Frenchie," came the reply.

Surprised, Jessie opened the door. As much magic as they might have worked on the ice together, they spent little time together outside practice and games, other than on road trips. As far as Jessie could tell, Frenchie hardly ever emerged from his room except for classes and hockey.

Jessie ushered Frenchie to the chair, then pulled a tin of cookies out of the bottom desk drawer. "Oatmeal and raisin. My mother baked them. They're good. Want one?"

Frenchie smiled as he took one. "Thanks."

Jessie took one himself, both to keep Frenchie company and also because they really *were* good. Jessie pointed to the door and the common room beyond. "I got milk in the fridge. Want a glass?"

Frenchie shook his head. "No thanks." He took a bite, nodded, and held the cookie up. "Good."

"Thanks."

Jessie debated whether to prod Frenchie along to see

what he wanted, but instead decided to let him choose his own pace. This was how conversations away from the rink seemed to go with the guy. Getting a word out of him felt like a lot of work.

"I hate it here," Frenchie finally blurted out.

Jessie thought of asking why, not because he couldn't think of the answer, but because the list of reasons ran so long. For Frenchie, the frustration with using a second language had to worsen the homesickness most students felt. Who knew, maybe back home, Frenchie was a complete blabbermouth, though Jessie had trouble picturing that.

"I'm leaving after the playoffs," Frenchie said. "Maybe even before."

"Before the playoffs?" Jessie asked. It was hard enough to believe Frenchie would consider leaving before the end of the semester; but that he might go before the end of the hockey season shocked him. "Why so fast?"

"Because I hate it here," Frenchie repeated, as if that truth should make the decision obvious.

And in a sense, it did. A senior would just tough it out, maybe even a junior. But a freshman? Why bother?

"It isn't much more than a month till the end of the season," Jessie said. He leaned forward ever so slightly and asked, "Are there problems at home?"

Frenchie cocked his head, as if not understanding the question. "No, Jessie, the problems are here."

"You got that right."

Frenchie shifted uncomfortably in the chair. "Did Stone really kick you off the team?"

"Sorry." Jessie groaned. "I thought you knew or I'd

have told you." When Frenchie said nothing, Jessie added, "Yeah, it's true."

"But why?"

Jessie explained what had happened, then Frenchie shook his head, dismay written all over his face.

"I'll leave now," he said. "There's no longer any reason for me to stay."

Jessie tried to offer some encouragement. "You guys can still win it. Any team can get hot at the right time." But the words sounded hollow even to Jessie.

Frenchie looked at him as if he were a fool but said nothing, apparently not willing to waste words on such nonsense.

"You won't be able to join any team back home this late in the year, would you?" Jessie asked.

Frenchie shrugged.

They sat there in awkward silence, Jessie not knowing what to say.

Finally, Frenchie spoke. "Would you come back?"

"Back here? If I'm healthy?"

Frenchie nodded.

"Stone isn't gonna let me come back."

Frenchie shrugged. "If he did?"

Jessie considered it. "Sure." It was a foolish hypothetical that would never happen, but he loved to play. "If I'm healthy," he added hastily. Two days in a row without a stick in his hand and skates on his feet were enough to drive him crazy this time of year.

"Good." Frenchie stood. "I'll talk to Coach Stone."

Jessie could only shake his head as Frenchie closed the door behind him.

39

Walking alone on his way to class two days later, the cold wind blowing in his face, Jessie met a succession of dirty looks. He wondered what people were so upset about. That he'd been kicked off the team? Wasn't that a reason for *him* to be upset?

Only after Mr. Richardson stopped him did Jessie figure it out. "Miserable cesspool, eh Stackhouse?" Mr. Richardson said.

"Miserable what?"

Mr. Richardson continued. "On a full scholarship and you'd say something like that." He shook his head and a sour look came over his face, as if he'd been sucking lemons. "Pretty ungrateful, if you ask me."

What was he talking about? And then it came to him. Franklin. Jessie remembered using that phrase with him, and apparently Franklin had blabbed it all over campus.

Taylor stopped Jessie outside the Freeman Humanities Building. "Am I one of the dozen?" Taylor asked, his arms folded, and his nostrils flaring.

"What?"

"I'd like to know if I'm one of the dozen who's worth a bucket of warm spit."

That had been another phrase Jessie'd used with Franklin. What else had Franklin spread around?

"Coach was right," Taylor said. "We're better off without you. You *are* a damned cancer."

He turned and walked away.

Jessie walked on, hurt and befuddled, until he saw a crowd gathered by a stack of school newspapers. Today was the day the *Springvale Record* came out. His heart sank. Faces buried in the paper looked up and turned away from him in disgust. One boy Jessie didn't recognize crumpled the paper into a ball and threw it at Jessie.

And the day was only just beginning.

●

Jessie caught his breath when he saw the excerpted quotes in boxed highlighted areas beside the front page story. In large bold face, one box read: "miserable cesspool" while another, larger one read: "There may only be a dozen people in the whole school who are worth more than a bucket of warm spit."

Jessie felt his jaw drop. With growing horror and rage, he read the story from beginning to end. By the third paragraph, his hands shook, blurring the words.

Stackhouse Suspended, Spouts Off
By Franklin Stoddard
The fortunes of the Springvale Academy varsity hockey team, winner of the last four New Eng-

land Championships, took yet another nosedive with the indefinite suspension of star freshman forward Jessie Stackhouse. The Warriors are now in danger of missing the tournament entirely for the first time in almost two decades.

"He's a talented player but one with disciplinary issues," legendary coach Frank Stone said. "We've had problems with him from the start, as most folks know. We can't have a player trying to run the team. This suspension is for insubordination. We'll take him back, but only under the right circumstances. He has to show that he's willing to be a team player and that everything doesn't revolve around him."

An interview conducted with Stackhouse illustrated vividly to this reporter why Coach Stone's patience finally wore thin.

The malcontent Negro recited a litany of complaints, ranging from the lack of black girls at an all-boys school to how his friend, Charles "Stick" Jones, was used, despite the assistance of tutors provided by the athletic department.

When asked how he felt, Stackhouse replied, "Fine," only to backtrack when reminded that he had missed six straight games to headaches and nausea, while senior co-captain John "Sully" Sullivan has continued to play with a separated shoulder. "I'm not fine," Stackhouse said. "Not really."

The outspoken freshman's assessment of Springvale Academy left nothing to the imagination. Despite receiving a full scholarship and a chance to escape a ghetto school with none of the amenities he has enjoyed since September, Stackhouse displayed no gratitude for his good fortune. Instead, he referred to the school as a "miserable cesspool" that is a "chapter of the Ku Klux Klan." (One wonders how many full scholarships other Klan chapters offer to prospective black students.)

However, his attitude toward the school was best summed up when he said, "There may only be a dozen people in the whole school who are worth more than a bucket of warm spit. The rest of them can all go to hell as far as I'm concerned." (This reporter apologizes to sensitive readers for the rough language.)

Stackhouse didn't even spare the townspeople of Springvale from his wrath, even though they have cheered his exploits on the ice all season long.

"The only thing missing from this redneck town is enough sun for the peckerwoods to get a sunburn," Stackhouse said.

It is easy for this reporter to see why the hockey team has been so deeply divided this year, failing to reach their usually lofty record largely because of the turmoil surrounding Stackhouse before the very first game was played.

It is this reporter's opinion that the hockey team, the school, and the town of Springvale will breathe a sigh of relief when Stackhouse is gone for good.

●

Jessie trembled with rage. Was there a single fact that Franklin hadn't twisted or distorted? Had a single quote not been taken out of context?

Jessie crumpled the newspaper and slammed it into the nearest trash can. Was there any point in his staying at Springvale any longer? If Taylor, who'd never really taken sides, could react with such anger, Jessie could only imagine what everyone else would say.

Jessie thought about turning back towards his room and packing his things at that instant, but he wondered about those vague possibilities at other schools that Mr. Whitney had mentioned before he left. And there were Frenchie's hopes that Jessie might be reinstated, most likely shattered by now, if they'd ever been a real possibility.

As another pack of students approached on the walkway, Jessie ducked his head down and stared at the ground. His ears burned as the boys' muttered insults flew—just loud enough for Jessie to hear.

●

Jessie's next English term paper came back with a big red F scribbled across the top. He stared at it, not believing his eyes. He'd put as much time, if not more, into that paper than all the others he'd submitted all year, none of which had ever come back with less than a B−, and usually much better than that. He flipped the pages, wondering what he'd done wrong, but he didn't see anything.

When he approached Mr. Richardson after class, the teacher's icy response was brief and to the point. "It's substandard work. Superficial and vague. Far better than that is required at an elite institution like this one." A cold smile formed on the instructor's lips. "Even if some people around here consider Springvale to be nothing more than a miserable cesspool."

Hearing his words thrown back at him, Jessie just stood there numb and unable to move.

"Move on, Stackhouse," Mr. Richardson said, his thin lips pursed. "I've got another class coming in. The world doesn't revolve around you."

40

The following Friday night, as Jessie stood by his window looking out at the students flocking to the game, he had a crazy idea—he'd join them. To him, Friday nights at this time of the year meant hockey games, and Jessie was desperate for slapshots, up-and-down action, and bone-crunching checks. After all the abuse he'd gotten in the days since Franklin's "interview" was published, Jessie figured there wasn't any insult or racial slur left that hadn't already been hurled at him. He'd no longer be able to sit in the section reserved for team members who weren't dressing, but he could show his student ID that granted him admission to the student section. Everyone around him would be watching the game rather than him, and he planned to keep quiet and mind his own business.

Jessie slipped a woolen ski hat on, trying to look less conspicuous, and then tossed it aside. Who was he fooling? He'd have to pull a ski mask over his face to disguise who he was, then shuddered at the thought of his masked attackers when he'd first arrived. He pushed the thought away quickly.

At the arena, an elderly man with thick glasses waved Jessie through after seeing the student ID, but even he shook his head in obvious disgust. Jessie walked along the concourse that circled the ice above the seats, ignoring all the heads turning his way as he continued toward the student section at the far end.

The catcalls began as he walked down the stairs to a seat. *Prima donna . . . . Why aren't you on the ice? . . . .* And *Go home if you don't like it here.* Jessie ignored them all and sat next to a vaguely familiar student, one who was wearing his Springvale Academy jacket. He held a hot dog with mustard in one hand and a box of popcorn in the other, a soda nestled between his legs. Jessie's mouth watered; even though he'd eaten only an hour earlier, the hot dog and popcorn smelled so good. He could almost taste the mustard.

Then the boy beside him did a double-take and wrinkled his nose. "Your kind makes me sick." He waved the hot dog for emphasis. "No matter how much we do for you, it's never enough. You don't appreciate anything at all."

Jessie, steaming, glared at him. "What have you ever done for me?"

The boy blinked. "The school, I mean. It's done a lot for you."

Jessie felt like asking the kid who'd clearly appointed himself as Jessie's judge, just what made him think he had any right to judge him or anyone else? But instead, Jessie defended himself. "I've done a lot for this school, despite what you may have read. I've studied hard, gotten good grades, and helped the team win a lot of games." He noticed as soon as the word was out of his mouth that he was still using *us*.

But the kid shook his head and said, "You just don't get it."

Jessie thought that he'd gotten it good enough. It was people like this kid who really didn't get it. So Jessie told him, "Eat your hot dog and leave me alone."

The kid recoiled and said, "See what I mean?"

Jessie stood for the National Anthem, hoping this would be the end of the conversation. But instead, as soon as the anthem finished, another kid scrambled to stand near Jessie and point in his face. "If you had any balls, you'd be out there with the team!"

●

The abuse toward Jessie subsided once the game got going and everyone's attention was riveted to the on-ice action, but then Jessie thought the first intermission would never end. He decided to leave midway through the second period, knowing he couldn't take another intermission filled with people coming up to him and railing at him about what he'd said in the newspaper interview. Besides, it was almost as torturous watching the team, especially Frenchie, as they struggled while he was helpless to do anything about it. Springvale trailed 2-1 in a game it couldn't afford to lose. Jessie's muscles tightened and he'd lean forward, adrenaline pumping through him, whenever he saw an opening to get Frenchie the puck or noticed a three-on-two rush developing the other way.

But it was all anticipation and no action, more of an exercise in frustration than anything else and he'd had enough.

When the whistle blew, stopping play, Jessie got up and walked out of the student section, heading for the exit at the other end. As he walked past the center ice seats where the townies sat, his blood ran cold. There in the back row, only a few steps away, sat a mountain of a man, someone close to three hundred pounds, and if Jessie waited to see him stand up, he was certain the man would be nearly seven feet tall.

As he turned to look Jessie's way, his mop of unruly black hair poking out from beneath a John Deere baseball-style cap, Jessie's mind raced back to the terrible night when he and Stick were attacked coming back from the movie.

The huge man, his face pockmarked without the mask to hide it, was almost obscenely ugly. Spotting Jessie, he grinned and nudged the man beside him. Jessie raced for the exit, nausea hitting him almost immediately from the effort, but he couldn't take a chance by slowing down.

Glancing over his shoulder, Jessie saw that the mountain of a man was not pursuing him, but then he accidentally slammed into another townie, knocking him to the ground. The man's drink splashed over his face and onto his jacket and he shouted at Jessie. "Hey! Watch where you're going."

"Sorry," Jessie mumbled. He bent over to help the man—middle aged, balding, and wiry—but nausea surged through him and everything began to spin. Jessie closed his eyes as the man began to shout.

"Who's gonna pay for this?" he yelled, sending icy pinpricks of pain through Jessie's head. Suddenly Jessie's legs wobbled and the nausea overtook him. Jessie's dinner came up and splattering the red-faced man before Jessie could turn aside.

Jessie bent over, his hands on his knees, as he gasped and spit. By now, the man swore even louder, sending white needles of light flashing before Jessie's eyes.

"Oh my God," the man groaned. "This smells—"

Jessie didn't wait for the description. With the disgusting smells filling his nostrils and his stomach still churning, Jessie walked away as fast as he could, heading for the exit as he wiped his mouth, his head ducked down in embarrassment.

"Hey!" the man cried out behind him.

Jessie took a quick glance behind him, but when he saw that the giant man had gotten to his feet, Jessie didn't waste another instant. He yanked open an exit door and headed for the dorm, a thin layer of new snow crunching beneath his feet.

●

On Monday, Frenchie grabbed Jessie between their Biology and U.S. History classes. A look of hope filled Frenchie's face, surprising to Jessie given the weekend's hockey results. The Warriors had lost the Friday night game, failing to come back from their 2-1 deficit after Jessie left. One night later, as Jessie stayed safely in his room, they outshot Tilton 51-17—a team they'd never lost to—but had to settle for a 2-2 tie because without Jessie and Rocco in the lineup, and with Sully hurting so bad, the forwards were no match for a Tilton goaltender playing the game of his life. A playoff berth was slipping through Springvale's fingers, but Jessie never would have guessed it from Frenchie's cheerful expression.

"You'll never guess who spoke to Coach Stone on your behalf," Frenchie said.

"You?" Jessie guessed, unable to think of anyone else.

Frenchie shook his head. "No, I already tried, but he doesn't listen to me."

"Taylor?"

"No, not Taylor. It was the last person you would ever expect."

Jessie couldn't fathom who Frenchie meant. Shrugging, he joked and said, "Dirk?"

With that, Frenchie's face fell and he said, "Who told you?"

Jessie stopped in his tracks. "I was joking."

Frenchie's face brightened again and he confirmed it. "It's no joke."

"*Dirk?* You gotta be kidding me."

Frenchie shook his head. "A couple colleges—what is the word, withdrew?—yes, they withdrew their scholarship offers to Dirk because of the suspension. We need to make the playoffs so all the scouts can see him."

All year, the talk in the locker room had been about how every scout worth anything attended the semifinals and championship game during playoff weekend. Teams getting that far were loaded with players the scouts wanted to see in action against the best competition to help gauge how well they'd do at the next level.

Frenchie went on. "Dirk's really worried. He knows we might not make the playoffs without you, so he talked to Stone about having you come back." Frenchie clapped Jessie on the shoulder and said, "What do you think of that? Dirk needs you now!"

Jessie couldn't help being amused at the irony. "That sure makes me want to stop trying," he said.

Frenchie's smile faded and he said, "You are kidding, aren't you?"

But a part of Jessie wasn't. Why should he help out his tormentor?

"We talked before," Frenchie said. "You said you'd come back if you could. It's the only reason I've stayed here."

Jessie recalled the conversation.

"You promised," Frenchie said, his eyes pleading.

Jessie couldn't remember actually saying it quite that way, but he had agreed to return to the team if he could. The prospect of the playoffs still made him tingle all over; if you played hockey, you didn't turn down an opportunity like that. But the idea of doing Dirk a favor galled him.

"I'll come back if I can," Jessie said slowly. "I'll do it for you, and for me, too. But I won't do it for Dirk."

Frenchie looked confused. "What do you mean?"

"Just don't ever remind me that I'm helping Dirk."

Frenchie let out a relieved sigh and said, "That's great." But then he started to look nervous and added, "There's only one thing."

"What's that?" Jessie asked.

Frenchie looked away and told him. "All you have to do is apologize to Coach Stone."

"Apologize?" Jessie asked, staring at Frenchie. "For what?"

●

A week and a half later, Jessie sat in Coach Stone's office with Dirk and Coach Chase. Jessie could see the hunger in their eyes, and their near desperation. As much as they still hated Jessie, he knew that they needed him even more. Stone had even taken down his George Wallace photograph to prove it. It had taken Jessie that week and a half for his nausea and dizziness to subside before he could rejoin the team, per his father's instructions. Day after day, Frenchie had looked at Jessie expectantly, only to slump his shoulders after Jessie shook his head, signaling that his symptoms remained. Now he was cleared and ready to go, but only two games remained in the regular season. For Springvale, it was like the playoffs had started two games early; the Warriors had to win both games to qualify for the playoffs, and a loss would end their season.

"So . . . what do you have to say?" Coach Stone asked Jessie from his seat behind the desk, then licked his lips.

"I'm ready to play," Jessie said. "I want to help the team."

Stone took a long drag from his cigarette, the tip glowing red. He turned and blew smoke in the other direction, then said, "That's not enough."

Dirk shifted uncomfortably in his seat when he heard the coach.

"I wish I could have come back sooner," Jessie admitted. "I wish I'd never gotten hurt in the first place."

Frowning, Stone turned to Dirk. "I thought you told him an apology would be required."

Dirk swallowed. "I did, sir."

Stone licked his lips again as he turned back to Jessie. A thin wisp of smoke curled up from the cigarette. "Well?"

A part of Jessie wanted to get up and leave—not just Stone's office, but Springvale Academy itself. He'd grown to hate the place and he wanted Stone, Chase, and Dirk to fail. He hoped Dirk ended up graduating without a single college scholarship offer—that's the punishment he deserved for his crimes. And he hoped Stone and Chase would never raise another championship banner.

But Jessie knew he couldn't leave. He'd promised Frenchie he'd stay, and unlike so many others at this school, Jessie lived up to his word. It was also to his own advantage to play. He'd written letters applying for admission to other schools in the next academic year. One other letter had nothing at all to do with next year, but directly involved what Stone, Chase, Dirk, and the others had put him through. His credibility regarding that letter, as well as his applications, would only be enhanced by Jessie suiting up and doing well in the playoffs.

But more than anything else, every muscle in Jessie's body twitched at the thought of skating again, of faking a defenseman one way and then flying past him the other, of ripping off a shot that nestled into the back of the net.

He'd never played in games anything close to the importance of the New England Championships; they were

338

the reason players like him pushed themselves in every drill in every practice. They were the reason he'd worked himself to the point of exhaustion, digging down deep for that little bit of extra strength most players didn't know they had. The championships were the reason to shoot just a little harder, to skate a bit faster, and to lift a heavier weight. Playing in games like these were what Jessie'd dreamed about before coming here.

But he wouldn't grovel—not to Stone or to Chase or to Dirk—not after what they'd done to him. But what he could do was outsmart them, and he was fairly sure he had.

"Coach," Jessie said. "I apologize for every single thing that I've done wrong." Silently, he added, *and that's nothing!*

Stone crossed his arms and nodded in satisfaction for a few seconds, a tight grin on his lips, before the grin faded and his eyes narrowed. He cocked his head and peered closely at Jessie, took a hard drag on his cigarette, and then, even though it was only half consumed, he ground it out in the ashtray. He drew in a breath of air, then licked his lips.

"Okay, then," Stone said, his glance flickering to Chase and Dirk for only an instant before fixing his gaze on Jessie. "Go get dressed for practice. I don't want any more trouble out of you this year. If you so much as look at me cross-eyed, I'm running you off of this team and out of this school. Understand?"

Jessie did, and he wondered if Harry Edwards would consider him an Uncle Tom for going back to play on this team. He hoped not, but even if he did, Jessie was sure that the Harry Edwardses of the world would soon be nodding their approval.

In the locker room before the game, Jessie slid on the jersey he'd thought he'd never wear again. It hung clean and crisp from his shoulders and he looked forward to playing in it. He'd missed all this—sitting in the locker room and hearing the team's buzz of nervous energy and conversation, eagerly awaiting the warm-ups and the National Anthem, and then, that very first hit.

Jessie knew this was where he belonged. He ignored the blank stares from many of his teammates; if they thought he'd taken too long to return to playing or was some kind of loud-mouthed *prima donna*, that was their problem. He knew as well as they did where the team stood: unless the Warriors won both of their last regular season games, there'd be no playoffs for them. Not even a win and a tie would be good enough to earn them a shot at the championship. For the Warriors, the playoffs had in reality started now.

If they made it past those last two games, they'd be going on the road for playoff weekend, but at least these two regular games were at home. Jessie'd assumed that would be an advantage until a chorus of boos greeted him when he stepped on the ice. The jeers grew louder, punctuated by catcalls, and from the first shift on, every time Jessie touched the puck, boos rained down on him.

Thank you, Franklin.

But Jessie pushed it all out of his mind; he'd just pretend this was a road game at Oak Ridge. Compared to the last time there, the crowd seemed very well-behaved.

For two periods, Jessie had trouble getting his timing back. Although he'd had no more symptoms, not even after a couple of big hits by Uxbridge defensemen, everything he did happened a half-second too late, or else was just a hair off. He'd missed a pass from Frenchie that should have been an easy goal, then botched a pass of his own to Taylor that should have required only a tap in to score. Instead of all the gears meshing perfectly to drive the finely tuned machine that had once been their line, everything seemed to grind the gears to a halt. Shots went wide and drop-passes were left hanging with no one to pick them up. By the time they entered the third period, the score was tied, 1-1.

Jessie knew whose fault it would be if the Warriors failed to get this win, but he was afraid his legs would give out on him. He'd lost the edge in his conditioning while he'd been sidelined, and it was in the third period that it would show.

But instead of that, the game seemed to slow down around him, as if the action was somehow in slow motion. Jessie knew exactly the right move to make, well before it was time to make it. He skated up ice one-on-one with a defenseman and saw he was cheating to the outside. Jessie faked that way, then cut back to the inside, and blasted past him. Jessie roofed the puck into the top of the net for a 2-1 lead, and then, two minutes later, threaded a perfect pass through two defenders to send Frenchie in on a breakaway. His deke and wrap-around made it 4-2, and Jessie's booming slap shot with five minutes remaining finished off the scoring.

After every goal, the crowd cheered wildly until Jessie's name was announced on the goal or assist. Suddenly the spectators, reminded that their supposed hero was in fact a villain, began to boo. When Jessie glanced up at the back row of the arena, he saw his huge attacker jumping up and down in celebration, only to jeer seconds later when he heard Jessie's name.

Jessie tried to continue the mind game that this was Oak Ridge, and that their fans were supposed to boo him, but it didn't work. The student section, filled with the same guys he went to classes with every day, had loudly vented their hostility all game long. One short scrawny boy had even climbed up on the dasher and hung over the glass to hurl insults at him.

Though Jessie wished he hadn't said a word to Franklin, he knew he'd been right. Most of these kids really weren't worth a bucket of warm spit.

●

The next night, with everything on the line in the third period, Springvale trailed perennial powerhouse Exeter 2-1. Time was running out and the Warriors needed more than a tie; they had to win. And the Exeter goalie was playing out of his mind. Jessie had scored once on the power play, but the goalie had stopped everything else the Warriors had thrown at him. Frenchie's frustration was reaching the boiling point. He'd already broken one stick, slashing it against the boards after getting robbed on a breakaway.

With less than ten minutes remaining, an Exeter defenseman gambled that he could get to a loose puck before Jessie—and lost. Jessie poked it off the boards and flew around the defenseman. He and Frenchie broke through center ice on a two-on-one, and Jessie carried the puck wide as Frenchie cut to the net. When a passing lane opened, Jessie feathered the puck across to Frenchie, alone on the opposite side. Frenchie ripped off a shot, one-timing it before the goalie could get set, and it looked to be labeled for the upper corner until the goalie dove, stabbed in the air with his glove, and picked off the surefire goal.

The crowd groaned. Jessie groaned. And Frenchie swore in his native tongue—at least that's what it sounded like.

On their next shift, Exeter kept them penned in their defensive zone with a fierce fore-check and almost scored off a turnover. Only a diving play by Frenchie, who poked the puck away from the Exeter player about to shoot, prevented a near-certain goal. When they got to the bench, gasping for air and exhaling it loudly, Jessie tapped Frenchie's shin pads with his stick and patted his shoulder pads. When he could talk again, he said, "Great play."

Frenchie nodded, but time kept ticking away. The tension grew on the bench. Everyone stood up, leaning forward in anticipation. "C'mon guys," came the occasional cheer, along with the slamming of a stick's butt end when something went wrong.

Six minutes.

Five.

Jessie shot wide from the left face-off circle. Frenchie matched him from the right.

"Put it on net!" some idiot screamed from the stands after play stopped—as if they'd been trying to shoot wide on purpose.

Four minutes.

Three.

"Let's do it," Jessie said, just before hopping over the bench. Taylor broke up an Exeter skater and the puck squirted loose at center ice. Frenchie and a defender raced for it, but Frenchie dove, poking the puck off to Jessie on the right wing. Jessie carried it into the zone, taking the defenseman wide. He looked to slide it over to Taylor on the far wing but the lane was blocked. Out of the corner of his eye, Jessie saw Frenchie breaking into the zone, trailing the play. Jessie faked a shot and dropped the puck back. When Frenchie one-timed it on net, the goalie flashed a pad out for another miraculous save. Except the rebound caromed to Taylor, and with a wide open net in front of him, he released the shot.

As the puck slid over the line, Jessie leaped in the air and let out a whoop. "*Yeeeaaaaaahhhhhhh!*"

But the euphoria didn't last long; a tie wasn't good enough to make the playoffs.

The seconds ticked down. "Let's go guys!" yelled one player after another. "This is our game!"

Then the buzzer sounded: five minutes of overtime.

Five minutes to score or the season was over.

"It's our game!"

The Exeter goalie made a great stop on Cheesie in the opening minute of OT. Then Jessie rang a shot off the post.

"Come on!"

Three minutes left.

Sully bent over in pain, cradling his shoulder as he skated to the bench.

Two minutes.

A tie would do them no good.

A minute and a half.

When would Coach Stone pull the goalie? He *would* pull the goalie, wouldn't he? He *had* to pull Shep.

With a minute and nine seconds left in overtime—and possibly the season—the Warriors got the puck into the offensive zone, shot on net, and the Exeter goalie hung on for a face-off.

Stone signaled a timeout and the referee blew the whistle. Stone waved Shep to the bench and pulled out his diagramming board. "You guys know the drill: six-on-five. This is why we practiced it all year." He glanced over at Sully bent over in pain. "Taylor's line. Cheesie, you're the extra man. Get shots on net. Look for the rebounds. No goalie can save every rebound."

Taylor lost the face-off, but Cheesie got right on top of the defender before he could clear the puck. It moved down behind the goaltender.

Fifty seconds. Forty-five.

Exeter players were just trying to hold the puck against

the boards with their skates and kill time. Jessie and Taylor tried to poke it free.

Thirty-five seconds. Thirty.

Jessie finally got the puck. He passed it along the boards to Cheesie on the right side. Cheesie back to Dirk. A big slapshot, deflected wide.

Twenty seconds.

Frenchie got the puck along the far boards. Moved to get away from a defender.

Fifteen seconds.

Frenchie faked a slapshot, freezing the defenseman. From the top of the face-off circle, Jessie cut for the net. He knew where the pass would go before Frenchie even released it, threading it through three defenders. The puck came to Jessie on the far post, and even though the goalie dove across the crease, he didn't have a chance. Jessie roofed the shot into the top of the net, only believing they'd won it when the red light went on and the siren sounded.

Jessie leaped into the air and screamed, "*GOOOAAAALLLLL!*"

The crowd erupted. Springvale had won it—with seven seconds to spare.

Jessie skated over to Frenchie, yelling as he did, "What a pass! Way to go, Frenchie!" He wrapped his arms around his teammate and hugged him. "You did it!"

The entire Springvale team spilled onto the ice, throwing their gloves and sticks into the air.

The crestfallen Exeter players hung their heads and skated off the ice.

Jessie spotted his parents cheering wildly. His mother

was jumping up and down. Pop had never worn a bigger smile.

It was only afterward that Jessie realized he hadn't heard a single boo.

42

The following week, the Springvale campus was abuzz with talk of the upcoming playoffs. Overnight, all of Jessie's perceived transgressions were forgotten. The same people who'd reviled him only a few weeks back were now slapping him on the back and congratulating his clutch goal.

Each time, no matter what Jessie thought of the person, he'd say, "It was all Frenchie. Give him the credit. I did the easy part."

But like it or not, Jessie was a hero. He may not have been beloved by all, but now the rednecks did a much better job of disguising their hatred.

"About that 'F' I gave you," Mr. Richardson said. "I might have been too harsh. I've taken another look, and let's call it an A–."

Jessie imagined a conversation with Stick:

"You know, I think somebody might even say he's got a sister he wants me to date." Stick would work his toothpick a second, and then say, "Nah. Not unless she ugly."

●

Oak Ridge, the number-one seed, would host the semi-finals on Saturday and the championship game on Sunday. Although Springvale didn't qualify for the tournament until the final regular season game, it took the number-three seed, based on a head-to-head tiebreaker, and would face St. Paul's, the number-two seed. Chartered buses were to transport nearly half the Springvale student body to the semifinal game, followed by a procession of townspeople honking their horns according to tradition for the first five or six miles and then again when they got with a few miles of the arena.

Jessie stared at the scenery and wondered if he'd con-found the fans again, making them cheer until they some-how remembered their hatred.

As it turned out, they must have decided he could say whatever he wanted—as long as Springvale won another championship. They cheered wildly when Jessie scored a goal and set up Frenchie for two and Taylor for another in a 5-3 win over St. Paul's.

Oak Ridge was all that stood between Springvale Academy and another championship.

●

After the game, Coach Stone gave the team a half hour in the lobby to socialize with family and friends before boarding a bus for the short trip to a local hotel.

Jessie slung his hockey bag over one shoulder and

grabbed his sticks. Food would be waiting for them on the bus, but it would feel like a long half hour; he was always so ravenous after a game.

Jessie pushed through the doors into the lobby and stopped, breaking into the biggest smile. Standing beside his parents were Rose and Stick. Rose was wearing jeans and a brown flowered blouse that made her look even more beautiful than ever. Jessie didn't notice Stick's attire.

"Girl, you are a sight for sore eyes," Jessie told Rose.

She ran to him and it was all he could do to drop everything before she wrapped her arms around him. Holding tight, Jessie practically drank her in: the faint scent of strawberries in her hair, the jasmine and honeysuckle of her perfume, and the way her body felt against his. It felt so perfect to have her head resting against his shoulder, her hair brushing his cheek.

It struck Jessie just how much he'd sacrificed to get where he was standing. He'd known it all along, had felt the pangs of loneliness and the monstrous cruelty from the likes of Dirk and Coach Stone. But holding Rose like this, feeling her kiss on his cheek, put a face on it. And what a face it was.

Rose looked up at him, her big brown eyes filled with tears, her smile melting his heart.

"I've missed you so much," she whispered.

"Me too," he whispered back. "More than you could know."

The thought of Leroy flashed through Jessie's mind but he pushed it away, hoping Rose's presence was a sign. Then he clung to her even tighter.

Stick spread his arms wide and said, "Hey, what she got that I don't?"

Jessie laughed. "Everything, man. Everything!"

While Jessie and Rose held onto each other, his parents ducked in for a hug. Jessie held out a hand for Stick to slap.

"Wow," Jessie said. "What a surprise!"

Rose finally let go of him, and as the jasmine and honeysuckle drifted away, he almost pulled her close again. He watched her smile and noticed the tiny diamond in her necklace glitter—the one he'd given her.

"Wow," he said again.

"Black Einstein be smart, but he not always so eloquent," Stick said, stretching out the last word to show it off. "You catch that, Einstein? *El-o-quent?* I got me something out of my Springvale education. Maybe only five vocabulary words, but that be one of 'em. *Eloquent.* I be so eloquent, I could just spit."

Jessie laughed. This felt so good. He wished he could stay right there forever, pull up chairs and never leave his people.

"Can we take you out to eat?" Momma asked, as if she'd read his mind. "We could drop you off at the hotel."

"No," Jessie said glumly. "I'd love to, though. Man, how I'd love to. But we only got half an hour, and then we gotta be back on the bus. Stone don't let us out of his sight for long, not during playoffs. They'll either have food for us on the bus or at the hotel."

Then Jessie asked, "You all are staying for tomorrow, right?"

Momma and Pop nodded.

"The track meet I was supposed to run got cancelled," Stick said, a sour look on his face.

"How's your knee doing?"

He shrugged.

Jessie took that as bad news, but decided not to press the issue for fear of dampening everyone's good mood.

"Great game, son," Pop said.

Jessie spread his arms wide, and with a wide grin, said, "Took you long enough to say so."

The half hour was flying by when Jessie spotted Frenchie standing alone. His parents hadn't been able to make the trip from Quebec, so Jessie waved him over and introduced him around. Jessie itched to introduce Rose as his girl; having her beside him felt so good and so right. But they'd only been together twice since September and he didn't want to assume what their status might be without talking to her. He settled for introducing her simply as Rose and left it at that.

When Coach Chase ducked his head into the lobby and told the team to be on the bus in five minutes or else, Jessie asked, "What time is it? It's been half an hour already?"

It had. In fact, thirty-five minutes had ticked by. But to Jessie, it felt as if he'd just said hello and the time was up.

"Aw, man," he said. "I gotta go."

Rose tugged at his arm. "Can I talk to you in private? Just for a minute?"

Jessie couldn't say no, but he glanced nervously toward the exit. "I gotta be fast. Stone doesn't mess around."

Rose pulled him ten feet away, then whispered, "I

broke up with Leroy. A while ago, actually. You're gonna be home in just a couple months and I gotta know. Do you want me to wait for you? You still wanna go out?"

Warmth flooded over Jessie and the widest smile spread across his face.

"What do you think, girl?" he said.

"I got to hear it," Rose told him.

"Yes, yes, yes, yes, yes! That enough for you?"

It was.

43

The championship game turned ugly right from the start. The Oak Ridge fans hadn't forgotten the last time they'd seen Jessie, and when he was introduced in the starting lineup, a thunderous chorus of boos rang out, punctuated by scattered shouts of obscenities and every possible racial epithet. Then Jessie realized the boos, at least most of them, weren't that at all. There was a distinct K sound; the Oak Ridge crowd was calling him a *coon.*

Coooooooooon! Cooooooooooon!

Jessie's ears burned. It was bad enough that *he* had to hear this. What he hated most was Rose being subjected to it; she was so sweet and innocent. He resented that it would offend his parents, but they'd heard it all before and could comfort each other. And Stick was tough as nails. But even though Rose had heard the words before, too, it was so much worse having to sit through a crowd of spectators shouting them and turning one into a chorus of unified hatred. Jessie felt sorry that she had no one to comfort her, with him on the ice. Then the image of Stick consoling her flashed through his mind. As he pictured his friend using his special moves on Rose, Jessie thought he just might have to mess up Stick's other leg.

But when the National Anthem began, Jessie shook off that notion and pushed everything but the game out of his mind.

He stared at Corey Simonton, the All-New England defenseman, waiting on the opposing blue line. He had to be 6-5 and at least 230 pounds; nobody was going to out-muscle that guy.

Simonton proved it on his first shift, when he slammed Jessie hard against the boards on a rush through neutral ice. The crowd whooped with delight and jeered.

Coooooooooon!

Jessie blocked it out. The only thing that mattered right now was what happened on the ice. Only the next shift mattered, and winning it.

But when a fight broke out in the stands on the opposite side where the Oak Ridge and Springvale sections met, Jessie couldn't help but notice. Some fans stood for a better look; others rushed to get closer to the action. The noise grew louder.

Jessie watched the fists fly as the police moved to break up the fight, slowed down by the fans packing stands. Jessie scanned the crowd, searching for his family and friends, then spotting them a safe distance from the brawl.

That's when Coach Stone noticed where Jessie was looking. "Pay attention, Stackhouse! All of you, eyes on the ice!"

For once, Jessie agreed with the coach. And that was

easy to admit, as long as the people he cared about were safe.

The game remained scoreless after one period, and by midway through the second, the worst of the racial slurs had fallen silent. The game was just too gripping for the spectators to focus on anything else.

Springvale took the lead off Jessie's feed to Frenchie in the slot. The Oak Ridge goalie made the save, but Taylor whacked in the rebound. Just three minutes later, Oak Ridge scored on a power-play goal to even it up, sending the two teams back to their locker rooms tied once again.

As the third period progressed, tied 1-1, Simonton never seemed to come off the ice. He was tough to beat—real tough. He could outmuscle a bulldozer, was surprisingly quick on his feet for someone so big, and he had such a wide wingspan, he could poke check the puck away even if you got a step on him. Jessie felt himself getting frustrated when dekes and stickhandling moves that worked on every other defenseman weren't working on Simonton. And he didn't just break you up; he made you pay with hard but clean checks. Jessie felt his head rattle a bit on a couple of the hits, but nothing too bad—just enough to get his attention.

A whistle sounded with 2:07 left and Jessie's line hopped over the boards. This would probably be their last shift until overtime, unless a team took a timeout. Simonton had been out there for an unusually long time and had been about to come off the ice for a breather when the Oak Ridge coach spotted Jessie's line coming on. At that, the coach waved Simonton back on the ice.

As the top seed and home team, Oak Ridge got to make the last change after a whistle. Its coach could dictate the match-ups, and he clearly wanted Simonton out there for Springvale's most dangerous line. But Jessie noticed that the big defenseman was bent over, leaning hard on his knees as he huffed and puffed. Jessie thought the Oak Ridge coach should use a timeout to give his top player a rest because as great as Simonton was (and Jessie had never played against anyone as good), the guy was still human. He had to be vulnerable right now, his legs turning into granite.

Twenty seconds later, Jessie took advantage of the defenseman's fatigue. He skated up ice on the wing, driving hard right at Simonton with Frenchie skating abreast. Jessie thought about just dumping the puck into the zone and making Simonton chase it, but decided to attack. He faked the dump-in and watched Simonton turn just a little to go after it—one tiny mistake made by an exhausted player to try and save what was left of his strength.

Jessie drove to the inside, forcing Simonton to overcommit to make up for his error, and when Jessie saw that weight shift in Simonton's legs, he drove hard to the outside. Jessie had him beat except for the poke-check, so when the defenseman's sweep of the stick neared the puck, Jessie pulled it back, spun one hundred and eighty degrees, drew Simonton to him, and then slid the puck across to Frenchie, sending him in all alone on the goaltender.

Simonton hit Jessie hard but it was worth it. Frenchie deked to his forehand, then to his backhand, and then pulled the puck back to his forehand—and into the corner of the net.

GOOOOAAAAALLLLLLL!

Jessie wanted to jump to the rafters but he couldn't. That's because Simonton held him pinned against the boards, as if he needed Jessie for support. His jersey reeked of sweat, and, gasping for breath, the defenseman swore loudly and pushed Jessie away in frustration. Jessie raced to Frenchie and joined in the celebration, hugging his friend and whooping for joy.

"Way to go, Frenchie!" Jessie yelled. Then he finally made use of something from French class. "*Quelle remarquable.*"

Frenchie hugged him back, saying, "*Bonjour?*"

The Oak Ridge coach called for the timeout he should have taken for Simonton twenty-seven seconds earlier, and all the players skated to their benches.

"Everybody sit down," Coach Stone barked. "Rest your legs 'cause this game ain't over. Have a sip of water, but not too much." He waited. "Okay, now. Here's what we're going to do. Taylor, Frenchie, and Stackhouse, you're staying out there. You too, Dirk and Hightower. But you guys aren't out there to score. No taking chances. Get the puck deep and make them beat us from two hundred feet. No dumb icings." He continued to bark out instructions until the referee blew the whistle to resume play.

The remaining 1:40 were the longest of Jessie's life. Taylor won the face-off back to Joe Hightower, who passed across to Dirk. Dirk got the puck over the red line, then dumped it in the Oak Ridge zone. For what felt like forever to Jessie's burning lungs, the Warriors kept Oak Ridge penned in their own end, keeping the puck along the boards until the whistle blew for another stoppage. Jessie glanced at the scoreboard.

1:19.

Only twenty-one seconds had ticked off? That couldn't be right. Was an Oak Ridge fan running the clock? Jessie's line skated to the bench and Cheesie's replaced it.

"Is that time right?" Jessie asked Matt Templeton, a fourth liner who hadn't played more than two shifts, and none since the middle of the second period.

Matt nodded.

Jessie shook his head and watched the clock as Cheesie lost the face-off and Oak Ridge broke out. The clock did seem to be working, but operating in slow motion. The Oak Ridge goalie raced to the bench for an extra skater as soon as the puck moved into the Springvale end.

Dirk, who'd stayed out with Joe Hightower while the forwards changed up, took the puck and sent it rimming around the boards to Sully on the wing. But Sully couldn't control it and Oak Ridge sent the puck back behind the Springvale net and raced after it. With the extra skater, Oak Ridge pressured until finally Joe Hightower had to whip the puck down to the other end to relieve the pressure.

Icing. Face-off back in the Warrior end. Forty-seven seconds left. Stone called a timeout, then got Dirk to sit down and sent Nick Caldwell out to replace Joe Hightower on defense next to Dirk. Jessie's line replaced Cheesie's. They probably had to get the puck out of the zone twice to eat up the clock.

But Taylor lost the face-off and Simonton boomed a slapshot that Shep had to stab at with his glove hand. A

Dave Hendrickson

save, but it took only five seconds off the clock. When was it going to end? Jessie wondered.

Taylor lost the next face-off, but Jessie anticipated a pass to Simonton, and with a sprawling dive, deflected it out of the zone. He glanced again at the clock.

Simonton collected the puck with twenty-seven seconds left and passed to a forward who dumped it in. The seconds ticked off slowly, slowly.

Twenty-one. Twenty. That clock had to be defective.

The Springvale fans, outnumbered by the hosts but vocal, counted down the seconds.

Eighteen.

Shep made an easy save and cleared the puck into the corner. *Sixteen.* Jessie raced for it and then pinned it against the boards, moving it along so there'd be no whistle. *Twelve. Eleven.* Body after body slammed against him, but he moved first one way, then the other.

Why were the fans counting so slowly? Jessie wondered.

Then another body crashed into him.

Nine. Eight.

Jessie couldn't move the puck anymore. Three bodies had him pinned, poking at his feet to jar the puck loose.

Six. Five.

The whistle blew. A face-off, with four seconds left.

No timeouts remained. Cheesie came on to replace Taylor. Everyone else stayed put.

Jessie could see Oak Ridge setting up its play for Simonton. He'd take a slapshot and everyone would crash the net, looking for a rebound.

No surprise there, but Jessie yelled, "They're going to Simonton. Keep the net front clear." It was obvious and easier said than done, but it didn't hurt to yell.

Oak Ridge won the face-off again, pulling it back to Simonton.

Jessie fought through a screen, and as the hulking defenseman wound up for his shot, Jessie dove sideways at him, his forearm sliding reflexively across his mouth to cover his teeth. But it wasn't necessary—Simonton's shot caught him square in the ankle, sending blinding pain up his leg and down into his toes.

And then, at last, the Springvale bench flew onto the ice, tossing sticks and gloves into the air, shrieking with joy.

Jessie watched the celebration on all fours, trying to get to his feet with his ankle searing with pain. Everyone raced to Shep, a time-honored tradition, but as the team surrounded him, Jessie crawled on the ice, alone. Somehow, it summed everything up.

Suddenly Frenchie noticed Jessie and raced over; Taylor, too, and then Cheesie and several others. His teammates helped him to his feet and Jessie hugged them all.

He enjoyed watching them all get their shot at raising the New England Cup high above their heads, and when he got his turn, it felt like he was in the NHL already and he was holding the Stanley Cup itself.

●

In the locker room, after Stone gave a congratulatory speech and all the whooping and hollering had died down,

Jessie held his jersey out and stared at it, burning the image into his brain. He'd never wear it again—he was sure. He'd finish out the semester, but then he was gone.

He'd already applied to six other prep schools with major hockey programs. Each one had a black student population, and four of them were actually within an hour of home. He liked to think that meant he'd be close enough to spend his weekends with Rose.

After taking a shower, his ankle still sore, Jessie hobbled out to the Oak Ridge lobby, its walls adorned with framed photographs of past teams, its polished trophy case loaded with the gleaming hardware of past champions.

Concerned faces greeted him there.

"Are you okay?" Momma asked.

Rose rushed toward him until Jessie put his hands up in a stopping gesture. "Don't tackle me today." Then he smiled and motioned her closer, saying, "Come here—I'll be fine."

As she hugged him, he smelled those scents that to him were all Rose, so sweet and so right. Momma added her own hug, telling him, "We're so proud of you." Pop clapped him on the back, and Stick nodded with a grin.

"I have to be on the bus in half an hour again."

Momma groaned and Rose shot him a disappointed look.

"Unless you drive me back to campus," Jessie added. "Then we can take as long as we want—" He grinned. "—maybe go out to eat. I sure could go for a pizza or three."

His parents exchanged a look, then Pop said, "It's okay with me, if Rose and Stick don't mind. They'll be getting home late."

"Yes!" Rose said.

"I ain't in no hurry," Stick said.

As they all headed for the exit, a white man wearing a sports jacket and tie called out, "Jessie?" He hurried over.

"Excuse me," he said. He looked to be about thirty years old and wore glasses. He held a thin notebook in one hand and a pen in the other. "Are you Jessie Stackhouse?" he asked.

Jessie nodded as he slipped his arm around Rose.

The man held out his hand. "Jonathan McClain. *Sports Illustrated*. We got your letter and I'd like to talk to you."

Jessie couldn't believe it—Jonathan McClain! He'd written some of Jessie's favorite *Sports Illustrated* articles, aside from the Jack Olsen series.

Jonathan McClain wanted to talk to him? *Sports Illustrated?*

McClain continued, "I'm looking at a follow-up story to Jack Olsen's series, one that might include something about black athletes on the prep school scene."

Momma and Pop stared, and Stick even stopped moving his toothpick.

Jessie couldn't stop smiling. "Remember those articles I read?" he asked his parents.

"How could we forget?" Momma said.

"Well, I contacted them. I figured a magazine that published those articles might be interested in what was happening to me at Springvale. But I never thought I'd be talking to Jonathan McClain." Jessie turned back to the writer, then said, "Have I got a story for you."

McClain chuckled. "I'm sure you do. I just finished talking to your coach."

Jessie's grin faded.

"He's a piece of work," McClain said, shaking his head. "I let him think he was talking one good old boy to another. He said some things he's going to regret, just like that athletic director in the Olsen piece. You know the one I'm talking about?"

"Sure," Jessie said. He remembered. He had the entire series all but memorized.

"Jessie, your Coach Stone is even dumber than the guy in that article — if that's even possible."

"He's not *my* Coach Stone. Not anymore."

"Smart move," McClain said. "I also got some interesting tidbits from that captain, Dirk Stapleton. He and the coach, they're two peas in the imbecile pod."

Jessie chuckled. "You noticed."

"Couldn't miss it," McClain said. Then he glanced toward the far end of the lobby as Coach Stone walked in with Dirk at his heels. "Speaking of the devil and his number-one disciple," said the reporter.

Stone slapped Dirk on the shoulder and surveyed the lobby, grinning broadly until he saw Jessie with McClain.

Stone's eyes widened. "Hey!" he called out and rushed over, a look of panic on his face. He turned to McClain and pointed to Jessie, then said, "You can't talk to him."

McClain raised an eyebrow. "Why not?"

"I won't allow it. He's —" Stone's face turned red. "He's a — just — he's only a freshman. It's a team rule that the press can't talk to a freshman."

McClain gave Stone a withering look. "Jessie Stackhouse is the only reason I'm *here*."

364

Stone blinked. "But I thought—"

"You and your captain Dirk Stapleton and the rest of your racist, pigheaded school are going to become famous, and for all the wrong reasons. *Sports Illustrated* is going to see to it."

Stone's jaw dropped. "But—"

"Not Jessie Stackhouse," McClain said. "He's going to be famous, too, but in his case, it'll be for all the *right* reasons."

Stone moved closer to Jessie and pointed his finger at him. "You tell this man right now that you're not interested in talking to him. Right now, *boy*! Or face the consequences—I swear it."

Jessie felt a sense of calm as he recalled the words he'd memorized at Pop's insistence. He turned to the coach and said, "Dr. Martin Luther King once said, 'Our lives begin to end the day we become silent about things that matter.'"

Jessie fixed Stone with a glare. "This matters, and *I'm* not going to be silent. Not anymore."

Stone opened his mouth, then closed it. His shoulders slumped and he nodded slowly.

Jessie understood it was the nod of a man who knew his day was over, that a new time was coming, and that the old walls were crashing down.

Jessie turned away from Coach Stone.

"Mr. McClain, would you care to join us for some pizza?" Jessie asked. "We have a *lot* to tell you."

ACKNOWLEDGMENTS

I owe so much to so many.

A special thank you to Richard Harris, who spent hours of his time describing his experiences as a black hockey player growing up in the late sixties (and to New Hampshire coach Dick Umile for putting me into contact with him). Your insights helped make this book what it is.

I also owe a debt of gratitude to Joyce Carol Thomas, Greg Neri, and Jewell Parker Rhodes for reading this book in manuscript form and offering their gracious endorsement.

Thanks to my daughter Nicole for being the most special of First Readers for this book and showing genuine enthusiasm at a time when it was very much needed. And to my son Ryan for making me a hockey addict. I love you two dearly.

Thanks to all my mentors over the years but especially Kris Rusch, Dean Wesley Smith, and Jeanne Cavelos. Jeanne's Odyssey workshop and Kris and Dean's many Oregon workshops, especially the Master Class where this novel was born, made all the difference in the world.

I'll always be indebted to my parents for so many things, one of which is filling our house with books and taking me to the library week after week. I love you, Mom. I miss you, Dad.

Thanks to the rest of my family for their support, especially my brother Steve whose frequent flier miles helped get me to those life-changing Oregon workshops.

Last but certainly not least, thank you to my editor and publisher, Evelyn Fazio, who believed in this book enough to make it a reality and then helped make it better.